CRACK IN

Secor

by

John Behardien

Duncurin
Publishing

Duncurin.com

Copyright © 2013

All Rights Reserved – John Behardien

No part of this book may be reproduced or transmitted in any form or by any means electronic or mechanical, including photocopying, recording, taping or by any information storage retrieval system without the written permission of the publisher.

This is a work of Fiction. Available in Paperback and e-Book.

First Published in England MMXI

Duncurin Publishing
Monton
England

Duncurin.com

ISBN : 978-09570982-7-5
'Crack In The Code': Second Edition.

Book Design : Moosey

DEDICATION

For Frances, Emily and Charlotte, the girls in my life, with whom each day has its "Fabienne" moments; and for my friend Eva, without whom this would not have been possible.

WITH THANKS

To Eva Jacobs for her limitless patience and steady hand in editing that, which at first glimpse, seemed 'uneditable'!

Roger Ellis for a wonderful picture of Salford Quays.

www.Theplacephoto.com

Jamie Runyan for another super book cover.

www.reese-winslow.com

OTHER BOOKS BY JOHN BEHARDIEN

Crack In The Code

Stars' End

The Last Great Gift

Dawn Over Vancouver

All That Time Allows (2016 release)

Final Horizon

Final Request (2016 release)

One Life Many Moments (2016/17 release)

Contents

Chapter I	"Paradise Flawed"	1
Chapter II	"Open Invitation"	23
Chapter III	"Bitter Betrayal"	53
Chapter IV	"Spellbound"	74
Chapter V	"Life Laid Waste"	101
Chapter VI	"Discovery"	124
Chapter VII	"New Girl in Town"	150
Chapter VIII	"Dinner for Four"	187
Chapter IX	"Found and Lost"	218
Chapter X	"Evasive Manoeuvres"	239
Chapter XI	"Loss and Profit"	269
Chapter XII	"Lethal Cone"	304
Chapter XIII	"Doctor Brown"	334

CHAPTER I

PARADISE FLAWED

It was a gloriously sunny day of the kind that most people loved; especially in early spring when, it seemed, that things were being renewed or reborn after a dormant winter. Though bright, the sunshine offered only a token of the ultimate power that it would be later in the year as it filtered through the trees: struggling to gain full ascendancy in the spring sky. A blue Jaguar saloon scrunched to its customary, secure halt on the gravel path. The driver looked up at the imposing beauty of the house with a new-found appreciation. Set in a substantial plot: the large, half-rendered, detached building was framed by the mature trees of the woods in the background, and before them came the meandering river that marked the end of his property. The sun was making a determined attempt to vanquish the moisture deposited by the recent rainfall on the clay-tile roof. Upon vacating the car, his shoes made a similar scrunching noise while he crossed to the porch: the damp gravel sticking just a little underfoot. Humming contentedly, he pinched the key-fob to lock the car.

Walking to the entrance, he looked up again at the magnificent house nestling in the woods on the outskirts of a beautiful, unspoilt English village. How fortunate that it was one of England's best-kept secrets; well-removed from the destruction that had accompanied discovery by the tourist industry of many similar villages. As he walked on to the porch, with its sandstone smoothed to a patina by countless such steps over the past hundred years, he turned to look out at the garden, and breathe in more of this moment. Whilst standing at this very spot, he'd been reminded on previous occasions, of how fortune had favoured him in purchasing the house. Today, other ideas would conflate quickly within his excited mind, creating a summit of wellbeing that he'd not noted before. Thinking about the work that he loved: a profession that had been a true calling, and the colleagues who helped to support and nourish him in an atmosphere of mutual friendship and respect. Although he wasn't yet twenty-eight, he'd progressed far in recent years. Financial security meant that he wouldn't have to worry about bills, the cost of a new car – albeit one not exorbitantly priced – or forego some of the luxuries of modern life. He had, he knew, a face accepted as nothing if not handsome, and a physique that training had made healthy, strong and toned. Recognising that most would be extremely envious of his life: they'd be more than happy with even a glimpse of such an existence. Fortunate indeed. How could he be described as anything other than happy: a contentment that could be measured by each and every second of such a life.

For some time he stood next to the porch rail. Looking back over the well-tended lawns and carefully planted shrubbery towards the two stone pillars that parted to allow his curved drive to connect with the quiet main road, which was used only by the locals. As he looked, he could see Walter Crossley, employed by the local street cleansing company, and who always made sure that the road in front of his house was regularly and efficiently swept. He gave Walter a cheery wave as he caught his eye: smiling, he turned to enter his house.

In that instant, as he began to open the door, even before he looked at the magazine that he had brought from the car, the moment was shattered. Throwing down the publication, suddenly, hoping that losing contact with it would recreate the mood that had irrevocably been lost. Entering the house precipitously as if being pursued, he left the magazine on the floor of the porch where the wind flapped gently against the glossy cover; oblique sunshine illuminating the words that he had seen and read a million times over, *'Fabienne Lands Leading Film Role'*. He avoided looking back at the porch: closing the door firmly behind him, with the determination of an alcoholic anxious to avoid picking up yet another full glass from the bar. He continued into the house as if being followed by a grim Nemesis, that he alone could see.

Evening's arrival would see calm restored, but would also see him returning conspiratorially to the porch, now in darkness, in order to retrieve his magazine – as a moth to the flame. Sitting indifferently on the sofa, he told himself that his aim was to spend a few minutes reading before turning in. Ultimately, however, he couldn't hide from himself, as he began poring over the contents of the magazine repeatedly and in painstaking detail: the cravings having defeated him once again.

The phone rang intrusively: he continued to revisit each sentence; every word of the article containing information that he had come across, in one form or another, many times over in the past months. Upon lifting the handset, his irritated mind was brought sharply back to reality by the familiar voice of the call-centre receptionist. "Just an information call, Doctor Sinclair. We've had a message from Caldbrook General about the patient you admitted there earlier. They'll be keeping her overnight and are planning to discharge her in the morning with urgent outpatient review."

Struggling to find his customary calm, polite tones, he thanked Melissa. Lingering briefly, she wished him a pleasant evening, and seemed just a little reluctant, in hoping that she would not be disturbing him again. Further calls would not interrupt his sleep, yet his dreams, not for the first time, would. Images of Fabienne intruded and found him, as he turned restlessly, in the dichotomy of begging the images to depart, yet desperately wanting them to stay. Another poor night's sleep, when twice he did something that he always told his patients never to do, if faced with a restless night; he looked at the clock at two am and again at three am, thereby unwittingly reinforcing the pattern for his subconscious the following night. Ultimately, sleep held sway in his racing brain, about half an hour before his alarm tugged him from his short-lived peace. He dragged himself from his chaotic bed, trusting that the warm shower would enliven him, just as it had done now, for so many mornings that had followed such restless nights.

Sitting in the conservatory, enjoying the first light of the day, a steady realisation crept over him. Things had shown no sign of improving after many months. If anything, his problems were getting worse. He gave a little shiver, despite the warmth flooding in, as he considered this. Holding back from admitting to himself that it must have been well over a year that he'd been caught in the trance: even though the articles, the DVDs and the CDs would all bear testament to just how long he had been mesmerized by the spell she had unknowingly cast. Only with that realisation came a strategy, perhaps a way out of his enchantment and back to the happiness that he knew, deep within, his life held.

Though his breakfast lay largely untouched before him, he finally grasped the point that something had to be done. With further thought came an idea as to what: brightening quickly as ideas crystallised like a crescendo within; his appetite returning, encouraging him to despatch the rest of the food with vigour. Taking up his car keys from the hall table, determination was written to his face, reflecting his new-found purpose.

He arrived early at the small surgery. The staff were amazed to see him at that hour because they were more accustomed to him appearing just after the first patient booked in, rather than some time before. They were similarly surprised by the speed with which he saw the ten booked patients and two 'urgents'. As the last patient departed, he quickly closed the consulting room door against curious ears and grabbed the phone, eager to make a start. Having decided on a plan, he wanted to waste no time in setting it in motion. Speaking with the switchboard operator at Mirfield General, his voice a little nervous as he remembered that this was where his most severe psychiatric cases were referred. However, he remained resolute as he asked for Doctor Collins, Clinical Psychologist.

"Hello, it's Doctor Collins here."

"Steve, it's Matt, Matt Sinclair."

"Matt, long-time no see. How are you?" Steve was joking; he'd heard from Matt only a couple of days before. It wasn't unusual for Matt to phone him or bend his ear about a patient, and Steve was usually only too happy to lend advice and support if Matt had a patient who'd presented with a challenging problem.

"Not bad thanks, Steve. Actually, I was wondering if you could spare me thirty minutes over lunch," Matt asked nervously.

"Well, if I can't spare my old room-mate thirty minutes, there's something wrong; how about one o'clock?"

"Fine, I'll pick you up," Matt replied in more relieved tones.

"Don't tell me, you have a tricky case you want me to sort for you?" Steve probed with resignation.

"Yes, I have actually. I'd really value your opinion," Matt confirmed.

Steve thought quickly as he replaced the handset. Though a telephone call wasn't unusual, it was rare for his friend to want to talk to him in person.

Steve Collins was a brilliant psychologist. He'd finished his psychology degree before taking up medicine as a mature student. He and Matt had graduated in the same year, having vied in so many subjects at medical school for the top places. On graduating, Steve decided that psychology was to be his calling. His medical degree had ensured rapid advancement, and he was now head of department. The nature of Matt's request would not be lost on him. The delicate pauses in the sentences had been picked up with a well-practised ease and the second-sense that all good clinicians had in abundance. Upon replacing the telephone he was already wondering to himself, 'why was it that his friend wanted to see him in person, rather than discuss things on the telephone?'.

Matt arrived a little early and waited in the car park outside the Psychology block. Aware that Steve would recognise his car, as he'd joked about the salary of GPs just a few weeks earlier, when Matt had first taken delivery. Steve, too, was early. Sporting the same tweed jacket that had seen better days, and the check-pattern shirt with a poorly-fitting collar; the combination seemed ill at ease, unlike the wearer, who was always relaxed and unruffled. His glasses, as usual, perched somewhere on his nose, but not necessarily along the line of sight: the brown hair clean but, typically, having missed even fleeting contact with a comb. Matt held the passenger door open as the door locks disengaged.

"Yo, Matt, how are you?" Steve said breezily.

"I'm fine, Steve, and you?"

"Not bad Matt, you know, at least for an impecunious psychologist - unlike these GPs with their new cars."

"Thanks for coming at short notice," Matt said as he seamlessly directed the conversation to other areas. Matt asked about Mary, Steve's wife, and also about their recent holiday. Their small talk continued as Matt drove to the café by the river; knowing it would be quiet at that time of day. It had been a long time since he'd visited the establishment, and it was clear that it had seen better days. They sat at the table that looked the least dirty, but even this was a difficult choice as each one had a red and white gingham tablecloth made from plastic that had long since faded and worn.

Steve gently rolled the menu between thumb and index finger while looking at his friend. Tilting his head, so that he could see comfortably over the top of his glasses which were interposed perfectly, for once, in Matt's direction, enabling him to look directly at Matt, and still focus on the menu. "Okay, Matt, fire away, what can I do for you?" A preamble would have been unwise; the young GP was clearly keen to unburden himself of something: the sooner he provided him with a forum with which to do so, the better.

"What do you know about obsession?" Matt began.

"You mean obsession-compulsion, as in washing your hands twenty times before you leave the house. That sort of thing?"

"No, Steve: I mean obsession as in towards another person," Matt clarified, suddenly looking very nervous.

Steve held his gaze on his friend, seeking more detail, his eyes flaring as he did so. "So how long have *we* been so obsessed?" He gently emphasised the 'we' to enable Matt to talk as if describing a case, should he wish to seek refuge in the anonymity that would bring.

"I've developed an unhealthy infatuation with Fabienne," Matt confessed, suddenly feeling a little less nervous.

"The one I see on the telly? Nice girl! Good choice." He couldn't quite conquer the smile that crept through at this point even though Matt's steely gaze revealed the serious nature of his admission, and the angst that lay behind. "So are you following her about; writing to her - the full stalking thing, or what?"

"No, no, not quite that bad. I stop short by buying all her CDs, all the DVDs, the magazine articles, every newspaper piece I can get my hands on, attending the concerts and so on," Matt explained whilst realising that the list would have grown ever longer had he not made a conscious effort to stop himself.

"So, we are talking here, more pictures on your wall, rather than dirty brown overcoats?" Steve suggested, determined to keep the conversation light so as to draw his friend out just a little more.

"I admire her from afar; have made no attempt to contact her or approach her," Matt confided sheepishly.

"How long has this been going on?"

"For six months, maybe longer, could be even twelve months or more," he admitted in such a way that Steve would know which answer held the truth.

The waitress arrived to take their order. Her pinafore was worn but also dirty. This was not the most worrying aspect of her appearance as Matt surveyed her carefully. Though he estimated that she was not long into her forties, the skin was already looking the worse for wear, most likely due to heavy cigarette consumption, and this was confirmed by the nicotine-stained fingers that applied the pen to her little notebook. Her nails were dirty with neglect, in keeping with her overall appearance. Matt started to worry about the standard of the food, when the waitress looked as if she could do with a good scrub. Looking nervously at Steve, wondering if his face was reflecting those same concerns, he needn't have worried. The buxom waitress had distracted the psychologist, whose attention had temporarily shifted from his friend. Matt smiled to himself and grasped the opportunity to scrutinise the menu carefully. Steve, apparently oblivious to everything else, seemed perfectly happy as he looked at her admiringly. Matt decided that his best plan was to order a bacon sandwich, as this was easy to cook and hopefully exposed to significant heat, thereby affording more protection - if the kitchen staff had similar standards of hygiene.

"So, what is it about this that worries you, Matt?" Steve asked, as he replaced the menu on the table, which was just a little too sticky for comfort.

Matt paused while he considered this unexpected enquiry. Steve knew very well why Matt was worried, and also with good reason. He had treated similar cases in the past, but knew that it was important for Matt to convey, in his own words, the extent of the problem.

"Well, I'm not sleeping, can't stop thinking about her, can't concentrate on anything, daydream a lot - and besides I can't afford the magazines anymore." Matt's smile flashed through, only for an instant.

Steve had deliberately asked his friend to frame the exact reasons for his concern; this was a useful way of gauging the depths to which he'd sunk. As with all good clinicians, Steve knew that the patient always held the answers, provided they were teased out in the correct way. "Seems to me that this can be pretty mild. Adolescents go through a similar phase," Steve began.

"Yes, but ...." Matt interrupted, nervously.

"Yes, I know, you're not an adolescent, but truth is, it can affect any age and may have been triggered by your Mum's death last year."

"Yes, yes I hadn't thought of that," as the new perspective dawned upon him.

"We psychologists call this CWS, *Celebrity Worship Syndrome*. You're exhibiting many of the signs. As I said, it starts off pretty mild, but then progresses with more symptoms. Poor concentration, poor sleep, daydreaming; buying the magazines, just because they have a mention of the person on the front cover. Planning holidays and days off so that you can attend concerts; or drive past where they live. Does any of this sound familiar?" Steve could see that his words were hitting home. He went on. "Everyone has a little of this inside. This is how advertisers sell us products. So-and-so uses such-and-such a hairspray; you should too. We're all happy to have products endorsed by famous people. It's one of the most powerful tools that advertisers use. Most influential are high-profile celebrities who allow their name, for a fee of course, to be associated with certain products. This really good athlete drinks this juice. This golf professional plays with these clubs. We're constantly being influenced by the media - with a message. To be a good person, use this; to be happy, more successful, buy this; good lovers use this. Advertisers then try to push us a little further along this pathway; from not just trying to copy that person, but to encourage us to live the same sort of life as they do. Of course it's not just to do with advertising, the whole basis of human attraction is in there. We all wanted to be the action hero, the handsome, good guy who could fight like Bruce Lee, look like Pierce Brosnan, shag like Casanova and, of course, get the luscious girl at the end of the movie. Who ever wanted to be the baddy? You remember the guy who did the shower scene in Psycho? Just how many other films have you seen him in? He became typecast as 'the psycho' not the handsome hero who got the girl.

As you might expect such forces are very powerful in the States. It's no coincidence that the war hero became president, nor should it be a surprise that the film star did. We all want to live that dream, and sometimes, separating the dream from reality is the hard bit. Life is hard; it has pain, like Monday mornings, gas bills and trips to the dentist. For those locked in these hero-worship scenarios, there's none of that; just cock your Kalashnikov, go shoot some evil baddies and end up in bed with Miss drop-dead-gorgeous. Escapism, truth be told, we all need a little of, but sometimes it goes too far, and that's when people become ensnared by the dream and depart from reality." Steve paused as he chewed his sandwich quickly.

Matt was hanging off each word almost as if a great seer was reading his palm. Steve continued, while a little food slipped down. "You remember the actors who received death threats after acting out a scene on the telly where they behaved like a total bastard to one of the really nice characters? This is by no means rare, and the people who then write in with those death threats are ordinary, intelligent human beings, not psychiatric cases." There came another slight pause as he munched again.

"I'd say that what you have is, very often, pretty benign, should self-limit and eventually you'll get over her. The problem though, Matt, is that many people never do move on. They continue to watch and wait; read and hope. The day they're waiting for, of course, never arrives, and quietly their real life fails to progress; placed on the back burner whilst they only truly live under the shadow of the life they aspire to. Or maintain a dreary, unfulfilled existence while they tick off the days as they wait for the next DVD, movie release or magazine article."

Matt shivered; there was worse.

Steve continued, "Then, of course, a few go on, they become low, depressed, why is this 'ordinary' life of mine worth living - when it bears little resemblance to the life of Miss megastar that I've read all about? They're attracted to a dream, a presentation, and a gloss, found in the magazines that even for that star, bears little resemblance to her true life. The magazine is pitched to sell more copy by pretending that that life is extraordinary and, of course, is hyped up. The star, surprise, surprise, doesn't live such a life; the magazine just puts out the best bits, or the bits that will attract readers." He took a quick slurp from his fizzy water as a lump of food lingered stubbornly: caught mid sentence. "Depression is very common; as are low feelings and misery – or worse. The person so affected tends to disengage from his or her own life, doesn't meet new friends, and then starts to withdraw."

Steve was the consummate professional: an expert in his field. Most significantly, he chose not to burden Matt with the true depths to which such people could sink. Neither telling him that the syndrome often led to a severe depression and misery, nor that one such patient had hanged herself before she could begin treatment. He was anxious to warn Matt, not scare him, and for this he needed to introduce his topic slowly, yet methodically, so that Matt could gain insight for himself and would, no doubt, have already started to recognise danger signs as he continued. "Maybe what you should do is concentrate on losing this bachelor lifestyle of yours and find a wife like the rest of us. That'll stop you pining for her," he said, with satisfaction.

Matt continued to soak in his friend's advice while he spoke.

"Obviously don't start hanging round stage doors for her, or wait on her street corner. What might not be a bad idea, however, is to try sending a card or two. You'll soon get fed up when she doesn't reply, or you just receive a mass-produced, signed photo. Under no circumstances start sending anything that's, that's..."

"No, Steve: stupid I may be, but not that stupid," Matt said.

"Cleverer men than us do worse, Matt," Steve reminded him.

"Yes, you're right," Matt acknowledged and continued, "I suppose I could write to her fan club and wait for the boredom effect you mention."

"If it's any consolation I don't think you're going mad, and I'm sure just about everybody goes through a phase like this at some time, though most ..."

"Don't tell me, I know, I know, most grow out of it by the time they leave their teens," Matt interrupted.

"Something like that," agreed Steve. "I suppose also, it's true that this obsession, this infatuation is stopping you from moving on. I remember, what was her name now, that redhead - Alison Grundy, yes, that was her name. We all had the hots for her, and you were the one who whisked her off on that balmy summer evening at Freshers' ball, I seem to remember, and then there was ..."

"Yes, yes, Steve. I know; I was very lucky." Matt shifted uncomfortably, his food untouched on the table.

"Yes, you handsome dog, you could have any girl you chose, and if I remember..."

"I know, I know I was popular," Matt agreed soothingly, hoping to change tack quickly.

"More than popular. I remember, yours was the only sample they refused when we all went to sell our semen to the sperm bank - probably because it was so dilute!" Steve chuckled, oblivious of his friend's discomfort.

"Enough Steve, you're embarrassing me in front of all these people," Matt offered, a little despair creeping in as he spoke.

Steve turned round at the almost deserted room and laughed. His friend had succeeded in distracting him with his usual skill, just when he was getting into his stride.

"As the song says, Matt, you've had some very fine things presented at your table, and it's perhaps a cruel irony that you want what you can never have." The head dipped a little as he peered over his glasses, while scrutinizing the GP more closely. "Tell me, do you feel lonely?"

Matt replied with enough vigour for the psychologist to know that he had hit upon a key tenet of the diagnosis. "No, of course not, Steve, I'm always out, always busy - postgraduate meetings, I work out at the gym, my surgery keeps me busy, my nights on call - I don't have time to be lonely."

Steve did his best to seem convinced: he had no wish to humble his friend by needlessly clarifying what he knew the young GP would realise for himself sooner or later. He'd learned enough, and said enough; before arriving at his conclusions.

"Okay then, just to recap. Make no attempt to see her; these days, stalking is bad news and you don't want to be on the wrong side of the law. By all means try to write, but nothing too serious, keep it light. I think you need to work through this 'crush', let's say."

Matt winced a little as, once again, his friend made him squirm by the deliberate choice of words. Steve continued, "Your Mum's death earlier this year may have contributed, and I do think it's important for you to keep up the dating that you were obviously so good at."

"Yes, yes, I know: that was few years ago now, when we were students," Matt interjected quickly, before embarrassment overcame him once again.

"This condition is usually fairly mild and self-limiting, but can turn nasty. I'd say poor sleep, poor appetite, lack of concentration, daydreaming and disengaging from one's own life, are all danger signs."

Matt swallowed hard: he was exhibiting all these signs and a few more that he dare not admit to himself, let alone to his friend.

"Okay." Steve adjusted his glasses as he acknowledged his friend's continued discomfort with more emollient terms.

"What I'm trying to say is: you were always a knockout success with the girls, and it seems strange that there's no one special in your life. Perhaps if there were, then you'd be able to draw a line under this and move on. That is, after all, the way most teens get over it. They lust after what they're never going to have, spend all those hours pining away, and then eventually meet someone who is approachable and attainable. Then, of course, they forget all about the fantasies they had for Miss Prom-Queen or whoever."

Matt nodded. He knew, without doubt, that his friend's words held the essential truth. Steve had voiced what had been many of Matt's own conclusions, though he hadn't appreciated that people could fall so far. He accepted too, that the way he was feeling about the person he'd never met, and would never know, was as false as the existence he'd allowed himself to be drawn into. The harsh reality declared itself before him as he acknowledged that his life, no matter how perfect on paper; was on hold, and would remain so until he settled this and moved on. The final truth would come to him, brutally, in the desolate early hours of the following morning as he despairingly allowed himself to look at the alarm clock - that he was lonely. Though the attractions in his life were all apparent, loneliness would be a constant distraction, until he had summoned the courage to confront it.

Matt settled the bill and drove them back to Mirfield. He remained subdued while considering his friend's words. Steve hesitated as he pushed back the heavy car door.

"Matt, you know where I am, so perhaps phone me in a week or two, so that we can talk some more?"

"It's very kind of you, Steve," Matt said earnestly.

"Don't worry, my invoice will be in the post, I can tell you, or at the very least I deserve an invite to your next Christmas bash, I hear they're wicked!" Steve suggested.

"Okay; I won't forget you, I promise," Matt said, as if making a mental note.

"You'd better not, my boy," and he continued more seriously: "Listen, what are friends for?"

"Give Mary my best wishes won't you? Matt remembered.

"Sooner you get a wife, my boy, the better you will be."

"I know, I know. I'll take on-board what you say."

The passenger door closed with its usual 'thunk' as the rubber sealed against the metal frame. The car growled, ever so slightly, as the engine bit against its weight and the X-Type swept down the smooth road towards the hospital exit.

Matt faced another distracted afternoon, as he mulled over his friend's conclusions. Just as he was about to start surgery, an urgent call came through. Mr and Mrs Murray were a lovely elderly couple, who troubled him rarely. Howard Murray was well into his eighties and his wife, Cynthia, though a little younger, at a mere seventy five had had problems with her heart. Mr Murray spoke.

"Doctor Sinclair, please forgive me troubling you in your surgery."

"That's no problem Howard, what can I do for you?"

"It's actually Cynthia who's poorly, Doctor."

Matt was just about to say that he was sorry to hear that, thinking that she perhaps had a chest infection or something of a similar routine status, when Howard continued:

"She's on the floor and can't seem to get up."

Matt repeated his words so as to make quite sure that he had heard correctly.

"You say she's on the..."

Once again, he was interrupted by Howard:

"Would you like to speak to her Doctor?"

Incredibly, he handed the phone to his wife who must have been lying on the floor at his feet. Matt could hear how breathless she was.

"Doctor, sorry to trouble you, I can't seem to get my breath and am having trouble getting off the floor."

Eventually, Matt got his words out: "Cynthia, put the phone down and dial 999, this minute." He spoke slowly and clearly so that there would be no doubt.

"Doctor, I'm sure that won't be necessary. I don't want to cause any fuss: perhaps if you were to come and check me over?"

Matt could hear how laboured her breathing was as she struggled with the words, "Perhaps after your surgery this evening?"

A hysterical thought rushed into Matt's head that the poor woman could be long dead by that time. "No Cynthia, please put the phone down now, and dial 999."

"Are you sure, Doctor?" she panted.

"Yes, Cynthia, I am very, very sure; we don't want you being poorly now do we."

Matt knew that a sudden collapse like this, especially in an elderly patient with a history of heart trouble, could be many things, unfortunately several of them serious. He knew that to leave her on the floor, even if he were to break off from his surgery that minute and visit, would introduce potentially fatal delays. An ambulance was the only course of action that made sense.

"Oh, very well then Doctor, sorry to trouble you."

Matt never ceased to be amazed at the toughness and the politeness of their generation. They complained very little, even when faced with serious problems, and sought his permission for action that others wouldn't have hesitated over. He popped into the office, so that his staff could telephone to make sure that an ambulance was on its way, and returned to his consulting room to start the surgery.

Patients came and went in a blur, as his self-occupied state had returned from the brief interlude of his phone conversation, and held him in firm embrace. Fortunately the surgery was quiet and the cases presenting were undemanding, thereby allowing him to continue in his reverie whilst maintaining the illusion of giving each patient his undivided attention.

At last he had things clarified. There were no more excuses; no way of hiding from what he now knew. He'd been forced to take a long, dispassionate look at himself; realising, in that moment, that there was a danger that he could lose the life that he had loved. For the first time, allowing himself to use the past tense. Now he had to find out if he could break free and recapture the paradise that had been lost.

Having seen the last patient through the door, he telephoned the hospital to see how Mrs Murray was. The casualty department at Caldbrook General told him that she had been admitted with a suspected further myocardial infarct, and that the tests would be through any minute. She was comfortable and her husband was with her. Events like these, though mercifully rare, brought it home to him that his patients needed, and expected, a doctor who was both focussed and alert, not one who was distracted and preoccupied. He would never be able to forgive himself if one of them had come to harm as a result of his neglect. Asking the doctor in casualty, if he would pass on his best wishes to her for a speedy recovery, and that, if Mr Howard would telephone when she got home, he'd pop in and see her. As always, the ones who troubled him the least, were usually the most unwell, and needed his attention and readiness to act, more than any other group. He hoped that he wouldn't allow himself to let them down.

Driving home: becoming aware of an all-pervading tiredness while flicking on the television, he smiled to himself because, suddenly, Fabienne appeared on the early evening news. He knew all about her film role and the multi-million pound sponsorship deal that had been rumoured with Pepsi Co. Fighting desperately, he dragged his mind from wandering along the lines that she was just an ordinary girl with ordinary human needs, as this avenue never helped. It was always easier to position her as some super-being, unattainable and aloof, who inhabited a very different world from the one that he, and others, lived in. This line, at least reinforced his belief that he knew they'd never meet, so she might just as well be some fairy-tale princess in a story beloved by children. Living, but not quite real: occupying space, but in a world he would never experience. This was the only way to preserve sane thought, the only way to move on and reclaim the existence that others would kill for - the one that was his for the taking. In so doing he'd cultivate an ordinary life without the intrusion of dreams about pop stars, which were no more real than any other fantasy. He picked up the *Radio Times* to look at the television listings: there on the back cover was an advertisement for her new fragrance!

Silencing the television with another stab of the remote: for a new thought formed within his mind. Steve was right about everything. He'd also been very clever: knowing that pride would never allow Matt to line up alongside those thousands and thousands of fans and write to her. The volume of post that she'd receive; the army of people who'd surround her, insulating and protecting her from those fans, invisibly, so that they'd never know they weren't in direct contact with the megastar in person. Even if she were to catch a momentary glimpse of his letter, what would he say? 'Really like you', 'Love to see you', or just, 'Want to know you?' The words alone seemed ridiculous as they crossed his consciousness.

How would they look if he were to even attempt to commit them to paper? Would the fan club send him a signed picture, perhaps swirled over by the pen of an assistant or a secretary, rather than by Fabienne herself? 'Thank you, for your lovely note.' Possibly even a pre-printed slip, 'Thank you for your kind communication'. Yes, his expression was more grimace than smile; Steve had been very clever. He'd known all along that embarrassment and self ridicule would be effective countermeasures to an obsession that otherwise had no basis - unlike the burning and stinging that was now pounding in his head. Even before the remote tumbled from his sofa onto the floor, he knew what he had to do. It had dawned on him as he sat there: desperate times, demanded desperate remedies.

He jumped to his feet. His lounge had several racks containing CDs, and others holding DVDs. The plan that formed feverishly within, coupled with his relentless determination, told him that this was the place to start. Scanning each one quickly, row by row and rack by rack: he removed each and every one that had a connection with Fabienne; including compilations, which might perhaps contain only one track of hers. Great gaps opened up in the previous smooth pattern of the rank and file of CDs. Their disordered pattern reflected many of the thoughts running through his brain. He moved to the DVDs, which were also selected by their content, and removed one at a time as he scanned their labels. Placing them all on the rug in the middle of the room.

Then came the magazines. Shelves lay on the bottom row of his large bookcase, in the corner. Each was stuffed to capacity with glossy publications and press articles. The only thing in common in such a wide collection of material was the star whose spell had bewitched him for more months than he could admit - even to himself. The magazines were harder in many ways to dispose of, as each held a slice; a different perspective on the person who fascinated and captivated him from afar - without any effort on her part. Leafing through them all, one by one, as if shuffling a great pack of cards, he knew most of them with an intimate knowledge that only repeated and careful study could bring. Either Fabienne's picture was on the cover, or her name. He looked at them all once again; with the interest that one might show photographs from a treasured family album. Suddenly his purpose returned from the torpor induced by gazing at her image on the covers of most of them. Tossing them all, apart from one or two, which even his determined state couldn't make him discard, on to the rug also.

There they lay, like a shrine to his infatuation that had continued possibly for two years or more. He shrank from considering exactly how long it had been, as exact knowledge, he was sure, would make his efforts to finally break free, seem even harder. Only when he was satisfied that he'd collected all items from the lounge, did he start to ferry them out to the bin. Grabbing his car keys, he went outside, the fading light hiding the resolve now etched on his face, as if his survival depended upon his steadfastness, while he removed more CDs from the player in the boot.

Everything with reference to Fabienne was hunted out and disposed of, in a systematic search that took over an hour. With the completion of that search came relief, a self-cleansing, that he was finally taking steps which would break the spell she cast. Pausing only for an instant as he held the latest CD, thought to be her best, its silvery surface catching the last rays of the spring sun, before the CD spiralled down into the bin. The task was finally over and he sighed contentedly. On closing the lid with finality, he knew that from this grim undertaking had come a peace; almost like banishment of unhealthy forces within him.

He smiled, as he thought of Steve, who'd planted a small seed within him: knowing that Matt would be unable to resist its influence once it had started to grow. The bin shut with a satisfying thud: returning inside from the cold night that now caused him to shiver as the beads of sweat reflected his frenzied activity.

Racing upstairs, he showered and changed for bed. Like an alcoholic who had cleared his house of all bottles, he knew that he'd made an important first step, but many more temptations would arrive: more CDs, more magazines, and more news articles. For the moment, he'd done enough; now came the tricky job of keeping it up - for as long as it took. The strategy would be just like that of an alcoholic. Tomorrow would herald a fresh start and he would, as he always instructed his patients facing addictions - take each day at a time. His temporary deliverance was to be echoed in his sleep, which embraced him with an uninterrupted flow, until the alarm woke him from benign dreams that he didn't remember. The following day would see battle joined for real. He could only pray that he was equal to the task, or suffer the consequences, which for most alcoholics, so entrapped, would mean losing everything, including one's self respect. He reasoned that failure would ultimately bring a similar fate to his door. Mercifully, Matt did not remember that fewer than one in fifty alcoholics would break free.

CHAPTER II

OPEN INVITATION

Matt was awake before the alarm sounded. Dressing with a typical frenzy of activity, he shaved while his mind thought of other things. The irony of his Saturday mornings - the day he didn't have to rise early - was that this was the morning he'd spend in the gym. Approaching his workout with unaccustomed vigour, he paced in time with the running machine, creating more bounce than his usual wrong-footed slog. Although it produced intense thumping from his heart, he left the machine eager for more. The rowing machine, too, failed to disturb the feeling within him that he could keep up that pace all day. He continued on to the resistance machines before re-entering the locker rooms so that he could change for a swim. He noted the young girl, who often claimed the pool for her own at this time of day, charging up and down the far left lane with her effortless, unassailable and smooth strokes. Though, as always, he was unable to keep pace with her, today's contest was to be closer than usual, and he left the water with the feeling that she'd had to try, just a little, in order to leave him in her wake. Smiling to himself, he sank into the relaxing fizz of the spa by the side of the pool, before showering and dressing quickly, as hunger made its presence felt after his morning activities.

A beautiful spring morning lay in wait while he walked from the country club to the café bar which was to play host to a drug company meeting, scheduled to take place just after lunch. Sophie Dewsbury, pharmaceutical representative, greeted him at the door.

"Nice to see you again, Doctor Sinclair." He remembered, just in time, her vice-like handshake, doing his best not to wince under its enthusiastic embrace. Sophie stood tall: he estimated her to be almost six foot two in the heels she always wore, and seemed to delight in the fact that most people she met would find themselves looking up at her. Matt was one of the few who could engage face-to-face. Rather like her handshake, she levelled her forceful voice in his direction just as their hands locked together.

"Nice to see you again, Sophie. Thanks for inviting me."

"No meeting would be complete without you, Doctor Sinclair," she boomed, as heads turned in the room in their direction. Matt disengaged his hand, doing his best to smile disarmingly so as not to attract too much attention from the voice that any parade-ground sergeant would be proud of. "Doctor Letworth is over there, Dr Sinclair; she asked me if you were coming."

Sophie's voice was a dual-edged weapon that served to embarrass, not only with its volume, but also by its content. Matt slunk away with a final 'thank you', took a plate from the large stack, and served himself from the buffet, which had been laid out along one side of the room, before heading in the female GP's direction.

"Rita, how are you? What have you been up to?" he said in a business-like fashion, as he sat, balancing the plate on his knees.

"It's been a while Matt; keeping busy, you know," she replied; her eyes homing in on him with precise, undeviating attention, like a trainer looking at a thoroughbred racehorse that had just secured first prize. Rita had obviously not forgotten the fling they'd had that summer's evening at medical school. Having both consumed just a little more drink than was wise; the morning light had brought an embarrassment to accompany the memories, as each had recalled the frantic passion that had been unleashed.

Now Matt sat facing her; the long legs swished silkily as they were uncrossed. Her eyes sparkled with renewed vigour because she caught the fleeting but unmistakable glance in their direction. Surveying him coolly, waiting for his next words: she mused to herself that perhaps some fire could be rekindled after all.

"So what are you up to these days, Rita?" he enquired, politely.

"Still at Parkvale medical, they made me a full-time partner about two years ago, now Matt." Her eyes continued to stare at him as if words were an inadequate means of communication. He hurriedly broke contact, as discomfort flickered within, transferring his attention to the room that was slowly filling with colleagues.

"Good turn-out," he suggested benignly, successfully employing his ability to move along an uncomfortable conversation.

"Miss 'crunching grip', over there always pulls them in - tell me, just what does she offer, besides your postgraduate allowance points?" she queried, as she surveyed him covetously.

"Nothing that I'm aware of," he volunteered disarmingly, and quickly tacked the conversation to calmer waters. "So are you happy at Parkvale?"

Parkvale Medical Centre was the largest practice in the region. No fewer than eight general practitioners worked there, and it was larger than the average, with a substantial list size, rumoured to be over sixteen thousand. Furthermore, it was held up as a model of smooth clinical efficiency, and was regarded as a leading edge, *Beacon,* practice as one government or other had christened them. Based in the heart of Shrigvale, it was some ten miles from Caldbrook, which itself lay some five miles from Matt's surgery.

"Yes, *very*," she said, "plenty there to keep me amused."

Once again he detected an enthusiasm in her voice that was in no way work-related.

"So, are you still messing about in that hamlet, Perrilymm?"

"Well, I know it's only a tiny village compared to Shrigvale, but it's a place I can call home and I'm happy there."

"I'd be bored out of my brains if I worked there," she said scornfully, and continued in order to underline her point. "What's your list size: a thousand, twelve hundred?"

Such talk amongst doctors was considered impolite. The equation here was a simple one: the more patients, the more money. It was rather like asking someone how much they earned. Matt knew that the national average was about sixteen hundred per GP, but rumoured to be even higher at Parkvale. Rita, as usual, wasted no time in asking simply what she wanted to know, without any concern for whether her words were actually polite or otherwise. "Tell me Matt, we'll be advertising for a new partner. MacGregor has finally decided to retire. The old bastard, with the wandering hands."

Matt wondered whether her version of events was the truth. She'd never been one to find herself unable to handle any physical attention that invariably came her way. She'd certainly been propelled very quickly into a full-parity partnership at Parkvale; perhaps old MacGregor had outlived his usefulness to her now that she was a full-equity partner. He wondered insightfully whether Doctor MacGregor had jumped or been pushed.

"We need someone with a bit of drive, enthusiasm, not afraid of hard work, who has uncommonly handsome looks, not to mention a great body - know anyone like that, who might be interested?" The eyes seemed to glow with avaricious intent as they homed in on their target.

"No Rita, I can't say that I do. I could ask around if you like. Have you tried advertising? The wording might need a bit of work but 'drive', 'enthusiasm' and 'hard work' seem good."

The eyes simmered to a glow as she continued, "Look Matt, you're wasted in that little village and that small surgery. Why not come and work with us, and see what real medicine's like? I know your Dad left you a load of money in his will, but it surely is time to enter the real world rather than hide away in that little hamlet." She slowly smoothed the line of her skirt as her hand stroked gently down her thigh. "We have a great deal to offer someone like you." The eyes, the steady gaze; the full lips, bubbling with passion, held much more than the promise of a new job, while she continued to gaze at him possessively.

She had chosen, as usual, the direct approach. This was the way she ran her life, and her interaction with that life was directly wired, with no messy cogs or chains to get in the way. If people found her abrasive or embarrassing, the problem was theirs; it wasn't her fault if they hid their feelings, or needed irrelevant platitudes and empty words to cushion delicate constitutions.

Matt had forgotten just how blunt she could be. The problem with this approach was that the person who practised it made no concessions at all to the frailty of the human mind, in forgoing emotions such as tact, empathy and the need to approach less-robust psyches with care. These thoughts were simply not in her emotional lexicon; nor did she see a need to acknowledge that fact. Doubtless, there was so much more on offer here than just the prospect of a new job. His mind flicked back to that night, now several years ago, when unrestrained passion had been the only medium through which their bodies had communicated. Would it be so wrong to take up such an offer, especially when her words and body language were indicating that it was one free from unnecessary complications? Logic and lust combined, for once, and were in full agreement. The sexual allure that she radiated must surely be as good a way as any to free himself, once and for all, from his predicament.

He turned to consider, not so much her offer, but her choice of words. Had the moment been more propitious he would have returned her words with a few direct ones of his own. What his list size was, and what his father had left him in his will, was no business of hers; that money could never make up for the loss of anyone, and certainly no one as close, someone he thought about constantly in his daily activities. Like all no-nonsense talkers, however, he mused that she wouldn't be able to receive what she gave out. This was the fulcrum of his indecision. Despite the beautiful packaging, the gorgeous looks and her undoubted interest, what lay within was a person less caring, more detached than he could ever warm to. Her every word made no secret of her direct, calculating stance to just about everything, and especially emotional matters which were seen almost as an irrelevance. Taking up her offer and using her would, on the face of it, be exactly what was being suggested: she was happy to effect that mutual trade. What seemed right in the midst of a flow of passion ten years before, as a student, wouldn't pass more careful scrutiny now. And the fact that she was a willing accomplice to his need for an uncomplicated relationship, just at that point, didn't give it more acceptability.

She continued to stare at him: the enchantress staring into the steaming cauldron of pure desire; she knew her spell with all the comfort of practised ease. He was certain that she licked her lips as he broke from the weight of her gaze. "Okay, look, suppose I have a think and maybe sleep on it. Perhaps I could call you?" His lame reply was precisely the one she was not expecting. Disappointment tinged with disgust flared at once within those eyes, now of steel. "Okay Matt, suppose you do that, but don't think too long, as an offer like this doesn't come, even your way, every day."

The lack of substance in his decision racked him mercilessly at that point. Perhaps he'd been foolish, and maybe it wasn't too late to take her wrist and guide her from that meeting room just as he'd done years before on that hot evening of the second MB ball.

Regaining composure, his smile flashed. "Look Rita, you're putting quite a lot on the table here. I agree, an offer like this doesn't come every day, nor do I take it for granted - but this is why I have to think it through. You wouldn't like me to rush and have regrets would you?" Her eyes continued to say much more than the voice, as 'rush' was precisely the urgency with which she sought an affirmative course of action. "I forget, Matt, you're used to a village pace of life rather than the twenty-first century one I'm accustomed to." The legs were crossed once again, the activity lingering only so long as to enhance the lush movement while the sleek flesh whisked together.

His instinct, as always, had been to keep options open as far and as long as possible, and whilst he recognised the attraction in the offer he'd just received, he suspected that it had been made to others on several previous occasions. He wondered whether Doctor MacGregor had paid in full for taking up a similar offer: or more prosaically, if the offer had been abruptly withdrawn as soon as events had turned to her advantage. Noting the banishment of any warmth from those eyes that took place at the first hint of disappointment: she obviously wasn't responsive to people who hesitated and certainly not to those who needed time to think. Finally, his thoughts crystallised in the icy waste that lay between them. Though he was unattached and yes, lonely, he wasn't about to slake his loneliness by using someone who was offering a no-strings relationship: and it was precisely because she'd be unable to grasp this point, had he offered an explanation, that he knew this to be the correct decision.

Later, when reflecting the events of the day, he would be unprepared to accept that Fabienne's influence held sway. Only in silent dreams, which existed fleetingly in the night, would he be able to visualise such a concept.

He was about to convey some of his thoughts to Rita, when Sophie's voice announced unequivocally that the meeting was about to start, and would they kindly take their seats. He finished his food quickly, returned the plate, and grabbed a cup of coffee before going in to the meeting room. Sitting next to Rita, however, their thoughts were widely separated: he being comfortable with his decision; she retained the frustration and anger of a hungry predator who had presciently detected that its next meal would elude it. Fortunately the consultant, who spoke, captivated his audience, so that little wandering of thoughts was possible, and any conversation too intrusive to risk in the hushed room, as he presented his findings with the steady click of a laser pointer controlling his laptop and projector. Only as the meeting closed did Rita venture more words in his direction, imparting with a hiss, "just have a think about things – there's a lot on offer here, and I wouldn't like you to miss out, Matt."

His composure, long regained and born out of confidence in his decision, flashed back in the full weight of his smile. She seemed just a little too keen, as if wanting to sell something before the unwary buyer had had a chance to think things through.

"It's lovely to see you again; Rita and I want to thank you for your kind proposal. I guess I'll always just be a village lad, and perhaps wouldn't cope with a move to the big league."

"Perhaps not," she returned, the look in her eyes now icier than he'd ever noted before, as they met his of placid but unwavering blue. His smile disarmed her just for a moment: as he bent to kiss her lightly he was aware of her brash and cloying perfume.

Risking another knuckle-shattering grip from Sophie's handshake, before leaving the room without looking back. Had he done so, he would have seen Rita now deep in concentration. A clever and determined tactician, she wasn't going to be diverted by what she now considered to be only a temporary setback. The predatory instincts, that had been honed within her, were also stimulated by the scent of blood in the way that he had glanced longingly at her legs; and the hunger in those eyes of solid but revealing blue.

Returning to the Jaguar in the car park, the engine caught, as usual, with a quick flick of the key. He activated the sunroof to let in the more persistent spring sunshine as he prodded the climate control back into a dormant state. The car cruised out of the country club and on to the main road that would take him back to the familiar comfort of Perrilymm, and his house at the edge of the village. Afternoon found him with the papers, settling himself in the warm conservatory: he reflected back on the day's events. In the not-too-distant past he would have accepted Rita's offer without hesitation, but he pondered that the passage of time had rendered such liaisons now inappropriate. Perhaps Steve was correct in that he was ready to settle down with a more enduring relationship. Maybe the mad imagery tied up around his fixation with Fabienne was simply reflecting his subconscious desire for that; and she was nothing more than a marker, a placeholder for such a need within him. Steve's observations were perhaps more relevant than even he'd grasped. Matt would certainly contact him again soon, as he'd suggested. What a clever man Steve was. Matt was constantly in awe of his clinical acumen and his skill with his patients. Having witnessed, first hand, what a detailed and comprehensive analysis he could tease from a consultation lasting perhaps only half an hour.

As the next few days passed, Matt considered that for the first time in months, some semblance of order had re-entered his life. He seized on this gladly. Hunted he may have been, and tortured by images of his own failure to counter the weight of obsession from re-entering his life. Instinct told him that speed was somehow of the essence and this was the defensive line that he drew. One based on a fast-moving life geared to the plain old-fashioned puritan ethic of hard work. One that had no time to stop and think: and certainly not to look back. If these fears were to pursue him, then he would not be found standing still, waiting for them to find him. In looking in more detail at his life and work, he also had to accept the painful truth that his surgery had marked time for too long. Perhaps Rita's words contained something of the truth, albeit couched in spite. Lots of changes had taken place within the National Health Service and also the field of Medicine, and he had paid little attention, let alone set in motion any of those modern practises. He intended to change this as soon as was practicable.

Though his surgeries were unusually quiet, even for this time of year, he applied himself to his work with as much enthusiasm as he could muster. The alternative was too horrible to think of, and Steve had intimated significant potential dangers in his state of mind so as to make further clarification unnecessary. To his ancillary staff he seemed buoyant and carefree; even his days on-call, failing to dent his new-found energies.

Matt's surgery was run by Mrs Simpson, a fifty-year-old ex-bank-manager who had been made redundant some years before. She was an honest and, when there was work to be done, a diligent worker who led by example. However, if workload was slack, and the surgery quiet, then she would turn her hand to less productive pastimes. Having been with Matt since he first took the surgery in Perrilymm, she'd had a lot of time on her hands in the past two years as the ship drifted and the captain remained somnolent in his cabin. This had given the practice manager all the time and opportunity she needed to perfect her own brand of mindless tittle-tattle with which to impress any who would listen for long enough.

The manager could only wonder as to the real reason for his enlivened attitude. Lack of firm knowledge didn't stop her from expounding her opinions as more-or-less concrete fact; what they lacked in proof, she happily made up for with a habit of exaggeration. Gossip between her and Janice, the junior receptionist, who was also a distant relation, turned away from patients to focus on the much more interesting, private life of their boss. Such hushed get-togethers occupied most of their break time and a significant amount of work time too. "It's a new woman I tell you," said Mrs Simpson, with the nodding, qualified authority that she normally reserved for patients who might be foolish enough to challenge her in some way or other.

"Funny, I haven't heard him mention anyone for well over twelve months," pondered Janice

"That's why it *must* be, it's the *only* thing that fits. Have you seen him on that new computer? It's only been installed a week, and he's working like a man possessed. Yesterday he typed in the *entire* Smear and Immunisation data himself, in just a day, without waiting for the secretarial support the suppliers promised us," continued Mrs Simpson.

"I've never seen anything like it," agreed Janice, smiling like a pixie.

"He's usually a cheery soul, but it's gone beyond that. It's a woman I tell you. That's the only thing that can bring this sort of change in a man. You mark my words." Mrs Simpson folded her arms triumphantly while offering her all-encompassing clarification as being final. Janice chuckled as she finished her coffee, her mousey ponytail flicking in time with the nodding head as she agreed with the practice manager's view. "Must be, you're right. I wonder who she is then?"

Mrs Simpson now did some nodding of her own. Her eyes narrowed just a little as they always did when she was about to enter her most discerning of phases. "Just wait a while, a photograph will appear in his surgery, we'll catch sight of her soon enough, when it does."

As spring continued to bloom, the days lengthened steadily and Matt continued to vent his energies into his work. The new computer system was commissioned more quickly than the trainer had envisaged. Janice heard him tell Doctor Sinclair that he'd never seen an installation go so quickly or so smoothly. Matt now sensed that he had to make up for lost time, as well as continue to nourish all the things in his life that made it unique. By strengthening his own ties with his existence, he hoped to demonstrate, once and for all, that everything else was simply the falsity that Steve had described. Rather like a man running, if he stopped for a moment, then the devils in pursuit would catch him. This strategy was made doubly difficult in that those demons were largely of Matt's own making, and existed only within him. Knowing, too, that Rita would love to see him fail, and would waste no time in gloating if he should find his surgery listed as a poorly performing one. It was no secret that the local Primary Care Trust, which regulated GPs' surgeries, was compiling statistics to do with performance data, patient satisfaction and uptake of new ideas and services.

Some days later, whilst coming out of the village Post Office his attention was caught first by the sharp toot from the horn of a sleek, red, Porsche Boxster sports car, its roof open in the spring sunshine. It slid to a halt along the kerbside as he turned, the wheels squealing a little as the differentials struggled with the rapid deceleration. He leant over the passenger door as Rita beamed from within, her sunglasses restraining the glowing concupiscence from those green eyes. He couldn't help noticing, as he looked unwarily into the car, that the wind had brought her skirt back to an immodest height, before doing his best to maintain the image of the smooth thigh so revealed at the periphery of his vision. Sensing his efforts, she stroked the offending thigh carefully, teasingly, just as her right hand simultaneously caressed the leather-bound steering-wheel. Her simper intensified as she focussed on him.

"What brings you to these parts?" he asked, suspecting that their meeting was not a complete coincidence.

"Oh, just out for a spin in my new toy," she offered with more than a hint of triumph.

"Yes, it's very nice Rita, suits you."

"The salesman gave me a very good deal, with just a *little* coaxing." Her hand tightened its grip ever so slightly, causing the knuckles to flare white, as she did so. Her nonchalant gaze was apparent even with her sunglasses on, and was reflected by her posture and her movements. "It's quite a ride Matt, you should try it sometime." She almost purred the words, as she now stroked the leather passenger seat with the same caress she had offered her left thigh. Matt risked a glance towards the indicated seat, breaking the intense gaze that was locked on him. "Yes, I bet it really moves, Rita," regretting instantly his choice of words.

"You need a complete change, I tell you Matt; get rid of that old man's car of yours. I can get you a good deal on one of these. The salesman would be *extremely* happy to do a little more business with me."

"Yes, yes I'm sure he would," Matt offered, honestly, and didn't have to use too much imagination to think of the inducements the salesman had been offered. "I'm sure that my Jag isn't quite as exciting, but I'm very happy with it, and I'd still be twenty-seven whether I drove one like this, or mine."

As was her wont, any words she considered at variance with her own, were rejected as irrelevant. She continued as if he hadn't spoken. "As I told you, offers like this don't come every day, Matt. The sooner you break out of your backwater lifestyle here, and move into the big league, the better. You're wasted here: sooner or later you'll come round to my view and I just hope that my proposal will still be available to you." She looked away. He'd been dismissed; the conversation was over. "See you," she offered with finality. She flipped the accelerator savagely, the engine connecting quickly with her mood as she selected first gear from the steering-wheel-mounted paddles. "See you around, Matt, don't die of boredom in the meantime will you."

"I'll do my best not to Rita, many thanks for paying us a visit in this quiet backwater." He almost had to shout after her as the machine revved without restraint. With a corresponding roar from the exhaust pipes, she disappeared, a red blur in the warm sunshine. One or two young men stopped and stared as she whipped down the road, her long black hair flailing wildly as the wind caught her.

Matt smiled to himself as he continued up the road to find his car; no doubt Rita had found what she was looking for and doubled back, so as to bump into him just at the right moment. He reflected as he walked. In many ways she was just the distraction his life needed at this time, to underline, once and for all, his break with the imaginary, and to engage with something that would be tangible in every sense of the word. The passion she'd bring to a physical relationship would also extend to her social and professional life.

For sure, however, any patient, who found himself in need of some assistance, would be offered the full weight of her advice. Matt formed a mental image of such a patient being rocked back on the chair, as it was given out, pitying the poor soul seeking warmth from her, perhaps at a time of bereavement or if they had just been made redundant. They would be told unequivocally to pull themselves together and stop wasting her time. This was in her nature, and no mental meanderings of his would change her. He recognised that she'd be lively, fun and interesting, only so long as her consort continued to play along with her view of things. Advice would be offered at every turn to enable that person to do so. He had little doubt also that the danger in having her as an enemy would exceed by a wide margin her skills as a lover. Though her looks and figure, assured sexual appeal; he had to admit to himself that embarking on a relationship held more danger than delight, and the only aspect of its failure would be when, rather than if, that would arise.

Prodding the steering-wheel control to increase the volume of the soundtrack he was listening to, as if by so doing he had closed that discussion in his mind; accepting his own conclusions. It would be better for him to remain as he was, for the moment, than to risk a hasty and ill-judged fling with such attendant danger. Years ago he wouldn't have subjected a relationship to such a detailed analysis, but simply got on with it. The passing years had brought caution in direct proportion to the things, most notably self-respect, he now stood to lose.

Driving the short distance home, he swung the car round to its usual spot on the drive and opened the large front door with its inset beautiful rectangular, stained and etched glass panel. Matching, but smaller, panels were set either side of the door so as to augment the light admitted, and the width of the hallway. He stepped onto the long, narrow rug that ran the length of the hall protecting the teak floorboards, which had been sanded and sealed to a lustrous shine that would grace any yacht. Placing his keys on the glass console table, he walked through to the kitchen. In doing so, he noticed that his answer machine was blinking to attract his attention, with one stored message. Upon jabbing the flashing button, the machine sprang to life with a loud click: recognising Steve's voice immediately.

"Hello Matt, Steve here. I was just wondering how you're getting on. It's a week or two since we met up. I'm free tomorrow lunch, if you fancy another bacon butty in the café by the river."

Matt silenced the machine with another prod of the button and dialled Steve's home.

Mary answered.

"Hi Matt, Nice to hear your voice. How are you? Where have you been hiding yourself?"

Matt felt sure that Steve would have discussed things with his wife, despite the fact that technically he held patient confidentiality. If that was the case, neither revealed that they had that information about the other. "Yes, Mary, Steve was reproaching me about not inviting you to my Christmas party. I plan to rectify that this year."

"I can feel a new dress coming on Matt, so be sure you do. I'll be looking forward to that. Your Christmas bash is *the* social event of the year. I hear tell. Perhaps you'd like to come round one evening for dinner and bring...bring a friend." Only the slight hesitation indicated that Mary knew of Matt's dilemma.

"Thanks Mary, I'd love to."

"Here he comes, let me hand him over. We'll look forward to seeing you, then?"

"Matt, thanks for getting back to me," Steve said, as he took the handset from Mary.

"No problem, Steve. About tomorrow, that would be fine I'll pick you up at one pm."

"Okay; sounds good, my boy, see you then."

Matt made another early start. The dilemma this raised for his staff was that they would have even more to gossip about, as they conjectured why he'd suddenly started to come in early, but have even less time available to do so. Matt worked quickly through the surgery, then promptly checked his post and signed the prescriptions. Janice had entered many on to the computer and Matt checked each one carefully before appending his signature and depositing them in the 'completed' file, ready for patients to collect. The new prescription paper had a green, almost luminous hue to it and as he handled it, a volatile substance was given off that stung his eyes and made him cough. Before leaving, he informed Mrs Simpson that he was popping out to lunch, but that he would have his mobile with him. As he turned in the office to collect his case, Mrs Simpson nodded knowingly to Janice.

"Told you," she mouthed, "out to lunch, with her, no doubt," she mimed, affectedly.

Janice could only nod as Matt turned towards them again. "Just one visit, Doctor Sinclair," Mrs Simpson said with a punitive grin that deflated him just a little.

"Oh, okay Mrs Simpson, who is it?" he asked, suddenly unsure as to why he'd assumed that there would be none.

"Mildred Gratt," came the reply.

Matt groaned, her words dispiriting him quickly as he registered who it was. Mrs Simpson stifled her grin as best she could, whilst she handed him the notes of the valetudinarian, which he took reluctantly: they were thick and heavy, reflecting the numerous consultations, investigations, visits and referrals that had been lavished upon her by specialists, nurses and Matt, over the years. No firm diagnosis had ever been established and he doubted that one ever would be. Perhaps, out of sheer desperation, some ten years before, a specialist had advised her to rest. This instruction had been taken literally. She had dutifully taken herself off to her bed, where she would hold court, while her long-suffering husband waited upon her hand and foot, delivering an endless stream of newspapers, TV guides, sandwiches, tea and, of course, library books to her smooth and unruffled eiderdown.

Matt had tried everything he knew to persuade her that recumbence was doing her no good at all, and that a little exercise would help her. She would look suspiciously at him; obliquely from one eye, while she reminded him of the instructions from a *specialist*, no less. "With the greatest of respect," she'd continue determinedly "how could, he as a GP countermand the orders of a consultant?" Matt laughed to himself as he grabbed his bag from the boot. In point of fact, Mildred was blooming while poor Stan, her husband, was a mere shadow of his former self. He had long since stopped sleeping in the marital bed, preferring the settee downstairs, either so that he could get some relief from the constant flow of instructions from his wife, or so that he could respond to her every whim quickly. Matt could never quite work out at which end of these two extremes his true feelings lay.

Stan met the GP at the door. Matt thought that he looked even more hollowed-out than usual. No doubt he'd had a bad night with Mildred.
"Hello Stan, how's things?"
"Not bad, Doctor," he said wearily, his grey eyes a little more sad than usual. "Its Mildred, she's had a terrible night, up every five minutes, she was, with her water."

Matt followed the elderly gentleman up the stairs, the stair-lift, initially put in to help Mildred get up and down, was now caked with the dust of many years' inactivity. Matt arrived in Mildred's bedroom, the spotless eiderdown, with its intricate tessellated pattern, as ever, piled high with many books, puzzles and, of course, cigarettes. Mildred used a special shuttered ashtray, which could extinguish her cigarette and exclude smoke, should she decide that her atmosphere was becoming too smoke-laden. As usual she looked at Matt obliquely, perhaps fearing that if she looked at him directly she'd have to accept the truth of what he was saying.

"Doctor Sinclair," she drooled lugubriously from her leathery visage, "I've had a terrible night. I've been off to the toilet every five minutes and my water stings. I was wondering, if it might be a water infection?"

As was her wont, she insisted on arriving at her own diagnosis, and would expect Matt to concur. He smiled with as much warmth as he could muster. "Well, Mildred, I'd agree with your diagnosis. People who are bed-bound," he couldn't quite defeat the slight icy edge creeping into his words, "tend to get more kidney and bladder infections. Now, if you were up and about more...."

She didn't wait for him to finish, "come now, Doctor Sinclair, we both know that Mr Stephenson, the eminent and *respected* Orthopaedic surgeon, told me to rest." There was a slight emphasis on the 'respected' as though she were trying to tell him that he failed in this way, by comparison.

"Ah yes, Mildred, but that was ten years ago, and I have a feeling that he meant only for a couple of weeks."

She laughed, as if dismissing a naughty schoolboy attempting to evade detention.

"No, Doctor, he told me that rest was all he could advise for my back, and I have followed his directions."

Matt could see Stan shift uncomfortably in the background. Matt almost laughed hysterically to himself, as he remembered their first encounter three years before. Matt was determined to get her up and walking, and had raced impetuously down the side of the bed. Picking up what he'd thought was a wicker chair; he'd begun to swing it around, to give himself more room. Only when it was far too late, did he discover that it was, in fact, a commode. All he could do was just look down, as his Macintosh, fortunately still belted, had become drenched. Mildred had screamed at Stan: "You've not emptied my commode!" Stan had looked incredulous and started to say somewhat redundantly, "Doctor, your poor Mac it's all covered in ...." before racing off to the bathroom to get a towel.

Matt would have to accept now, as then, that he was dealing with an immobile person in every sense of the word. All he could do at that time was retreat, placing his besmirched Mac in his boot in a curled bundle. Very little had changed from that day to this, apart from Stan's increasing weariness. He wrote a prescription for some antibiotics and proceeded to take her blood pressure. She smiled with an imperious grin as Matt bade her, "good morning," and retreated down the stairs, Stan following him to the front door. Matt paused just in the open doorway before turning to him. "Stan, are you getting enough rest? Can I get some help for you, a home help; social services; a relief admission to a nursing home for a couple of weeks?"

"Oh no, Doctor," Stan looked flustered again. "Mildred won't have anyone looking after her but me; it's very kind of you to ask, but no thanks," he said wearily, as if resigned to his fate.

"Oh well, Stan, you know where I am if you want me," Matt ventured, more brightly than he felt; patting him on the shoulder as he left, as if offering a tangible means of support, should he need it. He popped open the boot before depositing his bag safely inside and closing it with a firm thud. He jumped in the car and, setting the CD in motion, he drove in the direction of Mirfield hospital; thinking as he did so that poor Stan would succumb much sooner than old Mildred - no doubt from exhaustion and worry. Then, perhaps, Mildred would stage a remarkable recovery, and regain her mobility. Such was the way of things, and the GP couldn't change people or their lives, he could only encourage *them* to do so.

Steve was waiting for him in the hospital grounds, just outside the psychology block. Opening the passenger door, he slid on to the leather seat.

"Hi there, my boy, it's been a few weeks now, how are things? I've been watching the news and haven't seen you arrested for stalking."

"No, not quite Steve. I was going to take your advice but felt a bit of a prat. I just couldn't bear to write to her and be one of those millions of fans. Then it just sort of clicked and I came to my senses. I just decided that it all had to go. It was no use me constantly reminding myself of how miserable I was."

As he drove, Matt described how he had sought everything in his house that reminded him of the person he had never met and never would meet; and deposited it all in the bin. Steve remained silent as Matt continued. The café came into view. Matt parked the car and they walked in. It was as quiet as the last time they were there. Despite the attractive, riverside location it had the air of an establishment whose days were numbered. Matt had in fact suggested that they try somewhere else, but Steve wouldn't hear of it. They sat at the same table; the waitress attended wearing the same pinny, with the same smudges. Matt gave a little shiver as he wondered if there was anything on the menu that would be fried for longer than a bacon sandwich. Only then did Steve speak.

"You mean, all those CDs, DVDs, magazines, posters - all went in the bin?"

"Yes, yes," came the simple reply, almost as if he couldn't quite believe it himself.

"Whoosh! Could've given them to me."

"Pardon?"

"I said. Suppose it had to be." He avoided his friend's quizzical look.

"Well, since then I've felt a lot better. I feel as if my life has re-started - no longer on hold," Matt suggested. Steve continued to nod as positively as he could whilst still reflecting on those wasted CDs.

"So, go on, in what way?" he asked, still nodding.

"I'm sleeping better, I have more energy, I feel as if I'm taking an interest in things again, I've started one or two new initiatives at work, and I suppose what I'm saying is that I feel as if I'm over it." Matt deliberately chose the impersonal word rather than 'her' - a word he, just for the moment, couldn't bring himself to say.

The omission was noted by Steve, choosing to let it pass, as he continued to question his friend. "Do you feel better?"

"Oh yes, much."

"Are you comfortable with the idea that the life, the person you had in mind, perhaps doesn't exist out of TV stations, film sets and recording studios?" Steve enquired.

"Yes, I suppose so," Matt offered with more of a display of sincerity than he could echo inside.

"Well, not bad Matt, you seem to have done very well. I know this can't have been easy. But I'm proud of you, my boy. Can I ask you, is there anyone else on the horizon?" Steve intuitively knew that Matt's vulnerability was linked directly to his loneliness. This was why he was such a good psychologist; he could sieve the essential facts. Whether the GP would admit this to himself or otherwise, was academic. Steve knew that until there was a significant relationship again in his life, he'd be in danger of slipping back into yearning for a virtual one.

"No, not yet: one or two offers, but nothing I've wanted to take up," Matt revealed.

"Chance'd be a fine thing," Steve muttered to himself.

"Pardon?"

"Oh, I said 'that is something!' Well, Matt, you seem to be back on *terra firma* and it looks as though you've sorted all the steps to your own recovery very quickly. Not that I was ever that worried about you."

Matt had known his friend too long for him not to be able to detect when he was lying.

"I know that you'll think me crazy; it's just that I couldn't help but think that our destiny was somehow linked, and that we were meant to be together."

"I don't think you're crazy, but there'll be a million fans out there who think exactly as you do, and they're not the ones with this degree of *Celebrity Worship*."

"I know, Steve, you're correct as usual. In any event I am, I promise you, over it, been there, got the merit badge or whatever."

"You've made such rapid progress; I can't believe what you're telling me, well done, my boy. Now then, there's nothing more for me to say, except of course, Mary. She wants you round to dinner as soon as you'd like. Do you want me to invite another, or will you bring someone?"

"No, Steve, thanks for that, but I'll do my own guest list, if that's okay with you. I'm not keen on the blind date thing; I think it can put too much strain on relationships between friends, whether it works or whether it doesn't."

"I thought you might say that, and of course you're right. You know how it is, Mary has so many single friends, desperate to meet, and looking for that introduction to, 'Mr Right'," Steve said.

"Please don't think I'm not flattered, but I'm still hoping to do my own asking, if you see what I mean."

"You know these women, can't resist playing matchmaker. Only don't leave it too long Matt, before you do the asking. I'll have Mary on to me as soon as I get in tonight."

"I won't, I promise."

They finished their lunch, paid the bill and Matt fumbled in his pocket for his keys, before driving the psychologist back to his department.

"Busy afternoon, Matt?" Steve queried.

"No, not really, the surgery was only half full when I checked before I left, and you?"

"Oh, the usual caseload - six patients, two new, four reviews including one old lady who tells me that she hasn't been well since she caught the Margaret Thatcher virus some fifteen years ago!"

"Rather you than me Steve. Good job we GPs have specialists, like you, to whom we can refer these more difficult cases." Matt smiled. His friend knew that he had the utmost respect for him and knew also that there wasn't another living soul that he would have told, nor could have trusted with his predicament. "Many thanks, Steve, for your further advice," Matt said gratefully.

"All in day's work, my boy. Phone me if there are any problems. You start thinking you're Elvis, you know, that sort of thing."

"There won't be, I've left the building," Matt offered earnestly.

"I wish all my cases sorted themselves out as quickly as you seem to have done. Proud of you. Now, can I tell Mary that we'll hear from you soon? Please Matt, think of your old room-mate."

"I won't let you down. I'll start going through my old address book as soon as possible."

"That one that's as thick as a telephone directory?" mused Steve, mischievously.

"No, not quite," Matt corrected.

"Oh well, my boy, we'll both be looking forward to seeing you soon, with a guest of your choice."

Matt flicked on the radio and cruised back down the hospital drive. As his shoulders relaxed back into the soft but firm leather upholstery, he reflected back on recent events. For the first time in over eighteen months he could say that he felt truly relaxed. Once again, he was enjoying his work and looking forward to new challenges, like the computerisation that had been shelved for some time whilst he was imprisoned in his own reverie. Now that he had been freed from his enchantment, he detected that every facet of his life was entering a new phase. He knew too, that in awakening from his trance, it was time to make up for lost time. Computerisation was only one of many ideas his liberated brain had arrived at. With a steadily expanding list, he felt sure that the Medical Practices' Committee would look favourably on an application for another partner, possibly part-time, and also an extension to his surgery under the cost-rent scheme, whereby much of the cost involved was paid back to him in the form of rent that his premises would otherwise attract. If the extension were allowed, he would then be able to offer more services to his patients - like minor surgery, so that they wouldn't have to wait months to be sent for from Caldbrook District General for simple things that Matt could easily deal with, if he only had the facilities. In addition, extra space would mean that he could at last offer his practice nurse the full-time hours she'd been looking for, now that her youngest son had gone to university.

As he parked his car, Mrs Simpson was chatting to Janice in the office. "Here he comes; I can't believe the change in him. See that spring in his step - we asked him months ago about a computer and he wasn't interested, now we have a Cray supercomputer in our filing room and 'superdoc' here, types all the information in within a day."

"WITH a bit of help from me," insisted Janice after a slight pause, as she wondered what a Cray supercomputer was.

"You know what I mean," offered Mrs Simpson soothingly.

"I wonder who she is then, this woman," Janice pondered, any trace of offence, disappearing rapidly.

"Mark my words, sooner or later we'll find out. It's certainly about time: it must be two years since that floozy left," Mrs Simpson revealed teasingly.

"Who was that, then?" asked Janice, taking the bait.

"Cynthia Farramond - led him a merry dance, she did. We had frantic phone calls in the middle of surgery and everything. I think he was almost relieved when she dumped him."

"Dumped him?" Janice repeated with incredulity.

"Yes, so I heard." Mrs Simpson was at her most authoritative and liked to have a captivated audience at such moments. Janice avidly soaked up every word, as her manager continued to spout forth.

"Go on! Quickly he's coming," Janice implored her.

"Well, I hear tell that she phoned him in the middle of surgery and called the whole thing off. They were supposed to be flying off to Amalfi the following day. He had a locum booked and all sorts. Cost him thousands, I'm told."

"Sh.. here he comes."

"Good afternoon Monica, Janice," Matt said breezily.

Janice quickly busied herself with the filing. Mrs Simpson followed her boss down with the afternoon's surgery and a tray of second post. She sat on the patient's chair.

"Everything okay, Monica?" he asked.

"Yes, fine thanks, Doctor Sinclair - no messages. I telephoned the PCT to see if they would allow a part-time partner. They said they'd have no objections if passed by the Medical Practices' Committee. Your list size has grown so much that they can foresee no problems, but you will have to put in a formal application."

"Fine, Monica; perhaps you could draft the letter for me?"

"Certainly, Doctor Sinclair. Anything else?"

For months and months Matt had been quiet at this point and she had gone back to the steady routine of the office: today she was to be surprised. Just as she was about to get up from the chair and return to the office, he spoke. "Yes, Monica can you speak to the finance department at the PCT. I want to put in a Cost Rent application for a surgery extension. We need another consulting room and a clinic room where we can perform minor surgery." Mrs Simpson's eyes widened while she wrote everything down in her little notebook, almost as if by writing she would calm her thoughts, still reeling from surprise.

"Do you think that you could do that this afternoon?" he suggested, rather than asked. Not only was he a new man, but he was also one in a hurry.

"Why, yes of course Doctor Sinclair right away," she replied, her mind reeling as she looked at her pad for confirmation as to what she'd just heard.

"Okay, that's it for now thanks Monica, but stay tuned as I'm sure there'll be much more in the weeks ahead." A little smile played across his face as the steady, neutral blue surveyed her for a few seconds. It was almost as if he were putting her on notice that things would be changing, and her work pattern would do so too, in tandem with his. She looked back at him just for that instant, and the look in his eyes revealed more of his return and plans for the future. She cast a puzzled glance at him before standing finally, to scurry away and find Janice, leaving him to go through his post.

"Oh Doctor Sinclair, there's a drug representative in the waiting room who wonders if you can spare her a few minutes before your surgery?" she remembered suddenly. Matt looked quickly at his desk clock.

"Would you tell her that I have just five minutes, if she could be quick, Monica?"

"It's very good of you to see me Doctor. My name's Fiona Darling and I work for Etoille Therapeutics." She offered him her card, just after the firm handshake from the long elegant fingers. She sat down on the offered seat to reveal legs that matched the hands, themselves enhanced by the plain but fashionable shoes. Her eyes focussed on him, their keen attention holding him within an excited embrace. "I wonder if I could talk about our latest product which is a new non steroidal anti-inflammatory."

Matt knew that such drugs were hot products at the moment, as the newer ones offered much better safety from stomach ulcers and bleeding, than the older ones that had been out for many years. She fished out her detail aid from her leather valise and opened the pages as she placed the information on her lap rather than on the desk, as he would have preferred. The distraction of attempting to look at her legs rather than the information on the page, was a strategy used by many of her colleagues, who had worked out that the best way of getting their product remembered, was first to get themselves noticed. Matt did his best to remain focussed, but found himself staring instead at the full lips with the sparkly lipstick, which matched her shirt. He nodded enthusiastically as she enumerated the points that she had been taught to bring out from the detail aid.

"Okay Fiona, that seems clear enough and I don't see a problem in using this for a high-risk patient." A trick he'd learned was not to let them go on for too long, as such reps were notorious for taking up as much time as possible in order to hammer home their points. She beamed at him; obviously delighted that here was to be another contributor to her sales figures. Her area manager had promised her a Mercedes coupé if those figures were good. She replaced the paperwork within her valise. "Can I offer you a sample, Doctor Sinclair?"

A sample was placed on the desk, as she crossed her legs. The skirt rode up just far enough to reveal a couple of inches of the lacy top of her hold-ups as she did so. She was obviously a very attractive young woman who was determined to get herself noticed and propel her sales figures, and herself, ever higher within the sales structure of the drug firm. Matt could see why this strategy was effective, as she now certainly had his undivided attention. He wondered if it was perhaps a trade-off between lecherous GPs who looked to people like her to brighten their day, or whether she used this as a strategy to play upon the relatively weak male mind, that could be manipulated quite easily by the appropriate visual stimulation. Rather than attempt to calculate exactly what forces and motives were in play as they spoke Matt decided to wind up their meeting. "Well, Fiona, thank you for popping in to see me."

Matt knew that surgeries such as his, were of lesser importance on the drug reps' radar than, for instance, Parkvale Medical Centre would be, simply because of the far greater numbers of prescriptions generated each working day. He stood up and motioned to shake her hand whilst doing his best to focus on the sample of tablets placed on the desk, rather than her legs - which obviously formed a key part of her sales strategy. Standing, she shook his hand, looking at him with studied courtesy.

"No, no, thank you for your time Doctor Sinclair. I wonder if you would allow me to take you out for dinner one evening?" She surveyed him keenly without the slightest trace of embarrassment; obviously used to making such offers to the

GPs she met. Working for a large pharmaceutical firm and though still quite junior, she evidently already had a sizable entertainment budget - as it was known. Matt very rarely took up these invitations; always assuming that the young man or woman making the offer would have friends and partners with whom they would prefer to be out, rather than a stuffy GP, and he didn't like the feeling of being beholden to a particular rep or drug firm. She interpreted his slight hesitation in reply as likely to mean an acceptance and decided to enhance her offer still further. "I thought we could perhaps go to Danielli's." Matt had heard of Danielli's, which was a new and expensive restaurant on the far side of Shrigvale. Its reputation had travelled through Perrilymm already. Fiona had moved a little closer towards him, the pink lips glistening with expectation.

"Its kind of you to ask, but ..." he began.

"Don't give me a definite now," she said a little deflatedly. "Perhaps take my home number and call me in a few days." She wrote her number down on the back of the card and gave it to him again.

"Okay Fiona, it's kind of you to ask me and I'll phone you in a few days"

Matt was aware that each drug rep held secret and confidential information about each contact; what their interests were; whether they were nice or nasty; single, married or divorced. Such information was often passed from rep to rep as they switched territory. He knew that she'd know quite a bit about him, and though it wasn't customary for reps to invite out spouses, she would already know that he was single. It was unusual, however, for drug reps to give out home phone numbers: mobiles perhaps, but never, in his previous experience, a home number.

CHAPTER III

BITTER BETRAYAL

May arrived and was accompanied by warm, dry days holding promise of a long hot summer, only to turn wet and windy towards the end. It was said by GPs that their workload dropped in the summer months, though Matt didn't find this to be the case. The same number consulted, but with different problems. Instead of bronchitis, there'd be hay fever; and instead of falls on icy pavements, there'd be holiday injections and cases of sunburn. He enjoyed the seasonal variation in his work, and always tried to see the patient behind the disease or the presentation. He aimed for them to think of him as a friend, with skills who would help them, rather than some aloof and detached professional.

Mrs Simpson had been as true as her word. She'd typed the relevant formal applications and faxed them that very afternoon. If this new mood meant that he was impatient for change, then she had no wish to be the rate-limiting step. The surgery and the patients had marked time for months, ever since Cynthia's phone call that Friday morning, all those months ago. If he'd truly awoken from his slumber she considered it a good thing - about time, but a good thing, nevertheless.

Matt's applications were approved by the Primary Care Trust. No secret was made of the fact that his efforts with the computer system and his early adoption of NHS Net-link to allow electronic mail, transfer of laboratory results and communications, was something that the PCT approved of. His requests were assessed and passed in a short space of time. It seemed that even the PCT were encouraging change at the village surgery. Patients too, as perceptive as ever, sensed that things were on the move and that they had their dynamic young GP restored to them. Word travelled fast, especially in the close confines of a small village. New patient registrations continued to rise, many choosing to travel in from surrounding areas, in order to register with him. Janice looked at the new patient returns from the PCT. The transport bag contained no fewer than twenty-three sets of records, and there had been similar batches arriving earlier that week. She made up new case-note files and made sure that the registrations, now coming down the link from the NHS central computer overnight, were correctly installed on the new computer. Whatever it was, and whoever she was: Janice, Monica Simpson and the afternoon staff were all of one mind - Doctor Sinclair was on a roll.

As June appeared, Matt's plans advanced slowly but steadily, in keeping with the warm days slowly extending their influence over the night. Nights, which had once been a source of restless turmoil, now refreshed him, allowing him to continue to set such a breathless pace during the day. Only dreams that he didn't remember in the morning, would offer a different version of events. Had Matt's day on-call that second Sunday in June been busier, his life would no doubt have continued on its smooth but relatively uneventful path. Even if the call that came through at 11am had come through an hour earlier, little would have changed, and no deviation would have been seen from that path. As it was, events were to change his life, and the lives of many others, on to a very different course.

The paperboy had pushed the usual Sunday papers and supplements through the letterbox. Matt was up early, so that he could get some breakfast and have a drink before his calls started to come in. Sitting at the tiled table in the conservatory, he leafed through the glossy supplements whilst sipping a coffee. He'd long since stopped buying magazines; preferring to stick to newspapers and TV news programmes. He turned the pages reflexly, as little caught his attention, until moving to the next page. Something must have registered in the second or two, which it took him to move from one page to the next. He could never say just what had stimulated his attention or curiosity enough to make him turn back. Reading a few lines in more detail, his interest accelerating as he continued. Perhaps something had registered in his subconscious as he scanned the page, before turning it. In any event as he turned back to look in more detail, it wasn't long before Fabienne's name was mentioned. Turning the page: he saw her picture smiling back at him.

The central tenet of his recovery had been his acceptance of the separation of the world of the celebrity from the world of ordinary people. The people they knew, the places they frequented, or were invited to, were on a short and very restricted list. He knew too, that it was impossible for an ordinary person to be included on that list. Lesser celebrities might try all their professional lives and still fail: so, it was a reasonable assumption that a 'nobody' like him could gain contact with that world no more easily than fly to the moon. People who resided at the top of most-invited lists were as unknown to him as the workings of a nuclear reactor. This state of affairs had been useful to Matt and crucial to his recovery, for it meant that it was out of his hands and beyond his control;

therefore, why waste time thinking across a divide that he could never bridge.

The article he read held a very different view. Entitled *'Lunch with the Stars'*, it listed several celebrities whose company could be purchased, under very controlled conditions for an exorbitant fee. It continued .. *Access to the stars is assumed to be impossible for anyone who is not an 'A' list celebrity, or very wealthy, or both. However, several agents told us that for a fee, their clients would agree to lunchtime meetings. Some stars charge £10,000 others £15,000 for a half-hour one-to-one lunch meeting.* The author pointed out in the article that as such sums of money were involved, uptake would be limited, but it did illustrate that many things regarded as generally impossible, simply turned on price alone.

His key plank of defence had been shot away, and what lay in its place was an abyss that threatened to engulf him. Desperation rose within, as it might with an alcoholic who'd been bequeathed a brewery. He read the article again, hoping that it was a late April fool. Common sense told him immediately that such sensationalistic copy was included purely to fill space; to brighten an otherwise dull Sunday and sell papers: truth would be the last consideration in such an article.

Unbridled anticipation was now firmly in charge of his emotions, however, and more percipient thoughts were swept away without hesitation as he formed a daring strategy. Picking up the telephone, he began punching numbers, eventually getting through to the press office of the newspaper featuring the article, which provided him with more numbers. After more calls, he reached the secretary of the article's author who told him that the story had originated quite by chance and was initially thought to be simple gossip. However she'd checked with one or two agents to 'A' list celebrities; some of whom confirmed that the core assumption was correct. Those who hadn't heard of it phoned back later to say that their clients would probably wish to be featured. As news of the story broke amongst agents, more and more wanted to get involved. She admitted urbanely that it was more a case of the rumour creating the story. Matt asked her how he could go about booking such a one-to-one lunch with a celebrity. At this point the secretary became a little more defensive. They hadn't expected that anyone would actually want to take part, with such fees involved. People who could afford such expenditure on a whim were usually the sort of people who moved in the circles frequented by such celebrities in the first place. Matt tried very hard to convince her that his enquiry was genuine and that he was serious; eventually after much coaxing, he feverishly wrote down the number of Fabienne's agent's office.

The following day Mrs Simpson was poised nervously outside the consulting room door. Janice approached with a cup of tea. "I wouldn't go in, Janice. He's been on the phone for half an hour. I thought he'd done a 'Doctor Brown' over at Mitchelham. Came in one day, saw a waiting room full of patients, went into his surgery, opened the window, crawled through and was never seen again!"

Janice's tiny eyes widened with incredulity. "Is that what he's done - just when things were going so well? I knew it, I said to my Dad that something had to give, he was just too happy. Planning his escape was he?"

Mrs Simpson sighed calmly, "No Janice," followed by a slight pause, whilst she summoned more reserves of patience. "He's on the phone, I said, so he can't have crawled through the window now, can he?" Mrs Simpson looked at her with concern.

The heavy ash fire-door meant that only muffled sounds could be heard from within.

Had they been in the room they would have heard Doctor Sinclair talking to Lucy, Fabienne's personal assistant.

"Well, Doctor Sinclair, to tell you frankly, I'm not sure it's something she'd want to do. We only said we'd take part in the article for the publicity, you know, to try to pitch a more accessible image to the fans. Does the £15,000 not put you off?" Embarrassment made her continue, "To tell you frankly, we thought, well I thought, I mean, when I OK'd the article that no one in their right... I mean, well, it was a bit of a story you know. I didn't think..." Her voice trailed off.

Matt's strong intuitive sense, that had been honed with years of listening to patients, who only sometimes presented with their real reason for coming, was scarcely needed; the true meaning behind her words was obvious. He doubted that Fabienne even knew of the article's existence, and probably the agent and the PA had fleshed it out with the magazine. Having nothing to lose, he decided to go for broke.

"I wonder if you could, er perhaps ask Fabienne if she would be interested in such a meeting, and at her convenience?"

"Well, to tell you frankly, I'm not sure: she's very busy recording at the moment, then she's due to fly stateside for concerts in New York and Toronto. Perhaps some other time," Lucy said with an air of finality, hoping to terminate the conversation.

Sensing he was losing both control of the situation, and his unique opportunity to gain access to the person he'd been enthralled by for so long. He made one final, desperate appeal. "Could you just perhaps ask? I'd be ever so grateful," he pleaded beseechingly.

A pause, that seemed to last an eternity, followed. Holding his breath because it seemed so noisy to him, that he feared it would blot out her reply.

Bitter Betrayal

"Okay, why not, I can ask," came the reply. She added, "Give me some numbers I can contact you on, and I'll let you know what she says, but her decision will be final."

"Then, there's no more that I can ask of you," he said as hope rose within. Matt recited all the numbers on which he could be contacted.

Wild thoughts dared to flourish that there would be still a difficult phone call to come: the one to Steve. Just what would he say? However, he realised that his best policy was to wait for the return call. If the answer came back as 'no' then he wouldn't have to tell Steve anything. Matt put the phone down, his head swirling, with a million thoughts. Only his heart was making a brave attempt to keep up with the frantic pace set by his brain. How long he would have remained in such a state is uncertain. Mrs Simpson detecting that the conversation was over, gave a sharp knock on the door. She looked flustered and bewildered as she entered, followed by Janice trotting behind with a cup of tea that had long cooled, and a couple of biscuits, one of which she had nibbled, whilst waiting outside the door, as the tension overcame her! Mrs Simpson could only guess that the conversation must have had overarching importance. Doctor Sinclair's surgeries never overran, and now he was at least thirty minutes behind. Worst of all, she'd forgotten the reason for waiting outside his door in the first place. She recovered quickly. "Everything all right, Doctor?" she probed.

"Yes thanks Mrs S. I'll call the next patient if that's okay?"

"Oh, righto Doctor," she replied shakily.

Her interruption had shattered his cycle of thought, but paradoxically brought his mind back into focus. The two women shuffled out, no wiser about what they'd seen or heard. Matt's steady twinkle and neutral blue eyes had only served to mask his own turmoil, whilst increasing theirs by the same measure. "Oh, and Monica if there's a call for me from a Lucy Kwa, please put her straight through."

"Certainly, Doctor."

Janice just heard the name." Do you think that's her, then?"

"I'm just not sure. I hope it's not all starting again, the phone calls in surgery, the floods of tears as she berates him over something trivial," Mrs Simpson said gravely.

Had Janice had a more acute mind, she would have realised that the only way Mrs Simpson could have known such things, would be from eavesdropping on such calls from switchboard. As it was, she reasoned that her boss knew these things simply because she knew everything.

It was two hours later that the eagerly-awaited call from Lucy arrived. Matt was in his kitchen at home, having eventually finished the morning surgery and his visits. He listened eagerly to what Lucy had to say. He didn't dare to hope that her employer had given her a positive answer, especially when Lucy had done her best to downplay any possibility of such a meeting ever taking place. At least, he thought to himself as the split seconds flashed, after his first realisation that she was on the line, he wouldn't have to negotiate a difficult call to Steve.

"Hello, Doctor Sinclair, it's Lucy here. I've had a word with Miss Fabienne and we're 'go' at this end."

Matt nearly dropped his mobile on to the hot-plate of the cooker as he jumped with unrestrained delight, hit by the news.

"Hello, are you still there?" said Lucy, sensing a disturbance at his end.

"Yes, yes, go ahead Lucy, please," doing his best to control himself.

"Subject to the following conditions. Twelve, midday, two weeks Friday, that's 22nd June. Venue will be Luciano's, Salford Quays near Manchester. Cheque for £15,000 to be made payable to 'Brite Lite Entertainment'. Non-refundable. Lunch will last approximately half an hour. No newspapers, no prior notification to others, no recording devices of any kind, no photographs, no publicity. In fact we'd rather you don't discuss this with anyone at all. If these conditions are not met, Miss Fabienne will not appear, and no refund will be made of any kind. Do you agree to these terms?" Lucy continued, without giving Matt a chance to say he agreed. If they'd been talking face to face, she would have seen Matt nodding vigorously, despite his silence.

"I'll be posting you more details in the next couple of days. Please read the material carefully. Sign the top copy and return with your cheque in the stamped addressed envelope enclosed, and retain the other copy."

Lucy had obviously had time to collect her thoughts and regroup. From appearing initially surprised by his call, she was now obviously bringing more of a business-like slant to the proceedings. Matt being intrigued when thinking of the nature of the conversation between Lucy and her employer: remaining convinced that this was the first that his idol had heard of the proposal. He agreed to the conditions without hesitation, now so mesmerized by the prospect of meeting Fabienne in person that he would have accepted anything, and paid any price. He understood the need for discretion on his part, and assumed that a pop star of Fabienne's standing and resources would make sure that these criteria were met, before any appearance took place.

Concentrating on the afternoon surgery proved almost impossible. Doing his best to appear to focus attentively on each of his patients who attended: inevitably, he failed at several points; nodding when he should have shaken his head; grinning when he should have looked serious. Fortunately nothing remotely taxing presented and it remained fairly quiet. Thoughts he had to keep telling himself were foolish, kept crowding his brain - but this didn't stop their recurrence. The hardest to dismiss was the one uppermost in his mind; that this meeting was something he'd been waiting for, all his life. Finally, what brought him back down to earth was remembering that he had an even harder task to accomplish that afternoon than maintaining concentration and fending off wild thoughts; and that was to telephone Steve. Even this deflated him only a little, though he guessed that it would be a difficult conversation at best. Knowing that telephoning his friend was in no way mandatory: he could have kept his meeting and maintained silence. Although it was unlikely that he'd ever find out; Matt reasoned, however, that this could only be seen as a betrayal. A betrayal of someone whom he valued as a colleague and a friend: one who was trying to provide help when asked. Ultimately, Matt realised, that his silence would cause more damage than any response that Steve was likely to make.

Eventually, Matt tracked him down and found a time when he could come to the phone. He punched the numbers of Steve's extension, his hand trembling a little; thinking that this was not the time for pusillanimity. Steve listened for some time; 'active listening' as it was called, was very much part of his work, though its use at this point was more to allow him to try to control his own feelings, than think more rationally on behalf of his friend. Matt's already nervous state was heightened still further by the profound silence that opened up as a result. Active listening really needed face-to-face contact so that the person who was speaking could receive the little reassuring nods and other non-verbal clues from the party that remained silent. Only when Matt had said all that he could say on the matter, and had repeated a fair amount of it due to his nervousness, did Steve speak, sighing just a little before he did so.

"Okay Matt, we can deal with this," Steve began.

These simple words instantly conveyed to Matt that Steve had used the pause to order his own racing thoughts. It was now as if he was dealing with a difficult case where his first management plan, that he believed to be a success, had in fact failed and he now had to think of ways in which he could limit the damage and protect his patient. First came disappointment. "I can't believe what you are telling me."

Matt winced as the words that came: hit him, almost as if they had impacted physically upon him.

"Don't do this Matt. You're through this, and you've done very well. If you go back down this route you may not recover; suppose you start the whole thing off again and submerge your life in the half-light between reality and dreams. Suppose you waste what you've done, and how far you've come. Suppose you turn into one of these sad, lonely creatures who wait for the next single, the next TV appearance, the next snippet on the news, and somehow hope to place yourself in there to give it some special meaning. Suppose you try to tell yourself that this was meant to be, and she was really meant for you and no other."

He included these words deliberately to maximise the impact that it would have on his friend, this being precisely what Matt had told him. "Suppose the life she really has, and the life you think she has, are very different: and what if there really is no part for you to play in either of those. Have you thought about any of those things Matt?"

"Yes."

In many ways this simple agreement was the reply Steve had not anticipated. He assumed that Matt's so called 'recovery' was illusory and was simply a delaying tactic to wait for a better opportunity; and this was it. He hadn't made any recovery at all, and was simply delaying the eventual fall into danger from which he would never pull back, rather like an alcoholic who sank through several stages of destruction in his life, each worse and more prolonged than the one before.

He shouldn't have underestimated his friend so signally, but his own demons had hold of him by this time.

Matt continued. "I've thought of all those things and many more, I can tell you. I see this as a way of drawing a line under it. I know what I have, and what I want, and I'm not, I promise you, going to kiss all that goodbye. If I pass up this opportunity, I'll wonder for always what she was like, what she might have said to me."

Then, Steve's mood progressed to concern. "But Matt, it isn't *real*," he began, pleadingly, "do you think she really wants to be there with you; it's simply some stunt, suggested by her PR people and you're a pawn in that game. She doesn't know you. You don't know her - and what's more, you never will, even if you were able to afford a hundred of these meetings."

"I'm aware of that, Steve, but it isn't for her, it's for me. I have my own agenda here, and I know that one meeting, one glimpse up close, one-to-one, will be enough for me to satisfy my cravings forever. I won't go back on my word - not to you, and not to myself."

Steve told himself that he had to press his friend more vigorously to make sure that he had thought the whole thing through and wasn't about to travel down a slippery slope from which there would be no return. "Okay then, suppose it doesn't end there, and suppose you start writing, phoning and following and waiting on street corners; suppose you're no longer in control of yourself. Don't you think that people who are just as clever, just as accomplished as you, have done things like this; before they jettisoned their lives, *Matt*?" Steve's emphasis on 'Matt' indicated more worry than anger, at this point.

"It *will* end there. It's the not knowing what she's like, to see face to face, to talk to; that would destroy my life, not the other way round. Once I've done this, it's over. I won't go back on that, and I do know the risks. Steve, *trust me*. I know myself, and I know what I'm doing."

"Okay, so you're the alcoholic and you really think you can have just the one drink." Steve knew this would sting. It did. Matt would know that so many alcoholics believed they could just have one drink; nearly all were proved wrong - most of them fatally.

"The difference here, Steve, is that I've never tasted that drink, and once I have, I know I can put it behind me, and be the person I always promised myself I could be, but I can't do that if I have regrets, and I'll regret not doing this, forever. Now what do you say?"

Steve could sense that there was a pleading tone creeping in, almost as though Matt were looking for his friend's blessing. All was not done yet. Steve then tried to rationalise and to summarise. "OK then, Matt, just one promise." Sentences remained short and jerky as Steve continued to try to control his own feelings, ultimately failing, as disappointment and worry intervened. "When you've seen her. And met her. And *wasted* a *ferocious* amount of cash - the national debt of a small country - you promise me. We don't see her. We don't write; don't call. We do not make any attempt whatsoever to contact her again, *ever*. We settle down to a nice, *normal life* with trips to the dentist, sweaty socks, windows that have to be cleaned and bills that come through the door!"

Complex and contrasting emotions were still surging through the psychologist's head, and the only way he could attempt to keep them in order, was to seek agreement from his friend as they spoke. "Now are we agreed on this Matt.?" Steve asked.

"Yes."

Yet another most simple of affirmatives should have dissipated much of Steve's irritation. Not because of its brevity, or even that it was unexpected, but that it implied acceptance of all the points that Steve had tried to get across, and more. It signalled that Matt was fully intending to keep his promise to Steve and to himself, whilst not unaware that there was real danger here.

The simple truth was that Matt was now in too far. He'd committed himself to a high-risk strategy. Knowing what he now knew, that it would be possible to gain the briefest access to a person he had hoped to meet, for as far back as he'd known of her: meant that he *had* to see what that would be like. Perhaps if he hadn't noticed that article on that Sunday morning; perhaps if a visit had come in earlier, and he'd spent the rest of the day coming and going with no time to settle with the papers; all would have been different. His life would certainly have taken a different course. On the opposing face of that argument was the fact that Steve was extremely anxious about him: knowing that there were dangers here that he hadn't enumerated, and was obviously concerned that Matt would never regain the stability and grounding in his ordinary life. Incautiously entering a spiral of restlessness and worse, would eventually endanger his position as a GP, and put at risk his responsibility for so many patients. Both Matt and Steve knew that the psychologist would have to act if this came to pass, and that he would do so without hesitation - friend or otherwise.

All Matt could do, was to hold true to his feelings and hope that he could gaze upon the sun, briefly, without suffering blindness, or forever feeling that his life was in shadow. A wave of tiredness came over him; his brain had been stuck in that constant loop of thought since Lucy's call had come through, hours before. It all came down to one simple thing, clinging to his instinct.

The difficult words might have ended at this point, had Matt not made the mistake of saying just a little more. He'd forgotten the golden rule about being on the receiving end of someone's anger: say as little as possible, and agree as much as possible. Matt wasn't someone whose friendship could be damaged by a few harsh words once in a while. This was fortunate, as what was said next would severely test their friendship.

"I just can't help but feel that we were supposed to meet. It's almost as if our destinies are linked in some way, and I was meant to meet her. It's as though my life has something missing, that's why I want to go," Matt said unwarily as he tired of the discursive interchange.

Something either in Matt's persistent choice of words or the little flippant giggle he gave off as he finished the sentence was responsible for a Tsunami released within his friend that, once triggered, would inundate the breakwater and harbour wall that normally protected him, under all circumstances, against unrestrained anger; which is what followed. Steve's reply whipped quickly into a frenzy that Matt was unprepared for, and the psychologist was unable to restrain.

"You don't know what its like, do you, to be invisible? You don't recognise the word. Wherever you go, heads turn, women look; people pay attention. You could have anyone, at least within reason - you could be... anything. If you'd chosen surgery, you'd be professor of surgery at a top teaching hospital by now." His voice was loud and forceful, and also very quick, as if a pause now would stop the abscess from discharging its festering content. "People of both sexes love people like you. You have all those missing elements that some of us lack; and you have them in abundance; the voice, the looks, the physique, the poise, the air of gravitas that's exuded as soon as you walk into a room." He reeled off his checklist with an emphasis more vituperative than complimentary. "You're the guy who gets the table at the restaurant, the chap who gets served first at the bar, the one people gather round in the pub, and women always want to know. The man who would have commanded the squadron, or sent soldiers into battle. You don't know you've got all those things, because you've never had to wonder what it's like not to have them. Those of us who exist a little lower down the food chain, know what it's like to be invisible. I'm not saying you don't have to try, and certainly not that you don't have to work hard, it's just that you've never known the harshness of the comparisons that people make, even before words are spoken, because you've always come at the top of those comparisons. Now Matt, now you tell me that's not enough, that you're looking for more than that, and I have to ask you just why is that so?"

He'd continued his diatribe without pause for breath or pause for thought. Silence intervened once again, as a calm after a storm, but this time brutally so. The tempest might have abated but there was much wreckage in its wake. This wasn't about Matt so much; this was about his friend, and the message that came across, was just a little too hard to bear. Matt was glad that they were speaking down a telephone, as his eyes had started to sting painfully and he suspected that Steve's had too. Matt was humbled and disgusted with himself in equal measure; the emotions that burned within him, just a little too hard to bear. He knew that words would fail at this point; yet the silence hurt more, and had to be bridged at any cost. The only thing that Matt could arrive at, which could even begin to do the job was, "Forgive me Steve; forgive me if you think I've let you down."

This was it: the words were out and couldn't be put back. Not only was he viewed by a close friend, and a brilliant psychologist, as self-centred, but also his whole life was seen to have decadence about it. Precisely the things he'd always promised himself he would never be. Even worse, his friend was intimating that he'd betrayed not only himself, but also those who might have seen him and his life as an example to live by.

"I'll be a better person in future, I promise, and if you tell me to cancel; that's what I do, right now." Matt was by now exhausted and would have said anything or signed the most damning of confessions placed in front of him, if it meant an end to the pain which cut him more than if physical force had been employed.

"Look Matt you've got more going for you than any person I know or have ever known. You're a very lucky man. You have the sort of life that we all wish we had, and are the person we hope we'd wake up one morning to find staring back at us in the mirror," Steve continued. "You're not an uncaring person: you're the most caring person I know, the warmest and the most generous, there isn't a conceited bone in your body. I just couldn't bear to watch while you throw it all away."

The psychologist's more measured tones couldn't bring about the healing of those wounds that now lay gaping, and Matt knew instantly that closing such festering sores would be both painful and time-consuming: also would involve more self-awareness than his friend was hinting he possessed.

"I won't Steve, I have too many things to do: but I need to get this out of my system. I know how lucky I am, and I'm not about to flush it down the toilet. I just can't help but feel that I was meant, in some way, to do this."

There were those words again that Steve hated. Had he not already vented his spleen at this point, no doubt he wouldn't have let them pass so lightly.

"I don't want to hear that Matt. You go there and come back; and meet some astoundingly attractive, sweet, but ordinary girl; and for heaven's sake settle down and then I won't have to worry about you," Steve said, now with much more restraint. Calming still further, he said, "Okay Matt, enough said, I'll get off your case." Concerns for his friend had made Steve break the cardinal rule of psychology, or of medicine for that matter: never lose your temper. Steve knew that his anger had defeated him; the first occasion it had done so in a long time. His friend had been damaged by his words, and he wished that he could have recalled them as they flew across the ether, but it couldn't be. He made an ineffectual attempt to lighten the conversation.

"Just one more thing."

"Yes?" Matt said nervously.

"Can you get me her autograph?"

This was the nearest Steve could come to saying that, after the arguments had been presented and hashed through, he wouldn't allow their friendship to be damaged either. Matt laughed, more out of relief that the ordeal was ending.

"Sure thing, that's the least I can do." The tiredness written to his face was now appearing in his speech as it trailed off.

"Oh and by the way, you know Mary keeps asking when you're coming round to dinner. You sort yourself out, or I'll be turning her loose on you, they'll be queuing down that long drive of yours."

"As soon as I've done this, I'll be right round," Matt confirmed easily.

"OK Matt, I'll let you go. Please let me know how you get on. I'll speak to you soon."

Matt knew that this was more than politeness: that Steve intended to keep a very close eye on him. He knew too, that it would be so much easier just to cancel the lunch and get on with his life, as Steve advised; yet he could do that no more than stop breathing. Ultimately, Steve too, had realised this. Much had passed between them even though they'd known each other for many years. Matt guessed that their relationship would never be the same again: he could only hope that the change would be for the better, as being without Steve's objectivity, he knew, would make his life both poorer and more ordinary.

The next two weeks passed slowly. Matt considered that he was rather like a prisoner ticking the days off on his cell wall until the day of his release. Doing his best to remain focussed on his work, but close observers could see that there was something in the wind. Fortunately, a varied caseload presented in surgery to prevent him from ruminating on events too much.

Monica Simpson joined Janice for coffee in the common room.

"Well what's going on? No sign of a woman, no photograph like you said there'd be. He's still cheerful, but he seems preoccupied again like he was before, but more chatty now," Janice said a little impatiently.

Mrs Simpson sat back with all the contentment of someone who knew that she was right, and that time was the only factor needed to prove her so. "It's love, I tell you, mark my words, we'll see a photograph on that shelf any day now. I know him better than he knows himself. Only a woman can do this to a man."

Once again Janice accepted the Simpson view of things as being incontrovertible.

"What does he want that locum for? Do you think he's going to elope or drive up to Gretna Green and get hitched?" Janice pondered as she sipped at her mug. "Sooner the better, if you ask me, a handsome fella like that should settle down I tell you, it can only cause trouble. The suspense is killing me, when do you think we'll know?" Janice quizzed the all-knowing Mrs Simpson and gazed deferentially at her as one would at a fortune-teller.

"Soon enough, I tell you, mark my words." She tapped the side of her nose to indicate that Janice would not have to wait long to see for herself that the version of events as expounded was the only version worth listening to.

Matt telephoned James Farquar, his stockbroker. "James, it's me, Matt Sinclair."

"Hi there, Matt what can I do for you, need some hot tips to buy?" James said jauntily.

"No, actually I'm selling. I need to raise about £15,000 from my portfolio."

"Not a good time to sell just at present, Matt, are you sure?" James offered with caution in his voice.

"Yes; I can always approach the bank, but I'd rather just liquidate that amount, if that's okay?" Matt did his best to keep irritation from his voice at having to justify his actions to his broker.

"Well now, let me have a look here," James clucked his tongue against his cheek as he concentrated on the request. Matt could hear him typing on his terminal keyboard. No doubt Matt's portfolio and its current valuation was appearing on screen in front of James who continued to talk as he typed. "Haven't you just bought that car, not far off 30K wasn't it? What do you need this for; you've not got a woman on the go have you? Don't do it Matt, divorce lawyers cost you even more than you'll lose on these shares, believe me. I'm speaking from experience here. You can't see me bleeding down this telephone line can you, but I am; take my word for it."

James was always a little loquacious. Matt reasoned that he himself would be like that if he were stuck in front of terminal screens all day long, instead of talking to patients. No doubt when a client came on, it would give him a welcome relief.

"So a woman is it?" enquired James.

"No, not exactly," said Matt, keeping his tone as flat as possible so as not to excite too much comment from the broker.

"Don't tell me any more, I'm not sure that a young innocent like me should be burdened with what you're about to tell me."

Bitter Betrayal

Matt smiled to himself, he wasn't aware of intending to say any more.

"So, then, here we are; if you sell your holding in BP and United Utilities, that'll raise that amount and, you see how good I am to you Matt, there'll be a slight profit, though not enough to get the taxman man excited of course, but should just about cover my fees, now what do you say to that?"

"Okay James, go ahead with that, if you will?"

Matt could hear more keys being punched with an air of finality.

"Done Matt, no turning back, sold on ten day settlement. Cheque will be in the post - I'll send you the stock transfer form if you'll send me the certificates. Is that it then, Matt?" James said.

"Yes thanks, James, for now."

"She must be really pretty Matt, just hope she's worth it," James concluded.

Matt laughed - if only he knew!

"Don't use my divorce lawyer will you, lost my shirt to that bitch."

"Okay, I'll remember that: now don't work too hard will you James?" Matt said, just before replacing the handset. It struck Matt that poor James *was* probably working too hard, and also had bitter memories of a painful divorce uppermost in his mind. He'd wondered for a moment whether James was going to start admonishing him too, if he'd learned more detail about his plans.

Post from Lucy arrived and Matt signed the forms without delay; making sure they went in the next post, clipping his cheque to the form. Lucy telephoned two days later to confirm safe receipt and to warn him not to be late.

CHAPTER IV

SPELLBOUND

At last the day arrived. Matt was up even earlier than usual; anticipation and a steady flow of thought, preventing him from sleeping. However, despite the resultant tiredness, the excitement continued to course within: his face alight with expectation. Taking a rapid shower and devoting even less time in getting dressed; he then spent an age deliberating as to which tie and cufflinks to wear. Eating a light breakfast, despite not having the slightest pang of hunger, he made an early start, joining the motorway north at about eight o'clock. Being a Manchester medical school graduate, he knew Salford Quays very well, but remembered it from its more neglected days when the port had become largely derelict, and before its more recent redevelopment as a leisure, office, retail centre and, of course, expensive loft-style apartments - some costing almost seven figures.

Matt parked in the Lowry car park. Choosing one of the parking bays near the large fans, which he thought would be easier to remember, and which seemed a little wider than the rest, thereby hopefully minimising his chances of being 'car-doored' - by the adjacent vehicle's door being opened too enthusiastically, leaving him with a dent in his side panel. He vacated the darkness of the car park and walked out onto the old dockside. Several massive cranes remained to bear witness to the area's past activities but what he saw couldn't have been more different. Upon looking round, he was amazed at the transformation. When he'd last visited, it contained derelict land, poor housing and was one of the country's deprived black spots. He remembered as a GP trainee, parking his car one evening whilst he went on a visit not far from where he was walking now, and wondering if it would still be there on his return. How things could change in a relatively short span of time. Luciano's was an excellent barometer to the changes that had taken place. Warehouses and empty factories of yesteryear having been replaced by mirror-sided office blocks, hi-tech buildings and an influx of new money. Added to this, wealthy employees and entrepreneurs; looking for places to live, to work; and of course places like Luciano's, to eat or simply be seen.

    He walked past Luciano's several times, in order to get his bearings. Knowing that there was still plenty of time, but he didn't want to have to rush at the last minute, and risk arriving late, bothered and sweaty. The day was warm and sunny, however, the water looked cold and uninviting despite the presence of ducks and swans slowly coursing up and down. The bright sun shielded him against the wind that whipped along over the expanse of waterway. No doubt in the near future, the marina development would be expanded still further so that the cold murky water would be transformed too. Matt continued to walk: there was a lot to see, but his mind was really only focussed on Luciano's and his watch. For the millionth time that morning, he checked the time. The inelegant but functional diver's watch, purchased from Marks & Spencer for fifteen pounds, was not the most elegant of timepieces to behold; but it kept perfect time despite being over three years old and never having had a new battery. Notwithstanding this, he could have sworn that the hands were frozen in a time warp that had him trapped unknowingly inside.

Eventually after he had been pacing round for over an hour, the hands moved on to 11:55 and he quickly retraced his well-rehearsed steps to Luciano's. The door was locked. He tapped on the heavy glass with its thick chrome frame and substantial handle. A thin, keen-eyed, man appeared. "Sorri Sirr, we no open till twelf thir tee," he conveyed in a language that was obviously not his mother tongue.

Matt hesitated for a second, his brain befuddled by the unexpected information. Wild thoughts stampeded through his head. Was he at the wrong place, the wrong time, and the wrong day? Had he been set up? The turmoil, verging on panic crossing his face registered immediately with the waiter: his eyes narrowing a little as he realised that this was the gentleman he had been told to expect.

"You Matt Sin-clare?" he asked.

"Yes that's me," Matt voiced, with the relief of someone having been told that an impending death sentence had all been a mistake.

"You come inside, plise," he suggested as he stood aside to let Matt pass within.

The waiter showed him to a fully prepared table towards the bar, which looked as if it had been carved from a single gigantic block of black granite of Egyptian proportions: chrome finishes being applied as an afterthought. The glass shelves behind, were under-lit by blue 'running lights', their depth and contents enhanced by bevel-edged mirrors mounted on the wall. Discreet but powerful down-lighters illuminated the surface of the bar area, with its pumps, taps, blenders and huge Italian coffee machine, simmering satisfyingly as it gave off a smell that no taste could somehow ever duplicate. Larger wall lights, fan shaped, almost like Art Deco, but made from Murano glass wafers, provided illumination in the rest of the substantial room.

Spellbound

One person sat motionless by the nearest table to the door. Matt hadn't seen him when he arrived, having walked straight past him in his relief at being admitted. Wearing close-fitting sunglasses, with a gold reflective finish, so that it was impossible to tell if he was really looking at the crossword on the table in front of him, or scanning the entire room. The tense musculature, which stretched the suit just a little, despite its carefully-tailored dimensions; told Matt that he wasn't there by coincidence.

Matt sat down facing the door, staring toward the entrance: even blinking became a distraction as he continued to gaze with anticipation. The waiter asked him if he would care for a drink. He ordered a white wine spritzer. The waiter busied himself behind the bar; talking quietly in Italian to a young woman who was polishing glasses and placing them noisily back in the racks. Matt could see that their expressions were tinged more with curiosity than the expectation written to his visage. Matt received his drink with a grateful nod and a "grazie" in the best Italian his dry throat could manage.

The man by the door touched something in his suit pocket. Suddenly, the pavement outside was darkened by the rapid appearance of a large black Mercedes, which swept in. A driver leapt out and a tinted door was held open. The young waiter quickly moved to the door and put his weight behind it, to swing it wide open, in preparation for their guest. An older man with a grey moustache, and wearing a suit that was too tight for him, suggesting to Matt that these days it was an infrequent choice of attire, appeared from nowhere and also charged to the entrance. Each man was now ready to make obeisance to the guest.

Matt was used to feeling his heart pound in the gym, but even those rates were exceeded now: for he felt the uncomfortable kick lift his entire sternum at an unrestrained tempo. He swallowed hard and reflexly stood up, as if by some automatic movement not sanctioned by deliberation. All other thoughts had long since been put on hold while his brain awaited eagerly the information being fed in by the eyes. Nor could he, somehow, stop his mouth from falling open to reflect the wide-eyed entrancement that was engulfing him. Recognising, as he stood there in an agony of expectation, that his life had been but a preparation for this moment; and that if there were no moments after this one, that would be an exchange he would effect without hesitation. Ever since he saw her on a talk-show programme all those years ago, he knew that everything had been a rehearsal for this moment. Thirty minutes would be enough to last a lifetime, and there would be no regrets. He understood something of Steve's concern, but in those closing seconds Matt knew that he would do nothing to attract further opprobrium from the psychologist. Seconds expanded seamlessly into vast chasms of time, or so it felt, as his brain processed the information flooding in from his eyes and other senses, at a pace matched more intrusively by his heart which continued to thud away explosively.

He noticed first, the hat, which almost hid her face. All he could see were the full, pink lips, the delicate high cheeks as they swept down to meet the elegant jaw line; the slim neck, adorned by a simple but shimmering necklace that could only have been created by bringing together materials that were both precious and rare. Dazzling though it was, it paled in comparison to its owner.

He'd seen Dior dresses whilst glancing through fashion magazines. Black silk twill with a random pattern of white leaves. Slim, sleeveless, flowing and elegant with the slight drawing at the narrow waist. The hem skirting just above knee-height, liberating a pair of particularly fine legs to meet with the spiky heels of her delicate sandals. The older gentleman, Matt surmised quickly, was Luciano himself: having covered the distance in the time it took Fabienne to cross the threshold.

The door held open excitedly by the young waiter. Luciano grasped her hand quickly as if to shake it and then didn't seem able to resist raising it, more gently than the speed of his movement would have suggested, as he bent to apply his kiss.

Matt saw the pink shimmering lips part to reveal the dazzling array of teeth. His attuned sense of awareness picked up her words from across the room.

"Luciano, it's good of you to do this for me," she said, without interrupting the smile on her face. Luciano beamed back at her, helplessly, with a fatherly pride.

"No, no, no, La Signorina graces my humble restaurant, the pleasure is all ours."

Throughout all this, the muscular man by the door made no movement whatsoever; save for the steady clicking of his pen on the page of the crossword, as he worked out and applied the answers.

Suddenly, she was walking in Matt's direction. The hat was swept quickly, yet almost distractedly from her angled head, to reveal her cascade of blonde hair that had been uncharacteristically, but carefully, tied up. He'd seen that face a million times, beaming from TVs, magazines and newspapers. No camera had ever quite captured the delicate poise, the chiselled perfection of her features. A still image would always ultimately fail to convey that sparkle, that vibrancy and that flow. Even at concerts, when he'd been able to see her at closer range, something was lost in the transmission of that beauty: beauty that was in full surge now as she approached.

Then there was that walk, which itself was a thing of wonderment. The pace just a little brisk, the heels being applied precisely, in perfect alignment with the axis of travel: a metronomic cadence being set up as the sandals made contact with the floor of Italian marble. Despite the height of the heel, there was no dipping of the shoulders, which were held slightly back to straighten the spine; also, totally absent, was the lolloping, porpoise movement that many girls adopted, especially when walking in heels. A slight sashay of the hips in time to the perfect rhythmicity of the walk, as she transferred weight from foot to foot; the hips themselves at all times kept perpendicular to the forward direction, with no hint of rotation. The head held erect in keeping with the slight extension of the back, and she looked forward - not at her feet. The left arm kept at a comfortable perpendicular as it secured her bag, and the right allowed to move gently to counterpoise accurately the slight movement across the pelvis. Above all, was the smile that denoted a thing of beauty; of innate sexual allure, apparent to all who should gaze on her.

All his rehearsals - and there had been a great many of these - were swept away as her eyes, pale blue and sparkling like living crystal, engaged with his. Only by employing enormous effort did he stop his jaw from falling open because thraldom gripped him utterly. His heart continued to leap within his chest, almost as if it wanted to burst out and take a look at this vision, as she narrowed the gap between them. Matt prayed that his hand was not sweating, as hers was offered. That smile was turned now, full force on him, the eyes' contact only temporarily broken as their hands locked briefly. Their gaze re-engaged once again as Matt, bringing himself up to his full height, could only waft his free hand in the general direction of the empty chair facing him; his speech failing just at the most decisive point. Panic threatened to overwhelm him. He needn't have worried; her words appeared to hide any gaps created by his nervous state. A hint of a delicate perfume floated to his side of the table, subtle, but with notable highlights.

"Doctor Sinclair, I believe?" She hesitated only a second as Luciano attended in person with a white wine spritzer, before continuing. "Good taste," she said, as she nodded in the direction of his drink. His own smile flashed in reply as he, barely, overcame his nerves. Something about her easy poise and delirious smile made this easier. She was obviously used to dealing with star-struck fans. Moreover, he could only tell himself that her relaxed manner must surely be her natural state, rather than something that was crafted and displayed by artifice when faced with public inspection.

"Please call me Matt," he managed as evenly as he could, hoping that his voice wouldn't betray his nervousness.

Steve had warned him against considering her attention and her smile to be specific to him. "Don't forget," he'd cautioned, "this is a job of work to her, and she isn't meeting someone special: think of it as a stage show, more than a personal encounter". Matt knew the veracity of Steve's comments, and that he'd made them to ensure that the GP retained some perspective in all this. Yet, Matt could only trust what he was witnessing before him, and nothing would destroy that, or this moment in time. Everything he believed, everything that his sense of awareness could gauge, told him that this meeting was the genuine article, not some public relations stunt created by deception.

He was captivated by the way she glimpsed sideways at the peak of her smile, almost as if she couldn't contain its full force, the neck moving her head slightly forward as the smile matured, revealing the rows of teeth, once again.

"I was just wondering Matt, what sort of guy would want to spend fifteen thousand pounds just to have lunch with someone?" she asked, as the smile took on more of a playful quality.

"I was just going to ask you the same question," he responded as her mood caught him infectiously.

They both laughed in unison

"Go on then, you first," she suggested.

He could hardly believe the images being fed to his brain. How could it be: this superstar, living, breathing and so near as to be almost touching? Only in dreams had his mind been able to compass such an event, and yet here she was smiling before him.

"Okay, well, you know what I'm going to say," he began, suddenly more aware of the eyes now locked upon him as nervousness crept in again. He noted the way she perched the fine chin on her flexed palm, almost like a tripod making sure that the camera it supported was focussed only in one direction. Perhaps the ultimate compliment that she paid him was to afford him her undivided attention; and it was something he hadn't expected. There were no glances around, nor looks towards the door or towards the man sitting by the entrance: just for these few minutes, ticking by remorselessly, her attention was on him and, so it seemed, nothing else. Her beauty, anyone; man or woman, couldn't fail to see; her delightful smile, her relaxed demeanour; all these things would ensure that she'd stand out anywhere, yet all paled beside the one thing that exerted most moment on his consciousness: the attention that she bestowed on just him. Matt became aware of Luciano hovering discreetly.

"Your usual, Miss Fabienne?" he said.

"Yes please Luciano," she replied, with a polite glance in his direction.

"And for Il Signore?"

"The same please," Matt answered. At this point he neither knew nor cared what he'd just ordered. If a bowl of the most potent poison known to man was to be placed in front of him, he knew simply that he would drink deeply from it without question.

She smiled again as she asked, "How do you know what it is?"

"I don't; but if you're having it, then it must be a good idea."

There was just a slight hesitancy as she paused to take in a little more of this person who'd paid what for most would be an exorbitant sum for half an hour of anyone's time.

"Well, it's a smoked salmon and cream cheese bagel, in case you are interested."

"Bring it on," Matt said with conviction.

"Go on, you were about to tell me?"

"Well, Fabienne, ..." he began again.

"Call me Sylvie, all my friends do - and those who do lunch for large sums of money!" The smile glowed again as she added, "My first name is Fabienne, but I've always been known by my middle name, since I was a little girl."

"Well then, Sylvie, you know the adoring fan thing," he offered, still held, as if in hypnotic trance, by those effulgent eyes.

Steve had offered more advice, his demeanour, Matt reflected, rather like that of a manager in the dressing room before a cup final. He had warned him not to say too much, and emphasised his anxiety that if Fabienne received too much of an insight into Matt's true reasoning; she might become worried. He was perhaps correct in this assumption; Matt would consider later that he would have told her his darkest, innermost secret in return for another glimpse of that smile. Fortunately, his degree of restraint was not tested, she steered the conversation delicately, so as to maintain the flow and ebullience that mirrored her own personality.

"Most people would just buy a couple of CDs and a concert ticket, every once in a while," she suggested playfully.

"I've bought all your CDs and DVDs and, yes, the concert tickets; but people always stop me from clambering up on stage."

"So, it's *you* who does that?" The smile remained in abundance, as she stayed focussed on all that he said. "Local GP arrested in concert scuffle," she motioned as if reading newspaper headlines. "That wouldn't go down very well with your patients in Perrilymm would it?"

He wasn't surprised that his background had been checked. Lucy had had plenty of time to make sure that the person her employer was meeting was bona fide. He was surprised however by how much the star's sense of humour matched his own.

"You needn't worry, I'm sure those bouncers of yours would be too strong for me," he suggested, more calmly now, as he continued, "well that's enough about me, how about you? Forgive me, but surely this lunch must be a bit of a loss-leader for you? Would I be correct in thinking that your security precautions must have cost as much as I've spent?" He glanced towards the door. She nodded wisely.

"You're right, of course, the money is simply a filter to screen out, shall we say, undesirable elements."

She continued, more thoughtfully. "You know, Matt, any pop star..." she hesitated.

He filled in, "like you?"

"Yes, like me, has to arrange a fine balance between visibility, accessibility and yet not being overwhelmed by over-familiarity. We have to be seen to do ordinary things like lunch, and that's why Lucy agreed to feature in the article you read. A star who remains aloof from, and not in contact with, his or her fans wouldn't last two minutes. That's why we do concerts in far-flung places. It's much easier, believe me, to spend a day in a recording studio and sell a few CDs than spend weeks on the road. But without that, there'd be fewer CD sales, no adverts and no sponsorship. The whole thing is a bit like a house of cards, and I know that it could come tumbling down in an instant. Sad to say, I've seen a few go that way."

If there was the tiny flicker of sadness in her eyes at this point, it existed fleetingly before being subsumed by that seraphic smile that caused his legs to quiver, as it blossomed on her face. Straightforward and understated was how she came across, yet with those irresistible looks it would easy for people to overlook the fact that either quality existed in this young person in such abundance. He knew that she was only twenty-two, yet this belied the wisdom that could only have been learned out of bitter experience in that relatively short life. Many people would pass their whole lives and never gain such self-effacement.

"So you're not worried about being recognised by hundreds of fans and being mobbed?" he queried, with fascination now creeping in to join the emotions surging within.

She smiled again as the words gushed forth enthusiastically. "Funny one this, walk down a street wearing an old pair of jeans and plain T-shirt and no one would recognise me. Step out of a limo with sunglasses on, and loads of minders around, and then the fans will notice. Don't put sunglasses on, if it isn't sunny, people will only assume that there's someone here who doesn't want to be recognised; either a star, or perhaps a mass murderer."

"Which you bear little resemblance to," he suggested.

"Hopefully not!" she confirmed playfully. "It's a matter of bluffing people's expectations," she continued. "You could say that they see what they expect to see, but the opposite is also true; they don't see what they don't expect to see - if you follow."

He laughed at this simple, yet effective logic.

"The other thing is, I never draw attention to myself, never do the 'do you know who I am' routine."

"It's a bit like the story in the restaurant," he interjected, "the disgruntled star says to the waiter, 'Do you know who I am?' The waiter says aloud, 'There's a woman here who doesn't know who she is, can anyone tell her?'"

The grin flourished once again into a laugh.

"Yes, something like that, only, I never do that," she went on. "I try to maintain as much discretion in my life as possible, a bit like you doctors, are supposed to do" - the eyes widening as she gazed at him intently, "and hope for the best. Trouble is, Matt, publicity is never far away. Very little can be hidden for very long. Good job you live in a quiet little village, you'll escape the glare of publicity generated by today's events. The trick is to control it, and let little 'teaser' stories leak out, like this one."

Luciano set down the plates and the flow of words was temporarily interrupted by the necessity of eating.

Luciano's must have opened its doors as one or two people started filing in. Men glanced appreciatively at the beautiful woman in Matt's company and also at him, as the person lucky enough to be in receipt of that company. Only one person, a little girl, recognised Fabienne. She came up nervously to their table accompanied by an equally star-struck young mother.

"Excuse me, Miss Fabienne could I please have your autograph?" the little girl asked with quiet sibilant tones, giving a little curtsey.

Fabienne took the pen and napkin that she'd been offered. She quickly delved into her small bag and found a glossy photo. "Yes of course; what's your name, sweetie?"

"Elisabeth, Miss."

"To my great pal Elisabeth, Love Fabienne xx," she read aloud as she wrote across the gloss finish of the photo and the less-yielding surface of the napkin. "How's that?"

Matt had seen the flowing writing before and considered that perhaps, after all, she did most of the signing herself. She sensed his thoughts while Elisabeth swooned away, clutching the paper napkin as the most precious thing she'd ever owned in her life.

"I sign hundreds in a week. I like to do my own, if possible. It's a compliment paid to you when a fan asks for an autograph, the least you can do is to give them the real thing, though I must admit I do have some 'signers' working at the fan club."

"Yes, really? I was going to write in," he suggested cheerfully, suddenly remembering his conversation with Steve.

"Well, if you do, we'll send you a badge and a signed photo and enter you in the draw for free concert tickets - which reminds me." She searched in the bag once more and produced two tickets; an elegant finger was carefully and sensuously deployed to slide the tickets in his direction across the gleaming table. He swallowed hard at the sight of the delicate pink nails gliding across the table in this way. She paused momentarily almost as if giving him time to realign his surging thoughts. Perspicacious interest was matched in equal measure by delight as the smile broke across her face while she continued to survey him. "I'm at the MEN arena, here in Manchester, late this autumn: one for you and one for a significant other, as my guest. They're right near the front, so you might make it on stage yet." The long fingers worked their magic once more, tapping the tickets gently whilst she spoke.

He wondered as she did so whose company he could possibly want in future except for hers; anyone else's would be a pale imitation of the memories that would reside in him as of this moment. How could any interaction with another stand comparison, now that he'd met her? Steve would have been terrified of him drawing this conclusion - and would not have to know. He accepted instinctively that the price of loneliness was one that he would happily pay a million times over, and couldn't envisage a time when he would ever regret it.

"So, tell me about this village of yours. It looks lovely on the photos. We did a bit of checking before we agreed to do this," she mentioned, carefully and continued, "Do you have a nice life there?"

He wanted to believe that her interest lay just in him, but had to conclude that she was curious about, and fascinated by, all things and every person that she came across. It seemed that a simple, but all-pervading, fascination with life itself, and the human condition in particular, coursed through her veins.

"Oh, it's quiet, but I love my work and I wouldn't want to live anywhere else, I suppose. I'm a lucky man. It doesn't compare to international jet-setting, I'm sure," he suggested with a calmness that contrasted sharply with the thoughts flowing within.

"Don't be too sure." She nodded sagely. "Don't get me wrong, I love it, it's just that I see so many twisted souls around me, the alcohol, the drugs, the divorces, the suicides."

"Yes, they tell me general practice is a bit like that in some parts of the country!" he submitted.

"Not in that lovely village of yours, the one I saw on the photos?" Her voice paused delicately once again on the cusp of the question.

"I can't complain; the people are very friendly, so nice to work with and appreciative of all that I do, and yes, I count myself lucky to be amongst them - go on, you were saying." In that instant Matt knew that Steve had no cause for concern about him saying too much, as he hungered for each word that appeared at that fine mouth.

"I just wouldn't want you to think of it as being all autographs, beer and skittles. There can be a lot of turmoil, and sometimes it can be hard to find people who can be trusted," she said as a nuance of sadness existed fleetingly, once again, across her face.

"Everyone wants a little piece of you?" he volunteered knowingly.

"Yes something like that," her head nodding slowly, part in agreement and part in contemplation, "Anyway, for the next few years I'll be okay, but I can't see myself doing it, even if stardom persists ..."

"It will," he nodded quietly.

".... say for more than five years." She paused to sip from her spritzer before continuing, "there are always new stars coming along, just as I displaced some of the older, more established ones; my turn will come. The industry is very different these days. You see all the talent shows on the television that promise to make you a star if you get through enough rounds and enough people vote for you. There are the dance coaches, the voice coaches and the experts who judge or advise every week. It's a bit like a circus, and I think, maybe, the life of the stars is being oversimplified as a result, with the effect that we'll all have a sell-by date when the next batch come through," she said, almost as though she were thinking aloud.

"Unless of course you happen to sing in a way that a voice coach can't teach, or can dance with timing that can't be learned, and perform like you were born to do it, rather than created in some studio back room," he said sincerely.

"You're too kind Matt," she replied, suddenly looking away, not wanting to reveal the blush she felt rising on her cheeks.

"You don't read your own reviews then?" he asked.

"No, I can't bear that; I just go out there sing and dance my utmost, and hope that they come back for more."

"And boy do they come back: you were the highest selling....." he began.

"I can see you've done your homework Matt," she said as she blushed again. She had met a great many fans in her career and their attitude toward her seemed to span the whole panoply of human emotion. She realised too that the one before her now was at the upper scale of exuberance, such was the thraldom in which he was held, and it was this that was driving him, rather than any desire to embarrass. Remembering with a little twinkle, between her blushes, that she'd only agreed to do this lunch after much pleading from Lucy. She studied him a little longer; the young boy on Christmas morning, but behind the excitement lay a calm, quiet and kind man whose serious nature had been given a day's holiday. Ultimately she was glad that she'd given in to Lucy's plea, as there was little needing forgiveness, and much to admire.

Luciano interrupted to see if they wanted desserts.
"Just the usual please Luciano," she suggested politely.
"And for me please," motioned Matt.
"You are trusting, aren't you? You've just ordered a black filter coffee with a splash of cream."
"Perfect," Matt confirmed honestly.
"Are you always this easy to get along with?"
"Only when I'm out with megastars."
"Yes, I thought so; don't tell me, you're usually the sort of person who always sends the soup back because it's too hot."
"Routinely," he announced triumphantly, then went on, "no, no I'm a really quiet person who, like you, tries to be discreet and not to rock the boat. I have a comfortable, peaceful existence, doing work that I enjoy, and I've tried my best to smooth out much of the stresses others have to put up with in this type of work; like too many patients and things like that. I hope that I am, or perhaps continually strive to be, a good doctor."

"I'm sure you are," she said, the hand once again supporting the elegant chin, as the eyes of blue crystal met those of placid blue, while she continued to survey him closely, perhaps seeing something of herself as he spoke.

"Sylvie ... I wonder...could I?" he began.

Just then an unshaven man with a faded T-shirt and crumpled jeans interrupted them. Matt could see the minder by the door look across and stiffen visibly. Matt wondered if he could cover the distance quickly enough, were he called upon to do so. In any event he was sure that Sylvie was used to having things well under control.

"Excuse me Miss, have you dropped this?" the unkempt man asked with a gravelly voice that suggested to Matt, either too many cigarettes, or too much alcohol, or both. He held a small diary, which he proceeded to open as he offered it for her inspection and moved within a few inches of her in order to do so. Matt was also aware of his black greasy hair, dishevelled appearance and the overpowering smell of cooking fat as he leant over the table. Fabienne glanced briefly toward her minder who had removed his glasses and was rising from his chair. "No, I'm sorry it isn't mine," she replied pleasantly but briefly, the flat cadence in her voice much less inviting than the tone she employed with Matt.

Matt was aware of a fleeting shake of her head toward the minder who sat down carefully. The man lingered only for a second or two; then was gone. Matt paid him no more attention than he did anyone else in the restaurant, so spellbound had he become, so wrapped in her company and intoxicated by her charm.

"Matt, you were saying?"

"I can see that you really are that pleasant with people aren't you?" he noted.

"Well, I do my best not to appear strung out, but I do try."

"I think I might charge that stage after all," he suggested mischievously.

"I don't mind, but you'd better watch out for Peter over there: he's very quick off the mark."

"Perhaps not," said Matt gauging once again how those muscles were stretching back that suit.

"I was just going to ask," he hesitated, and then continued: "I hope you don't mind," he began again.

"Well, go on then, what!" she replied as the suspense over what he was about to ask built within her.

"You couldn't sign this for my pal Steve could you?"

"Yes of course - another admiring fan?" she said, taking the pen and the little pad he offered her.

"Well, let's just say, that he's your number two fan."

"OK then, in that case, how could I refuse? Perhaps you could give him your second ticket?" she suggested.

"I don't think he'll speak to me ever again if I don't. The other thing I wanted to ask you about was *'Not In Love'*, they say it's your greatest hit ever?"

She smiled as she considered his enquiry. "I have to confess, here, Matt that it was more good luck than good management. We had a bit of space left on the last album. I hate cover versions and try to do as much of my own material as possible. If I can't write it, then I buy it in, but at least it's mine, if you catch my meaning? Anyway, one of the team starts humming the track –*'Not in Love'* and asks me if I could sing it.

I didn't think we could go head-to-head with 10cc who, as I'm sure you know, wrote and sang the original. Anyway we reworked it just a little, changed the words ever so slightly. Where the girl used to say *'big boys don't cry, big boys don't cry'*, we decided, as you may know," - he nodded, she smiled. "I know, you can recite all the words can't you - you're that sort of fan, I can tell - you are a doctor really, aren't you, and not a professional fan who follows us from concert to concert?"

He smiled placidly as he wondered what Steve would have to say at this point. He said, "I think your version is more up to date, where you have the guy saying *'It's OK for boys to cry.'* I prefer yours even over the original, as of course do so many others."

"We hoped it would be well received, but it was really just to fill a bit of space, so we weren't too worried as long as people didn't think it absolute rubbish," she continued. "As you may know," he nodded, she smiled again, "it went Platinum after two weeks, and the track was in such demand we had to release it as a single."

There was a pause. "Very well, then, Matt."

She seemed to be winding up; there was a look of leaving in her eyes, the professional now breaking through within her. He saw Peter nod as she glanced briefly in his direction. "Is there anything I can do for *you*, before I go?" she asked, as the eyes held him, once again, within their bewitching embrace, there was a slight emphasis on the 'you'.

"I don't suppose …?"

"Well?" she said, and continued as he paused, "go on, I'm listening."

She looked ceiling-wards as if he were trying her patience, but the smile, as ever, belied this pretence, while she locked her gaze back upon him.

Producing a camera, he said, "Lucy warned, no cameras and I do understand if you refuse. I thought it couldn't hurt to ask - but I wonder if - a quick shot for my - meet the celebrity album?" He paused as hope flickered in that sliver of time.

She sighed good-naturedly. "OK, why not. Just for you?" The intonation in her voice rising with the question.

"Just for me," he confirmed.

She beckoned to the young waiter who attended immediately. Handing the camera to him, and stood next to Matt. He estimated that she was about five foot, ten inches in the heels. Briefly touching her shoulder: they posed for the shot. A little prickle ran down his spine as he made contact: hoping anxiously that she couldn't feel the shiver that coursed through him like electricity. The smile for the camera was more rehearsed, though no less exhilarating. The camera flash fired once, then again as the waiter took two shots.

She motioned to Luciano for the bill. Luciano hesitated, his expression grave behind the wire-rimmed spectacles, but he could see by the look on her face that she wasn't leaving without it, so he dutifully brought it without protest. Matt too, withdrew his wallet, but she gave him the same look. The black Mercedes appeared on the pavement outside, as Peter rose to his feet, tucking the newspaper under his left arm. Fabienne offered a black American Express card. Matt had heard of their existence though he'd never seen one, but then again, he'd never been in such company before.

More people had recognised Fabienne by this time, and some were starting to appear in front of the restaurant; staring in through the windows. A flash fired from outside as a tourist's camera went off. Luciano despatched the young waiter and waitress who had been polishing the glasses to stand by the entrance, to filter those who might be wandering in purely out of curiosity.

"Time for me to leave Matt." She looked directly at him as she said, "Are you going to be okay?"

Her words echoed across the ether as she uttered them, almost as if she had peered into his very soul. Could it be that those intense blue eyes had detected far more than he'd hoped while they surveyed him?

"I will be, now," he returned, as honestly as he could. "Thanks for this Sylvie. I've had a great time."

"Me too, Matt, give my love to Steve."

She turned, hesitated, just for a second, after shaking his hand, as if coming to an unexpected decision and asked, "Are you ready to be in the papers?"

"Pardon?"

Matt stood motionless as myriad thoughts queued for his urgent attention. Without further word she stretched, suddenly, in his direction and kissed his right cheek. He saw the whimsical smile move playfully across her face, and in that instant she turned, replaced her hat; while covering the distance to the door in easy strides; the heels echoing through his mind in synchrony with their journey across the hard surface.

At first he could only stare. When movement returned, he stifled an overwhelming urge to scream across the room and beg her to stay, or run to her and ask to go with her; wherever that may be. He knew this to be impossible since such action would not only betray her trust in him, but also create embarrassment for which she would not thank him. He could only continue to look as she walked, after what had seemed to him a brief glimpse of paradise, towards the door, and out of his life forever.

It hadn't been enough, not by any means. An eternity wouldn't have sufficed, but he knew that it would have to do, and he was acutely aware of the promises that bound him. She turned to glance back, as Peter, who looked even larger when standing, held the door open for her. Matt stood dumbstruck by the enormity of what he had seen and experienced; an encounter he could not have imagined in any of his wildest dreams. The Mercedes' door opened and she disappeared behind the inked windows. More people were gathering now, and random flashes fired from people who had suddenly realised just who was in their midst.

In the commotion, as the Mercedes floated away, Matt was ignored. He thanked Luciano and shook his hand gratefully.

Luciano gazed at him intently for a few seconds, no doubt wondering who this man was, who could command the presence of one so special. However, he returned the GP's smile benignly, with one lacking any trace of suspicion. Matt sought and tipped the waiters before walking out into the warm sunshine. He was not aware of the short man in the raincoat who settled his bill as soon as they had both left.

Matt walked along the quayside: only then was his head flooded by the things he'd wanted to say, and the things he'd wanted to ask. Things that he would never know, either because he had forgotten to ask them, or perhaps more likely, didn't want to interrupt the calm grace she exuded: characterised by that lovely smile and those glinting eyes. Just how could she dance like that? Was it learned, or was she born with that innate rhythm? How could she hit those notes whilst dancing with such energy? How did she feel about being described as the female equivalent of Michael Jackson? How did she manage to come up with such original song material? Why did she never mime, always singing live at each and every performance? Was she happy: was she sad? In any event, as he would never know the answers to those questions: they had become of academic importance only. One thing he did know; was that his life would never be the same again.

Upon finding his car, next to the large fans: he wasn't surprised to see that an old wreck of a car had been parked uncomfortably close. Matt could see the swathes of rust on the body from the far side of the car park as he approached. However, he no longer cared about such irrelevancies. His obsession with his car was part of his old life; so many emotions were invading his brain, begging for time so that they could be addressed more fully. He put his hand to the cheek that had been kissed. He could still feel the light touch upon him, one that he would never know again. Smiling to himself, he was reminded of a classmate at school who had touched his favourite footballer in the tunnel at Old Trafford, and who swore that he was never going to wash that hand again.

He couldn't get over her parting words. Just why had she asked him if he was going to be OK? Was it simple politeness, or had she detected far more from within him than he'd planned to reveal. The eyes had seemed to see right inside him, and that was why he could trust no more than fleeting contact with hers; for fear of revealing more than was wise. Perhaps he hadn't been as careful as he thought. In any event, he'd never have the opportunity to ask her, so he would be unlikely to ascertain the truth.

Steve's outburst in their conversation a short time ago had been a wake-up call and made him view one or two uncomfortable truths. The most prominent reason, however, was that any attempt by him to seek her out, and abuse the access that he'd been granted, would embarrass and betray her in equal measure. Most crucially her good nature would be traduced by such an attempt. For these reasons he knew that he would live by his promises, and that whatever course his life was now about to take, he would never complain about having done so. Though he ached for her company, and would sell his soul to regain it, he knew there was no course of action open to him that could bring it about. Life without her, with just this day for his memories, would be enough: this simple fact would sustain him in the years ahead. Ultimately, knowing with certainty what the answer would be, were Steve to ask of him, 'would he do it again?' Of that there was no doubt, and this conclusion, more than any other would serve in the days ahead.

He took his time driving home. The car was longing for a high-speed run: initially seemed to be pulling him faster and faster, but after a few minutes, the wheels synchronised perfectly through the gearbox to that mellifluous engine, and conveyed him in perfect comfort, at a speed that would not attract opprobrium from the Police. He didn't drive directly home, but called in to the surgery to collect his post, sign some prescriptions and even managed to catch the print shop before they closed. Leaving the precious memory card with them, he asked simply for the two images to be printed at the highest quality available and he would collect all in a day or two.

Mrs Simpson surveyed him with a quizzical eye. Despite giving Janice the exact opposite impression, she was puzzled by what she saw. Sensing the turmoil within him, yet she saw there was also a calm about him, almost as if a ghost had been laid to rest. The last time she'd seen that look was when his previous girlfriend had dumped him. Realising that she was no nearer to knowing just what was going on, but she was sure that she would have enough figured by the morning to tell Janice and others the latest, in the way of news. She knew too, that in such a small village, all would be revealed, sooner or later. Secrets couldn't be kept in such a place, and she would make sure that she was in prime position to discover them, when the time came.

While the locum finished off the surgery, Matt breezed home, feeling tired; yet relieved. He'd promised to phone Steve upon his return, and he attended to that promise immediately.

"Well, my boy, how did it go? Are you still in one piece?" Steve asked expectantly.

"I had a really good time. It was so nice to meet her, and she was everything I suppose I could ever dream she could be," Matt offered honestly.

Steve did his best to just listen. Fortunately, Matt couldn't see the concern engraved to his face. "So how do you feel about things?" Steve probed using the open questions beloved by psychologists.

"I feel calm: I think I've got it out of my system, and I feel as if I can return to my life," Matt said, in part knowing that this is what Steve wanted to hear, but also that it had a high content of truth.

"So, Matt, do you think that you'll be able to return to that life a little bit more ordinary?"

"You know, Steve, I think I will. I accept that what I've seen and heard and felt today isn't real, and I understand that no part of my life can relate to that, or indeed, that nothing of her life can relate to mine. But I'm still glad that I went, saw her and met her, because otherwise I would have always regretted not knowing," Matt concluded.

Steve had to take those deductions at face value. He regretted that, by not controlling his own feelings, he had been unable to help his friend, using the skill and objectivity that the GP had every reason to expect. Steve spent his professional life with such cases and with the consequences of not accepting that the truth, sometimes, was harder to see than people realised.

"I got you her autograph and she sends her love," Matt said quietly as if frightened to hear the response.

Steve could hardly believe what he was hearing; his friend spoke almost as if he had met a friend or an old acquaintance, rather than being the willing participant in some publicity stunt. Knowing that it would be cruel to attempt to shatter that, but if Matt did find himself sinking into that dream, Steve would have to do more, much more, than expose the painful truth. He was nevertheless pleased for his friend, having gone along with what Steve could only consider was a whim, and had returned with, at least, a promise that the whole business was concluded. Perhaps when it came down to it, he realised that he should have trusted the GP more, despite the fact that so much seemed to be at stake. He recalled with a slight shudder how his anger had mastered him.

"Very well, Matt, my boy, so how do you feel about putting all this behind you and getting on with the rest of your life?" Steve said, using an open question once more.

"Positive and optimistic." Matt lied a little to Steve, but he knew that by applying himself to his work and his life with his usual energies and enthusiasm, sooner or later, these emotions would creep in. He could only hope that Steve couldn't sense the restlessness that still resided within.

Steve did detect that Matt had been as true as his word, and this was enough to re-assure him through the slight pauses in the conversation. He thanked Matt for phoning him, and each returned to their private thoughts. There was still much unsaid between them. Matt could neither pretend not to know Steve's true feelings, nor manage his life, any longer, in a self-indulgent way. Perhaps he'd been on his own for so long that he'd forgotten the fundamentals that others lived by in their daily lives: because of this he'd come over as uncaring and vain. Steve had shaken him, Matt realised, in his best interests, but he also knew that there was much work to be done to confront and rebuild the relationship with his friend that he believed had been imperilled. His aim now, without quite knowing how, was that he would make it right with Steve; and he would pursue this end tirelessly.

CHAPTER V

LIFE LAID WASTE

Matt was in the gym even earlier than usual the following morning. Feeling a little embarrassed about waiting by the door whilst they opened up, he always tried to avoid appearing either so shallow or so sad as to be incapable of avoiding this. In truth he was up and desperate for some physical action, to expunge some of the feelings that bubbled within: almost as a penance would absolve a sinner. He set the cross trainer onto its highest level and started on a punishing hill profile. Twenty minutes later he was sweating profusely, but showed no signs of letting up. The other gym users, beginning to file in, could detect that this was a serious work-out and left him to it, without even the odd 'good morning' coming his way, while he charged onwards. In the pool he swam the fastest time of his life: even the young girl who had hitherto fought off all challengers, was left seemingly becalmed as he tore after her, overhauled her and continued at this pace for a further twenty laps.

He tried to keep himself busy all weekend. Inevitably, in quieter moments his strategy failed: the concentration lapsed as he went over things said and not said, a million times. Many of his thoughts centred on his conversation with Steve, as the stance taken by his friend still troubled him. The more he analysed it, the more depressing his conclusions. On a brighter note, Fabienne's words, too, continued to run through his mind endlessly, especially her parting comment, "*Are you going to be OK?*" echoed from consciousness, to hypnogogic state, to sleep itself. Slowly, but determinedly, he steeled himself for the Monday to come. If work was to be his salvation, and he was never to set eyes on her again, then he'd embrace his fate and not be found wanting in this respect or dreaming about what might have been. The pact, he mentally agreed, would be ready by Monday - a clear action plan for the years ahead.

Arriving in the surgery earlier than usual, he even preceded Mrs Simpson: making himself a cup of tea and took the box of notes down to the surgery. The manager wasn't surprised to see him quietly tapping into the computer on his desk as she got to work. He was the sort of person who would lead by example, and if more work were in prospect, he'd be the first to get stuck in. Something was driving him; of that she was certain, and that stimulus had occurred recently. Not being able to define it more closely would in no way spoil her discourse to other staff members. The turmoil within him being widely apparent to all who might look, she'd just have to come up with something plausible. Making him another cup of tea, she waited for Janice to arrive, before making more. The patients eventually started drifting in, as another week began.

Amanda O'Reilly presented in surgery. She'd lived in the village for some years but originated from Ireland. Though she was a frequent attender he received the impression that she'd never quite summoned the courage to tell him exactly what was on her mind, despite his leaving plenty of open questions before her, to give her a forum to do so. Today was to be very different.

"Doctor Sinclair," she began. He could sense that he was about to be told something profound, and he decided that listening was his best ploy. "Thirty years ago I was young, single, alone and... pregnant." Matt knew that she'd been married; her husband had been killed in a road accident leaving her with three grown sons, about ten years ago. "I was jobless, homeless and penniless, without a roof over my head. The nuns who looked after me suggested that my only course of action would be to have the little girl adopted, which I reluctantly did. Nobody knows about this, none of my family. I put it all behind me, but never, of course, forgot the little girl I'd left behind all those years ago in Ireland. That baby is now thirty years old, and just recently my brother, who still lives in my old village, has been contacted by that thirty year old woman who wants to trace the mother who abandoned her all those years ago."

Mrs 0'Reilly was always a pretty tough customer; bringing up three boys on her own had made her so, out of necessity, yet the tears were falling now in silent cascade.

"What do I say to her? What if she asks me why I didn't keep her? What if she's angry with me? And how can I make her believe that I never, ever stopped thinking of her from that day to this? I wanted what was best for her. Just what kind of life would she have had with me?"

Matt passed the box of tissues that he always placed strategically on his desk. He had known for some time that there was something, and now here it was, out in the open. There were obviously a lot of emotions coiled within, fear, shame and, of course, deep sorrow. Matt's strategy was to confront them one by one and seek clarity in the morass of charged feelings.

"Amanda, I don't think your daughter is contacting you to blame you, or to make you feel guilty, perhaps her main reason is that she just wants to meet her natural mother. Could it be as simple as that? If you were that thirty-year-old woman, what would you want after all these years? You'd be looking for answers - answers that we all either have, or that we seek. She's no different, and I'd bet that there's more of a hug on offer here and 'can I get to know you?' rather than an accusatory finger. Who can judge you now, on the actions you took when you were what, fifteen, sixteen?" He paused whilst she digested the information, before continuing, "she'll have questions of you, because she needs answers for herself and, perhaps, her own family; but I don't think she's going to criticise you. Have you thought that this could be a healing process for all of you?"

The tears still flowed, but she looked a little more composed.

"I'm not trying to tell you that this is going to be easy, but it's about discovery, about healing, and about her future as well as yours. Truth is, it's never left you, has it, that guilt over something that you did, quite understandably, thirty years ago? I've seen it on your face before, and perhaps you owe yourself the opportunity to lay that guilt to rest. I wonder if you'd like to think about some counselling to prepare you..." Matt knew that Steve's team had several counsellors who would see Amanda at short notice to help with the issues she faced.

"Yes Doctor: I think I would like that. I feel so much better just telling someone."

"I'll arrange it. Counselling will help you more," he assured her.

They talked for a few more minutes. A more positive Mrs O'Reilly left his consulting room with a promise to return when she'd made contact.

As she departed, he reflected on what had passed. There was certainly a lot of suffering, bubbling below the every-day lives of ordinary people. Perhaps this is what Steve was alluding to. Could he be trying to suggest that Matt's decadent lifestyle had insulated him from the lives of such people, who had stresses and strains on them that the GP couldn't understand? Perhaps he was trying to tell Matt that he came over as being vainglorious and bored. Despite his introspection and the devastating conclusions that this led to, Matt couldn't agree. He wondered if Steve had, even now, not gained sufficient insight into his true character, his desire to learn from, and help, all his patients. Whilst it was true that Matt was lucky to have a comfortable existence, this reinforced his desire to help others, rather than stifled it. Was it possible that Steve's usually keen insight into the lives of others had deserted him, at least temporarily, where it came to his colleague, his friend and his old room-mate? He remained optimistic about his ability to learn from setbacks, especially painful ones and whilst he retained this, he knew that the future was to be anticipated eagerly, rather than feared.

Despite Mrs O'Reilly being in longer than expected, Matt still managed to finish on time. After surgery he met up with Mrs Simpson so that she could update him. She began, reading from her notebook, "the Medical Practices Committee have passed your application for a partner. The Primary Care Trust see no reason why you shouldn't go ahead and advertise, unless you want their finance chief to go over the cost implications with you before you do?"

"No, I think we'll just go ahead. Monica; will you contact the usual weeklies so that we can get an advert out?" he suggested, wanting to get going straight away, now that he'd made his mind up. There were several weekly GP publications that were widely read by the medical profession, and these would allow rapid and far-reaching access to other doctors who were looking for a job or fancied a change of environment. As there was a shortage of doctors, Matt knew that they'd have to do their best to make an advertisement look attractive so as to tempt good candidates.

"Any ideas you have about how good we are, and how attractive we'd be to a new doctor, would be most welcome, and I'll come up with a few ideas of my own. We can perhaps get our heads together with it on Friday?"

"Righto, Doctor Sinclair," she said, and moved on to the next point on her list. "The architect has been and had a good look round. He was here for hours: couldn't get rid of him. He had lots and lots of questions. He'll be contacting you in the next two weeks with some quick sketches he wants you to have a look at, just to gauge your opinion."

"Sounds good, Mrs Simpson: I don't care if he talks, as long as he's good at his job and is thorough."

"No doubt we'll soon find out, Doctor."

"True enough, Monica."

Matt smiled contentedly as she left with another tranche of gossip to feed Janice and the administration staff in the office. He couldn't help but recall the events of last Friday, but permitted his thoughts to stray only for a brief moment before checking his post, signing prescriptions and collecting the visits. There were only two visits so he had plenty of time to call into the photographer's to collect his prints. He smiled: the two people in the picture made a handsome couple, that was for sure - but were no more real than the dreams that came to him most nights now; eventually sublimating as the dawn claimed the sky at a very early hour. He placed one of the pictures on the shelf in his consulting room and one at home in his lounge.

In Tuesday's post, a letter arrived marked *Private and Confidential*. He groaned; such official looking documents as these nearly always contained aggressive letters from solicitors retained by disgruntled patients, wishing to make formal or serious complaints about some aspect of their NHS care. He opened the envelope cautiously. From inside he withdrew a little note: the handwriting he recognised immediately. Moving into his consulting room, from reception where eyes seemed to be upon him, just as Mrs Simpson's antenna of curiosity was tuning in.

'Dear Matt,

So nice to meet you!

I had a lovely time in Luciano's, but I couldn't have you podding out this sort of cash for something that gave me as much pleasure as hopefully it did you.

Might see you clambering on the stage at the MEN.

Yours,

Sylvie

PS. Love to Steve

PPS. This is my own handwriting too!'

Pinned to the note was a cheque for £15,000. Matt couldn't resist glancing back at the photo on the shelf behind him, and smiled again. He wished that he could simply pick up the phone and try to get through to Lucy, but knew that this he could not, and would not, do.

The photograph's appearance was immediately detected by Mrs Simpson, who couldn't hide the self-satisfied look of triumph when telling Janice, "Told you, told you," she repeated a little more loudly, so as to emphasise her delight, and to firmly establish her reputation as someone who was all-seeing and all-knowing; at least within the restricted confines of the village surgery.

"Who is she then?" asked Janice, anxious to limit some of the gushing posturing coming from the practice manager.

"Now, that I don't know, *yet*, but I'll find out, you'll see," Mrs Simpson replied emphatically.

"She looks familiar," said Janice, gazing myopically at the picture, brought out of Matt's consulting room by her manager, as a trophy to verify still further her pre-eminence in such areas as gossip.

"Some blonde bimbo no doubt. I'll give her a couple of months. He's never been one to pick the right woman," Mrs Simpson said knowingly.

"Has he been a bit unlucky perhaps?" suggested Janice, more kindly.

"Told you about the merry dance the last one put him through didn't I. Mark my words, this one will fare no better."

"Yes you did," interjected Janice quickly, anxious to move the conversation along, as her boss's tone was becoming just a little too self-congratulatory. Fortunately, Doctor Sinclair arrived at this point, and Mrs Simpson had to dive quickly into his room to return the picture to its spot on his shelf.

The next two weeks saw Matt involved in feverish activity as drawings had to be finalised, submitted and eventually passed. The architect was obviously someone who liked to take his time and couldn't understand why there was all this haste. It was only when Matt reminded him that they were hoping to finish the project this year, and that the glorious summer weather was almost certainly not going to hold through the winter or even the autumn, that he saw Matt's view.

He was able to continue to resist urges to try to contact Fabienne, and also those to purchase more magazines. Just occasionally, she'd be mentioned on the national news. If Matt was half listening to the television whilst he got on with something else, his brain would detect such information within an instant: his attention then being held rigidly until the next item was introduced. Evening would often find him switching on the late night news to see if there was any mention of her. Noting that on one such programme, reference was made to Fabienne's two city concerts in New York and Toronto that had been sell-outs; and that she'd returned to the UK in time for the imminent release of her new CD.

Matt continued to use his work as a foil to counter the ever-present desire to telephone Lucy with the hope of speaking to Fabienne: the urge slowly passing, from daily to weekly. His dreams quietened in their immediacy; in tandem with his sleep, which returned to a more refreshing pattern. July came and gave witness to a blur of activity, as Matt's plans continued to mature. The adverts had been sent off and the number of replies he received surprised him. It seemed that a great many young GPs were deserting city life for the quieter, but more rewarding life, in rural areas. No doubt Rita would be aghast at this.

Matt took all the replies home, as did Mrs Simpson. They each compiled a short-list and then held a meeting where they compared their choices, and the reasons behind their selection. Matt knew that he'd have final say, but he was interested in the opinion of his practice manager, as she'd undertaken this sort of activity when she'd been with the bank. Eventually, after some discussion, a short list of three was drawn up, and those applicants invited. Matt and Mrs Simpson held the interviews for the new post, and were impressed by the calibre of them all. Matt settled for a young man fresh from finishing his GP trainee year; being amazed at how young he looked. Mrs Simpson also picked him out as the one she believed to be best suited to the job. It didn't seem that long to Matt since he'd been in that position: the past five years had flown so quickly.

Janice had surveyed each of the young doctors as they arrived, sat them down in the office, and made them tea while they waited for their turn. She informed them that she'd be available to show any of them around the small surgery, and was delighted when the handsome young doctor, Greg Stevens, took up her offer. She took her time in showing him round, and devoted undiluted attention towards him until Doctor Sinclair asked him to enter the consulting room for interview. Janice was even more ecstatic when she learned that he'd been offered the post and had accepted. Mrs Simpson had carelessly left his application on the table in the office and Janice had noted that he was single and apparently unattached.

July remained hot and dry. Matt knew that the weather wouldn't hold forever, and thus became impatient to drive his plans along. Doctor Stevens was due to start on the first of September. Matt was very keen that the surgery should be seen as a model of efficiency, so he redoubled his efforts with the administration and the computer system, to make sure that any doctor who had occasion to look, would be most impressed. He remembered the words that Rita had chosen on this subject, and was keen to banish such descriptors: not that she'd ever seen his surgery, so what she knew of the matter he couldn't guess. In any event, his main thrust was to make the new partner feel at home, rather than impress an outsider like Rita Letworth.

That evening found Matt relaxing lazily in front of the television. Though he was usually a morning person, he spent so many nights on call that his habits had had to be changed: often staying up in case a late call came in. He wasn't really paying attention to the television, which was on more as background noise, and was about to switch it off when his attention was grabbed in one of the most unexpected and brutal ways possible. The headlines flashed across the screen, transfixing him to the spot with horror and alarm in equal measure. The detail he missed, but the essence was to be indelibly engraved upon him while he stared at the screen, horribly drawn in by the story that had broken that day.

The evening news was dominated by the discovery of a body at Fabienne's London home. All the British channels carried the shocking news, and many of the international ones, too, ran the story as their main lead. More and more bad news unfolded as he watched, in disbelieving silence.

'Fabienne arrested.'

The words echoed like explosions going off in his psyche. He could only stare in panic and incredulity as more news was released.

'It can be confirmed that the body of a male was found dead today, in the London home of Fabienne. The pop star was interviewed for two hours in Bow Street police station.'

Hordes of press and photographers were shown crowding around the entrance to the police station. Fabienne and her solicitor were mobbed on the way in, and the press remained while she departed. Her solicitor had this to say: "I would emphasise that Fabienne arrived here this evening voluntarily, to answer Police questions about the death of a thirty year old male - the body being discovered at her London home. Fabienne has agreed to co-operate fully in any way that she can. We would wish to point out that Fabienne does not know this person, has no idea how he came to be in her home, nor how, or why, he met his untimely death. She would like to extend her condolences to the dead man's family."

Streams of shots followed as the newscaster continued to fill in more detail: images of Fabienne arriving at the police station. There were shots of her six-million-pound London home, and then some of the dead man, a Barry Miles. Reports continued to flood in and were given out initially in a haphazard way, but later news programmes had more details, as further facts had been unearthed.

'Barry Miles, believed to be an unemployed former stage-constructor, was found dead in Fabienne's multi-million-pound London home. Police are treating the death as suspicious. The pop star was interviewed this evening at Bow Street for almost two hours, but allowed to leave pending further police investigation.'

Matt could only stare in disbelief, the salient points of the reports hitting him as if making a physical impact.

Disbelief was the emotion that he tried desperately to cling to. For the briefest of moments he was able to use this as an anchor point and, from there, to tell himself that none of it could possibly be true. Words that were much beloved by Steve when he was relating a fantastical tale from one of his patients; *'You couldn't make it up,'* came to Matt at this moment, and he realised that such a truism was in force now. Harsh reality had created events much worse than the most alarming of grim nightmares: these events were in the process of stampeding brutally and devastatingly through the middle of Fabienne's life.

His desperation, tinged with panic, meant that he was determined to phone Lucy to ask if Fabienne was all right, and if there was anything at all he could do. Looking at the telephone, as a patient dying of a fever might stare at a lifesaving serum. At that moment, Steve, sensing Matt's turmoil, telephoned in order to lend support to his friend, and also to infuse restraint. Steve tried to calm the GP with an objective analysis of the situation, though he acknowledged that calm was the last word that could be used to describe Matt's state of mind at that juncture.

"Just what can you do?" he began. "This is a game that will be played far above our heads, and don't you think that she'll have her hands full at the moment, with calls coming in from all directions? The poor girl won't know where to turn," Steve's voice sounded an increasingly desperate note.

Matt then considered writing, but couldn't commit himself to words on paper: they just wouldn't come, and the thought of sending them to the fan club, the only address he had for her, left him cold. Eventually he had to accept that Steve's view was correct, and all he could do was watch, as millions of others did around the world, while the story unfolded. He could only guess at how Fabienne was feeling at this time, but what he knew of her, dictated that she'd be devastated. She'd recognise this as the worst kind of publicity that she had at all times sought to avoid. The maelstrom that now bore down on her was not just beyond her control, but was likely to have an obliterative effect on her, her fan base and her career.

Every newspaper gave top billing to the story that morning. The tabloids, which could be easily swamped by just one prominent story, devoted most of their available space to the events unfolding across a national and international stage. She would know that the tabloids, in particular, could be either your best friend or your worst enemy, depending upon which approach was likely to sell most copy. This lesson was to be hammered home with malign intent in the days that lay ahead. Matt still had great difficulty in controlling the overpowering urge to phone Lucy, but Steve's sage counsel acted as a restraint.

Worse, much worse was to follow.

The next day one tabloid, the *Daily Scorcher*, published a picture of Barry Miles talking to Fabienne. Matt knew the scene immediately: it was inside Luciano's, and could only have been taken the day that they had met there. He wanted to kick himself for not recognising the pictures of the dead man before. Barry Miles was the man who had produced the small diary. The angle of the photograph gave the impression that both were in deep conversation whilst looking at the book. Matt could still recall the all-pervading smell of burnt chip-fat, which seemed to trigger memories readily from the feverish activity within his brain. The caption couldn't have been worse. *Come clean, Fabienne. Tell us what you know.* It was almost an appeal to her to confess and get it all off her chest. The article continued:

'Fabienne told the police yesterday that she had never met Barry Miles, the thirty-year-old who was found dead in her Kensington home; yet exclusive pictures taken by our staff reporter reveal a cosy tête a tête at an exclusive Manchester restaurant recently. You can clearly see the star in deep conversation with Miles. The police confirmed that they are still investigating the circumstances of Miles's death, and that further enquiries are in progress. We feel that the public have a right to know just what Fabienne knows, and why she was less than honest when her solicitor made a statement on her behalf. Just what could the multi-million-pound superstar be hiding, and when will she come clean?'

At this point Matt's urge to do something became overwhelming. He telephoned Lucy. "Lucy, it's Matt Sinclair," his voice wavering in keeping with the trembling hands as he tried to grip the handset. "How are things?"

"Terrible, Doctor Sinclair; this is what she'd always feared. Her worst nightmare has come true, and is now splashed across the newspapers," Lucy offered dejectedly.

"Is there anything at all I can do, Lucy?" he said, still unable to compose his voice.

"To tell you frankly, no, Doctor, I don't think so, unless you can work miracles?"

Matt wondered with alarm if Fabienne suspected him of being in on the snare, and of setting her up in some way.

"How did they get that photo Lucy? It must have been taken when we were sitting together," he queried.

Lucy picked up on his mood quickly. "Doctor Sinclair, don't blame yourself: Fabienne's always a target. The reporter must have been in the room - maybe she stayed just a little too long - and the photograph was taken with a sophisticated camera that would have given you no clue that pictures were being taken - probably from some distance away."

"I know it's a setup: that chap, Barry Miles asked her if she'd dropped her diary, no more than that - she didn't know him." Matt realised that no words or actions that he might make would be able to assist her: all he could do was watch, as did millions of others.

"We know that, Doctor Sinclair, but when tabloids sense a story they don't worry so much about accuracy, only if it'll sell, and if people will believe the headlines long enough for them to hand over their money. And believe me, it is selling," Lucy said with a little more objectivity in her voice.

"Lucy can you tell her I called and how sorry I am." He wanted to say more, but couldn't compose words that would have any meaning other than underline his own impotence in this situation.

"I'll be sure to do that Doctor. I must go, all the lines are ringing."

Though having broken his promise to Steve, he could not have sat back as this horror unfolded in her life, without at least leaving a message, which hopefully she would get. Each day brought worse news. The picture painted by the *Daily Scorcher* became widely held. The media tore into the events like a pool full of Piranha, and Fabienne was clearly the bait. Film contracts and sponsorship deals were cancelled because the bandwagon that had her, somehow, implicated in this death, began to roll and became unstoppable. The papers held up each piece of bad news for public inspection, so that this, too, became a totem of her obvious guilt. Her management company, *Brite Lite Entertainment*, was also hit hard. The day before the story broke, its share price was around £3.87. As details of the story spread, the price collapsed as the stock was heavily sold: the rationale being that, though other stars were managed by the company, if its main client and majority shareholder, Fabienne, was suddenly holed below the water line, then the company might well not survive. The run on the shares continued, until the Stock Exchange stepped in and suspended them at 38p. Financial commentators then worried openly about the viability of the company, and so, several of the stars managed by the firm, cancelled their contracts, thus endangering it further. Matt knew that Fabienne would have lost millions within hours.

Overnight, the golden girl whom everyone loved; everyone wanted a piece of, became devalued currency. Graphic details describing how the body had been discovered in her bedroom, and in what condition, were leaked. The tabloids sucked it all up in the story-making machine, as more and more sensational headlines were spawned. It became clear that the body had been asphyxiated by a rope tied around the neck. Newspapers spared no gory detail as they picked over the events, not caring about the people who were now most mixed up in them; the dead man's relatives, and, of course, Fabienne herself. The frenzy didn't allow for human frailty; not when there was a story in the offing and, though the aim was thinly disguised as uncovering 'facts' that people had a right to; few failed to realise that it was simply about selling more copy. The pursuit of truth became the banner under which she was slowly crushed, and the tide upon which Barry Miles' relatives were swept away. One newspaper ran the banner, *Kinky sex sessions in Fabienne's bedroom*. She immediately sued, but the publishers retracted the story only after ordering two extra print runs, each of which sold out instantly.

Another led with: *He died with her boots on!*

Public revulsion at how the poor man had met his death became linked, as newspapers had hoped, directly to Fabienne: the damage became as dry tinder in a forest fire. Economics of the tabloid world meant that even punitive damages that might possibly be awarded, some time in the future, would have little influence on the here-and-now, as more and more stories surfaced, and a deluge of revenue cascaded into their coffers.

The police interviewed Fabienne again. One newspaper ran a story that she'd been arrested and was remanded in custody. Despite being forced to issue a denial, as her lawyers intervened to try to protect her again; but having acted as quickly as they could, they were simply too late: the media frenzy had brought its prey to the ground and was now picking over the bones of the dead carcass that had once been her career.

Professional advisers would no doubt tell her to tough it out, to be seen going about her usual business. But Matt knew that her strategy would be the opposite of that. To lie low, if at all possible, to keep out of the public gaze; and hope that the hurricane now sweeping through her life, would sooner or later blow itself out, or move on. Seeing clearly that the house of cards she'd referred to so presciently, was in free fall now, he wondered how much of it would be left standing once they had all had their fill. Matt wished, with every ounce of his being, that there was something he could do. Ultimately, he could only agree with Steve that the atmosphere in which this game was being played was very rarefied indeed: nowhere that he could reach, let alone breathe. Concerts were cancelled; the release of the new CD was deferred. Fabienne sank out of sight. The absence of riposte from her, to the tumult of accusation and innuendo, was taken to proclaim her guilt rather than her innocence. She was condemned and sentenced in the court of public opinion: the very air that she needed to sustain life, being denied.

Some relief came the following Monday, exactly a week after the news first broke. Professor Harrison, an eminent psychiatrist at Nottingham Medical School, came forward to announce that he had been treating Barry Miles for some time, with schizophrenia linked to an abnormal fixation with Fabienne. He explained his late announcement by the need for patient confidentiality. Doctors weren't permitted to release confidential information about their patients, generally, without their consent. On consulting his defence body, however, he'd been advised that if he had material facts about a case, then his primary duty now lay with the living, and necessitated divulging what he knew to the police: this superseding his duty to his ex-patient and to the relatives.

The police then announced that they had completed their enquiries and that they were not looking for anyone else in connection with Miles' death - generally a polite term for suicide. A coroner's investigation would be convened, and they would be passing information to that. Immediately the media focus was switched from Fabienne the murderer, to Miles the stalker. It then becoming apparent that Fabienne was an innocent bystander, mixed up as the coincidence of being the unknowing object of his attention. Only then were facts, that had been known all along, released by the press - that Miles had broken in whilst Fabienne was not at home; that her statement that she neither knew him nor had ever met him, was perfectly true. The shifting emphasis was too late, far too late, to save her. Never had a celebrity's fall been so rapid, so tragic or so complete. Her life had been de-constructed in the same time span as that attributed to the Creation.

The days had become a blur as Matt finished his surgery each day, only to return home to catch the news and find the most objective reporting of events he could. He couldn't bear to read the *Daily Scorcher* or the *Sunday Scoop*. These two tabloids had run the most aggressive campaign against Fabienne, and were owned by the same entrepreneur, Mervyn Boomer; keen to promote them as the pre-eminent force within the field of tabloid journalism. Any other consideration was widely held to be of secondary concern. Clearly this included such things as truth and a person's career.

Matt telephoned Professor Harrison the day after his press release. Doctors were excused from observing patient confidentiality, providing the matter under discussion would benefit one or other's patient. Matt explained that he was a friend of Fabienne's. Inactivity, whilst watching her life being shattered before her very eyes, had been hard to manage, and in phoning Professor Harrison he at least felt that he was doing something. The professor told him that Barry Miles had been working as a labourer on a set for one of Fabienne's concerts some years before. He was medically retired from that work having become mentally ill; and had developed a fixation with Fabienne. Incredibly she hadn't been warned of this, despite the fact that Miles had exhibited violent behaviour when frustrated. Policy for so-called dangerous patients in the community, Professor Harrison reminded Matt, had changed dramatically in recent years, but unfortunately too late to save either Barry Miles or indeed Fabienne. Barry had been given a large sum of money as part of a redundancy package and compensation for an accident at work. Apparently, it transpired after his death, that all of this had been spent in following the star around the country on her various tours. He had been referred late in his illness to the Nottingham team and attendance was patchy.

Miles had been stalking Fabienne without her knowledge for many months before his death. He'd come to the attention of the psychiatric services after a violent outburst while in a Nottingham pub. A drinker had been grievously assaulted, and the judge hearing the case had insisted on psychiatric reports before continuing with the proceedings. It was felt that Miles wasn't dangerous enough to be admitted for treatment against his will. They hadn't known that, though he was attending his appointments regularly and gave the illusion of a co-operative patient, he was secretly following Fabienne. Having defaulted only on the last two appointments; a few days later he was found in such circumstances in the star's home. Professor

Harrison told Matt that Miles had taken a university degree in mathematics, been employed briefly as a college lecturer some years earlier, but had left his job after his divorce. Loss of contact with his family about twelve months earlier, being thought to be responsible for triggering his mental illness.

Matt gave a little shiver: perhaps this was the side of obsession that Steve was used to seeing, and one of the reasons why he had been so worried for his friend. Matt thanked the professor for speaking with him. He felt as if he were helping in some small way, but still felt restless and impotent; fighting a desperate urge to contact her every time her name was mentioned in the newspapers or on television -and that was still on a daily basis.

He also telephoned James Farquar, his stockbroker. Knowing that he couldn't help Fabienne directly, but he could at least show moral support, albeit somewhat peripherally. Without doubt, he was tired of sitting on the sidelines and was ready for some action: that others would have called foolhardy.

"James, Hi, it's Matt Sinclair here," Matt began.

"Hello Matt, don't tell me she's bled you dry and you want to sell more shares. Oh well, let me see now. Just as well you're good for it Matt. I tell you these women; they are simply not worth it..."

"No, James. I do want to sell, but also to buy," he interrupted, sensing that James was at his most loquacious.

James's interest picked up. "Okay then, Matt, what have you got in mind?" he queried.

"What is the total value of my portfolio at present?"

"It's around £200,000 last time I looked, why Matt?" suddenly sounding more alarmed.

"I want to sell the lot and put it in *Brite Lite Entertainment*."

Life Laid Waste

James laughed. "Good one that, really got me going. Love it, Matt. Now what can I really do for you?"

"I'm deadly serious," Matt corrected firmly.

"Go on Matt, tell me you're having a laugh?" A little hint of desperation crept in to his voice as he sensed that Matt, far from joking, was very serious.

"James, I haven't taken leave of my senses, please get me the figures," he said, as patiently as hurry would allow. He knew that if he thought too much about his plan, he would simply not have the courage to carry it out.

"Don't do this to me, Matt. It's been a really bad day. Just had that bitch's solicitor on to me - ripping me apart, they are. Go on Matt tell me you're joking," pleaded the stockbroker.

Matt confirmed calmly, but unequivocally, that he was not joking. He didn't have to remind James that he was an execution broker only, and wasn't paid or retained to provide advice or comment as to the wisdom of a given investment. Eventually James confirmed that by selling everything, Matt would raise £212,303 and that the shares in *Brite Lite* had come out of suspension that morning but had continued to fall. James spoke very slowly as he released each fact to Matt, hoping that even then he would come to his senses.

"They're now at 32p fallen a further 6p on the day, so far Matt." James paused hoping that even now Matt would admit the joke.

"The whole lot to be invested in *Brite Lite*, please, James."

James coughed nervously. Matt could hear him swallow hard as though someone had just told him to stick his fingers in a light socket whilst standing in a bucket of water.

"Very well, Matt, that's 663,400 shares; are you sure?"

"Do it, James. I know you think I've taken leave of my senses."

Matt heard him take a deep gulp of air, holding his breath, as he punched the instructions through the terminal. If he'd been there in person, he would have seen the stockbroker's hands shaking and sweaty as he carried out his instructions.

"Done, Matt. Once my fees are paid there'll be a small balancing cheque, which will arrive in due course," he paused once again before continuing. "I'm sweating here for you, Matt, but I wish you luck," he confided generously.

James was burning to ask Matt if he knew something that others didn't. He knew, however, that alluding to inside knowledge on the part of another, or so called insider-trading, was illegal, and such a suggestion could easily cause outrage to an investor who was simply following his instinct. James understood that he couldn't put such an enquiry to Matt, or, indeed, any of his other clients in a polite way. Nevertheless, putting the phone down, he decided to contact his supervisor to ask if he could buy some *Brite Lite* for his own account. Matt Sinclair was no fool and perhaps he knew what others did not.

As Matt replaced the phone, he knew only two things. First, that his future was now inseparably linked with her recovery, of which he had no doubt in his mind, but if she were to fail, then, he'd fail with her. Though he wouldn't tell him of this, he wondered if Steve would see it as a cleansing of his cosseted lifestyle, or simply a misguided act from a confused person. Second, if he lost everything, and there was a danger he would; then, he'd be just like everyone else, and have to work for a living. In a strange way Matt received considerable comfort from this fact.

A very troubled James Farquar was given the go-ahead to make a purchase. Deciding to place his entire week's wages on the shares, as he reasoned either that Matt was on to something, or he had indeed taken leave of his senses. James's financial predicament could be made no worse by the gamble. James' supervisor had telephoned his own wife, who was a fund manager for an investment company, with twenty billion pounds under management. He asked her if she'd heard of anything on the grapevine about *Brite Lite*. She confirmed that all she'd heard was bad news. She, too, decided that there must be something in someone buying so many shares at this time, and promptly contacted the market to purchase a million shares, which were offered, now, at thirty-three pence.

CHAPTER VI

DISCOVERY

Matt drove home that evening to his house on the edge of the village, just as the sun's increasingly oblique rays began filtering through the trees at the end of another day that had borne witness to its all-pervading power. Leaving the car, as usual, on the drive without bothering to put it in the garage. He knew that the car would come to no harm in the sultry evening. At first he sat in the conservatory with some newspapers, but after a few minutes, threw them aside with unsettled disgust: no longer able to read even the broadsheets, which, as always, had maintained a more considered analysis of the situation. No one, however, had thought of Fabienne or what she must have been through. The tabloids, having destroyed her, were now wondering where she was; no doubt thinking that their stories could do with the oxygen she generated. One newspaper ran the headline, *Just where is Fabienne?* The article continued, '*Having had her version of events confirmed by Professor Harrison's statement about the schizophrenic stalker Barry Miles, Fabienne is nowhere to be seen. Her press office denies knowing where she is. Having cancelled all her current tours and latest album release, just where could the missing star be?*'

Moving into the lounge, he absent-mindedly flicked on the television. What prompted him to do that, he didn't know. He'd become sickened by the endless stream of gory pictures, of conjecture and the media's failure to grasp that there was, whatever he'd done, a real person in there, who'd lost his life, as well as a person who'd done nothing, but who'd had lost everything *except* her life; simply because she'd been the object of focus in the poor man's illness. Switching off the television after a few seconds, restlessly, he walked into the kitchen to make himself a drink. The village was very quiet at this time of night, yet he could swear that he could hear a car engine and the rustling of gravel on his drive as tyres rolled across it.

He gave a weary sigh. Occasionally patients would turn up at his door, carrying various wounded soldiers; usually children with acute ear pain, or sometimes cases of appendicitis that had come on after the surgery had closed. Though he did his best to discourage such moves by his patients, he knew that living in a small village, where everyone knew where he was, and whether he was at home, simply by seeing if his car was on the drive; it was a price he'd have to pay. GPs working in larger conurbations often lived well away from their surgeries to prevent such occurrences, but he was of the view that it was worth it, given the area in which he lived. Greg had asked him about this very question, and Matt had been pleased when he revealed that he was looking at a small cottage on the outskirts of the village, not a mile from the surgery. Matt usually kept his medical bag in his boot, so he made his way to the front door and took his keys from the small table, flicking the porch light on with his free hand simultaneously. He could see through the stained glass as he approached the door that someone was struggling with a heavy weight, no doubt a child prostrate with abdominal pain. Depressing the handle, he pulled open the door. His brain could not have been less prepared for what he was about to see. A sight as unexpected as those he had witnessed recently in the media, but infinitely more welcome. There, illuminated by the porch light, stood Fabienne wrestling with a large holdall.

"Sylvie!"

Disposing of his keys quickly, so that he could take up her burden.

"Matt, forgive me, I ran out of places to hide. The reporters are looking for me everywhere: could I impose on you?" Her pride held things together, barely: the poor girl seemed devastated. The confident, worldly-wise, young woman he'd met just a few weeks ago, had been replaced by a hesitant and tired little girl, who looked frightened and alone. Despite the warm summer's evening she looked cold and shivery; sadness hung about her like a damp, sticky blanket that she no longer had the strength to shrug off.

Matt stared at her, his shock and disbelief centred as much on how her appearance had changed, as on her presence on his doorstep. An uncomfortable pause opened up at this point. His racing mind struggled to process information that even the most lateral thinker couldn't have foreseen.

She continued uncomfortably, "Just for a few days Matt, until some of the attention dies down and I become yesterday's news." This unfortunate choice of words made her look even more vulnerable and isolated. Matt realised that the shock at finding her had made him hesitate more than her discomfort could bear just at that moment. He spoke quickly.

"Sylvie, you can stay for as long as you wish. Come inside; let's sit you down; you're welcome," he offered, as his brain finally engaged coherent thought and action.

Having to rely upon someone who was essentially a stranger signified the dire predicament in which she found herself at that point. She tried to summon that smile, but it seemed like more of a grimace. He wasn't sure if she were on the verge of tears or exhaustion, or both. The silence opened up again as words couldn't carry the emotions through such a charged encounter. Reflex movement from him eventually overcame that awkward pause while she perched, seemingly for life itself, on his doorstep.

"Here: you look as though you could do with a hug." The arms opened and she half collapsed, half fell into their muscular but gentle span. He was wearing a fleecy rugby shirt that almost felt like one of the warm towels that her mother would wrap her in, when she jumped shivering out of the bath, on a cold day. Burying her head against him seemed easier and less painful than either attempting to speak, or hiding the moisture that was welling from the corners of her eyes, swollen and sore. She remained there for vital seconds. Seconds where each could calm and attempt to quantify a nexus of complex emotions arising from the unfamiliar circumstances into which both had been plunged precipitously. Her dominant emotion was sheer relief at her deliverance from abject exhaustion; and his, wide-eyed incredulity that even his inventive mind was unable to span.

"Sylvie, it's really lovely to see you, but I wish it were under better circumstances. I was so sorry to hear the dreadful news. It must have been a bad time for you."

"Matt, I've had better weeks," she managed with what little vigour she had left.

He looked past her on to the drive at the little blue Beetle. "Nice car, not your usual mode of transport, I'd guess," he wondered aloud as he desperately tried to move the conversation on.

"It's all I could hire at short notice, and it's got one of those horrible gear lever thingies. I haven't used one of those for a while. It took me five miles to figure out how to change into second. I left my car in London: it's a little less anonymous than the Beetle, so I reasoned this one would assist with my getaway."

Squeezing her hand: his other arm closed the door, whilst still grabbing the holdall. He guided her through to the kitchen and sat her on one of the chrome and beech bar-stools along the island that divided it. He turned off the main light, after switching on the under-lighting, thereby creating a more diffuse illumination, which would afford respite to her inflamed face and eyes. The last thing she would want, he reasoned, was the glare of bright lights in those tired and sad eyes.

He busied himself in the fridge, after placing the kettle on the boiling plate of the Aga. A few moments later he perched a white wine spritzer in front of her and, a minute after that, a mug of tea, having dismissed quickly the idea of a good slug of Scotch. She drank most of the spritzer quickly, and sipped the tea more slowly. His flurry of activity whilst she sat on the stool and watched, meant she didn't have to feel pressured into talking if she felt unable. The drink both calmed her and slaked her thirst. More importantly the time delay it introduced, allowed her fluttering heart and shaky legs to settle just a little.

Ultimately, what he wanted to demonstrate to her was a routine as if her arrival was the most natural thing in the world, so that she could immediately disengage and wind down if she so desired. Making a big fuss at a time like this was definitely the last thing she needed.

"I couldn't believe it when I saw the news stories unfold one after the other. I could only guess at how bad it must have been for you. What a horrible thing to befall you," he said, desperately hunting for words to ease her discomfort.

"It just happened so quickly, the news and the stories, most of them untrue, arriving at such a relentless pace. I just couldn't cope: the pressure, the calls and the aggressive pursuit for pictures, for comment. They hounded me like some wild animal in a hunt: each reporter hoping to get that one story to out-scoop his rival, or to improve on the scoop that he thought he already had. I just had to get away - all my friends, suddenly, they were either being watched, or I found out that they weren't my friends after all," her voice modulated by sadness.

Her eyes swelled with tears once again, and the effort of trying to restrain them made her feel even more wretched. Matt was unsure as to whether to just let her cry, or to try to cut in quickly with a diversion. He judged, after the briefest hesitation, that unstoppable tears in front of someone she barely knew, would make her feel more unhappy still. He couldn't begin to discuss what he knew she'd be unable to voice, that friends whom she had trusted had either shunned or betrayed her. Simple non-verbal measures were the only way he could proceed: opting for a squeeze of the cold hand that had been slightly warmed by the mug of tea. Hoping that this would begin to acknowledge the embodiment of unremitting pain in which she found herself.

"I'm so sorry, Sylvie." The words seemed redundant, but he could think of no others that would help at this time.

"I hope that I'm not inconveniencing you, Matt. I'm not in the habit of turning up on the doorstep of people that I don't know very well," she ventured.

"In that case then, I hope you know me well enough to believe me when I say that you're not inconveniencing me at all; so you can put that thought right out of your head."

His breezy manner was designed to draw her out a little more, away from those painful thoughts and also to provide reassurance, reasoning that this might be an effective strategy in guiding her from wretchedness to brighter emotions. If established friends had turned their backs on her, it would probably hurt more than the excoriation at the hands of the media. His activity about the kitchen served another very useful purpose; it allowed his mind to focus on one task at a time, thereby limiting awestricken thoughts that otherwise would have swamped him. By clinging to simple, every-day tasks he avoided stalling at the knowledge that one of the most famous personalities in the world, one whose influence spanned continents and was followed by millions, was at this moment sitting on a bar-stool in his kitchen! This, above all, he reflected later, helped him to create the sense that her presence was as natural and low-key as a friend, popping round to watch a match.

"This is a beautiful village even at night. It looks even nicer than the photos," she said, still preferring to look more at the mug of tea than at him, as she struggled to effect small talk.

"You wait, there's a lot more to see and it's quite a peaceful little place, perfect for megastars relaxing between performances," he assured her. Once again the smile tried and failed to break through. She continued to look wretched.

"I'm just pleased you knew where to find me," he admitted, with more emotion than he dared display.

"I only had the file that Lucy had created before we agreed to the meet in Salford Quays, and I remember thinking that I'd never heard of Perrilymm. To be truthful, it was a bit of a long shot, a shot in the dark, so to speak," she replied.

"One that I'm very pleased that you made," he said honestly. He continued, "There are some lovely walks; just head out of the front door or the back and you'll be surprised what you'll find, especially for you city types, it'll be a nice change for you. The village is fairly small, at least we don't have a music or CD store, and no one will expect to find an international megastar in their midst." A mixture of his own nervousness and her desperate plight made him chatter as enthusiastically as he could, in the hope that it would deflect her more painful thoughts. "It'll also allow you a good opportunity to test that theory of yours about not being recognised. If you can get away with it anywhere, our little village must be the place." He sensed that she needed a little more time and kept up the conversation so that she could just listen. "Ordinary pair of jeans and plain T-shirt; let's see how you get on. You can tell people you're a friend or a long-lost cousin of mine, if you like, and hopefully they won't be any the wiser, at least for a little while. We'll have a bet - of a tube of Smarties - how long you can go undetected. What do you say? I say twenty-four hours." He stopped to gauge her response.

On this occasion there was the slightest flicker of a smile. His calm but genial manner, his obvious desire that she should feel at home and comfortable here, made her feel more reassured when such feelings were in short supply. He wanted to demonstrate that her unexpected arrival at this time of night was perfectly natural, and not something that fazed him in the least. She hadn't heard him talk of a wife or family, as he had used 'I' so much in their previous conversations. Not knowing exactly what she'd find, and had simply seized a chance that was borne out of desperation. The fact that this was a quiet village, well away from the spotlight of publicity, wasn't lost on her and that, she told herself, was the main reason for making this trip.

"No, Doctor Sinclair, wrong diagnosis on this occasion. I say much longer than that - just how long do you think you'll be able to put up with me?" she queried.

His playful light stance was drawing her out of herself, and she seemed just a little brighter. This was his plan. His instinct following their meeting in Salford had suggested that her sense of humour was similar to his own, and he would play that instinct for all it was worth. He had to check himself, just a little, as wild thoughts wanted to reveal to her that a permanent stay would be entirely suitable: recognising that such a confession would be the last thing she would expect or need just at this point. "At least as long as it takes me to run out of cornflakes," he offered. "Talking of food, can I get you anything? Bet you're starving."

Food had been the last thing on her mind. Her need to escape had been so urgent as she had driven across country, hoping that no one would recognise her. Instinctively she'd left behind not only all the things that reminded her of who she was, but also the ghastly events that she'd just gone through. Shivering within, she recalled some of the events of the past ten days. "I'm not sure I could..." she began,

"Wrong answer, Miss Fabienne," he corrected playfully.

Busying himself in the fridge, once again. "Perhaps I can tempt you to a personal favourite of mine," he suggested triumphantly, as a couple of minutes later he produced a plate for each of them containing smoked salmon and cream cheese bagels.

"You didn't know I was coming here tonight did you?" she said, with a hint of a smile.

"No, I swear, I always eat this stuff. You thought I was just trying to impress you in Luciano's, didn't you, with my good taste, or ability to creep when in the company of a celebrity?"

"The thought had crossed my mind, or at least something like that," she said, curiosity now starting to replace some of the pain.

It became apparent that though she was doing her utmost to break free from the bonds of pain that beset her; the task in her weakened, exhausted and distracted state was simply too much for mortal flesh to accomplish. It tormented him to gaze on the scene before him, as one might at a beautiful butterfly caught in a killing jar. The media contagion that had surrounded her was that killing jar, and they'd had more thought for making money than for any regard to the suffering that their actions had generated - as if deliberately excluding oxygen from that vessel.

"Didn't know I can cook did you!" he smiled, the solid blue of his eyes surveying her intently. When the plate was set in front of her, she ate enthusiastically, despite the tiredness that was firmly etched into her face. Replacing the kettle on the hotplate, he boiled some more water.

When she had finished the bagels, he delved into the stainless steel refrigerator once again and produced a large slice of lemon meringue pie, which he placed in front of her along with a small carton of cream. He suddenly feigned a serious look on his face. "Just don't tell my patients I eat any of this stuff will you? I'm always lecturing them about cholesterol, that's why I keep a lock on my fridge, just in case I get broken into and one of them gets a look inside."

She tucked in enthusiastically, mouthing between spoonfuls that her lips were sealed. When the kettle had boiled, he made two cups of coffee using a small quantity of the cream to add just a splash to each.

"This is a real home from home, Matt. I'm glad now that I didn't bottle out and stop at that Travelodge twenty miles back," she said, as she managed to meet his gaze more steadily.

"So am I Sylvie - I would have been gutted."

Suddenly, she looked extremely tired; for the exertions of the past minutes had finally consumed what little reserves of energy she had remaining.

"Come on, let me show you to your room," he suggested, as he detected her worsening state of near exhaustion.

Finishing the last drop of coffee from the mug, she followed him back into the large hall with the beautiful teak floor. He found her bag that had been left in the hallway, and motioned that she should follow. The wide staircase climbed away from the hallway, and met with a gallery rail of polished mahogany and the spindles painted white, which ran the width of the first floor. At the foot of the stairs was the substantial front door which had announced her arrival not an hour before. She looked back beyond the hexagonal brass lantern, which provided illumination, toward the front door, to take in more of the stained glass panels, and noticed an even larger one set in the wall above the front door.

"It's a lovely house, you have here, Matt. Forgive me for being nosy, but is there just you in this great house?"

"Yes. Truth be told, I snore so loudly that guests can't bear to stay for more than a few nights! Fortunately, for you, the guest room is over here."

He turned left along the gallery rail as it intersected with the stairs. The first door off the landing, so formed, was the main guest bedroom. He opened it and placed the case on the bed.

"Through there is the en-suite," he indicated the white door with the raised panels to the left of the large window now facing them, and continued, "you'll need some towels. Don't go away, I'll be right back." He doubled back on himself, a little, and went further along the landing to the main bathroom where he extracted two warm towels from the airing cupboard. Instinct dictated the choice of the lightest and softest he could find.

"Matt, this is lovely," she said as he returned. "You're a fortunate man - and that view!" She had moved over to the large window. Despite the darkness she could make out the majestic trees that came right up to his palisade fence, framing the large back garden. They formed part of a more densely-wooded area, and the black ribbon that snaked between, she assumed was a small river or stream. "Even a city girl, like me, can see just why you've fallen in love with this place. Beats a Travelodge any day of the week."

He smiled gently. "I'll leave you to settle in and unpack and so on, perhaps see you downstairs?"

"It's good of you, Matt, to take me in like this."

The solid blue eyes focussed on her less-than-robust form. "Look, I'm flattered that out of all the people you know, you should think of me as someone you could turn to in a crisis." He looked at her seriously again, but just for a moment.

She knew that she couldn't go into too much detail about the crisis in her personal life that had brought her here, but a summary of her predicament was enough to convey something of its gravity.

"That's the problem. As I said, people whom I thought I could rely on, who wanted to know me when things were going well, suddenly seemed to be either unavailable, or dropped me like a hedgehog in a temper, when the storm broke."

Her eyes glazed again as once again she fought with unwelcome tears, now stinging her lids under the bright light of the bedroom.

"Sylvie," he said quietly, "either they never were your friends, or they simply didn't know you. In any event you're best off without them, I'd say." His perceptive analysis of her situation served not only to reassure, but also furnished validation as to what even a relative stranger should be expected to provide to another at a time of unremitting distress. "Listen, we'll get through this, you'll see. It won't always be dark at seven, as my Mum used to say to me, and besides I've been given two tickets for a concert in Manchester later this year, and I know that the girl who's going to perform there can really sing; and she told me that I can leap up on stage."

"At this rate you'll be the one doing the singing!" she managed, with more bravery than she could sustain. Blinking fiercely, she managed to replace the tears with a faint smile once again.

"Okay, two towels, more if you need. I'll leave you and perhaps see you in a while?"

She showered quickly and changed. The hot water that stung her skin just a little seemed, for the moment, to wash many of her cares away: feeling rejuvenated, she towelled herself dry. She found him in the lounge listening to a CD of Vangelis, the Theme from *Bladerunner.*

"Nice music, Matt; always loved this film and the soundtrack," she began as she gazed at the racks of CDs and DVDs. "Hey, I thought you said you had all my CDs and DVDs' I can't find one here. There's Steps, even Bucks Fizz - what's this doing here? I remember my granny telling me that they won the Eurovision song contest before I was born. If I'd known this was your taste in music I'd have thought about checking in at another establishment or I could have brought her!"

"Hey, these aren't mine, they were left here by a former ... friend," he suggested, far from convincingly. Not for the first time he was amazed at the restorative power of a good hot shower. She seemed much brighter and obviously keen to have a joke with him.

"A likely story: they're too well used for that. I thought I could hear you singing along to Bucks Fizz when I was in the shower. Besides, don't change the subject, where are all these CDs of mine you're supposed to have? I bet you haven't got one. Have you even been to a concert?" That playful smile was back in force, and the shower and change of clothes had obviously reawakened it.

Matt shifted uncomfortably. "Well it's a bit of a long story."

"I have time - in fact lots of time," suddenly sensing an interesting tale.

Just then the telephone rang. "Saved by the bell," she mimed as he grabbed the receiver, with more than a little relief crossing his face. "I won't forget to ask you again," she continued as he mouthed that it was Steve calling.

"Steve - nice to hear from you!"

"Look Matt, you know why I'm phoning, Mary just won't take 'no' for an answer," he said, sounding a little worried. "She says if you aren't going to bring someone, then you can come on your own. She's wondering about Wednesday? Matt, my boy, I have to tell you, this is not optional," the disquiet in his voice increased as he continued.

"OK then, Steve, thanks to Mary for asking me, and to you also." Matt sensed that he needed time to think; Steve was obviously under pressure. "I left my diary in the car. Can I nip out and get it and phone you back in two minutes?"

"I'll get killed if you put this off again," Steve assured him.

Matt reasoned that there was more substance in Steve's comment than he would have liked. "Minutes. I promise," he confirmed. Replacing the receiver, he turned to Fabienne, who was still gazing at the rows of CDs.

"Not 'Johnny Hates Jazz', who are they?"

"Now, that *is* mine - and they're very good," he confirmed, doing his best to look serious and placing emphasis on the adverb, before continuing, nodding as if trying to lend authenticity to his comments, "*You* could learn a thing or two from them."

"Matt, all I can say is that you're obviously not getting out enough. I'm amazed that you turn up to my concerts, if this is your *real* taste in music. If my security team knew you were singing along to this lot, they'd politely guide you to the pensioners' day-centre down the road. I'm certain you'd find a few like-minded fans of err.. music in there; you could have a whale of a time with them. I take it you have been to at least one of my concerts?"

She picked up a handful of CDs from the rack as if she was about to throw them.

"I'm against all sorts of violence and besides, hold on a minute before you do, so that I can at least return his call," he replied cheerfully.

"Okay then, a stay of execution for the doctor," she agreed.

"Steve wants to know if we'll go round to dinner this Wednesday," he asked in as neutral tone as he could manage.

"*We*, what's 'we' got to do with your invitation?"

"Well, me, but he says ask someone, and I'm inviting you," he suggested lightly.

She suddenly became serious again, almost as if her confidence had deflated in that instant. "Look Matt, forget about me. I'll house-sit and look after your plants or polish your Bucks Fizz CDs or something. Dodgy area this, you know, by the looks of it someone could break in a steal your entire Bucks Fizz collection, not to mention the David Cassidy I've found over there."

"Now, a true star, if ever I heard one, not like this rubbish you get today," he said as he managed to stifle the smile forming within.

"Is Steve an expert then, at retrieving CD cases from difficult places? Or perhaps, better let me have those tickets back, please, so I can shove them up your left nostril - or worse?"

"Stop changing the subject, you. Now, how about Steve? Will you come with me?"

Matt could see that she was agonising on the cusp of indecision, no doubt exacerbated by her tiredness.

"I don't want to intrude on your social life, Matt and I don't think I'm very good company at the moment. Why don't you go on your own, there must be someone you had planned to take?" she asked reasonably.

"No, Sylvie, not really, so it seems as if I'm totally stuck unless you'd care to help me out here? You might just enjoy yourself, and often they play very good music like Abba and Karen Carpenter," he continued, as if stopping now would cause the decision to go against him. "It'll do you good, besides Mary is a great cook and I'll make a real pig of myself if I go on my own: now how about it?"

She opened her mouth as if to speak, but no words were produced.

"Fine, it's settled. I'll take that as a yes," he concluded happily.

Fabienne recognised that further argument was futile, and also that in her drained state, decision-making was not at its sharpest. For a while, at least, it might be better to simply rely on his. She nodded, a weak smile surfacing again fleetingly and with some difficulty. Matt picked up the phone elatedly and dialled Steve's number.

"You'd better be giving me good news here, my boy. Mary is a lovely girl, and I love her dearly, but she's not keen on hearing 'no' -ouch!" Mary must have been next to him.

"Hi Steve, Wednesday did you say? Yes, that'll be fine; many thanks for asking, we'd be pleased to come"

"*We*, like the sound of that Matt. Does it mean what I think it means?" Steve asked excitedly.

"Oh, just a friend: no one you'll know," Matt replied with deliberate disinterest.

"Is she pretty?"

"Is she pretty?" He paused slightly as if having to consider this question carefully. "Well - I *suppose* she is, in a kind of *ordinary* way," he repeated the question as if having to deliberate on it.

Fabienne's eyes narrowed as she determined what punishment would be suitable. She took out a Bucks Fizz CD and motioned as if she were about to snap it in half.

"Is she intelligent and witty?" Steve continued.

"Yes, in abundance."

"And is she just an ordinary girl?" Steve asked, expectantly.

"Just an ordinary girl? Yes I suppose she is," Matt replied, as if realising something for the first time.

"Just the person to take your mind off that other woman, then," Steve concluded. "Great, we'll see you and Miss-ordinary-but-gorgeous then. How about eight for eight-thirty?"

"Oh, just one thing Steve, she loves Bucks Fizz, Karen Carpenter and Abba - I don't know if you have any of their CDs?"

"OK Matt we'll see what we can do. A bit quirky, I can tell, this new girl of yours."

"Yes, that's right Steve, a bit quirky all right. I haven't heard those, myself, in a long time."

"Many thanks for getting back to me, Matt, you don't know how much easier you've made my life. Bye for now," Steve said, the relief evident in his voice.

"Tell me you had your finger on the little button whilst you were talking to Steve, or that you were just yanking my chain?" Fabienne queried with feigned menace on her face. "Are there many murders in these parts? Many GPs strangled by disgruntled house guests who turn up on their doorsteps in darkness, then?"

"Oh yes, it happens all the time in these parts - we lost two last week."

"Yes I can see that, driven to it were they?" she suggested knowingly.

He laughed by way of reply.

"So, I take it, Steve doesn't know who I am?"

"No, he's no idea, and won't hear it from me," Matt confirmed.

"Well, at least you telling him I want to hear Abba and Karen Carpenter can only add to my cover," she suggested archly.

"I wonder if they'll recognise just who has been invited to dinner. Surely they couldn't foresee such a thing in a million years," he acknowledged.

"I must confess, there's a big difference between just appearing in an old pair of jeans and a plain T-shirt, and facing someone over the dinner table all evening," she pondered.

"Don't worry, Sylvie, I'll take a bottle of my strongest red, and hide Steve's glasses. If they do recognise you, we'll just have to admit everything," he advised.

Matt wondered for a moment how Steve would take this. An unusual dilemma opened for him at this point. Should he calmly state that Fabienne would be attending with him, and risk the likelihood of Steve concluding that Matt was having a psychotic breakdown, or say nothing, and let events simply take their course? Things had moved so quickly, that Matt hadn't yet had a chance to reflect on whether her presence here with him was real, or part of an elaborate dream, with his alarm clock about to sound any second. He desperately hoped that it wasn't psychosis that had stepped in, and he'd really been talking to himself for the last two hours! In any event, she'd be the last person that Steve would expect to find in his house, so perhaps her 'bluff their perceptions' theory might just work. At least it was about to be severely tested.

"Okay, well, we'll see what happens," she mused as he arrived at the same conclusion.

She sat back in the large chair. All at once, though she had shown a flicker of her former self when they were joking about the CDs; exhaustion descended over her like a dark cloud blotting out the sun. One thing that he could see, however, between the all-encompassing tiredness, was that she looked more relaxed than he'd seen her, at least since she'd arrived, and, he guessed, probably for the first time in over a week. His very different surroundings and lifestyle could be more than a refuge to her; they could also be the chance for a complete rest while she regained her strength and thought about her future. It came as no surprise, therefore, when she rose and said,

"Matt, would you think me rude if I turn in?"

"No, of course not, Sylvie."

He, too, rose to his feet, his face crossed by concern; his eyes delved to their deepest blue whilst surveying this incredibly strong person, who was just about exhausted.

"Can I offer you anything? Gin and tonic, brandy, cocoa, sleeping tablet - not one after the other, of course?"

"No, I'm fine, honest. Thanks again for doing this for me."

He gazed after her as she left the room and ascended the stairs.

Matt's sleepless nights and days on call had encouraged him to keep later hours than his body clock would have thought wise. It was about an hour later that he went up the staircase quietly, so as not to wake his guest. His ears were well attuned to every sound the house made, in all seasons. The quiet sobbing coming from the direction of her room became obvious by the time he'd reached half way. At the top he turned right very quietly towards his own room, thinking that his concern would only cause her embarrassment. She'd obviously been close to tears several times that evening. Although the strong person within had been severely tested by recent events, he knew she would probably prefer to keep her current turmoil to herself rather than have someone who could almost be considered a stranger, appearing at her bedroom door.

On reflection, however, he considered that embarrassment was a much lesser emotion on the pain scale, than the ones she was presently feeling. Turning quickly, he tapped on her door, waited for a few seconds, and then slowly pushed it open. She remained fully dressed on top of the bed, the room illuminated only by the softer bedside light: her face, now very puffy, with the steady flow of tears.

"Oh Matt," she sat up and the flow became a flood. Perhaps more than ever, he wanted to hold her at this point, and to continue to do so until the stars had burned through to the blackness of space. Yet, with his emotions in turmoil, he needed to be certain that he could hold his own thoughts in check, and not allow them to get out of hand. Doing nothing, however, was impossible, as her suffering was clearly intense. He sat next to her, touching the same shoulder he had when posing for the photo in Luciano's. How different the circumstances then, and how different the person now! Leaning forwards, she tried desperately to stem the flow of tears cascading into her hands. He squeezed her shoulder harder by way of support.

"Matt, I keep seeing him there, all strung up in my bedroom. It was terrible, switching the light on and finding him in that way."

In their thirst to dish dirt, none of the tabloids had mentioned who had made the grim discovery. No doubt they were in receipt of this information, yet sympathy for the poor girl's horror at coming home to that hideous scene, wasn't the image they'd tried to convey. When pitching their stories, nobody would've wanted to have her seen as the victim, since it might have sold fewer papers than if they painted her as a perverted lover whose deviant exploits had gone wrong. They'd deliberately leaked the gory details; the rope around the neck; a bag over his head; and the scene being her bedroom. But all had been strangely silent when it came to analysing how it must have felt to walk in one evening, on your own, to that sight: and what effect it would have on anyone who'd done so.

Matt realised immediately the full significance of the sketchy details she was able to voice. Near-asphyxiation, where the brain was starved of blood and oxygen was known to produce heightened sexual stimulation. The difficulty with using these methods was that of retaining control for long enough, to loosen the ligature around the neck before the brain became incapable of instructing the body to do so. There was a very fine line between maximising the stimulation, and death. Matt had come across cases where the person who practised such methods had inadvertently strayed across that boundary, and continued irretrievably down a terminal slope, as Barry Miles had evidently done. Matt shivered as he recalled the details of cases he'd read about as a medical student. The study of which was bad enough; confronting one face-to-face must be truly terrifying. He could only guess at the horrors she'd seen, and understood the need for her escape. Her bitterness at the tabloids' handling of the details of the case had potentiated the trauma she suffered: quite apart from the disgraceful response to the situation by her so-called, 'friends'.

She continued. "How could they print that about me? I've stopped, I've allowed photos, I've chatted, given the interviews - and then they turn on me like that." She shook her head by way of denouncing a cruel and corrupt enterprise that fed off misery.

"I'm sure you know better than I do that the press can't resist the lure of what they consider to be a ground-breaking story. They can also be very good at ignoring such things as truth, if it would tend to get in the way of exciting straplines and sensationalist copy. I suppose, though this won't be any comfort for you, that it isn't a personal thing – they'd tear the flesh from anyone's bones if they though it would make good copy. *Because* you're such a good, caring person, who maintains discretion in her life; that flesh was made much sweeter. Now, if you'd been an absolute bastard they wouldn't have made so much of it, because most people would be half expecting it anyway! That's the irony of all this."

The crying paused. Perhaps more reflexly than deliberately, Matt had entered his caring professional mode. Though he had no responsibility for her whatsoever as a patient, this means of handling himself was expedient, in that it stopped him from becoming too emotional. Ever-present were those thoughts that wanted to cut through lesser considerations, and simply state that staying with him would be the best solution for them both. The surging maelstrom would have mastered him at this point, had the stimulus of necessity not intervened to assert that this approach would help neither. Tears and sentimentality were the last things she needed, he judged: patience, a listening ear and a cool head, were the skills his medicine would bring, to augment the care and common decency that he hoped he would have shown anyone, this far down the emotional barometer. Pushing the tissues gently in her direction, he stood up. "Come with me, I want to show you something."

"Is that what you say to all your patients?" she posed nasally.

"Well, I try not to, certainly to the pretty ones, but in your case, I'll just have to make an exception."

The smile flicked temporarily as she grasped what he said: at least the crying had stopped.

Grabbing her hand firmly, he led her downstairs, through the house and exited via the back door of the kitchen. Though it was nearly midnight, the maturing summer had continued its influence through the quiet of night, with sufficient ambient light to guide anyone who was used to the various paths and trails. Continuing out of his back garden and through a gate in the fence, along the river, now black against the available light. The ducks had long since returned to their nests; a pair of magnificent swans paddled effortlessly past on the river of black glass. He led the way over the little footbridge spanning the river, on the far side of which stretched the woods, now enlivened with the sounds of owls, and animals whose eyes could cope perfectly with lower levels of illumination than the human eye could perceive, and for whom night was their day. Stopping on the bridge enabled them to look back towards the house; beyond, which lay the quiet village: a couple of streetlights making their best efforts against the all-enveloping darkness. He remained silent for perhaps a minute. She rested her arms on the rail as she stood beside him. "What can you feel?" he asked thoughtfully.

She could feel the smooth timber rail of the bridge, made so by thousands of such hands as hers leaning on the frame, as people rested at this very spot. She could hear the owl in the nearby woodland, and, of course, the gentle lapping of the water as it accommodated the bridge supports within its sweep. A gentle warm breeze impinged against her cheeks, made sore by the flood of tears and the rub of tissue in a futile attempt earlier to stem their flow. Her eyes had started to register some definition in the darkness. Most of all, she could just feel the night: its calm permanence seemed to instil its own presence within her. Having always lived in the city, she'd always been surrounded by the light and noise, such that no matter how dark and still, the night could never defeat their man-made intrusion. Yet, for the first time, here, she could drink in its calming influence. What light there was, only just able to convey to her the smile that flickered on his face, as he saw the realisation dawn within. In that moment, she understood why he lived here, and what made it so special.

Speaking slowly, he didn't look in her direction. "I can't know or feel the suffering that you've gone through. I'll never be able to say exactly how you felt as you walked into your bedroom, or when you read some of that drivel they wrote about you. I can only guess how much that's hurt you. I believe, simply, that you'll need time, and you're forgiven for wondering if you're ever going to feel stronger. I'm not trying to tell you that I understand exactly how you feel, how can I? My world hasn't been shattered like yours. I do know that that there is a peace and a depth here, that may well nourish and support you, if you can tap into it." Only then did he glance in her direction. "Come on," he offered as he walked over the bridge, grabbing her hand quickly. His studied, calm words, which seemed to resonate with the tranquillity of the night, conveyed infinitely more than the artifices of rhetoric ever could. She found herself staring, despite the dark, in his direction, toward the voice with its rich, mellow timbre.

Continuing along the far side of the river at the edge of the wood, they walked into the village and on past the small pub. Bill Scrivens, one of Matt's patients, was ambling along chaotically, not making much progress toward home. To say that he looked a little inebriated would have been a polite, but understated, description of his state. Matt stopped. "Hi there Bill. You OK?" he asked solicitously.

"I'm fine, Doctor, thank you for asking. Absolutely fine, never better. Good evening Miss," doffing an imaginary cap, that he must have left his house wearing, and probably had left in the pub.

"Are you off home Bill?" Matt queried. Bill seemed just for that instant to be unsure of exactly where he was headed, and seemed grateful for Matt's reasonable suggestion. "Come on, we're going your way, we'll see you home," Matt offered comfortingly.

"There we are Miss, what Doctor would come out and care about a man's welfare at this time of night, eh, now tell me that?" Bill queried. "You'll be quite safe with him, my dear, I can tell you," he said with as much clarity as eight pints of best would allow.

"Oh, I'm sure I am, Bill," she confirmed lightly, mirroring his good humour. They came to a rundown, mid-terrace, stone-built cottage. "Ah yes, seems familiar." Bill suggested, now struggling to remain upright.

"This is you Bill: have you got your key or are we going to have to disturb your wife?" Matt asked.

"No, don't you be doing that, I have it here," Bill replied as he retrieved a key from a pocket, in the nick of time to save his marriage. "I'll be wishing you young two a very good evening and thanks once again for seeing me to me front door, Doctor."

Matt helped him with the tricky job of sliding the key into the lock and slowly turned it the right way so that he would gain access. A steady hand guided him carefully but quietly over the threshold. Matt suspected that his wife, Eileen, would find him asleep in the hallway the next morning.

Matt and Fabienne walked back along the road, eventually arriving back at Matt's house. "So what do you think of the village then?" he asked expectantly.

"Absolutely lovely. I can't get over the quiet, the calm and the deep night. London is such a noisy place by comparison. I loved my walk, Matt, and I hope we can go again. I feel much better: thank you for taking me." Her frantic and complex life had shown itself to be a cruel illusion that was incapable of supporting her at the first time of asking. Here, a much simpler existence was evident, and one that seemed to engender a calming resonance deep within that would heal and nourish her.

She returned to her room, and once again gazed through the window at the garden and woods still very dark; moreover, she could imagine the area better and retrace the route they'd taken. She made a mental note to compare this image at the dead of night with that on display during the day. In the days ahead Fabienne would look back with relief at the events of that night. Recognising that, somehow, she'd reached the lowest point after a catastrophic sequence of events: and having defined it in this way, the next step could only be upward. Not being sure whether instinct or desperation had brought her to his door; in the darkest of dark nights and the loneliest of nightmares, she faced the truth that there was no one else to whom she could have turned.

His attempts to help her limit the depth of that low point were deeply moving, and she knew that he was genuine in his offer that she could stay for as long as she needed. This was especially useful at the moment, because she really couldn't see how she could get back to a life with which she had been perfectly happy until switching on her bedroom lights that fateful evening; a life that was now at the mercy of malignant ruin.

She changed and slipped into bed before turning off the bedside light. Leaving the curtains open deliberately, so she could at least see some of the night and the calm that seemed to retain a steady influence as it permeated through her, and her new surroundings. There wasn't much that she could be sure of at that time, but one thing was certain; she was glad she was there: whether simply because it was the last place people would think to look, or a place where she could recover - or something more than she could quantify. Convinced that sleep would be elusive, she decided that she could stare through the open window until the dawn arrived. But the still country air had exerted its influence upon her which, combined with the gentle exercise, conspired to bring sleep on within minutes.

Matt had hesitated very quietly outside her door, before finding his own bed. All was quiet, meaning that she was either asleep or hopefully, at the very least, not still sobbing. Stealing away to his room, with a million thoughts of his own. The overriding one that he would do his best to help her in whatever way he could.

CHAPTER VII

NEW GIRL IN TOWN

He rose at his usual early hour. Though morning showers were routinely an energetic and noisy business, when on his own, he silenced his radio alarm before it went off and hummed gently to himself rather than perform his usual, noisier Caruso-impression, vocal work-out. Placing his feet on the bed and his hands on the floor, so that he could do his thirty press-ups, as he did every morning. This morning, however, he lost count as his mind wandered; therefore, he continued until his arms ached more than usual, thereby hoping that he had done at least that many. Dressing, leaving his hair to dry in the warm but overcast morning, he went quietly downstairs and swirled round the end of the balustrade to head for the kitchen.

He hadn't expected to find Fabienne up at this hour, sipping a cup of coffee, an empty bowl in front of her.

"Morning, Matt. I hope you don't mind, I helped myself," she began, a little uncertainly, still not used to being in an unfamiliar house.

"As I told you, my dear, my humble home is yours," doing his best to assume the tone of a middle eastern business man about to secure a massive arms deal, as he rubbed his hands together in an obsequious fashion. "Nice to see you," he nodded in her direction appreciatively, "looking more like your sunny self." He noted that she still couldn't quite meet his gaze, but she did look much better.

"Yes, the best night's sleep I've had in weeks."

"They say it's to do with this fine country air, but I'm, not too sure of that. Anyway, I'm pleased you slept; it'll do you good. So, what are you going to do today?"

"I thought I'd head for the village. Tell me are there any shops hereabouts? The village seemed very quiet last night."

"Yes, you noticed; bit of a problem there, I'm afraid. If you drive out of the gate, turn left and keep going, you'll see the row of cottages where we left Bill Scrivens last night. Keep left there by the church, and continue for about five miles. Eventually you'll come across Merton. There you'll find a lot more than the basics we have here in Perri."

Making himself a piece of toast, he put the kettle back on the hot plate for a quick cup of coffee, before popping back upstairs to brush his teeth, find his jacket and mobile phone.

"Can I get you anything before I go, Sylvie?"

"No, Matt you've been super, you know I can't, thank...."

"Stop it right there, my dear, or you'll have me embarrassing this clean shirt I'm wearing," he interjected lightly, so as to stop her lingering in more painful areas. Smiling and nodding, she conceded that there was no need to revisit ground that was considered settled. "Here's my mobile number, if you need me, and this is the surgery number," - he jotted down on a little pad. "Usually it's surgery, visits, lunch, surgery, then home." Looking at her carefully, he tried to anticipate things she might need. "Oh, and let me give you a key. There's no need to lock the door if you leave, but you may feel safer, I understand." He reasoned that unexpected exposure to unspeakable scenes within her own bedroom would make her feel insecure for months to come.

"Okay," she said quickly, determined not to dwell among areas of thought that would only drag her back to the turmoil of previous nights.

"Have you a mobile, Sylvie, I mean, one with you?"

"No, Matt, I left it behind deliberately. Each time it rang, there'd be a desperate plea from yet another reporter suggesting that I'd feel better if I confessed, and got it all off my chest," she admitted with a further flicker of sadness crossing her face.

"In Merton you'll find a mobile store. I know the owner, Stan Fellowes, very well. He'll sort you out with 'pay as you go'. No one need know, unless, of course, you want them to, where you are and who you are. Stan's a lovely chap and will help you; just tell him you're a friend of mine. Sylvie can I ask..?" Suddenly he looked awkward as his words paused mid sentence.

"Well, go on," she implored, the suspense rising. She smiled and looked quickly at the shelf over the radiator in the kitchen, which held the photo of the two of them taken in happier days in Luciano's.

"Spit it out," she suggested.

"Are you all right for cash? You know, credit cards and cash machines can be traced?" he ventured at last.

His nervousness broke through between the pauses in his words. Asking anyone about the state of their finances was never easy; let alone, one of the richest women in the country. He realised, however, that the tabloids had put much more sensitive areas of her personal life under sustained scrutiny. A simple question as to whether she needed some cash or otherwise, would pale into insignificance, beside their assertion that she had virtually murdered her lover in her own bedroom. Her imperturbable nature about such lesser things as finances was very much to the fore: acknowledging his momentary discomfiture with a grateful smile.

"Oh, thanks for that Matt," she replied easily. "Don't worry, I have access to funds, shall we say, that no one knows about, save me - and the Inland Revenue, of course."

"So the tax man won't be doing you for tax evasion then?" he smiled.

She offered him a reproachful look." No, not today thank you. I'm in quite enough trouble as it is."

"Okay I'll go then, in that case." He paused again, trying to make sure that he'd remembered everything. "See you later; help yourself to whatever you want and use the house as your own. Just to say that the magazines in the third drawer down in my study aren't mine: I'm keeping them for a friend!"

"They all say that," she laughed." I thought you were going to say that you found them in the bus shelter."

"No; I think that's where he got them from."

Mrs Simpson was hard at her usual activity, gossiping, with Janice in wide-eyed attendance; Matt's car swooped at higher speed than usual into his parking spot; the front of the car dipping as he applied the brakes to ensure a shorter stop than was normally required.

"See, here he comes, now," said Mrs Simpson hurriedly and added, "whoever she is, she's doing him a power of good; he's running round like a two year old. Must be this floozy in his life. Can only be a woman that can have that effect on a man, any man; they're all the same when it comes to, to such matters." Mrs Simpson suddenly remembered that Janice was quite naive, and altered, at the last minute, the words she had intended.

"I wonder who she is, then?" Janice asked again, hoping that by posing the question at this point it would slow the self-congratulatory tones that were coming unremittingly from her boss.

"You mark my words, Janice, I'll find out. Small village such as this, how hard can it be for a perceptive person like me?" Mrs Simpson folded her arms across her chest, the movement, unfortunately, serving only to make her short, rotund form even more so.

"She does look *so* familiar; I can't help but think I've seen her somewhere before," suggested Janice, as though forgetting something that was on the tip of her tongue.

"Perhaps, Janice, but don't worry. I'll be telling *you* who she is, soon enough," affirmed Mrs Simpson firmly but dismissively.

"Where do you think he found her?" asked Janice.

"I don't know," she admitted quietly, such unaccustomed words. "I hear he was a *right one* in his younger days, different girl every week." As was her wont, Mrs Simpson always counterbalanced with other knowledge, areas in which she might be found lacking.

"Seems to have calmed down a bit, then?" Janice enquired and continued, "did you say he hadn't had a girl in ages?"

"Well, I know," Mrs Simpson tapped the side of her nose in her ultimate show of inside information. "I reckon that's why he's been a bit dreamy up till recently, maybe missing-." She replaced the end of the sentence with a knowing nod, leaving the interpretation to Janice's own imagination rather than be too explicit. Janice was, as always, held rigid by Mrs Simpson's knowledge: perfectly happy to accept her version as being the unabridged truth. Suddenly, Mrs Simpson stood up as Matt came in. "He won't be pleased. Gertrude Willy is in today, she'll be in for at least half an hour and she's his first patient. Hope he's not meeting *her* for lunch today." She chuckled wickedly.

"Is Gertrude the one who brings in those lovely cakes?" Janice queried.

Mrs Simpson had views on this too. "Guilt, Janice, guilt, I tell you."

"What?" Janice said, suddenly finding herself lost.

"*Guilt*," the manager confirmed, "I know what goes on. I tell you, after what she did to that poor husband of hers, found him at the foot of the stairs, they did." She tapped her nose again as if tipping Janice the wink on another exclusive. "I could tell you a thing or two, my girl," typically, the outline of a story more intriguing than facts that she could confirm.

"Morning Monica, Janice," Matt said breezily.

Janice hurried off to make Doctor Sinclair a cup of tea.

"Monica, could you pop into my surgery for a minute?" he asked.

"Yes of course Doctor, I'll be right there," sensing that she needed a moment to compose herself, she grabbed her notebook. "Here we go, I wonder what we're doing today?" she mouthed to Janice leaving her in the little kitchen as she ran after him, her short legs at twice the rate of his. She sat on the patient's chair.

"Lovely girl, Doctor," she said expectantly, nodding at the photo on the shelf behind him.

Matt didn't take the bait; his thoughts were on other matters.

"Oh, Just a friend, Mrs S. Any news?"

"Ah yes, the builder is coming to see you. I wondered about Wednesday, one pm, before your half day?"

"That's great, I've been hoping he'd be able to come fairly soon, so we can get on with things. There's a lot on the boil just at present, but it should be worthwhile," he ventured.

"Yes indeed Doctor," she found herself nodding enthusiastically.

"Anything else Monica?"

"No, everything else is fine, Doctor."

"Very well then, I saw Mrs Willy in the waiting room, suppose I'd better make a start."

Mrs Simpson got up to go, holding her notebook a little more firmly than usual, reflecting on her failure to further her quest as to who the person in the photo might be. No matter, sooner or later she would know. Like most men, he was an open book; she would read that chapter in good time.

The surgery finished a little late because of Mrs Willy taking up her usual leisurely consultation. Matt made no attempt to rush her. She was a gentle old lady and had never really got over losing her husband. Matt knew that it was a kind, but sudden death, for he was thought to have suffered a catastrophic stroke as he went up the stairs. The GP had been unable to issue a death certificate because Mr Willy had been fit and well when last seen. Matt, therefore, had no idea as to the cause of death. Any death under unusual circumstances had to be reported to the coroner, who would then organise a post mortem. This was doubly distressing for the relatives, but made sure that there was no foul play, or negligence on the part of doctors. For those left behind, such deaths were always harder to handle, and he liked to allow Mrs Willy time to talk things through with him, if she so wished. Today she hadn't really dwelled on the death for too long, so perhaps she was seeing a little light at the end of the tunnel.

Matt only had one visit, so he took his time signing prescriptions. He deliberately asked Janice to bring them, so that he would have to remain and do them, thereby countering his urge to dash home and see if Fabienne was still there. Janice had entered most of them on the computer, and the patients were getting used to using the pre-printed order slips rather than the little blue cardboard folders they'd used previously. Matt looked at her as she brought the box of prescriptions in with her and placed them carefully on his desk. Despite being young and a bit dizzy, she was showing promise, and always tried her best. Though, perhaps, not the most agile intellect he had met, she was willing and hard-working, and this would more than make up for any deficiency in her brain power. Matt was of the view that he would rather have a hard-working person of modest intellect, than a brilliant one who was lazy or who couldn't see the point of doing something, and therefore didn't bother.

Matt managed to get home for a sandwich and also caught the lunchtime news. Fabienne had left him a note to say that she would see him later and she would cook an evening meal.

Smiling to himself, as he thought, 'What a girl! Not only does she look like that, but she can cook too.' He knew so little of her private life that he just couldn't picture her remaining at home and cooking for herself or friends. The image he had of her was visiting top London restaurants, where ordinary folk were unlikely to be seen: either because of the cost of the cover, or the difficulty in getting a reservation.

Driving back to the surgery, he suddenly realised as he glanced at the passenger seat, that he'd forgotten to post the mail. Stopping off at the village post office, he was just about to turn back to his car, after slotting the post into the box, when a frenzied call caught him. He knew the voice without turning. Stella came running out of the hair salon she owned. He groaned to himself just before he turned. She often caught him in this way, as her shop was next door to the post office. Usually parking down the road, so that she wouldn't see his car, but today he'd been in a hurry and hadn't observed the usual countermeasures. He was amazed that the nature of her work allowed her such latitude to be able to run out with the frequency she did. No doubt some poor pensioner was left cooking under the drier for a few minutes longer than was absolutely necessary. Matt preferred to think of this as his reason for avoiding her, though in quieter moments he would probably have to accept that the real reason was that she knew just too much about everyone, including him.

'Too late,' he thought as her high-pitched voice sailed across the pavement. The large, winged glasses in sparkling diamante, that reminded him of an old Cadillac, could be seen long before the rest of her came into focus. He was always transfixed by their appearance, and would have to make a conscious attempt to look at her, and not at such impactful frames.

"Now then, Doctor Sinclair, you're a dark horse. Who have you got in your house then?" she posed knowingly.

'So much for Fabienne's theory,' he thought. 'Rumbled straight away, no doubt with a quick drive into the village that morning.' It was perhaps naive of her to expect that someone so famous wouldn't be recognised very quickly. Possibly, he'd overestimated her people-management skills, which she seemed to have in abundance at their first meeting. Maybe he'd been so captivated by her, that he hadn't seen that she was just an ordinary person with human weaknesses and failings. In a way, this was the real damage done to her by the press. At the height of her success, fame was just one of the many trappings that had accompanied it. She was the star for whom everything had gone perfectly: the girl who could do no wrong. Suddenly, it was almost as if the Fates had decided that her life had blazed just a little too brightly, and the time had come to cut the enchanted thread that gave life to her career. Perhaps the papers had done no more than point out this very possibility, and her days in the sun, with infallibility as her constant companion; now ended. He was about to voice her name by way of confirmation that he knew the game to be over. Miraculously, in the last sliver of time, as his reply was formed, caution supervened.

"What do you mean?"

"What do you mean, what do I mean?" she asked, looking askance at his unexpected reply. "That gorgeous girl, of course - Sylvia!" she continued, her excitement brimming.

"Sylvia?" he replied flatly.

Stella always sported a perma-tan, which unfortunately was not because of plenty of foreign holidays, summer and winter, but due to the presence of tanning tubes in her salon. She was evidently the greatest user, and no amount of urging from Matt had managed to dent her enthusiasm for their use. Though she was only forty-five, her skin wasn't coping very well, with the regular doses of irradiation. Without doubt, Matt reasoned, it was now starting to addle her brain just a little; either that, or he hadn't had as much sleep last night as he thought, and had missed something very important that morning.

"Yes, now don't you try to keep her a secret from me," she went on, before confirming, "I know all about her."

As luck would have it, Matt was so confused at this point, that he simply kept quiet and let her do all the talking, which she did with relish.

"Your visitor, your girlfriend, you kept that very quiet," she said struggling a little against his blank expression.

Matt was no nearer to any form of answer and decided to say nothing. The first rule of being in a hole, as they said, was to stop digging, and he judged this maxim must apply now. He decided not to pass on this secret to Stella who was still in full flow: doubting that he could have got a word in edgewise anyway. Adding further details, she continued, so that he would know that his secret was well and truly out in the open, and also to gain a little more response from him, rather than the bemused look that was fixed on his face. "Been in for a haircut, hasn't she?" she nodded, by way of ultimate verification of the words she uttered. "Told me everything, she did, so it's no use trying to deny it: you can stop that innocent look with me. Real pretty one she is." Her face contorted briefly. "What beautiful hair! Wanted it all off, well I don't mean that, but she wanted it short didn't she. Say, you didn't talk her into that did you?" suddenly looking accusingly at him.

"Who? No, not me," he decided, would be a perfectly safe reply at this point.

"I can't think why then, what gorgeous hair," she continued, looking a little mournful at the loss of such beautiful tresses. "Anyway, she told me - it's no good smiling".

Matt had finally understood something of the events of that morning and was piecing them together quickly.

"I know," Stella nodded again. She had firm control of the conversation, and Matt realised that all he need do was to continue to nod in reply. "Here for a week or two. She's a drug rep, met you at a meeting was it?" Only a slight pause came at this moment of lack of certainty in her recollections. "Been going out for about a month. Lives in Evesham. Well, I want you to know, you're a lucky man. Not that she ain't a lucky girl 'n'all, but what a pretty one she is. Said to my Patsy," Patsy was Stella's daughter who helped in the shop in her summer holidays, "she's lovely lookin'. Could be a model without a doubt, that one."

Matt smiled again as he thought that perhaps it would be her uncommon looks that would give the pop star away.

"Thought you might try to keep it a secret eh, that she's staying with you. I've been asking Patsy to keep lookout for you all morning; thought you might pop in next door with the post."

Matt continued to smile and acknowledged the pause that was now long enough for him to form some sort of coherent reply. He chose flattery as being the most suitable vehicle.

"Stella, I should have known better than to try to pull the wool over your eyes. I might have known, out of everyone in the village, you'd find my little secret out."

New Girl In Town 161

Obviously Stella was thoroughly delighted with her exposé of the person she'd discovered was his girlfriend, and accepting this version of events, as to who she was and why she was here; might stop her for thirsting for more information. He'd been surprised, and pleasantly so, at Fabienne's cover story as his 'girlfriend', but perhaps, he reflected, she might just be right. Maybe her theories would hold, and she would pull it off for a week or two, after all. Perhaps the best way of hiding something was to put it right in front of people's noses, with a label, albeit a false one, that people could identify quickly. In any event, Fabienne would be delighted when he told her later. To think; he'd almost blown her cover with his very first word.

"Thanks for that, Stella, must go, surgery and so on," he said, as a mixture of delight and relief crossed his face.

Stella hopped back into her salon, glowing with her discovery, then with more hurry: no doubt suddenly remembering the customer who was still perched under one of her driers. They both knew that news would be right around the small village by close of business that night, at the latest. Matt could only hope that it wouldn't backfire, and couldn't decide whether Fabienne's plan to pass herself off as his girlfriend was brilliant, because it settled people's questions about her quickly; or foolish, because it drew more attention to her. In any event, he conceded, with looks like hers, heads would be bound to turn wherever she went.

The afternoon surgery was very quiet. Matt took the opportunity to get through a lot of paperwork and also to pull out the architect's drawings: being very pleased with the plans. Extensions of small premises in villages had to blend in rather than stick out, and Matt was delighted with the architect's grasp of that central precept. He decided to leave a little early. Mrs Simpson was on a half day and Janice was at college on her day-release at the nearby technical college learning computer skills. Mrs Jenkin was covering the office, and he told her how to contact him if there were any problems. He drove the mile to his home.

Fabienne was struggling with some bags from the Beetle. Light rain had begun to fall and she was desperately looking for the house key that Matt had given her. He popped onto the porch, made sure that the door was open and went back to help her.

"Here, you stand on the porch and I'll grab the bags," he offered reasonably.

Looking at the shopping bags that had been placed in the back of the Beetle, he saw that she'd evidently found the Tesco store, which lay a short distance beyond Merton. He deposited them on the porch and went back for more, while Sylvie ferried them inside. Another trip and he had them all. He went back to close her door and joined her in the kitchen.

"I like your hair, Sylvie: it's magnificent, you look lovely." He held back from staring too closely or for too long, in case more was conveyed than was wise. He continued to talk, so as to hide his embarrassment, as she caught him surveying her a little too intently. "Did you fancy a change?"

Her long hair had always been one of her most distinguishing features. It was usually crimped, sometimes braided, and occasionally straight; but always well onto her shoulders.

"Yes," she confirmed, "it's the new me. No nonsense, discard some of the past and look forwards, you know, and also, to be truthful, thought it might help with my disguise."

What she didn't say, was that ever since her discovery of the body of Barry Miles in her bedroom, in conditions that she did not wish to dwell on, even in her own mind, she'd felt unclean. Having her hair cut was almost like a baptism that she subconsciously hoped would deliver her from the feeling that her home, her life and her very body had been sullied by his presence and actions.

"Talking of disguises what's this 'Sylvia, drug rep?' he queried.

She smiled. "Sorry about that: I thought if I could give people something to get their teeth into, then they would simply accept me as your girlfriend, and not look too closely at me and wonder. I should imagine strangers in a village of this size always attract a lot of attention, especially when no one knows who they are. So, I thought that if they knew, or thought they knew, who I was, they wouldn't wonder too much." She continued: more of her old confidence seeping back, "I hope you don't mind, me going around calling myself your girlfriend. I won't offend anyone, will I, and have some young woman come up to me and punch me on the nose?"

"No, I don't see that happening ..." he paused, trying to stifle delight from appearing on his face... "at least for a week or two," he added with as much gravity as he could muster. Matt, of course, was delighted at her passing herself off as his girlfriend, and had to try very hard to keep his expression as impassive as possible.

"Are you sure it's not going to embarrass you? Maybe I should have checked with you first?"

Matt fought even harder to control his expression, but managed a few words that seemed plausible. "No, no I suppose not. You know; not if it helps you anyway," doing his best to remain imperturbable.

Looking again at her hair, his struggle being waged within as he tried very hard to take his eyes off her. How he would love to reach out and caress those silky locks and tousle them through his fingers, as he filled his lungs with the gentle fragrance emanating from her direction whenever she moved in close proximity. One thing was for sure, despite her penchant for running out of her shop at every available opportunity to grab him about something, Stella could certainly cut hair.

She caught him looking again out of the corner of her eye. "Well thanks, for the compliment. Perhaps you'd better phone Steve and tell him that, let's see now what was it? Ah yes, 'pretty in an ordinary way - but nice hair'."

Matt looked away briefly from the gaze locked upon him. "Let's just say that, you look great?" he offered as openly as restless thoughts would permit.

She smiled and was about to speak, but decided that further words might embarrass one or more of them. The smile he had identified at their first meeting was returning with more intensity. The eyes, still a little wan, seemed to be regaining some of their sparkle. The skin around them wasn't nearly so puffy this morning, as it had appeared last night.

"Oh that reminds me, I forgot one or two things on the back seat," she remembered aloud. She darted out to the car although the rain fell more densely now. Returning with a couple of other bags, she was clutching a new mobile phone. "What a sweetie Mr Fellowes is. He told me that this phone was on offer and I could do 'pay as I go' or 'pay as I went', whatever," she beamed with delight at her purchase. "I told him that I was your girlfriend, too, hope you don't mind?"

Matt was still struggling to hide his delight at her new-found energies, fighting desperately against his desire to stare for just a little longer than would have been wise. In facing the battle within he did his best to remain passive, while fortunately, she continued to talk. "He let me have it with an even bigger discount: saying that any friend of yours was welcome, and wanted to make sure that I got a really good deal." Though Matt had no doubt this was a factor, he didn't fail to grasp that men of all ages would sell their souls to Lucifer himself, just to have a glimpse of her smile, that would brighten the darkest day and the most miserable of lives. How could she not succeed in getting a discount? Even women couldn't fail to be refreshed by her cheery, relaxed manner. Her new hairstyle seemed to enhance her features and bring out those eyes more vividly than he thought possible: the little pert nose also being liberated by the masterly trimming of those long, lustrous tresses. Looking away quickly again, before his expression betrayed more of his thoughts than he'd wish; to those crystal blue eyes that were so perceptive, and were now looking at him as they anticipated a reply.

"Oh yes, nice phone that," he began suddenly, sensing a way of hiding his fascination for her new image. "He let me have that one last year. Let me see." Matt took the offered phone and turned it in his palm. He pointed to an imaginary mark on the back plate. "Oh yes, that's the one, with this little mark on the back."

She hesitated ever so slightly, as if unsure whether this could be true or not, looking at him intently for non-verbal clues, his voice being imperturbable. Staring at the phone as if making its acquaintance again, he turned it in his palm but also to avoid her penetrative stare. Having been correct in not underestimating her astuteness, she'd quickly gauged his sense of humour.

"How much did he charge you for it?" Matt asked.

Her face now brimming with delight, sensing that the game was in play, "thirty-nine ninety-nine," she said.

"Really, it's gone up!" he began with incredulity, "he let me have it for twenty, traded it in for a new one last Christmas. Still these old phones are quite good you know," he offered with reassuring tones.

"That's funny; he told me you couldn't work this one, it was too complicated for you."

"No, no, not at all, old Stan must be getting confused," he assured her.

"He seemed pretty clear to me: gave me a free case, charger, hands-free kit, as long as I didn't tell you, in case you got upset."

He sensed that he had met his match. "I'll have to have a word with Stan, I send him new customers and all I get is cheek." He couldn't quite stop his face from breaking into a smile: realising that her agile thoughts were more than happy to play along with him.

"No, he was really nice and told me to tell you that he'd let you have one of these at the same price, as he made his money, on the one you bought last Christmas."

"I'll just pop over there and put some grease on his step," Matt said, as if thinking aloud.

"No don't do that," she sensed she had him on the run. "He told me that you're his best customer, nobody loses more phones than you."

"This is what I get when I try to help someone. We GPs are expected to keep people's confidences and not spread around gossip and tittle-tattle about our loyal customers. New haircut and what happened to that polite girl I met in Salford?" he queried playfully.

"You mean that pretty ordinary one?" she corrected.

"Right that's it! I'll phone Steve and call it all off."

"Now don't you bother, I had a word with Mary today and told her that you'd be bringing your Bucks Fizz collection."

His laughter conceded defeat.

"You're right Sylvie, he's a lovely man, and this is a great phone," restoring it to her as she looked gleefully at him.

"Right, Doctor Sinclair, you get off upstairs and change out of that suit. I'll get this stuff into the kitchen and start tea."

He went upstairs for a quick shower and changed. On descending the stairs he was greeted by encouraging and hunger-inducing smells from the kitchen. He popped his head round the door and asked if there was anything he could do.

She held out a white wine spritzer that she had just made, on hearing his steps coming down.

"Can I do anything to help?" he offered.

"No Matt, you go and sit down. I thought we'd eat in the conservatory. I like to watch the rain through the glass roof, if that's okay?" she suggested.

"Lovely," he replied as similar thoughts crossed his mind.

"You go and put some nice music on - if you can find any in that collection of yours! Which reminds me...." He shivered a little as he realised what was coming next, "just what did you do with all my CDs? I'm sure you told me you had them all, and I can't find one in that, uh...extensive collection of yours."

"I'm sure they're there, somewhere," he voiced. Lying was not his strong suit.

"You haven't got *one*, have you, and me thinking you were my greatest fan," she concluded.

"I'll just go and see if I can find them and put some music on while I'm there." He sat in the lounge thinking furiously, hoping that desperation would provide answers. She'd clearly not forgotten to ask him again, and no doubt would return to the subject. He wondered just how many of her CDs were still in the shops. The nearest CD store was in Tesco beyond Merton.

A short time later she called him into the conservatory. The rain hissed slightly as it hit the glass roof and coursed down in tiny rivulets. She preferred the sun, but loved to see the rain fall; watching from some dry vantage point or from beneath a large umbrella. The conservatory served to afford both. She placed two plates on the table and went back for a bottle of wine. He sat down uncertainly. The smell that he'd caught earlier, with much promise of the food to come, had evaporated, and unfortunately the offerings on the plate before him, unhappily pierced his expectation. It seemed that he'd been a little hasty in assessing her culinary skills so favourably.

She returned, looking so excited. He wondered if he could suddenly feign illness, or perhaps the phone would ring with an urgent call. She'd be sure to notice any attempt at scraping some of the food into one of the potted plants. Ultimately he decided that he'd just have to sit there, and grin and bear it in every sense. She sat down facing him. "Oh, do start, don't wait for me. I don't get much chance to cook, but I do so enjoy it. I prefer to cook it rather than to eat it."

Matt was suddenly crestfallen: his worst fears about what was in front of him had been realised.

He would never cease to be amazed at how much of that food he managed to get down. Doing his utmost to make reassuring and grateful noises, he wondered feverishly by which means he could keep her out of the kitchen. Her desire to cook and take part in the running of the house was undoubtedly a novel experience for her; but he knew simply that his stomach, which hitherto had never been known to refuse any food, would not be able to withstand more of her culinary efforts. No doubt assertive people would advise him to simply explain his dilemma in calm dispassionate terms.

"It took me a little while to get used to your Aga. I haven't cooked on one of those before."

His initial thought, perhaps unkindly but accurately, wanted to confirm the evident nature of that comment, but his words were much more emollient and sensitive.

"Oh, but Sylvie, you did so well."

As she removed the plate from in front of him, not a moment too soon, he prayed that she'd simply bought a ready-prepared pudding. He knew that the supermarket had any number of excellent ones that his stomach would welcome just at this time. Unfortunately it wasn't to be. It seemed that her cooking skills also extended to the dessert, which was retrieved with a flourish from the oven. Neither sight nor smell could help him in assessing just what kind of pudding it was, and he looked towards the bowl that was brought in, doing his utmost to hide his trepidation. Fortunately he could beg her to give him a small portion, blaming the previous excellent course on making him too full. Looking a little disappointed, she halved the portion she'd intended to give him. He rubbed his stomach as contentedly as he could, and told her that he was really very, very full but that it looked delicious. With a fair quantity of wine and even more gulps of water, he managed to slide most of the contents on his plate down his gullet. He deftly whisked his own plate off the table before she could see how much was left, and carried it along with hers into the kitchen, where he could safely slide the remainder into the bin. Clicking 'on' the percolator, he dropped in heaps of coffee; hoping this would expunge any aftertaste.

"Coffee Sylvie?" he called.

"Oh, yes please, Matt."

Returning to the conservatory, he felt rather queasy. He hoped and prayed that the familiar taste of the coffee would persuade his stomach that what he had eaten was at least digestible.

"It's so kind of you to cook Sylvie."

"Oh, not at all, I really enjoyed it," she replied honestly.

He concluded that cooking wasn't one of her strong points though she approached it, he suspected, as she did all things, with an abundance of enthusiasm and a desire to create; sadly the wonderful attributes that she held in spades weren't enough to nudge the food, on which she worked so hard, even to approach tolerability. Despite voices nagging at him within, he realised ultimately that he could no more have told her this, than he could have left her standing on his doorstep. He'd do his best in future, either to get into the kitchen ahead of her, or to suggest that they ate out, if at all possible.

Later they sat in the lounge, talking whilst the dishwasher chugged away at the dishes.

"So *Sylvia*" he emphasised deliberately, "seems like you've had a good day? I take it nobody recognised you, and your *bluff* theory is intact?"

"Well, I think my new haircut helped a little, and I did cheat a bit today." She produced a red baseball cap with the words '*Wokingham Working Men's Club*' emblazoned on the front. "I found this on the back seat of the Beetle - what do you think?" She tried it on for him. Even this couldn't diminish her looks, the eyes sparkling with renewed vigour from under the peak.

"Yes, not bad: so, you wore this today?"

"Yes, I thought, it might throw them a bit?"

"I can see why you thought that – I don't think you'll come across another quite like it here in Perri."

"I tell you, they won't expect to see a pop star walking in their midst. If they're especially curious, then I tell them what they want to hear, or something that they can instantly believe," she continued with illustrations, "me and Stella got on like a house on fire, especially when she thought I was your girlfriend - and lovely Stan in Merton."

"Yes I know, don't rub it in," he began, "you twisted the poor fellow round your little finger. A quick flash of those nice jeans and that smile, and he was putty in your hands," he suggested, almost thinking aloud.

"I think that despite what you say, they're just nice folk. Even the people in Tesco, a bit further out, were really friendly. Helped me with my bags and couldn't have been more polite."

Matt grasped that much of this was new to her, although she'd obviously retained an interest in, and empathy towards, people, in whatever circumstances she found them, he doubted that she was used to interacting with them in this way. Reasoning that these weren't the sort of people she'd come across in a typical day as Fabienne; it was doing her good to have the freedom that arose out of being someone completely different. The person who'd discovered an asphyxiated stalker in her bedroom, and the star who'd been ruined overnight by the tabloids, was someone very different and, at this point in time, very far away. Her instinct in seeking him and the life he enjoyed in Perrilymm, was excellent. Not daring to hope that it was anything more than instinct, he knew that for a wide variety of reasons, just at this juncture, her place was in this village and with him, until such time as she was fully restored.

Suddenly, she leapt from the chair. She rose so precipitously that he gave a little jump. "Oh, I nearly forgot," she went back to the hall to rummage through one or two bags that presumably hadn't come from Tesco and returned with a glitzy carrier bag. Matt's heart sank when he saw it.

"I see you've been to *Razzle*," he said unenthusiastically.

"Yes, indeed, and what a lovely dress shop, and not far from here. Good job I managed to find it, though," she said, brightly.

"Yes," he offered with even less enthusiasm.

"The owner knows you very well, Matt." The gleeful grin was making more of its presence felt and even becoming tinged with a little mischief as she sensed his awkwardness. "Yes, Jane Tomkins," she said triumphantly and went on, "we had a really good natter."

Matt gulped. He and Jane Tomkins had dated some years before, when he'd first arrived in Perrilymm. Hoping that Jane hadn't revealed as much, but he knew that this was a forlorn hope: sensing from that little playful twinkle that there was more on the way. Fortunately, she was looking at the shiny bag and concentrating on it, or she would have seen him glaze over just a little, as he remembered that night, not so long ago. Having had a little too much to drink, in a moment of coital ecstasy, he'd told Jane that he loved her and asked if she would she marry him. Fortunately, perhaps for him, she was a little surprised by this, so early in their relationship and had played for more time. The ardour had cooled and they'd parted some time later.

"She did have a lot to say."

"Did she mention me at all?" he managed as casually as possible.

"Oh yes, as soon as she knew that I was staying with you, I couldn't shut her up."

"So what did you two talk about?" he wondered.

"Oh this and that; she mentioned you quite a lot."

"Really, what did she say about me?" doing his best to seem surprised.

"Oh, you know," she replied carelessly.

"No, I don't, go on."

"Well, I wouldn't want to break confidences."

"I'm sure you won't. You were saying?"

"Oh it was only girls' stuff," she concluded.

Matt could see that he wasn't going to get too far. He shuddered within as he recalled the events that summer. Remembering the brief passionate liaison that both parties had enjoyed could surely be forgiven by even the sternest critic; but why for the life of him had he suddenly proposed? Cringing again, he thought of the words that appeared seemingly without logic, without thought and - the most shameful aspect - reflecting emotions that he no longer recognised the following day. It was perhaps not surprising that the poor girl had been shocked and unsettled: desperately playing for time to consider his words. The sober light of day had shown his words to be as false as they were embarrassing, and he knew with a further helping of shame that he heaped upon himself, that he'd been grateful for that pause. Her uncertainty, and his guilt had put paid to the relationship, and he berated himself still further for having treating Jane – for treating anyone - this way. It had been some time since they had spoken.

"Well I'm sure there isn't much to tell," he thought aloud, more with hope than expectation. "It was all a few years ago."

Fabienne's spontaneous grin remained in place. He couldn't fail to see that there'd been quite a transformation in his guest. Within a span of just twenty-four hours, her appearance had changed. She was certainly much brighter, and that smile that he'd seen at its height in Luciano's was returning with increasing vigour. He detected another change, however, which encouraged him more. In Salford he had met a charming and vivacious businesswoman; at all times studied and careful in the way she handled herself, and the interaction she allowed with others – fans and acquaintances. Her close proximity to him had revealed just a little more of the playful, insouciant streak that ran through her, and he could only conclude that her less formal manner would rest her physically and, more vitally, emotionally, from her recent trauma.

Suddenly, she jumped up again.

"Say, Matt do you fancy a walk?" she asked excitedly.

"Why not," he replied.

The rain had gone, leaving a warm and slightly humid evening. Weak sunshine had appeared, but seemed to be sinking quickly as night waited in the wings to claim the sky for its own. He withdrew a truly massive umbrella from the car boot and, as the ground was still a little wet underfoot, they walked a short way past his house along the road, before reaching the path they'd taken the previous evening at the edge of the wood. They walked for over an hour, talking as they went. Matt spoke about his work, and his hopes for the future. She listened for the most part, occasionally asking questions or seeking clarification over some point that he'd raised, or pointing to something that she'd seen. She seemed content to let him talk about his work; and by doing this she could exclude, for that time, some of the horrors that were still close to the surface within her own mind. Though he was a physically large and muscular man, he retained a calmness and a restraint in the words he spoke; and in his movements. She could quite easily picture him propping up a bar with enthusiastic friends after a rugby match. But the person she'd discovered was oddly at variance with this image. Finding his manner was responsible for instilling a similar calm and an inner strength within her, and she could see exactly why medicine was his calling and his life.

Although once or twice their hands brushed fleetingly, he remained a model of rectitude, and such a stance seemed to permeate through his physical presence, which was at all times friendly, attentive and warm, but never intrusive, pushy or contemptuous. It was almost as if he was being still held by the awe she detected in him at their first meeting. Awe that he hadn't quite been able to dispel or to modify. Despite this, his eyes hinted at something of the deeper thoughts he held within. Being convinced that she could see more than a flicker in his eyes when she caught him surveying her: she couldn't know that he was restraining himself with every ounce of effort available to him, in keeping more vigorous instincts towards her firmly in check.

"You're a lucky man, Matt. I can see why you love it here. It has everything that anyone could possibly want."

As she spoke, he could only reflect that there was only one thing in his life that was missing - and that was a person in very close proximity.

They continued to walk until darkness came. For each of them this was an amnesty, a sort of anonymity so that he could gaze across at her without feeling he was staring; and she could look at him without wondering what was going on within those deep blue eyes. He continued with most of the talking and she listened contentedly. Remembering that he seemed to be so in awe of her in Luciano's, that she felt more comfortable continuing to talk, rather than have silences open up. Now that he was in his own surroundings, obviously so precious to him, he had enthusiasm and an energy that none could fail to realise, and all but the most unfeeling would be engaged by. Another ineluctable fact was that his life, his surroundings and the people he knew, had provided the most welcome and the most crucial of distractions, in the same way as a luxurious holiday might. Even in Tesco, whilst wandering between the aisles, she'd heard two young women swooning over their dishy doctor and hadn't been at all surprised, while she deliberately lingered among the chocolate biscuits, to hear that it was that "scrummy" Doctor Sinclair.

What a marked contrast between his simple life, which was filled with straightforward, genuine people; with no dark corners, and her own life that was in many ways just the opposite. She shivered next to him as she thought about all the things she'd left behind, and all the things she'd have to face, in order to regain a semblance of a life that she could call her own. This was a mountain that she couldn't even contemplate, let alone climb at that point. Instantly detecting the shiver, as it rippled through her, he said.

"I'm sorry Sylvie, are you cold? I'm rambling on and not realising how dark and cold it's become."

She was just about to correct his assumption when he grabbed her hand, rubbed it with his other, and moved a little closer to her. For that most fleeting moment, just before he was able to correct it, she could see a slightly less formal side to him, and her mind's eye saw afresh the popular chap, standing in the pub, surrounded by his mates with whom he could enjoy a few drinks and a little knockabout humour. Studying him carefully, she could only conclude that even in these uncomplicated surroundings, he was something of an enigma. The more answers she uncovered: the more questions remained.

"Come on, let's return to the house and I'll get you a nice cup of tea and a piece of lemon meringue pie," he said quickly, but without realising the full implications of his simple words.

"Perhaps I could heat up that crumble I made?"

"Oh the crumble," he said, remembering what action self-preservation had dictated. "I am sorry Sylvie, I'm afraid I unthinkingly put it in the bin when I cleared the dishes for the dishwasher. Do forgive me!" His words of regret at this point were almost genuine, because he'd been convinced that it was, in fact, bread and butter pudding. Fortunately, the gathering darkness offered him absolution in this area too. They walked briskly back to the house along the road, the umbrella not being needed.

They drank their tea in near silence, his stomach grateful for the chance of food that wasn't just edible but palatable also. She excused herself, the walk reminding her body of the sleep deficit that had been built up over the past days, and the unaccustomed air also playing its part. She climbed the stairs to her room after bidding him a good night. Matt remained for half an hour or so, but he, too, felt suddenly very tired. He changed and slipped into bed. A warm glow came over him as he ran back through the day's events. The last thoughts he remembered before sleep took him; that she seemed to be not only rested in the village, but also just seemed to fit in, as if she'd been intended for this life, with him, rather than the one that she knew. Knowing that Steve wouldn't be at all pleased with his assessment and his conclusions, but all available evidence was with Matt at that time: his friend not privy to his innermost thoughts, which was just as well.

The following day, brilliant sunshine flooded into his room. He often deliberately left the curtains open, as he found in the summer months he enjoyed the sun intruding in this way, and it seemed to set him up for the day. Only the nearby woods overlooked his room, and the views at this time of day were as invigorating as they were stunning. He showered quickly, but as quietly as he could. He hadn't heard Fabienne going downstairs but she, too, was quiet in the house and made very little noise. Deciding that her absence from the kitchen meant that she was still asleep: he poured out cereal and made coffee and toast.

He popped back upstairs for his jacket and the phone that he always left by his bed, in case he was needed in the night. Despite other doctors joining in the out-of-hours rota, he, like every other GP in the land, still bore ultimate responsibility for each and every patient, twenty-four hours a day for 365 days of the year, and if the on-call doctor was unable to go on a visit for any reason, he'd be expected to attend, or face the consequences of his inaction.

Fabienne appeared sleepily as he was just picking up his car keys from the hall table. Her hair was tousled and chaotic, and she looked like a little girl as she blinked the sleep from her eyes as she descended the stairs. Looking rested and refreshed, however, and more and more like the person he had first met.

"Morning Sylvie, sleep well?" he asked.

"Oh. Hi Matt, oh yes thanks, like a baby. Great place this for sleep, you should bottle the air or the water or whatever; I'm sure it would be more effective than sleeping tablets."

"Good thinking: might just do that; perhaps we could sell genuine village air?" he suggested.

"Yes, I could do with a new business direction."

"Have you any plans today?" he asked.

"No, I thought I'd stay home today. Do you mind if I do a spot of washing? I won't pin undies on your line or anything and I promise not to add to that pile of washing that nearly buried me when I opened the door to your utility room!"

"Sylvie, you can pin whatever you like, where you like, I'm sure the villagers won't raise an eyebrow. They might be a bit nosy, but they aren't really into others' washing," he assured her.

"OK thanks Matt you're a real pal. See you later."

"Oh, don't forget Steve and Mary's tonight," he reminded her.

"No, don't worry, I'm looking forward to it."

Matt could only think, at this point in time, of Mary's excellent cooking. "I have a half day so I might see you later?"

"Okay Matt. Bye."

Fortunately there were no visits and Matt was waiting for the builder when he arrived, having cleared his desk so that they could view the plans and discuss the project in more detail. Matt was impressed from the outset, by the way in which he'd discussed the project and his work - even though his quotation was higher than some of the others tendering - Matt picked him for this reason. Mrs Simpson sat in the meeting with the two men, making notes on one or two points that had been raised.

The builder was hoping to make a start before autumn set in, if possible, as the roof had to come off, to allow for the extension. Temporary accommodation for the surgery was to be set up in the adjacent car park to allow the workmen unfettered access at all times. The local PCT had firmly got behind the scheme, and promised that the full cost-rent allowances would be available, and would also include an uplift for Matt's new partner. They'd even intimated that if he were to bid for equipment upgrades; using local incentive monies, they would consider such a request favourably. It looked as though Matt would be not only able to afford a generously-proportioned extension, but also to equip it.

Driving home after the meeting, he arrived at about two o'clock. He found Fabienne relaxing outside, where only the gentle gurgle from the nearby stream disturbed the otherwise quiet rear garden. She'd found the teak steamer chair and cushion, in the shed, and was reclining in the sunshine. Looking from the kitchen window, he tried not to stare at the lithe, firm body, wearing denim shorts and a T-shirt. Though he had seen her wear skimpier clothes at concerts, she'd never been this close before: close enough to smell and to touch. As restless thoughts coursed through his brain, he did his best to control their influence.

Just at that point, she seemed to sense his presence; looking into the kitchen, waved and moved to meet him in the house.

"Hi there, Sylvie, another lovely day."

"It's just so peaceful out here Matt; is it always this quiet?" she asked, the surprise still apparent on her face, after being accustomed to living in London for so long.

"Just about. In fact the noisiest day of the year is usually Christmas Eve, when I have my party."

"So, who do you put on the guest list? Do you invite all those old girlfriends?"

"No, just the young, sexy ones," he countered, sensing that the mischievous grin was about to return. "And, of course, any megastars who happen to be staying with me."

"Good, I might just hold you to that, but I'm not sure I could fight my way through all those adoring people."

"Talking of adoring people, I popped in to the newsagent on my way back. Pete Timms? More fans of yours in there," he assured her. "Just what are you doing to all these men?"

He didn't really need an answer to that question. Knowing exactly what effect she was having on these men, having had to battle with his own thoughts on the matter on more occasions than not.

"You know, Matt, these people are just so friendly. I just popped in to get a card for a friend, and they were all really pleased to meet me. They're not like this in London, they seem a lot more standoffish."

Matt considered for a moment that they were probably all dirty old men, looking excitedly at those denim shorts, which seemed to hug her figure most flatteringly.

"Well, you know, small villages, they need to get on with one another: either that, or they're all nosy and want to know each other's business."

"They all speak highly of you Matt, especially the blind, confused ones," she teased.

"Hm, I think I'd be better going alone after all tonight, Steve told me not to bring any trouble-makers."

"No, you're not going to get rid of me that easily: besides, I've got to listen to those Bucks Fizz albums and pretend they're really good. What do I do if I feel sick when they start to play? Anyway, as I was saying before I was rudely interrupted, they haven't a bad word to say about you."

"Well, they're uncomplicated, straightforward people, who always seem grateful for what I can do. I wouldn't want to be a GP in a stockbroker belt; there'd be too many worried well, and too many people making their own diagnosis on websites. Most of them would have private medical insurance and would come in to pick up referral letters to specialists, rather than to get my opinion."

He sensed the conversation needed a new direction and quickly said, "Come on, I'm hungry let me make you a sandwich."

She sat at the island whilst he made some sandwiches with smoked salmon and brown bread. He pushed a plate over to her, and a glass of flavoured water that had been chilling in the fridge.

"Seriously Matt, are you sure you'd better not go on your own?"

He held his hand to his ear feigning deafness. "Sorry, did I hear something then? Now, I thought we'd had this discussion and settled it."

"Well, what if they recognise me?" she offered initially, but knew inside, that this was not the real reason.

Matt understood that if they did, Steve would have a great many questions to ask of him, and no doubt would think him duplicitous. Much worse, however, Matt knew that Steve's stance before he'd admitted to Fabienne's influence would be very different from his having gained this information. Mindful of recent history: Matt was no longer sure that the psychologist would be able to view events with his usual equanimity.

"Not getting cold feet are we? I thought that you had it all sorted," he replied as he looked carefully at her.

"Well I guess that I haven't been up so close for that length of time. I agree with you there's a big difference between popping into a shop for something, and sitting facing someone for the whole evening."

"From what I hear, you've been doing a lot more than just popping in to shops. The whole village keep coming up to me to tell me what a lucky man I am, having a girlfriend like you," he said, doing his best to keep the unbridled delight out of his voice.

"You've got to admit, it's good cover," she reminded him.

He could only consider, that he longed for it to be real, and not just a good cover, and that she were here because she wanted to be, rather than because she'd run out of places to hide, against a swirling tide with an undercurrent ready to pull her back to deeper waters as soon as she was located. Dismissing his own thoughts quickly, he knew that they wouldn't help him.

"Look, Sylvie if they do recognise you, we'll just have to come clean: I know they'll keep your secret."

Matt wondered if he should have phoned Steve to reveal all, but in truth things had moved so quickly: her needs had been so pressing, that it wouldn't have been possible. The other point was that before doing so, he'd have had to discuss it with

Sylvie, and he wasn't sure she'd wish to hear everything that she'd have to learn when he did so. In any event, the solution to his dilemma had been to do nothing, and he'd just have to live with that: together with any admonishment from Steve, if and when that time arrived.

"I suppose you could always wear your working man's baseball cap and perhaps I could find a stick-on moustache," he suggested.

She realised that her true reasons for holding back had little to do with her detection, but more to do with the fact that she would prefer, just at that time, to talk about anything and anyone but herself, and by going with Matt, as his girlfriend, she couldn't escape their enquiries.

"Matt, seriously isn't there someone you'd rather be taking. I turned up here unannounced, you must have had plans?"

If only she knew, he thought instantly. The crystal gaze was upon him, clear, yet perceptive with refined accuracy. He could look away and lie, or meet her gaze full-on and speak the truth: either way she would know.

"Well, to be truthful, no there isn't just at the moment. I guess after a while, in a little village like this, you just run out of people to ask out," he said, almost flippantly in order to hide embarrassment.

She nodded as if recognising that at least some of that sentence was correct. "I can see that: from what I've heard *you'd* soon run out of people to ask. Okay, then, we're a date," she said with the gleeful insouciance that was making more and more of its presence felt. "Come on, let's have a sit in the garden."

Finding another steamer chair in the shed, he sat next to her.

"I can't get over how peaceful this place is, and what a magnificent garden."

"To be truthful, gardening isn't my strong point: I can just about cut the grass without making it look worse than before I started. Fortunately Tom Scrivens, that's Bill's brother, comes once a week in summer, to help with the tricky bits. "

"So how did you end up here?" she asked, her ever-present curiosity surfacing once again.

"I grew up in the Midlands. My Dad was an engineer and - obviously this was a long time ago - had an idea to make smaller and more efficient electric refrigerators. In those days, they were all large, bulky inefficient things. Many of them didn't use electricity at all, but ran on gas."

She looked incredulous.

"Yes really! His could be made smaller, lighter and used less electricity. He started his own company and turned these things out by the lorry-load. Demand soared through the roof, and he'd initially work round the clock producing his fridges. Unfortunately, a not-so-good idea was to use asbestos as an insulator and liner for the cold compartment, to keep it cool. At that time asbestos was thought to be safe. The disadvantage with it, as you may know, is that it often causes problems only years after someone's exposed to it. My Dad was working seven days a week and running eighteen-hour days. The company grew and grew. More efficient materials came in and eventually asbestos was replaced. Unfortunately it wasn't substituted nearly soon enough to save my Dad, as it dawned on people just what a dangerous material it was, to those who had been exposed to it. He'd been working with it for so long that he must have breathed in a really high dose. He developed mesothelioma, which is a fatal lung tumour, linked to asbestos.

For me, as a young teenager growing up, it was really sad to see, such a great man, who'd never had a day's illness, being consumed by this dreadful disease. He was really wealthy by this time. His factory and patents had been bought out by much larger companies, and they paid handsomely: but all his money couldn't save him. I suppose, I learned an important lesson there and then; about which things in our lives are really precious, and as I'm sure, you'd agree - money isn't one of them. The other thing that it taught me was that when you lose your health, you lose everything. Money isn't important all of a sudden, whether you've got it or haven't, it becomes irrelevant, as all you can see is the health that you've just lost and will never regain.

    I got into medical school in Manchester. He died that same year. I wanted to quit, but my Mum wouldn't hear of it. She made sure that I went, and that I stuck it right through to the end. I worked really hard and did well. There were lots of career opportunities in medicine and many of my tutors wanted me to stay in hospitals and take up a speciality. Steve qualified my year, and we've known each other since that first week when we were both spotty freshers. He and his family were very supportive when my Dad died after this long, horrible illness. Anyway, when I qualified, I did a GP training scheme in Merton and just when I was about to complete it, I saw this job advertised. People thought I was crazy, wanting to move to such a quiet backwater. They all envy me now, I can tell you. The elderly GP before me, had died whilst still in harness, and they were looking for someone to take over quickly. By this time, I knew the area very well, I'd bought this house when I was still a GP trainee so I was lucky to find work so near. The house had been owned by an elderly couple who both died within a week of each other. It was in a bit of a state when I took it, but over the years I've slowly restored it - I hope - to its former glory.

    My Mum never really got over losing my Dad. She wasn't that old either, when she died, about eighteen months ago, from breast cancer. I think that a broken heart killed her really, and the breast cancer just happened to be there too. It wasn't easy at first being in the village very much on my own but, as you know, Steve happened to get a job in Mirfield General, and one or two other members of my year don't work too far from here. I was left comfortably off, but, as you might guess, at first, more than a little lonely. Fortunately, you've seen for yourself, the folk are very friendly: after a while you feel as if you've always been here. They never make me feel like an outsider."

"Yes I can see that Matt." she said quietly and continued, "I'm sorry that you lost them both when you were still so young."

"Worse things happen, Sylvie. Some kids don't have their parents as long as I did. Divorce, separation and so on, can sometimes be more upsetting."

She nodded but remained quiet. Sensing that he had touched a nerve, he moved on quickly. "Some people think I'm lucky, living in a place like this, whilst others think me lazy and that I should be working at a teaching hospital or doing VSO or something. I just know this feels like home, and I don't feel as if I lack anything."

His eyes broke contact just for a second at this point: realising he'd been staring again at the exception to that rule.

Her smile returned. "I think you did the right thing, if it's any business of mine, and I think many people would kill to live in this house, in this village. I've met a lot of people and seen a lot of places in a lot of countries, and this must rate pretty close to the top, bar none: so don't let them talk you out of it. I think maybe one or two of these people giving you their opinions are just jealous. So, you sit tight."

He snoozed; she read; the sun slowly lost its control over the sky, and shadows steadily lengthened as night approached. He woke after about an hour. Looking at him for long seconds, she was still trying to assess this man: his life so simple, yet the man more complex - much more complex. Perhaps it would take a long time to learn of those thoughts that seemed to stir so deep within. In any event she was pleased that a wild idea had brought her here, almost out of desperation, but she now knew that there could be no better place to recuperate, hide from the teeming world, and discover much about people and their real lives that she'd hitherto not experienced. Eventually, she got up and said, "Well, it's the shower for me," and went up to her room to shower and get ready for the evening.

He remained and stared up at the sky for some time, its hue deepening almost imperceptibly, at first, as the sun continued to decline: its ultimate glory being denied to him by the dense tree line. In those final few minutes, night descended quickly and was accompanied by a chill in the air as soon as the sun had departed. Putting the cushions back in the shed, leaving the teak frames outside, he went inside to shower and change.

CHAPTER VIII

DINNER FOR FOUR

He was ready in his usual unfussed manner and popped downstairs to wait for her; flicking on the TV to see if there was anything on the news. A short time later he could hear her on the stairs, and moved to the hall table to collect his keys. Looking up as she came downstairs, he'd been amazed by her physical appearance on more occasions than he could remember. However, the vision that he beheld didn't disturb that conclusion for a moment; yet the aspect that presented uppermost in his mind as he gazed at her, was the change in her in so short a span of time – from exhaustion to exhilaration and from despair to deliverance. The long tanned legs, just lightly sun-kissed, in the spiky mules, the skirt above the knee and a pale-blue, strappy top that enhanced the slim elegant arms and curvaceous breasts. Her wrist had the usual 'Patek Phillipe' wristwatch as its only adornment and she wore a gold chain around her neck, heavy enough to look expensive, but not thick enough to look vulgar. As she continued to descend, he tried, but failed in the attempt not to stare. "Wow," he said, "you look stunning."

"Thank you Doctor, not bad yourself," she smiled, sensing the weight of his stare and asked, "will I do? Am I pretty ordinary?"

"No, Sylvie, I'd have to say that you are inordinately pretty," he admitted simply.

She smiled; he felt his heart leap and his knees quiver.

"I bet you say that to all the girls," she offered.

"So, is that what Jane Tomkins told you?" he asked.

"Oh no, she told me much more than that," she confirmed with an air of mystery.

Stepping on to the teak floor next to him, the delicate breeze of her perfume washed over his senses, adding its contribution to the intoxication that had submerged him. Smiling contentedly, as myriad thoughts crossed through his mind; emotions more enthralling than even the most vivid of dreams could suggest. "Nice legs," he commented as he looked down, appreciatively.

She looked down at the spiky heels. "I never go anywhere without my Manolos, they can make even stumpy legs like mine, look good," she assured him.

"Look great to me," he said, reflecting that 'stumpy' was probably the last word he would have chosen to define those particular legs. He reasoned further, that there again was the quiet unassuming grace that she exuded in all things she did, and each word she spoke. People would perhaps forgive her if there were a seam of conceit running through her, for she had much that would support such a flaw. He had yet to see even a trace of it, after observing her in a wide variety of conditions. The treatment meted out by the press, he reasoned, would be doubly hurtful to someone who'd always gone out of her way to treat all those she met with the same unpretentious grace.

"Come on then let's go," he suggested, deciding simply to stick to the mechanics of one necessary action after another. His mind was racing so fast that it didn't pay to think too much at any one point, in case more-detailed thoughts betrayed him.

"You've just been on the news," he remembered to say.

"Oh yes?" she said defensively, as if afraid to enquire what new revelations had been made available.

"They're still looking for you!" he beamed contentedly, "Little do they know that you are charming the inhabitants of Perrilymm."

They went to the car, and she slipped her shapely rear carefully onto the cold leather seat as he entered on the driver's side. The engine caught, and he prodded the climate control until it promised more comfortable temperatures against the evening air, which held a slight hint of a chill and the promise of more to come later. The car sped serenely through the quiet village. The fifteen miles to Steve's house was accomplished in a short, fuss-free, interval and he parked on their drive.

The post-war semi-detached was typical of suburbs of more industrialised towns than Merton. The curved bay windows extended the full height of the house, and the top lights were of stained-glass panels. Many of the houses in the road had had theirs removed and replaced with modern plastic frames, but Steve's still retained the original ones, both in the top lights of the bay and also in the front door. The top gable end was part-tiled, as was the front of the bay between the first-floor and ground floor windows. Matt walked with Sylvie up the drive, which was little too steep for the Manolos to be entirely comfortable: lending her a firm elbow with which she could gain support. Steve had left the porch light on, so it wasn't too hazardous an exercise.

"Well, here we go," he whispered as he motioned toward the bell. "Too late to back out now, they've seen us," he said quietly.

"If I forget to tell you later, thanks for bringing me," she offered, as if suddenly arriving at this conclusion that she just had to voice.

He looked at her quickly but carefully, as if uncertain as to what to say. Fortunately, before he could form a reply, Steve opened the door just as they approached. As usual, his glasses were perched on the end of his nose, a badly-fitting, home-made, jumper doing its best to hide his ample stomach.

"Matt, you devil." He held out his hand, suddenly captivated by the person in Matt's company. "Who is this gorgeous woman?" he asked with fascination. Matt deliberately turned round to look over his own shoulder. "Who? Where?" he queried. Sylvie toyed for a moment with the idea of standing on his foot with a spiky heel. On seeing his boyish, excited manner, however, she realised this she could not do. Steve offered his glasses to Matt.

"Put these on, you so-and-so." He continued, "I don't need them to see this vision of loveliness."

"Thank you, you must be Steve, and I'm Sylvie, Matt's newly-suffering, girlfriend," she said as she held out her hand.

Mary appeared at the door. "Sylvie, so pleased to meet you" she said effusively.

Steve interrupted quickly, "and this is Mary, my wife."

"Steve you old schmoozer. Don't listen to these men, my dear, they get worse with keeping, let me warn you. You look lovely Sylvie, what a gorgeous colour," she nodded, indicating Fabienne's top.

"Thank you Mary, and I just love your hair," Sylvie remarked.

Mary blushed just a little, she wasn't used to compliments, but Sylvie had picked out immediately, the beautiful, shiny, mid-brown hair that was cut to perfection in the shape of a bob. "Tell me, does Stella cut your hair?" Sylvie enquired.

"Correct, I can see you've made her acquaintance as yours is lovely too. Yes, she can certainly cut hair as long as you prepare yourself for the raft of gossip that comes your way as soon as you sit down," Mary confirmed.

Mary was a pretty girl, whose features had been made a little more ample than her genes had intended, by her abilities as a cook and her tendency to sample freely of those abilities!

"Come and sit down, my dear: let's ignore these two," she suggested.

She shot Steve a reproachful look, but much more endearing emotions queued in its wake. Fabienne could see immediately, that this was a love-match; the two being very comfortable with each other, in a way that could only be inbuilt; never learned or feigned for inspection. Matt seemed strangely quiet in Steve's company. Fabienne wondered about a distance between them, and whether words had been exchanged in the recent past. It contrasted sharply with the close relationship between Steve and Mary who seemed entirely at peace together, like a pair of well-worn gloves.

Doing her best to give Mary her undivided attention, Fabienne's curiosity was driving her as she tried to monitor the interaction between the two men out of the corner of her eye. She handed over a box of chocolates, and Matt a couple of bottles that he'd brought. "Oh, these are for you and Steve; it's really kind of you both to invite me, Mary."

"Well, put that thought right away; we've been asking Matt here, to come round for months and months, so I think we have you to thank for his eventual acceptance," Mary assured her.

"I must be very flattered then, as half the village seem to be chasing him," Sylvie said playfully.

Steve immediately seized on her words. "Ha, what about that then, Matt, hoist by your own petard here. You've got his measure pretty quickly," cut in Steve, a little acidly, as he turned to Fabienne and continued, "he kept telling us that he had no-one to bring. When we were medical students, this old bugger used to have every female medical student chasing him - and most of them caught him."

"Steve!" Mary said by way of reproach, as she shot him a further glance.

"Yes I can see that," said Fabienne. His words supporting her own conclusions. Something wasn't right between the two men, the atmosphere that stretched between them was palpable. She could see Matt's discomfort and that he was searching for words even now to make it right. Knowing that it was rude to listen to another conversation, whilst talking to Mary, didn't help; she just couldn't stop herself from straining her ears, so desperate was she to learn what had passed between them. She could just make out Matt's words.

"Steve it's good of you to invite me. I want to apologise for..." Matt began quietly.

"No Matt, I should be apologising, I gave you a really hard time and I'm sorry, I should've trusted you," Steve corrected him.

Matt continued. "I just wanted to say ... I'm sorry if I've appeared ...." pauses breaking up the sentence.

"Look Matt, just forget it," from Steve.

"But Steve," Matt said a little more loudly.

She could hear that Matt was desperate to get something off his chest; which he felt the need to apologise for; yet Steve had issues of his own. She wondered what or whom it could possibly be about.

Mary had sensed her distraction. "I just love that pretty top you're wearing," repeating herself as she desperately tried to restart their conversation.

"Oh thank you, Mary I bought it locally actually, in *Razzle*. Nice lady, Jane Tomkins, do you know her?"

Mary felt Matt squirm immediately at the mention of the name, said with more emphasis than was necessary, "Oh yes, I think, - well never mind about that," she corrected quickly.

Matt shifted uncomfortably again; detecting that Mary's diplomatic streak had been forced into play without knowing that Fabienne was teasing him just a little.

"Would you like a glass of Bucks Fizz, Sylvie?" Mary asked expectantly.

"Mary, I'd love one."

"Is it you, Matt, who likes Bucks Fizz? We thought we'd get it just for you, and it's very refreshing," Mary said, deliberately, bringing Matt more into their conversation, as she tried to disperse the awkwardness between the two men.

Fabienne shot Matt a glance, framed by the glowing smile, which he couldn't help returning as they shared the joke for that instant, despite his difficult conversation with Steve.

"It *is* Bucks Fizz," said Mary; detecting at once that something had passed between them, triggered by her words, which on the face of it appeared so simple.

"Oh yes, indeed, Mary, he just loves Bucks Fizz and, in truth, so do I," Fabienne said urbanely, so as to ensure that she extinguished the private joke quickly: taking pains that Mary was in no way embarrassed by not being part of it.

Steve and Matt moved into the kitchen to get the drinks. Fabienne heard the conversation resume, although Steve was doing his best to keep his voice down; she could make out only snippets.

"Forget it, Matt, it's all in the past, and I think she's lovely." Steve was signalling that he wanted the conversation to move on. He was desperately trying to change the subject, and Sylvie seemed a good choice. Matt wanted to let him know that he'd learned his lesson: that he was disappointed in himself and the image that he projected to others: either as a self-centred person, or a vain and decadent one. Steve had accepted that his worry over his friend and also perhaps a tinge of jealousy, had added to the problems, but had discovered that such words were hard to convey at a party with the two women sitting in close proximity. Fabienne detected that it was settled whatever it was.

"She's lovely," Steve repeated, quietly. "Just the thing to keep your mind off Fabienne," he continued, "She's having a really bad time isn't she? The press have really ripped her apart. I don't blame her for disappearing for a bit, when she's that cut up."

"Yes I am afraid she is," Matt voiced under his breath.

"Pardon?" Steve asked.

"Yes, I'm sure she is," Matt corrected quickly. At this point, Matt desperately wanted to reveal all to Steve, so as not to continue to mislead him. Realising, however, that he'd supported Fabienne's need for anonymity, which in turn required discretion more than confession. Knowing that he had her needs to consider; and this held precedence over wanting to assuage his own guilt.

"Now, just where did you find Sylvie?" Steve asked with fascination.

"Oh, on my doorstep," Matt mumbled.

"Pardon?"

"Oh, I said 'she's a rep!'."

Mary's intuitive streak, being the equal to Fabienne's, sensed that she was curious about the debate passing between the two men. Mary concluded that they had been absent for far too long: raising her voice. "Steve, darling, I was just about to ask Sylvie that very question, why not bring the drinks through so that we can all talk?"

They both reappeared, Mary's voice lifting in tandem with her curiosity. "So, go on Sylvie, I'm dying to know, just how did the two of meet? It all seems to have happened so suddenly. One minute Matt here is saying that he's no one to bring and now, here you are!"

Fabienne took a little sip from her bucks fizz. She'd been asked this many times in the past day or two, so much so, that it had become a well-rehearsed pathway: words that that she could trot out automatically, which added an air of authenticity.

"We met at a drug meeting, I organised a few weeks ago," she began carefully, and went on, "Matt was present, and we sort of got going from there, really."

"So, are you a drug rep then?" asked Steve.

"Yes, that's right," she affirmed.

"So, who do you work for?"

Matt intervened quickly, before she could begin to feel embarrassment. "Astra Zeneca, would you believe."

Fabienne did her best to nod seamlessly with agreement, and synchronised this as best she could with taking another sip from her glass, giving Matt more time to intervene.

"Good firm," said Steve; "they have some pretty good products, so which ones do you promote?" Mary cut in at this point, sparing Matt from having to intervene once again, albeit unknowingly. "Now darling, don't start talking shop; I can feel you dropping back into work mode."

"Yes Mary, I'm quite sure these doctors get quite enough of drug reps pushing them for appointments and meetings," he mused.

"Are you a doctor too, Steve?" Fabienne asked, wanting to shift the conversation without revealing that she knew the answer already.

"Yes, for my long suffering sins. I'm a consultant psychologist and as I'm sure you know, these days we're in more and more demand."

He talked for a while about his work. Fabienne could see Mary glow with pride: obviously deeply impressed by her husband. Although it couldn't be said that he was the most handsome man she'd seen, he had a boyish, mischievous charm that she could tell Mary, in particular, found compelling.

"Now don't you go on, you boring old fart," Mary said, whilst really meaning the exact opposite, since the harsh words were illusory. The smile and the concentration; the way she hung on his every word, told a very different story.

"How long have you two been married?" Fabienne asked.

"Well, that's another story: we were married five years tomorrow," Mary said, the pride still brimming.

"Oh congratulations, Mary. I'm so pleased for you."

Fabienne had seen a lot of people in her life. She'd witnessed the break-up of her own parents' marriage, and the screaming, shouting, as well as emotional levers they used to hurt each other. The bad blood that existed between them as their relationship deteriorated knew no bounds: any vehicle was used to inflict pain and hatred; the little girl that each professed to love had been one of those instruments. At all times, telling herself that each party loved her deeply, yet she could never rationalise why, if that were so, they sought to use her in that way. In her daily life she came across many superficial relationships. People who went to great expense to make ostentatious, public displays of their passionate love for each other, often declared publicly on television programmes or in glossy magazines, only for that love suddenly to be over, by the time the next issue of that magazine had hit the newsstands. Acknowledging that she had no answers: her experiences had made her frightened of any firm relationships, however, for the first time, she'd witnessed two people create an invisible but unbreakable bond. Moreover, this was nothing elaborate; there were no public demonstrations, no displays of excess, or of empty, vainglorious gestures; just a relationship that would withstand the test of time and the vicissitudes of human nature. She couldn't help but feel happy for them.

Mary had detected much of her wonderment. Having simultaneously assessed their guests, she too, could sense what passed between them: the little smiles, the nods, the things that each said that the other would instantly recognise; almost as if they were talking telepathically. Above all of these things, was the joy reflected on each of their faces. She hadn't seen Matt like this for some years. He'd always been bright, friendly: displaying both energy and his loyal friendship to Steve. Notwithstanding these, there was something written to his face and his whole persona that was entirely new. Whether he recognised it or not, Mary could see that a big change had taken place within.

Further consideration sensed that a tiny but crucial piece of the jigsaw was missing, and though she detected its absence she could not define it more closely. Ultimately, witnessing two people entirely at ease, yet strangely awkward when it came to displaying that to one another. Had she asked each of them, neither would have been in a position to supply any more detail than she had surmised already.

"I love this house, Mary, it's quiet, peaceful and just seems so friendly. It's the kind of place in which you could keep a wild animal, and, I suspect, it would just curl up and go to sleep on the rug."

"No dear, Steve usually sleeps in the chair," Mary suggested cheerfully. They both laughed.

Matt sat next to Sylvie. Despite detecting the barely-concealed passion burning in his eyes, Mary noticed there was very little physical contact between them; no rubs of her shoulder and no patting of her knees. In fact, the only things that gave him away; were the sideways glance at the revealing top, enhancing her figure so beautifully; and plainly, lots of looks at those long, slim legs, complemented by her gorgeous shoes. Mary was aware that they'd only recently come together, yet she'd seen at first-hand on several occasions that Matt had never hesitated to develop a relationship quickly, especially when the feeling in him that she sensed, was palpable beyond any doubt. This, coupled with the almost shy glances he directed toward Sylvie when she looked at him, was similarly most uncharacteristic. When Sylvie had handed over the chocolates and Matt the bottles, it was almost as though two very separate people had each contributed, rather than a joint present, as any stable couple - including she and Steve - would do. In discerning that something wasn't quite right, Mary couldn't say exactly what, but she made a mental note to speak with Steve later, and see if he'd picked this up.

"So, Sylvie, I hear you're from Evesham, is that right? It's a lovely area. We nearly settled down there, after we got married," Mary began.

"Yes, anything to get away from this man who keeps sending me these impossible patients to sort out," Steve cut in, and continued, "oh, saw your patient, the one who had had her drink spiked in the club and now is frightened to..."

"Now you two don't start talking shop again. Steve, you promised." Mary intervened quickly, sensing that her husband had inevitably been transported back to the work he loved so much.

"Oh, yes, love, sorry," he said, and then to Matt, more quietly, "don't worry, my boy, I'll tell you later," as Mary got up.

"Let's see now, folks; time to go through - if anyone's hungry?" Mary announced.

Matt, unsurprisingly, was starving, his stomach beginning to crave food that wouldn't be a burden to swallow, but a pleasure. Knowing that he was on safe ground, this evening, because he'd never had a bad meal at their house: Mary's cooking being on a par with the very best that he'd tasted. He wondered how Fabienne would judge it; would she compare it at all to her own, and if so what conclusions would be drawn. Realising, inevitably, that he could never ask her this, without damaging the sheer delight she habitually displayed: he'd rather eat a hundred of her meals than do that to her, now, or in fact – ever.

"Come on through then, let's eat," Mary repeated.

Steve took charge of the table and sat Matt facing Fabienne. He hadn't noticed the interplay between their guests, but was preoccupied by delight that his friend had recovered so quickly, leaving behind his celebrity worship at a stroke, by embarking on a new "ordinary" relationship. The GP had been correct all along: the psychologist recognising guilt and regret that he hadn't trusted him more. Matt was obviously trying to tell him something. However, the sight of him with this gorgeous woman in tow - what more could there be to tell? Knowing that he'd been correct in encouraging his friend to move on, and forget it.

The meal went very well. Matt was both grateful and delighted with Mary's cooking: eating with his usual gusto. Fabienne had developed, very quickly, a liking for this couple. What they lacked in physical attributes, they more than made up for in depth of personality and strength of feeling. The people she was familiar with were shallow and false in comparison. Feeling at home with them: also noting a peace and sincerity that she could see complemented Matt's personality. Crucially, it was all so far removed from the horrors she'd traversed in recent weeks. Their total acceptance that, as Matt's friend, she was their friend, being both reassuring and humbling.

Owing to the fact that Matt had been the person who'd known each person in the room before that night – he should have looked forward to a relaxing evening. Recognising that Sylvie would be made more than welcome, however, he worried about their deception. Moreover, he retained worries about failing to tell Steve what was on his mind. In revealing many of his inner-thoughts, the psychologist's words had struck home – even more so by being unequivocally, and, some would say, brutally, aired. Ultimately, Matt knew he was going to have to sit Steve down, sooner or later, and make him listen to what he had to say, although he recognised that such a pleasant evening was neither the time nor the place to do so.

Matt's instinct about bringing Fabienne had borne fruit, for it was plainly a good move. Most importantly, he could tell that she'd seen for herself the attractions of a stable, peaceful existence in their home, hopefully as she had in his. Such experiences, he believed, could only support her and rebalance her views of a world that had clearly harmed her. Despite the fact that both he and his friends were ordinary people, he couldn't help but believe that such views were nevertheless more closely aligned with her own, than those who'd surrounded her until very recently.

Mary was deeply impressed by Sylvie; she felt delighted for Matt, but the more she looked, the more curious she became. There was something that wasn't quite right between them, and she couldn't quite penetrate exactly what it was. She doubted that it was something terminal: for no one could feign that delight of being in each other's company; she could only hope she'd meet this young woman again.

Steve, for his part, was delighted to see his friend restored, and was oblivious to the undercurrents that his wife's perspicacity had detected. Under normal conditions Steve would have quickly detected many of the clues that Mary had amassed all evening, yet for each of the four, and for different reasons, there was very little that was straightforward. Undoubtedly, each shared the comfort at being in the others' company, but deeper thoughts, that each held privately, made further deliberation, at best, indistinct.

Three hours had passed so quickly. Mary and Steve were seeing them reluctantly to the door.

"Matt, it's been too long, please don't leave it this long again," Mary said genuinely.

"I won't, Mary, I promise. In fact, give me a week or two, to find my feet, and I'll have you both round to me. Thanks for the lovely food."

"My pleasure, Matt, and we'll look forward to that. Will you still be staying with Matt, Sylvie?"

There it was again, an awkward pause accompanied by the glance in his direction. None of the delicate, almost hesitant interplay between them was lost on Mary.

"Oh no. I'll be back at work then, besides I am not sure that Matt could stand any more of my cooking!" Fabienne said awkwardly.

Mary saw it for what it was; a reply that had been hastily assembled, but Matt squirmed uncomfortably beside her.

"Mary, it's so nice to have met you and many thanks for inviting me," Fabienne said much more confidently.

Mary hugged first Matt, then Sylvie." I do hope we see you again," she offered honestly; Fabienne's agreement genuine. Mary noticed, once again, that she shot a slightly nervous glance at Matt as they moved towards the door. Steve was effusive and gave her a long hug.

"You leave that poor woman alone, before I call the police," Mary said.

"Matt, you old dog, you leave me speechless: and this beautiful woman, so pleased to have met you."

Steve had drunk a little more than was wise, but was never less than his usual affable self - if a slightly more loquacious one. Mary stopped him before he could say too much: their guests being allowed to depart.

Matt offered again the strong arm as they descended the slope to the car, so that she didn't slip on the drive; now wet with a little rain. As the car slowly slipped by gravity back down the path and onto the road, where Matt engaged drive, they waved through the open windows.

"So, Sylvie, what do you think of my friends?" he asked curiously.

"What a lovely couple. Steve can get a bit carried away, but he's really nice. They look so good together. Matt, what was Steve saying to you in the kitchen, things seemed a little awkward? " She had been bursting all evening to ask her question.

"Yes, Steve had been worried about me some weeks ago."

"Yes go on," her level of curiosity now rising, not otherwise.

"Oh, nothing more to say. Let's say that the situation was resolved and I just wanted to know if he was mad at me."

"Mad at you or worried about you?" she asked.

"More worry, than anger I guess," he confirmed.

"So, go on, why was he worried?" she continued.

"Oh, something about meeting Fabienne in Salford Quays," he admitted.

"So, was he not in favour?"

"No: I suppose not," he replied.

"So why was that?" She could sense that Matt was tensing, just a little, and she didn't wish to push things too far and spoil what had been such a pleasant evening. Rather than pursue the subject with him at this time, she decided it would be more diplomatic to offer him an escape route. "Well, I suppose it was a lot of money, even for a new-Jag-GP," she interjected mercifully.

"Yes, I suppose so," he laughed, more with relief than anything, at not having to clarify the true reasons for Steve's concern.

She continued, "*and* my cover held up really well."

"I think that in many ways they were quite easy to convince, as they're not up-to-the-minute pop fans," he suggested incautiously.

"They had two CDs of mine. That's two more than you," she informed him quietly, still grappling with the reason why this should be so: making a mental note that there were now two matters to revisit when things were a little more opportune.

"So did you enjoy yourself?" Matt asked, quickly changing the subject.

She paused for a moment. How could she not have enjoyed herself? Once again, she had been transported from a world of double-dealing and a place where commercial priorities reigned over people, and certainly over their feelings. Having been allowed to escape for several hours, she couldn't express her gratitude to him and his friends nearly well enough, for that deliverance. At least she could see that there was a real world; a world where people were genuine, meant what they said and expressed true feelings: rather than ones that looked good, or were just expedient at that time, not earnestly held.

"Matt I had a super time - the time of my life," she said, as if in a clear-sighted moment.

Her unexpected words made him pause. He'd read much of her lifestyle; the trips to the South of France, and many more exotic destinations; the multi-million pound villas and yachts she frequented, and the people she'd be seen with, at those venues. He hadn't expected her to describe tonight in such terms.

"Thank you for taking me," she said with a simple humility.

One of those expectant silences opened between them. Had this been a normal relationship, the girl would perhaps have taken the opportunity to hug or kiss her consort at that moment. Both shifted a little uncomfortably on the warm leather of their seats. He risking an amorous glance in her direction, sensing that she'd glanced away a second earlier. Fortunately, the darkness granted some immunity from their discomfort, while each thought quickly of a way to re-join a conversation that would be appropriate.

"Well, I'm so pleased; and I thought it would do you good," he said hastily.

Matt steered the car homeward. Habitually, at this time of night, the Jag seemed even smoother than during the day. Something about the still night, the cold air coming into the intakes, the calming influence of the all-pervading night; all conjoined to make the journey effortless and as smooth as contact with a road could be. Their progress was measured by the car speeding past the cats' eyes, as the beam from the headlight caught them; serving as countdown markers to a journey that he wished would never end. A rabbit hopped to the verge and was held mesmerised by the headlights. Matt saw it in time to flick the steering enough to avoid it, the car giving a temporary lurch in its otherwise smooth progress. They reached home, after what seemed a fleeting moment in time.

"Come on, would you like a cup of tea?" he asked as he placed the kettle on the boiling plate after filling it with water. She sat a little precariously on the stool, his pulse kicking as she had to hitch the skirt just a little to get on. He placed the tea in front of her.

"You're lucky to have such friends," she reasoned; as she drew comparison with her own friends.

He sensed the failure, and the danger for her, in that comparison.

"We're perhaps more simple folk than the ones you'll be used to Sylvie, but I'm sure your friends are no worse for that, just different."

His kindness, as usual, was tuned in to help her avoid painful confrontation with her recent experiences.

"They seem so much in love and so compatible with each other: do you think that's rare?" she probed, as if faced with a situation of which she had absolutely no experience.

"Truth is, they *are* comfortable with each other, and they're not looking for anything else. They don't have the greenback fever that many people have, they don't look at the telly and ask, why we haven't got that? What do they call it? Ah yes, the constant inflation of desire. They're happy with what they have - and I don't think, by and large, they look round and want, want, want. They haven't got the worry of what I call the lottery-winning scenario destroying their lives."

"How do you mean?" she queried.

"Okay, here we go. Joe Public wins five million on the lottery. He swears it won't change him, and I'm sure he means it. But overnight he's richer by five million, and whether we accept it or not, that's a pretty life-changing experience. If not for Joe, then certainly, for all those around him. All his workmates are jealous, and they want a piece of him or of the money. His relatives will also want a bit of a slice and - of course - his girlfriend, and his best friend, and so on. Not forgetting all those who are quite happy to write to him and beg him for a few bob.

Joe continues at his job at the smoother ball-bearing factory, or wherever. His mates have changed, because they're now working with the man who's a multi-millionaire. Suddenly, 'Oh they've changed: they aren't my mates any more: I'm going to retire. Also this old house, it's a bit small, could do with one with a pool table. I need to move.' Joe moves to a nice posh area. All his neighbours hate him because he's just a working man with loads of money, and they've had to scrimp and save to get there - they earned it: he was just lucky. It's mainly jealousy, of course, but all his friends desert him: meanwhile he's surrounded by acquaintances who just want what crumbs fall off his table, rather than because they're interested in him. Sooner or later poor Joe doesn't know which way's up from down. Everything he's ever known and every person he's ever known, including his relatives, of course, are now very different people - and he's surrounded by people who aren't friends and not genuine. As I say, this scenario could destroy you, not make you happy: far from it."

"I suppose it's a bit like me really?" she considered. It was another comparison he hadn't intended to make, but he couldn't stop it now, nor deflect it. She continued, "People around me are especially wealthy; they can go anywhere and do anything. Trouble is, if they don't need to work, they get bored. Spending a few months of the year in Cannes or Monte Carlo, even, will lose its shine in the end. Some of us have had to work very hard in the past just to get there, or to stay in the running, but after a while, the constant striving is too much of a hassle, and they get fed up. 'Why should I get up, when I don't have to; why should I do that, when I don't like it; or put myself out?' In no time their lives lose purpose too, as well as that hunger to succeed; that drive, that each of us needs to keep us on our toes – the best we can be. What goals does a person have who's worth a hundred million? Because of boredom, they try other ways of putting back a little excitement in their lives. 'I'm worth a whole lot of money: I should be having a really good time, so why am I not?' Then they move on to too much drink, start the drugs, or lots of bonking; or all of those things. Probably worse than any of these, is the star who hasn't kept up, but still has a load of conceit. 'Do you know who I am? I am fantastic. I don't have to try hard, or bring out new songs, the old ones will do, and so what if I turn up drunk – I'm a star aren't I?' So where do they go from there?"

"Well, I'm afraid I can't answer that - buy a bigger Jag?" he suggested.

"Yes, very well," she nodded by way of recognition, "but even that wears off sooner or later - so now, you buy a bigger

Jag - and what then, you find you're still bored or your bigger Jag still makes a bit of a noise when it goes over a pothole, so you think 'I'll get a Rolls', only that's a bit slow, or whatever. You're striving for perfection, an ideal that can't be found - eventually your life has no meaning and you, too, are surrounded by people who weren't as honest or as trustworthy as you thought."

The use of the past tense was not lost on him. "So what's the answer?" he asked.

"Well, no use asking me for answers," she admitted, with more cheer than she would have done a day or two before; "but I suppose, set yourself goals, and when it doesn't seem like fun anymore, get out, and do something else. Oh, and of course, most important, don't do the lottery: it could really ruin your day!"

Matt knew that she did lots of other things, her charity work for instance, but he wondered if she were now so damaged that she could never see herself returning to that life. Tomorrow, after a night's sleep on both sides, he would have to ask her, because he sensed that she too recognised that the time was approaching when she'd have to face the torment that was her own life, and decide how much was salvageable. There was a trace of sadness across her face as she spoke about the lives being led by her contemporaries. However, even when discussing such difficult things with him she seemed much more resilient, and there was no trace of tears in those eyes of living crystal that were now sparkling with resurgent intensity. Sitting facing her on another stool, they sipped their tea: few words were spoken, but each was thinking furiously, turning over the day's events. Eventually gathering tiredness and a desire to seek solitude, to clarify some of those thoughts in her mind, made Fabienne bid him a good night.

Remaining for a short while in the kitchen: he then went to sit in the lounge and put some music on, with the volume turned down very low. As she settled in bed she thought she could hear music being played very quietly. At first, she didn't recognise the artist. It must have been a very old CD, which, unlike more recent works like hers, he seemed very fond of. Eventually, she made out the artist and the track as Cat Stevens' *How Can I tell you?* She drifted off to sleep as she pieced the words together, and wondered if his moods were reflected by the choice of music he played. She would have to find time to ask him that, too. His own thoughts had made him restless, the music exerted its usual calming influence as he listed to Cat Stevens' *Teaser and the Firecat,* but eventually he too, succumbed to increasing tiredness and he went upstairs.

The following morning, he rose early, as usual. He didn't see her before he left, for she was evidently still asleep: he crept carefully out of the house and drove to work. The steady influx of new patients meant that surgeries were a little busier, and he was glad that Greg, the new partner, was starting soon. A quiet revolution had taken place at Matt's practice, but at a breathless pace. The surgery, however, was much more efficient. New staff had been interviewed, appointed and were starting in the next month; the new partner's imminent arrival, meant that everything had been looked at, and new working methods set in place. Without doubt, the new computer was already starting to deliver some of those efficiencies, as were other things that accompanied it; like electronic mail and the transmission of pathology reports. Blood tests taken in the morning would now come back that afternoon. Under the old system, results could only be delivered that quickly if marked 'urgent': routine samples taking several days.

The building schedule had been finalised and the portable accommodation was to be delivered the week after next. Greg Stevens visited several times just to make sure that he was familiar with things. Neither he nor Matt wanted him to be dropped in at the deep end. Janice somehow made sure that she was in work whenever he was due to appear, and would always be on hand to help him in whatever way possible. She had begged Mrs Simpson to change her rota at the last minute; offering to work all through Christmas for the next five years, if she could swap her rotas in this way!

Matt missed Fabienne at lunch time. She left him a note to say that she had driven over to see Mary with a 'thank you' card for the previous evening and some flowers for their anniversary. Matt couldn't help but wonder if the conversation would expand a little, and smiled as he did so. Fabienne was certainly curious about him and about his life: having a penchant for bumping in to his old girlfriends, so that she could embarrass him later. Having nothing to hide, he was happy for her to do this, even if she seemed to delight in making him squirm just a little: for, at least, it stopped her brooding on events back in her own life. He knew, however, that Mary, without doubt, would have a lot to tell her if the conversation did stray in this direction.

The afternoon surgery was very quiet. Janice was wearing make-up and her hair had been beautifully cut at Stella's. Matt reasoned this could only mean that Greg had telephoned to say that he was going to pop round. The two GPs spent a long time together in the consulting room going over future plans, drawing up rotas and talking a little of financial matters. Janice found it necessary on three occasions to interrupt them, and Matt could only smile to himself on each occasion that she did so. Greg seemed oblivious to her on these appearances; but the third occasion - when she practically deposited the cup of tea on his knee - did produce a flicker of recognition bordering on interest. No doubt Janice would read quite a lot into that, and take heart that at last he'd noticed her. Certainly her interest in Greg was not lost on any of the staff at the surgery. The way she hung on every word that he uttered: her habit of appearing seconds after he did, and the fact that even the slightest query was either answered or actioned within seconds! Matt concluded that a little romance in his surgery would probably raise efficiency and morale, all round. Even Mrs Simpson had started to talk about her husband with sentences that no longer contained the usual words 'lazy' and 'good-for-nothing', but far more emollient, even endearing terms. He could only hope that re-focussing on her own marriage would reduce some of her interest in other's relationships, including his.

Before leaving for the evening Matt telephoned Fabienne to say that he had bought a Chinese takeaway, and not to bother cooking. She seemed a little disappointed, but he did his best to provide a covering excuse, telling her that Mr Chan, his patient, had offered him the meal and he didn't have the heart to refuse. This account was not widely at variance with the truth, as Mr Chan always gave Matt extras in his carrier bag, that he'd discover when he got home, and which weren't charged for.

They chatted as they ate. She told him about visiting Mary who'd been delighted with the flowers that she'd taken. "Matt, she's a remarkable woman. We got on really well."

Matt could only agree. He and Mary had dated long before she married Steve. As soon as she met Steve, Matt having introduced them, he could see without a doubt that she was really in love with him, almost from the moment that she'd set eyes on him. Matt knew it, as did she. Steve and he were already good friends from medical school. There was a little awkwardness before Matt found the courage to confront her. Moreover, his relationship with Mary had for the most part been platonic. All parties were relieved that it was out in the open; Matt withdrew, thereby allowing the two to start dating. Six months later, at their wedding, he was best man.

Though Matt didn't voice this to Fabienne, he wondered what they'd talked about. Certainly the choice of topics would be pretty vast. Making no attempt to pry, he knew Fabienne well enough by now, that she would tell him if and when she was ready: incautious enquiries of his would be met by the engaging but mischievous streak that was coming increasingly to the fore as each day passed. Sensing more than a hint of awkwardness within her as she paused: seeming a little embarrassed, as if she were about to reveal something. Certainly this wasn't what he'd expected. Eventually he could bear it no longer. "Sylvie, go on, just tell me."

She laughed. "Mary knew there was something going on; she just couldn't put her finger on it. She discussed it with Steve last night as they went to bed and he, of course, had noticed nothing: men! I knew that Mary was especially curious about me, but also about our relationship - me and you - if you see? "

He nodded, not having noticed, but he wasn't surprised. Mary was one of the most perceptive people he'd ever known: he recognised that Fabienne shared many of those skills; perhaps this was why they got along as well as they did.

"I hope you don't mind; I just came out and told her who I was."

"What did she say?"

"Well, let's just say, she wasn't expecting to hear that!" she said, the delight still in her voice. "She laughed and laughed when she got over the shock, and couldn't wait to tell Steve."

Mat swallowed hard at this point, his heart now racing: he wondered how Steve would view this latest revelation. He knew that both had seemed delighted to meet his new 'girlfriend'. Having felt the lash of Steve's anger, however, his anxiety levels rose precipitously as he desperately tried to hide this from Fabienne.

"Sylvie, did you tell Mary how you came to be here?"

"Yes, I think she was most surprised by my explanation. For some reason she thought that you'd phoned me - of all things!" she said incredulously.

"Well, fancy that. I wonder how she could come to that conclusion," Matt said, doing his best to recreate the surprised tones of Fabienne's sentence, rather than those of sheer relief.

"I don't know, she didn't say why she thought that at first. Anyway, I told her how I turned up on your doorstep. The Travelodge was full, and so on."

"Oh, full was it! That's not what you told me," feigning damaged pride.

"We had a long, long talk, and we spent a wonderful afternoon. She told me about the two of you. Said you were marvellous; just came out and asked her one day. I bet that wasn't easy. So, how did you feel about being given up for Steve?"

"Sylvie, it happens," he admitted.

"Not often, I bet", she probed mischievously.

"That, I'm not going to say." Hoping the simple words would somehow cap her interest: but he also knew that once those crystal blue eyes were upon him, there wasn't a thing he wouldn't tell her were she to ask, and not a request that he wouldn't grant, if she were so desirous. Still, her curiosity about him continued unabated.

He continued, "I could tell they were meant to be together and it seemed churlish of me to get upset, or jealous, or whatever. They looked so good together, how could I possibly stand in the way of their destiny?"

"She thinks the world of you; you know that," she said, as she continued to survey him: more surprises awaited her at each turn, whenever his name arose. She considered as she looked at him: that he had loved Mary wasn't in doubt. The intensity and character of that love was harder for her to define. It might well have been more of a platonic relationship that one might show to a mother or sister, but that in no way devalued what she must have meant to him.

Matt wasn't at all sure that he could admit to himself, let alone to this beguiling woman, who seemed able to look into his life and some of his very thoughts, that he'd loved Mary for one very simple reason. She could see beyond the physical attributes of a person and into their very quintessence. This was why she'd chosen Steve, and not him. He could only wish that one day he could summon the words and the courage to be able to say that to him: having assumed that he held this knowledge deep within. More recent events, however, cast doubt on this theory.

"They seem really pleased to have you as a friend, each of them." She moved the focus of conversation just a little, sensing that she'd embarrass him if she persisted down that route.

"I know that I can count them both as my friends, so I guess I am the lucky one."

"Yes, I think you are," she agreed.

She went quiet again as if deep in thought. Perhaps she was reflecting on all the things that underpinned his life, here in Perrilymm, as compared to all the things that were missing in her own.

"Sylvie, I've been meaning to ask," he paused and looked uncomfortable.

It was her turn to say, "Matt, go on, just tell me."

"Have you had any thoughts about your future strategy?"

Looking suddenly crestfallen, she said, "Matt, oh I'm so sorry: I promised you it would only be for a day or two. I knew I must be getting in the way."

"No, Sylvie that is *not* what I mean," he beamed at her bemusedly. "I told you that you could stay as long as you want, and that promise holds good. The reason I'm asking was simply whether you'd had any thoughts about your career? I know it's a bit soon, but a spot of planning, working out a strategy, won't hurt."

"What do you have in mind?" she asked, brightening visibly.

"Well, you won't want to hide here forever, or they'll know that you're really hurt badly. You need to think about getting back; that'll hurt them the most. I'd sue the pants off the two tabloids that published those lies about you. You must surely have a good case, and go for punitive damages: perhaps offer the proceeds to charities, assuming you don't need the money that is."

Her face was neutral, but she was listening intently. "Select a children's charity or one that researches mental health." She never talked about money. This was one of the things that so impressed him. It seemed that she, like him, had reached the conclusion that money was by no means an essential component of happiness: no amount of it could create that state, if really precious things were missing, or in danger of being lost.

"Good. Like that, Matt, go on," she nodded enthusiastically.

"You need to be seen to be coming out fighting. This'll hit them where it hurts, in their pockets, and also demonstrate to the world that they've underestimated you," he continued animatedly. "Launch your new CD, the one you put on hold. Restart the tour. If that's what you want?" He paused again: hoping desperately at this point that she'd say that wasn't what she wanted, that she was going to delay her departure, perhaps indefinitely. Certainly he wanted to scream at her to stay, with the same uncontrollable urge he felt when she'd walked away in Luciano's - which he'd only just managed to hold in check. Similar forces were building within him now.

Logic stepped in, as then, to restrain his impulses. Knowing only that, despite the thoughts that continued to pass across his brain like clouds on a stormy day, he could, and would, never ask her to stay. How could he allow selfish desire, strong though it was, to interfere with another's life of which he knew so little? Realising that sacrificing her usual life at the behest of another, could only cause resentment sooner or later, and perhaps even hatred for the person who'd asked for that change. He accepted that he could no more ask this of her than suspend the moon's rotation about the earth.

"I'm not sure what I want," she said uncertainly. She was aware that he wasn't trying to force her hand, but she knew, too, that she couldn't hide forever. He seemed perfectly genuine in his comment that she could stay for as long as she wished, but just how long would that be in practice, if she were to take him up on it? A further week perhaps: or a month; a year? Reasoning instinctively that the trauma that she'd been through, could best be healed by taking each moment and each day, one step at a time.

They continued to talk for some time; then deciding to take a short walk along the river. As they did so, the day faded and dusk gathered. The moon appeared large and hazy at first, just on the horizon, but soon rose and sharpened into a textured, silver disc that seemed to punch out a well-demarcated hole in the gathering blackness of night. They returned to the house, as the ground quickly gave up the heat that had been gifted ceaselessly by the sun, and a chill gathered about the air. She made him a cup of tea before bidding him a good night. Though tiredness had steadily crept up on her, she sensed that more than sleep; she needed time alone, in which to think.

The moon continued to rise into a clear, still night as owls awoke to begin the search for food to nourish themselves and their young; the occasional screech or hoot indicating their presence in the impenetrable darkness. She brushed her teeth, changed, and slipped below the soft duvet. Smiling to herself, she wondered whether Matt had washed and ironed that duvet, or if some ex-conquest were still on hand to provide that service: having seen, first-hand that ironing was not his strong point.

It was a restless, but not unproductive night. Her mind retraced some of her steps as far back as she felt comfortable, in an effort to plan her future strategy. She'd arrived, unannounced on his doorstep, having run out of places to hide and people whom she could trust. Her desire to escape had been as acute and as pressing as someone needing to vacate a burning house: Matt had accepted that and her presence, without hesitation or precondition. Just what lay in those eyes as he turned away? Though she had seen the look of pure sexual desire on men's faces before, Matt had made no attempt to take advantage of her vulnerable and weakened state - when many would have tried to do just that. The appreciative looks being more welcome than lecherous or intrusive. Having experienced her share of men undressing her with their eyes; she conceded that only a proportion of her fans would be there for her voice, or her dancing routines, alone: others would be more attracted by the revealing apparel that she and so many pop stars of her generation wore, and it was part of her work, whether she liked it or not.

What had Steve been whispering to him in the kitchen, and just why had Mary diverted the conversation quickly but discreetly? One day, she hoped that she'd be able to seek answers from Matt, face to face. The other question nagging at her was why, when he assured her that he was a great fan, did he not possess a single CD or DVD of hers in the house? It didn't matter to her, she tried to assure herself, one way or another, but if that was the case why did he simply not just admit to never having bought one in his life?

Try as she might, the pieces wouldn't quite fit for her at this point, and her strategy in such situations was one beloved by Matt - pull back and try a different line of thought. She turned to her own future. Decisions here were a little easier to encapsulate, and long before the dawn chorus, she'd formulated a plan of her own. Despite the long night, she was keen to gauge Matt's views; rising to catch him, before he left for the surgery.

CHAPTER IX

FOUND AND LOST

Sun streamed into the conservatory. Matt had opened the windows and roof ventilation, but more relief eventually came from a few dark, lazy clouds, which blotted out the sun's uncomfortable heat. Sitting facing him in a business-like way, she'd been thinking for much of the night: now being keen to express her thoughts and sample his opinions.

"Matt, I've been thinking."

He put down the newspaper to give her his undivided attention. Anticipating that the conversation in which he was about to be engaged was of significant moment, as she clearly had pressing matters to discuss.

"Do you know how it all started?" she asked.

Having read so much about her for so long, he knew much of what, he guessed, she was about to tell him. He recognised, however, that the question was more rhetorical and his chosen response, therefore was simply to nod and say, "Go on", exactly the line he would take with a patient, anxious to get something off their chest.

"My Mum and Dad divorced when I was five. Mum went back to France, and my Dad stayed in the Midlands. I spent a lot of my school holidays and weekends in airport lounges, waiting for connecting flights, one way or the other. I must've been about fifteen. They were running this karaoke competition, a bit of a laugh, at Manchester airport. Anyway, I stood up and started singing this song that I knew."

Matt continued to listen attentively: he didn't interrupt, nor did he reveal that he knew what that song was.

"Well, the machine broke half way through, the backing track died off, leaving just me, solo. I carried on singing. A record producer just happened to be passing through the foyer at that time, and had stopped to listen, like a few other people. They usually say, at this point that the rest is history, but that isn't quite right. Since then it's been constant hard work, tours, learning dance sequences, writing some of my own material, buying some in and, of course, rehearse, rehearse and rehearse again. People think you just stand up there and sing. They don't see the work that has to go in beforehand, to make it look effortless, to make it look as if it's just second nature.

For sure, they don't see the creeps, the hangers-on and the sycophants around you. These weeks, I've discovered that there were more of those than I'd reckoned: people who'd switch loyalty so quickly that Judas himself would be surprised. But this is what I do; this is what I like to think I do well, and I don't want a few newspaper hacks telling me that the fat lady is about to sing and destroy the life and the career that I've built from that beginning."

Though her night had achieved little in the way of rest, it had caused a simple conclusion to form from the wide-ranging thoughts and tumultuous dreams that had passed before her. She believed that her next step had to be to fight for the career that had made up almost her entire adult life. Only then would she be able to formulate whether this would be enough for her in the years ahead; or to seek a different direction. She drew strength from the realisation that she was no longer at the mercy of the incalculable. "So I want to fight for it back. How does that sound to you?"

His own advice would have been along similar lines. What was the alternative? Simply to retire hurt, and never be in the public eye again? It was unlikely that the tabloids would realise, or feel in any way responsible for, their contribution to her fall. The only regret they were likely to feel was that they'd have to move on to another target, and then only after posting the usual story about the ex-pop star, shopping for a pair of tights in Sainsbury's, or similar. Hearing her declare her intentions in this way, also gave him focus, and stopped the restless thoughts which he realised were ultimately selfish ones, based on his needs, not hers. He looked at her face, set rigid in an intensity of concentration. This was the correct strategy for her career, for her life and ultimately, he suspected, her happiness. Promising himself, in that instant, that he wouldn't allow misplaced desire to countenance any other measure.

"Okay, Sylvie, welcome back. I agree; I think you should go for it, or you'll forever wonder, and though I don't believe it's a personal thing for them, your retirement would be seen by some as a sort of vindication, in a warped way, of their stance."

"Right then, Matt, can I pass this by you?" She outlined her strategy to him. He listened carefully, as she explained her thoughts, making suggestions where he could, and nodding supportively as they agreed the plan of action.

He knew this wouldn't be easy. He guessed that she was wealthy enough to retire, even though the tabloids had published full details of the owners of the concerts taking Fabienne to court, who were seeking to recover their losses and sue for breach of contract. This was given more momentum when venues had been cancelled with little or no notice. Knowing, too, that such retirement would have the same effect on her as never taking breath again. He understood the difficulties at *Brite Lite Entertainment*, her management company, and after his covert investment he hadn't dared to look at the share price. Looking at her as she finished, he paused in careful study. Right from their first meeting he'd discovered that she wasn't some empty shell, pretty on the outside but with no substance within. Newspapers would be wrong to underestimate her; in fact by doing so they'd only sweetened the potential satisfaction in making a return – if, she could just pull it off. Ultimately, he concluded that every aspect of her inner strength, her courage, her desire to succeed and even her faith, if only in herself, would be tested – he could only hope not to the point of destruction. He smiled, his face brimming with pride in her as he spoke.

It was her turn to look away, the crystal becoming suddenly moist on seeing his response as the deep blue gazed at her.

"Sylvie, I'm so proud of you. I know it's a bit soon, but I think you'll be ready when the time comes. I'll get to work: you make the calls."

The distraught and desperate young woman, he'd found on his doorstep just a few days ago was gone: in her place he saw increasingly the confident one he'd met in that restaurant all those weeks ago. The eyes were no less attractive, but now a much deeper shade, reflecting the determination written to her whole expression while she contemplated the not inconsequential obstacles that lay in her way; and the memories that were strewn in her wake.

Despite the warm summer's day, the gentleman in the khaki-coloured Mac pulled the belt a little tighter, as he waited in Merton train station car park. He always wore this coat because of its ample pockets, which could carry a variety of cameras, binoculars, high-powered microphones, recording machines and, of course, his mobile phone and handheld computer. A story or a photograph could be on its way within seconds, bound for the highest bidder, anywhere in the world.

He knew the four people he'd followed, very well. That was precisely the reason for following them in the first place - the fact that he knew who they were, and the person that they were, most probably, on their way to meet. Naively they thought that by parking their nondescript Ford Mondeo in the station car park, and then by calling a taxi, they could elude any follower.

"Soddin' amateurs," he said to himself under his breath.

Though holding them in contempt, his career depended on such people: they were easy to follow and just when they thought they were safe, there he would be with his camera and 'click' another scoop would be on its way. Such people always underestimated him, his resilience, his hard work and his desire to get that scoop at any cost. He loved this game; he just wished he could see their faces when they appeared in one of his spreads, the following day. Bitterness, jealousy and spite, especially toward those he believed had no right to the exalted lifestyles they led, had made him restive, determined and, when coupled to his long hours, extremely dangerous to the celebrities he liked to debase. His emotional range varied from taciturn to aggressive, and each of his limited moods had a core of menace that he gave off readily in a wide variety of situations. Often working alone: over the years this had created a modus operandi of thinking out loud and self-praise, which was invariably applied to gratify his own vanity. Laughing again, to himself, as his powerful digital camera was brought to bear and his quarries photographs' were captured, with neither sound nor flash.

"Bloody, soddin' amateurs," he said to himself again, as he fired off a few more shots.

The taxi arrived, just as he knew it would. They all piled in as quickly as they could.

"That's right, mi darlin's, you jump in quick, all nice and safe in case that nasty reporter is followin' you. Too bloody late, mi darlin's: I'm gonna have you lot, ''n 'er when you've led me to 'er."

He spat quickly in the general direction of the pavement, and stubbed out his cigarette. A little girl, out walking her dog, had unwittingly strayed into what he considered to be his space. Glaring at her menacingly, he caused her to pull the dog towards her in a defensive reaction while attempting to hurry past. Then, pulling on the battered car door precipitously; with neglectful disdain as to whether the girl or the dog would be hit, as it swung wide open. The engine started at first bidding and, without bothering with his seatbelt, or the whereabouts of the little girl hurrying past, he wrenched the wheel quickly so that the car thudded off the kerb and on to the road.

"Now, just follow the taxi, mi old son," he said to himself, in a self-congratulatory tone. The taxi went about ten miles: they were never out of his sight. "Like takin' candy from a bleedin' baby," he continued as he steadied the wheel just a little while he lit up again. "I'll soon 'ave yer, yer bleedin' amateurs: and there you'll be mi old son with another scoop." He stretched over in order to preen himself in the rear-view mirror, as if rehearsing the accolades that would come his way: the car swerving wildly as he did so. The taxi pulled into a large medical centre. Parking his car quickly, he got out to gain a vantage point. The four vacated the taxi; the older gentleman paying the driver, before they all hurried inside quickly. "No use hidin' in there, yer bastards, I've got yer now, and Jim ain't gonna let yer out of 'is sight. Time for back up," he said, again to himself. "Hello Bill, it's me, Jim. Got her; she's in this medical centre, Parkvale it's called. Send backup so we can scoop 'er when she comes out."

Bill Wetherly was the features editor of the *Sunday Scoop*. He punched the air. Jim Duggan never let him down. "Knew you'd do it Jim, if anyone could."

"No problem, easy pissin' peesy - just remember me bleedin' bonus like ye promised, eh."

"Counting it as we speak, Jim mi boy," said Bill.

Jim moved over to stand by the main entrance, his camera within his grasp, but in his pocket, charged and waiting. Knowing that she wouldn't escape him now: he'd spent too long looking, to let some toff girl beat him. "Like a spider to the fly, come on out, mi darlin'. Just time for another cig I reckon, Jim, mi old son."

Jim, in his haste, didn't see an immaculate blue Jaguar glide by behind him; the three-litre engine gurgled temporarily through the twin exhausts as it negotiated the last speed bump, slowly picking up effortless speed. The four people waited for a couple more cramped minutes, as they bent down as far as they could, into the front and rear footwells. Finally, Matt then gave them the all-clear as he saw, receding into his rear view mirror, the man in the khaki mac, keeping vigil by the front door.

"Okay, should be safe to sit up now," he suggested. The gearbox selected another ratio, the engine growling for an instant as the speed whipped up. One person, however, did notice the metallic blue X-Type and its distinctive personalised plate. Rita turned agitatedly to Sue Hindmarch, practice manger of Parkvale medical centre, as she gazed from the first-floor common-room window.

"What's Matt Sinclair doing here?"

Sue rushed to the window. "Ooh it's that sexy Sinclair, wish he was picking me up," she drooled.

Rita looked across at her distastefully, thinking that Matt could never fancy a nonentity like Sue.

"Meeting you, what do you mean?" Rita half spat the words.

"He phoned yesterday to say that he was picking some friends up: they didn't know where he lived, and could he wait round the back while we showed them through the building and out of the rear door," Sue explained.

"Well!" Rita looked across at her with mounting impatience. "Why was I not told about this?" she demanded.

"We didn't think anyone would mind, we only showed them to the rear exit; and he did ask *very* nicely," Sue offered innocently, with just a slight emphasis on the 'very'.

"If that's the case, why didn't he pick them up at the front, then; and besides he's not that good in bed, so you can stop drooling like that," Rita insisted, her jealousy running with unremitting fervour so that the sparkle from those striking green eyes was masked, by the flow of negativity bubbling within, like smog blotting out the sun.

Sue decided that she'd welcome the chance to see first-hand if her boss's opinion of Dr Sinclair was correct or otherwise. Both women had been distracted by events and in Rita's case almost catastrophically. Believing that Matt had arranged things in this way to avoid her. Had she not been lucky, such feelings would have prevented her from discovering essential facts that she would use to her advantage in the days ahead. Events would show later, that fortune was to favour her, as she gained information that hundreds had hitherto ignored.

The Jaguar continued its steady progress, leaving Jim Duggan far behind.

"Hi everyone, I'm Matt Sinclair. We'll meet up with Fabienne in a few minutes."

Lucy Kwa leant forward from the middle seat through the gap between the front seats.

"Hello Matt, we've spoken once or twice on the telephone, I believe."

Matt, of course, remembered Lucy, Fabienne's manager's secretary. "I know everyone then, Matt so I'll do the introductions," she said. "You may remember Peter."

"Peter, ah yes, you're the guy who's good at crosswords."

A strong arm came forward to pat him on the shoulder by way of a handshake.

"Rupert Allison is my boss, Fabienne's manager."

"Hello, Matt, pleased to meet you."

"And last is Wayne Dasschler, Fabienne's choreographer."

"Hi there Matt, sure nice of you to do this."

Matt noted an unmistakeable American accent.

"How is she Matt?" came from Rupert.

"She's much better I think. She's obviously had a bad time, but her instinct now is to get her life back."

He saw the three in the rear nod, and look at each other encouragingly as they did so, a wave of relief appearing on their faces: for this was the first good news they'd heard in a long time. Though continuing to do his best to answer their questions, ultimately each person in the car realised that they would just have to form their own conclusions when they met up with her. The car covered the fifteen miles to his house in no time.

Fabienne was waiting, looking from the dining room window as the car swung into view. She came rushing out. Each in turn gave her a hug, by way of greeting, her eyes growing a little moist as they did so. Matt had no doubt that, though she had borne the brunt of the tragic events, they'd suffered along with her. They followed her into the conservatory. Rupert was obviously in a hurry, as he clearly had pressing matters that he needed to discuss with Fabienne.

"What a lovely setting," said Lucy, as she looked through the conservatory windows and to the woods beyond the large garden.

They sat at the table in the conservatory. Matt brought in a tray with coffee, cold drinks and biscuits that Fabienne was preparing when he left.

"Can I get anything else for anyone?" he asked, as he placed the tray on the table.

"No that'll be fine, that's lovely Matt," they agreed in unison.

Fabienne turned towards him as she sat at the table. "Matt, feel free to sit in with us won't you?"

"No, Sylvie, I'm sure you have a lot to discuss, so I'll go and cut my grass, paint my toenails, and wash the car, that sort of thing."

More and more, he could see the self-assured business woman's return, and he had no wish to intrude on this, or remind her of more vulnerable times. She needed to be confident and strong in front of these people, if she were to get the best co-operation and advice from them.

"Well, you know most of what I am going to say, and I'll fill you in later - so I hope your nail varnish doesn't run - that pink blush you had on yesterday, really suits you."

The four looked at each other quickly, as they saw how comfortable these two appeared in each other's company. Placing her hands on the table in front of her, signifying her determination and also indicating that she was in charge of events.

"Thank you for coming everyone, I'm sorry to have left so quickly." The pain flicked upon her face for an instant. "I just couldn't go back to that house, that room."

Lucy spoke up in an attempt to help her boss at a difficult juncture. "The police have finished their forensic examination. I've had a team of cleaners in, and I've personally removed your things. Anything that I thought had been touched, I've removed and burned. Decorators are in now, and when they've finished, the cleaners are due to go back."

Neither woman could bear to clarify even within their own minds, the condition in which Barry Miles had been found. A pause opened up that allowed each person in the room to recognise their horror, having learned just what had confronted her that night.

"Thanks so much, Lucy. I do appreciate you doing that for me. I'll be selling the house just as soon as," Fabienne said with an air of finality.

There was another pregnant pause. They all knew how much she'd loved that house, but no one was surprised to learn of her decision. Lucy spoke hesitantly, "Just let me know if there's anything, anything at all I can do, Sylvie."

Fabienne gave a little shudder, as if trying to free herself from all those painful memories: she moved on quickly. "Very well, then, Rupert. How about releasing the new CD, now that things have calmed a little?"

"Yes, it's as good a time as any, Sylvie. We're all set to roll, as soon as we've got the all clear from you. We need a bit of advertising, so we thought about buses and illuminated bus-shelter signs. One or two of the big supermarkets have agreed to co-promote it, if we offer a good price. We're planning to have several bus companies repaint their buses with our material: should get you noticed again, for all the right reasons."

"Okay then, do that, please," she nodded in agreement and asked, "are we going to use the advertising material we shot some weeks ago?"

"Yes, that'll save a lot of time," Rupert agreed. "I've also got some runs on MTV. It's expensive, but it'll raise your profile a lot for the new launch".

"I agree with you, now's the time: so *go* on that Rupert please," nodding again. "Next, *concert*." She went down a small list that she'd prepared to jog her memory. "I wondered about a re-launch in the MEN, Manchester; that'll give us eight weeks. It's going to have to be big, and I wondered if we could extend it. Back the warm-up act a little, so they play for half an hour, then I take the rest."

Wayne looked up at her; each person was furiously making notes. "That's a lot of material, Sylvie; are you sure you're up to it?"

"I've got to be, Wayne," she said simply.

Each person knew that this was true.

"No way back now," she added with finality.

"Now then, Lucy, can you liaise with the Manchester team? We'll need advertising, go for radio and broadsheets. I've had it with the tabloids, so pull all those, as soon as we can," she said, as she looked at Lucy.

The crystal was now more like ice, as she spoke those words.

"More coffee, anyone?" Matt had popped his head round the door.

"Me please," said Wayne.

Matt disappeared, to refill the percolator.

"Can I pass some other ideas by you, and see how you feel?" Rupert asked. "We've been offered a TV talk show slot. Now, are you up to that? I'll insist on vetting all the questions before it goes live. The MEN arena would have been the last of the UK tour. I was wondering about a couple of concerts in North America. Even though Pepsi Co. have pulled your ads and cancelled their sponsorship, together with most of your stateside backers, sales have held up fairly well. There might just be the slimmest of opportunities to get things back on track. I've been talking to Nichols plc who wonder if you'd do a Vimto promotion. They have a new ad campaign *'It's Stronger than it looks'* and apparently they want you."

"Yes," was the uncomplicated answer.

More than anything, the single unequivocal reply, underlined for them her strength, her determination to continue.

"Yes to what?" said Rupert.

"Yes to all," she confirmed, simply.

She continued down her list. "Lastly, the libel case."

"I've retained Mason, Hilldigger and Finkelman to represent you. They're ripping apart the *Sunday Scoop* and the *Daily Scorcher*," said Rupert.

"Yes, we avoided Jim Duggan their 'scoop man', as they call him, on our way here. We think he was the one in Luciano's," suggested Lucy.

"I should've spotted him," said Peter miserably.

"No problem," said Fabienne, as she admitted, "I shouldn't have stayed so long; you warned me, thirty minutes max."

"In summary: we've lost a lot of sponsors, and so many of our *friends* have turned their backs. It's going to be expensive, and you'll be at risk of ruin if it fails. Are you prepared for this?" warned Rupert. "If the reviews at the MEN go against us, it'll be especially bad. We can risk a slow start to the CD release, but not poor reviews from there also."

"We'll just have to make sure they don't, won't we, then?" she said with finality.

Once again the short words held more impact for them than long sentences could.

"Tell our solicitors I want them to squeeze very hard," said Fabienne.

"Injunctions forbidding them from printing anything about you, are being served now. Just as we re-launch, they won't have anything. It'll hurt them quite a bit. We're asking for punitive damages," Rupert replied.

"Fine. I'll donate half to mental disorder charities and half to children's. I want to expose them as slime, not be seen to be profiting."

Matt brought in the coffee.

"I hear you," said Rupert, "it's just that, if we do badly in the MEN, the money would be welcome."

"No Rupert; I understand what *you're* saying, but it's do or die. I fly without a wire on this one."

They saw that she was determined and not about to change her mind. They continued to talk for some time, settling finer details, so that her return would go as smoothly as possible. Even so, everything seemed to depend on the MEN concert. The consequences of its failure were not lost on anyone around that table, and least of all on Fabienne.

Jim Duggan shifted uncomfortably.

"Bleeders 'ave bin in there two hours. Must break cover soon. What are they doin' in there, anyways?"

He'd been joined by Michael, his assistant, who'd set up a tripod with a camera and long lens.

"She'll be out, you see, Jim"

"*Sunday Scoop* never fails, Jim Duggan never fails," Jim reminded his young colleague.

Matt continued to busy himself, while his guests continued to talk. Some time later Fabienne came to find him. Looking tired, however, she seemed satisfied with the day's events.

"I wonder, Matt if I could borrow your car to run them back to the station?"

"No Sylvie, I'll take them back, you're all in. You look dog-tired. First, however, I wondered about a little food?"

Whilst Fabienne was conducting her meeting, Matt had prepared a simple meal of mixed salad, together with garlic bread baguettes and an enormous dish of lasagne, cooked in the largest roasting tray that his Aga would accommodate. Peter had wandered into the kitchen after Fabienne.

"Can I interest anyone in some food before you go?" Matt asked the appreciative group. They all sat and ate enthusiastically, but in near-silence as they each reflected on the items discussed at their meeting, and the strategy that had been outlined and agreed. Each person knew their precise role and the role of others. Half an hour later Matt was driving the four visitors back to the station to collect their car.

"It's kind of you to do this, Matt," said Lucy.

"It's also good of you to look after her in this way. I'm sure a lot of her recovery has been due to you," interjected Rupert.

"Thanks for that, but she's a remarkable woman and I'm amazed at her resilience and fight."

"We all know that," agreed Peter.

A short time later the station came into view. Matt saw them out of the car, shook their hands and bade them a safe journey. Returning to his car, he began retracing his steps, without lingering.

Back at the medical centre, the car park had steadily emptied as patients had come and gone, and staff started to leave for the day. Both newsmen continued to wait: the cold associated with inactivity had crept upon them, despite the warm afternoon. A red sports car stopped just next to them and the power window opened.

"Just what do you think you're doing here?" Rita said abrasively.

"We know she's in there," challenged Jim.

"Who?" she asked, looking puzzled.

"Fabienne, of course, and don't try tellin' us otherwise, darlin', we know, we ain't stupid," snarled Jim.

Their words died an uneasy death on her facial expression. Looking straight through them; she shouted, "Idiots!" and closed the window with dismissive disfavour, driving off rapidly as though she couldn't bear their very sight: a cloud of sulphurous exhaust smoke appearing because the catalyst hadn't had the chance to heat through.

"We've been rumbled son. Back to the station, quick," said Jim, hurriedly.

Packing up the tripod and camera quickly, they stowed everything in Jim's battered car. Michael left his, even shabbier, car at the medical centre to save time. Jim drove like a maniac. They made the distance to the station very quickly, arriving just in time to see the Mondeo pick up speed on to the dual carriageway, bound for the motorway south.

"Drat; bastards 'ave got away, given us the bleedin' slip they 'ave."

"No scoop then Jim?" Michael asked dully.

"No soddin' scoop, you prat," Jim confirmed, as he clipped Michael on the back of the head in recognition of his voicing the painful truth that confronted both men.

Fabienne was waiting for Matt as he returned.

"So, Sylvie, do you think it went well?"

"Yes, as well as I could expect," she replied.

"And how do you feel about things?"

"I'm very scared. It's all riding on the concert in Manchester. I'm not sure I can do it."

It had seemed so easy, to slip back into her professional mode when her friends had been there. Now they'd gone, a crisis of confidence had made its uncomfortable presence felt, and she was looking very shaky and nervous.

"You can do this, Sylvie, I know," he suggested, calmly. "I've never seen you give a bad performance yet, and I've seen a few," he continued unwarily. Feeling worry on her behalf, he searched desperately for words that would insulate her from the traumas within.

"That's what *you* say," she said accusingly. Self-doubt had extended its influence, and she had to bite back hard to prevent herself from asking him if he'd ever been to *one* of her concerts. Sensing her turmoil and what it was doing to her, he continued calmly.

"Do you remember your concert in Glasgow 2006? Right at the very end: you chose *Love so Late,* as your closing number; you sang to the hushed crowd. There was a little tear in your eye: there wasn't a dry eye in the house. Anyone who can do that to fifty thousand Glaswegians can't fail."

Staring back at him, she felt very guilty for her expostulation. All was not done. He reached the drawer behind where he was sitting and pulled out a magazine. He tossed the glossy in front of her.

"Remember this? This is the only one I kept, of hundreds, believe me."

The deep blue surveyed her earnestly, though she still couldn't quite meet his gaze. The article was entitled *Act of Mercy* and, as usual, with all the magazines Matt had purchased, she was on the cover. Looking at it without speaking, she was glad of the chance to look away again from his steady gaze.

"That children's home: it was going to close with debts of two million. Did you know, *Sylvie*?" there was slight emphasis on her name, "that a mysterious benefactor intervened to save it, not with two million, but it says in here, five. Five million pounds donated just like *that*," he clicked his fingers. She gave a little jump at the sound. "It was about the time that you ran an extra concert in your World 2007 tour, I believe. Rumour held that the person who gave that fortune was a *superstar*, someone who could pull in capacity crowds at the click of her fingers, and at short notice. This article says that that person donated the *entire* proceeds from a concert, or tour perhaps, and *others besides*, to go to that children's home. Not that any credit was ever taken, which, I believe, is *typical* of the star behind this. I believe that that person is so much more than a performer, so much more than a singer, a dancer; someone who's *spellbinding* to watch on stage; and someone to whom the money is a lesser issue than doing what she's very, very good at."

Something told him that he had to keep talking, as just then, the stinging in his eyes warned of the consequences if he should falter: her eyes having broken contact, seconds before.

"I can't *believe* that it's about to end for that person. I can't believe her next concert will be her last, and not just because she's a great artist, nor even a really kind, generous soul who shines light in the lives of people that she's never met, but because there's so much more for her to do. I think that that person is in this house, oh yes, and that I'm looking at her. *You* were responsible for that, and lots of other donations to desperately sad causes up and down the land. I can't foresee it ending here for you, because your story isn't yet written: your destiny holds more, much more. I know, deep inside that your work will go on. It isn't over for you Sylvie, the fat lady hasn't even washed her hair, let alone reached the stage."

His voice rose as he spoke, its tone admitting no possibility of dissent; she just had to risk a glance at those eyes, at their deepest but burning blue, fuelled with a passion that she'd only glimpsed on previous occasions, but which was now all-consuming as he spoke.

"*How* do you know it's me? Lots of people could have done that," she countered.

The eyes flared again. He laughed. "That's just it, Sylvie, precisely my point, *no-one* could've done what you did, and no one *would've* done what you did. It might be because they're bored, it might be because they're on sex, drugs and rock-'n'-roll, or they simply want a new yacht. But in any case, the only person who could've carried that deal is *right here,* before me: and her time isn't over, not over by a long chalk. I know, Sylvie, trust me, I know." He nearly said that he knew those things because he'd been following her career and her progress avidly for years, thinking about little else in that time, but stopped himself short. He looked at her steadily, the eyes calmer now. "You can't fail now, not at this point."

"I'm just not sure any more, Matt. I keep seeing him, cold and lifeless; strung up like that. I keep seeing those horrible headlines in my mind, and I guess that the person you think you knew, who did *all* those things, died with that stalker in my room."

Now, more than ever, it would have been easy for him to say to her that she should abandon her attempt, pack it all in, and retire to the village with him. At this point, she might just have agreed and gone along with his plan. He would have her, and everything else he'd ever wanted. Knowing, however, that one day; perhaps a week, a month or a year; even longer; she would wake one morning, look at him, and hate him for what his heart desperately was begging him to say. Realising that when that point was reached, his life and everything that he held dear would be reduced to ashes. His brain intervened before the words were uttered. "You do this, and you won't fail. It's now or never."
"If I do fail, it'll ruin me and all those who've depended upon me. Just about everything rides on this one concert."
"I know Sylvie."
"You will be there, won't you?"
"What, and miss my chance to rush that stage? *No way*, am I going to miss that. Come on, I'll get that case upstairs."
Lucy had brought a case with more of her personal effects. He carried it upstairs while she sat alone in the conservatory. He returned a few minutes later.
"Sylvie?"
She'd learned to recognise that look, when he felt awkward about something that he was about to say, a skill that was mirrored in him.
"Go on, Matt."
"I can see you're bitter about the tabloids, and I understand why, but don't let that cloud your thinking: it'll eat away at

you, and they won't be the wiser. By all means pursue them through the courts, just so they know they haven't got away with it."

"I know Matt, you're right of course; I'll feel much better when this concert is over.

Thanks Matt, you've been super. You know that I couldn't do this without you."

She leant forward and kissed him.

How that light touch, just for that instant, electrified him. Desperately needing something to distract him: to allow him to break eye-contact without appearing too obvious. He couldn't reveal how much he ached for her; nor could he complicate her plans by even attempting to make manifest his own desires - just when things were at their most crucial phase. Moreover, he could never allow her to witness the barely restrained passion in his eyes. He spoke quickly, "Sylvie, I just believe in what you do."

"Thanks for that Matt: at this point in time, you're one of the few who does," she said, the sadness written temporarily on that pretty face.

The other thing he read from those eyes of crystal; just before their gaze parted, was that leaving look, the one he had seen in Luciano's, just as she drew everything together in perfect synchrony, like the consummate professional that undoubtedly she was. He knew that it wouldn't be long before she left: ready to face her greatest challenge - herself.

They continued to talk for some time. Opening a bottle of wine, they relaxed as he put on some music. She approved of his choice of Madonna's greatest hits; saying that at least it wasn't Bucks Fizz. After a while he stood.

"Right, I'm up early in the morning, are you coming to the gym with me for a swim and a sandwich?"

The twinkle banished the sadness instantly.

"If I'm up, then yes, if I'm still asleep; I'll see you when you get back?"

"Fine, sounds good to me. I won't slam the door on my way out, I promise." he said, with a daring look in his eye.

CHAPTER X

EVASIVE MANOEUVRES

He was awake, up, dressed and ready to go with a typical precipitous start to his Saturdays. He crept downstairs slowly, and with frustrating care so as not to wake his guest - only to find her dressed and waiting. She sat in the kitchen, her chin resting on her arm, itself supported by the worktop, her legs swinging randomly as slim fingers tapped the surface in a perfect study of boredom. Creating a long-suffering sigh, she looked at her watch in mock impatience. However, her posture couldn't obscure the seraphic smile, nor the glint in her eyes: a glint that had replaced entirely the sad and tormented, lustreless features of those same eyes of only a few days ago.

He stopped and stared at her in silent, fleeting study, accompanied only by a delighted smile modulated with pride more than covetousness.

"About time, let's go. I'm sure the gym will be open in ten minutes; if we leave now we can start banging on the door to be let in," she suggested jovially.

"Just like these city types," he said brusquely, feigning distaste to mirror her playful mood.

Wriggling from the bar stool, she stood before him in a plain vest top, covered by a cotton jacket, and jogging bottoms, with white New Balance trainers, finished with flashes of bright pink. Pausing again, he looked at her, terrified that his eyes might convey something of the tumult within. Standing there, her outdoor clothes in a cheap plastic bag, she looked just like any other girl; but then came the flashing smile, the array of teeth, the glorious hair that seemed to refract any available light to its advantage, and the erect athletic poise. In those few moments, he could glimpse the ordinary girl, before being reminded of the rock star, whose fame spanned the world. He understood, in that moment, the forces that underpinned her recovery: the central one that, by just being in this village she could be absolutely anyone other than herself. Surely not even a holiday in an exotic location could offer such escape: the chance to forget who she was and her troubles

"We're not going in the car are we? I thought you'd jog there."

"Are you sure you wouldn't rather stay in bed. I'm quite safe to be let out on my own, you know." He could no more have left her behind than the Earth depart from orbit around the sun.

"No, I'm going wop your ass in that pool, and besides, all the young women in this village need protecting from men like you," she said teasingly. She raced out to the car and pulled impatiently on the passenger door; jumping excitedly up and down.

"You watch that car, you, some people have never been used to nice things. First, I get insulted, and now my car gets vandalised."

"Sorry Mister, can I clean your windscreen for a 5p piece?"

"Get in and stop causing trouble. Okay, let's go."

She signed in as Sylvia Faber, his guest at the country club. The young woman on reception stared intently at

Fabienne as she handed over a towel, her mouth opening on the cusp of recognition. Matt stepped forward quickly and gave Fabienne a knockabout hug, as one might give a young sister. "Oh, this is my cousin from Melbourne," he offered, as if acknowledging her suspicion whilst simultaneously defusing it with something tangible.

"Gudaye, cobber Howw arr yu?, Pretty lil village n'all," Fabienne offered spontaneously.

The receptionist blinked and smiled, her thoughts being distracted just enough, as they went through to the lockers.

"Was that supposed to be Australian or from the deep South?" he mumbled sotto voce.

"What d'ya mean? I'll set my Roo on yu mate," she said in a much louder voice, the giggle permeating from within.

He joined her in the gym after changing in the men's locker room. She looked down at his shorts - just a little too short, and the legs just a little too long. "Nice legs mate!" she opined, placing an Australian bias loudly on the last word, for more effect. "Shorts could do with an iron, though," she suggested, as he looked down a little self-consciously.

"Nobody irons their gym shorts," he said with more surprise than rhetoric.

Her answer came simply by way of a knowing smile, the action communicating more than any words. As she did so, the thought presented within, that a woman's presence in his life would have sorted those shorts before he was allowed to leave the house. She winked, initially seductively: not being able to hold back a deep "Cor!" said with just a hint of tease that she couldn't restrain. Even his knees blushed at her words.

"Matt, you're stunning," she offered initially by way of apology, but then realised that her words contained more truth than otherwise.

She went on the treadmill, while he started with the elliptical trainer, and followed this with some stretches and then the exercise bike. Fabienne moved on to the rowing machine. Unable to stop his curiosity, he noted that she ran the machine on the highest level and even after fifteen gruelling minutes didn't seem to be unduly out of breath. He remained thankful that he hadn't selected a machine adjacent to hers, in case he was shown up by the fitness, created out of years of dance routines, training and endless rehearsals. Even after a punishing fitness routine she still looked fresh and unflustered, whereas he was beginning to look more like a greasy chip, as the sweat rolled off him.

After the gym, she joined him in the pool. He swam his usual frenzied lengths while she started at a more sedate pace. The young girl he often saw at this time being absent on that day. At first he left Fabienne well behind, but then noticed that her speed was increasing, smoothly and steadily: her lithe form powering through the water more like a dolphin than a human. He managed to keep ahead of her, by the slimmest of margins and the maximal use of effort, but it was only with difficulty that he avoided embarrassment. Concluding that there had been little time for drugs and alcohol with the rock-'n'-roll, on her part.

He stopped. Further movement had long since become impossible as his muscles screamed in pain. His heart could beat no faster, and his lungs already scorched him from within, as no more air could be supplied. All he could do was wait - panting - whilst his muscles made every effort to call in the loans from the heart and lungs, taken out during exercise that simply couldn't be funded.

He was shattered; barely managing a depleted smile. She appeared as fresh as a daisy, completely unperturbed by the demands made by the same exercise on her body. Doing his utmost to hide the relief forming on his face as they got out of the water. She looked as if she could do it all again: he looked for a sun lounger - with an urgency he'd never previously experienced. Smiling as best he could: deep within, however, he knew that she'd held his all-important male pride, within her grasp: deciding at the last minute to preserve it intact. Much more than this, she grinned magnanimously as if beaten in a fair fight. He reflected later that this was typical of her self-effacing manner: she wouldn't have wanted to bask in victory that was hers for the taking. After a brief spell in the spa pool they went off to shower and change.

He waited for her in the reception; she appeared after a short delay. Once again the receptionist looked at her with curiosity. Fabienne handed back the towel for the laundry bin, as she did so the movement gave prominence to the magnificent watch on her left wrist. "Wow, nice watch," the girl said; her face lit with expectation once again.

"Strewth, mate: it ain't a real one. Couldn't afford a real one o' these on moy salary. Thank heavens for Choina, that's what oy say," Fabienne offered with sufficient incredulity as to how anyone could have thought the watch real. The girl nodded; seeing the 'truth' for the first time; this vivid image, enough to decouple any thoughts that she'd just bumped into someone famous.

Matt waited, his face full of bemusement, rising from his chair when Fabienne joined him just outside the café bar: they went in for an early but leisurely lunch and coffee. Glancing carefully in his direction, puzzled by him, as usual, she wasn't used to people standing as she entered: something he'd always done reflexly. Surely such a practice had long been confined to the aged and forgotten annals of things such as etiquette.

"Come on, they do magnificent smoked salmon and cream cheese bagels here; nearly as nice as Luciano's," he suggested excitedly. Her eyes lit up. Hunger always followed vigorous exercise, and especially swimming. They were both ravenous.

Moments later he sat facing her, like an excited schoolboy who'd just won tickets to the chocolate factory, being separated from one of the world's sexiest women by the width of two plates with cream cheese bagels on them. Not for the first time, the surreal moment stunned him into silence, as he allowed himself to think a little too much, instead of living moment to moment as he'd promised himself he must.

"So, do you think that girl nearly recognised you?" he wondered aloud, as he recovered a moment later.

"Mm, you were quick off the mark there, Matt, sending me to Australia in the blink of an eye," she mused, her face still alight with enthusiasm.

"Yes, I thought you'd like that. Shame about the accent though. I think she was so puzzled after a few words that she couldn't tell which way was up." It was his turn now, for the mischievous smile.

"I'll have you know that I'm famed for my Australian accent. They just love me down under," she assured him, knowingly and with a reassuring nod.

"I have no doubt about that," he replied with honesty. "But I'd stick to the singing if I were you."

They laughed in synchrony, something much more complex stirred in the simplest of circumstances.

"I take it that your watch is the genuine article?" he asked; drawing her attention to the elegant wrist that sported the magnificent timepiece. Hesitating demurely, which he reflected was typical of her, before she spoke: leaning towards him, deep in thought, while supporting the chin with her palm as she considered her words.

"Well, the man in the shop assured me that it was, before he took rather a lot of money from my credit card." She paused again, before deciding that jealousy wasn't a facet of his character. "This was a present to myself when my first album went platinum." Touching the watch gently, she relived the moment upon hearing the news that day, now several years ago.

Matt realised that to qualify for Platinum in the UK, six hundred thousand sales would have to be made, whilst in the States the threshold was a million. He knew that if he revealed that he was aware that such targets had been achieved in both countries, she'd be embarrassed, and as a result decided to keep his own counsel. The free wrist extended in his direction so that he could view its crystalline elegance at closer range. Not daring to point: his hands, he felt, would surely tremble. Looking directly at her, he accepted the protection that the circumstances had afforded him, as he said, "Beautiful, Sylvie, absolutely beautiful." And he remembered, just in time, to look at the watch.

After lunch they drove home slowly. Matt retired to the conservatory to read some papers. Fabienne asked him if she could borrow his car to pop to the shops. Throwing her the keys, "No speeding, now, the village policeman isn't my patient."

"Don't worry, I'll keep a low profile," she said as she pulled the Wokingham Working Men's Club cap low over her eyes. "Besides, I hope you'd never try to persuade an officer of the law not to do his duty."

"Never, Miss, unlike you in that short skirt of course."

"Chance'd be a fine thing," she replied, taking the keys as she spread the hem of the skirt with a little mock curtsey, as if acknowledging the interest that he'd restrained with every ounce of self-control.

Fabienne parked his car on the main street of the village. Stella gave her a cheery wave as she passed, but fortunately she was in the middle of cutting and couldn't dash out from her salon, despite the overwhelming temptation to do so. She wondered just why Dr Sinclair's girlfriend saw the need to cover such wonderful hair with that red cap, and quickly had to cut out her mistake as she did so, from the customer who remained in blissful ignorance.

A shiny red Boxster was on the prowl, and Matt's car was detected instantly. It drove down the main street and turned to park up behind the blue Jaguar. Rita had been waiting for this opportunity and was very keen to know why he'd been at Parkvale Medical Centre. This being her first chance to investigate and she waited, poised like a Panther. Surprise accompanied by even more irritation came over her as she saw the young blonde girl in a short denim skirt, come out of the newsagent's and flick the boot to open. Vacating the Porsche quickly, she raced to close with Fabienne, who was still sporting the baseball cap.

"Excuse me; are you a friend of Dr Sinclair?" She looked her up and down with disdain, thinking what a revolting cap she was wearing.

"Matt, oh yes, I'm his girlfriend," Fabienne said, naively.

Piercing green eyes shot a disbelieving, then curious look at her. How typical of Matt to have gone for some pretty 'nobody', when he could have had someone with education, brains and substance.

"How long have you known Matt?" Rita began, her questions queuing, and fuelled by jealousy and spite.

"About two months," Fabienne offered slowly, as her mind raced: the conversation reminding her of ones from the past rather than the present.

"Are you from round here?" Rita continued quickly, as if desperate to ask her next question, and the next.

"No; I'm staying with him for a few days," Fabienne replied, attempting to keep a calm in her voice that she couldn't reproduce inwardly. Sensing that the line of enquiry was more scrutiny than friendly questioning. The eyes upon her appeared to be trying to bore into her, to elicit truth without relying on her words.

"Excuse me, but who are you?" Fabienne asked calmly, unlike her interlocutor who seemed far removed from that frame of mind.

"I'm Doctor Letworth, a colleague of Matt's," the reply snapped, as if Rita was talking with an impertinent inferior.

Her own question brought only temporary respite from the onslaught of Rita's line of enquiry.

"So how did you meet?"

"We met at a meeting, I gave."

"Are you a drug rep?" she concluded, almost with triumph. This would figure; another young, pretty drug rep in a short skirt had turned many a GP's head, even the married ones. Matt would have been easy meat. She wouldn't last long. Rita was surprised that they'd known each other for two months already. No doubt Matt hadn't quite had his fill, but he would tire quickly of this vacuous bimbo.

"So, what meeting was that?" wondering why she hadn't been invited to the same meeting.

"Oh, some weeks ago," Fabienne couldn't evade her aggressive tone: it felt like a physical weight upon her.

"Who do you work for?" Rita asked, after deciding to shift the focus of her interrogation.

"Astra Zeneca."

Something wasn't right. Rita's directly wired emotions cut through preamble and smokescreens and she detected one such now. Her eyes narrowed as she homed in upon her prey. "So which are your products then?"

"Symbicort." Fabienne remembered just in time.

"Is that the tablets or the inhaler?" the question hung in the air expectantly: the trap was sprung. Fabienne had never met this woman before, and couldn't know the depths she would plumb in order to uncover the truth that had been hastily and incompletely hidden.

"Oh, both," Fabienne said innocently.

Rita smirked with satisfaction, like a hyena that had just managed to prise a chunk of meat from under the gaze of a hungry predator with its kill. The green eyes now glowed more with menace than with enquiry. Any drug rep would know that Symbicort only came in the form of an inhaler, and the enquiry about tablets, though ridiculous; easily able to expose the unwary.

"Well, tell Matt I'll be along to see him," Rita said dismissively, grasping that she was in a much more important game: one that would render this short-skirted floozy irrelevant.

"Oh, very well then, Dr Letworth. Nice to have met you," Fabienne held out her hand, but Rita was already turning to get back into her car. Fabienne hesitated for a second or two, not quite knowing what had just passed between the two of them. Sensing that the other woman had grasped something of substance from their conversation, and she now seemed keen to meet up with Matt in order to declare it.

Rita watched her from the car. Fabienne closed the boot, opened the driver's door and got in. Rita scrutinised every inch of her as she did so, with a piercing look that not even a male in a stimulated state could replicate. She recognised Manolos on her feet, as the suntanned legs were retracted into the car. Rita was sure that the watch she had on her wrist was a Patek Phillipe, Nautilus, which, if genuine, would have cost £20,000. The necklace, too, was not within the sphere of accessibility of a drug rep's salary.

One thing had become patently clear – drug representative she wasn't. Given this fact, Rita wondered as to her real identity and why she had gone to the trouble of creating a web of lies that had taken Rita herself only seconds to tear apart. There was also something not right about her very appearance. She doubted that Matt would have been able, or willing to spend such significant sums of money on any girlfriend, especially one who would be jettisoned long before the credit card bills arrived; and still further, one who had declared where her real taste lay with that ridiculous red cap.

She reminded Rita of someone. Suddenly, an incredible idea had formed in her brain. Remembering the two idiot reporters waiting for hours outside the surgery and information that she'd noted but dismissed at the time, came back to assist her thoughts. Why had they stood there all afternoon? They said they were waiting for Fabienne. Matt had met some people, but why there, when there were easier places to meet strangers from out of the area? Two reporters wouldn't be sent on a wild goose chase - even two dim-wits like those. Why had Matt asked that his friends be escorted through the building so that he could pick them up at the back, rather than collect them at reception?

Just what was Matt up to? It wasn't possible, yet the idea that rose within was the only one that seemed to allow each piece of the puzzle to fit, no matter how remote the chances. A call to the newspapers would settle it one way or another. Waiting for the girl to drive off, she wasn't going to alert her by following her.

Deciding to go straight back to Matt's, Fabienne was deeply troubled by her meeting with Doctor Letworth. She needed to ask him about her; with a feeling that Matt would be hearing from her fairly soon - for one reason or another. Matt looked up as she rushed in, sensing immediately her excitement and also her discomfort.

"What, tell me?" he said urgently.

"Matt, who is Doctor Letworth?"

Matt bowed his head. "Oh no, Rita! I am sorry I should've warned you. I just didn't think she'd show up here again."

"Well?" Fabienne said with impatience now coupled to her sense of alarm, as she saw the unease cross his face.

"We had a bit of a fling some years ago," he explained.

"Tell me, Matt, is there anyone you didn't have a fling with some years ago?" The question was more rhetorical, but she too had picked up on his anxiety and was desperate to make sense of it all. Matt paused, but decided that the question was unanswerable, and selected the politician's response of bypass and distraction.

"Rita's poison, what did she say?"

"Why did she ask me if I sold Symbicort tablets or inhalers. Surely a rep would sell both?"

Fabienne had asked him about the part of their conversation that had troubled her the most; as she sensed the look of triumph replace hostility on Rita's face.

"Sylvie, they only make it in an inhaler. She was testing you deliberately. A plain old trap designed to deceive you."

He thought furiously about the implications of Rita being alerted in this way, and the reasons for her ensnaring the pop star. "Oh, this is bad. Sylvie: just how ready are you for your discovery here? "

He knew that she could do with a few more days, that she wasn't quite ready. Press camped out on the drive would be the last thing she'd need, while her recovery was both fragile and uncertain. His mind raced feverishly: knowing that he'd need to play for more time. Things had been going so well; now she was about to be plunged back to an existence she wasn't quite ready to resume.

"Surely she couldn't put that together. I didn't even take my cap off," Fabienne suggested.

"Trust me, this woman is sharp, and misses very little. How many people do you see in the village with your looks? People think they see someone special because they think you're my girlfriend. Rita sees a competitor, someone to tear down, devalue, expose, and that's why she scrutinised you carefully. If she hadn't known that you knew me, she wouldn't have given you the time of day, if she'd fallen over you. You've met some nice, kind people in this sleepy village, who are straightforward, trusting and honest – she's not one of them," he summarised; his thoughts becoming frenzied.

Matt had seen first-hand one of Rita's defining characteristics; when her plans were frustrated for whatever reason, other less pleasant emotions were unleashed. Her disappointment at not bumping into him; was the price that Fabienne was about to pay, in full.

"Sylvie, what were your plans, for this afternoon?"

"I was going to pop out to Tesco." She grew more worried seeing the disquiet verging on panic coursing across his face. Not having seen him this worried, she reasoned that Rita Letworth must be a formidable person.

"Right then, would you take your car?" he requested, whilst continuing to think quickly.

Matt didn't underestimate Rita: he knew how she burned within and wouldn't settle until she had this puzzle exposed; if necessary broken in pieces, but all within her grasp and under her control. Trying to contemplate her next move, he decided that she would either appear in person, or phone the press, or both. Matt had devised a desperate plan to buy more time.

"Okay, Sylvie, off you go, don't hurry back; take your mobile with you. The one you inveigled out of poor old Stan."

Smiling, she held it up for his inspection. "Okay, I'm going; missing you already." Fabienne wanted to ask him more, to learn more of this woman and why just the mention of her name was enough to make Matt so disconcerted.

"Look, just go!" he implored.

"Okay, understood, I'm on my way. Bye." Her grin rose in tandem with the flicker of confidence that had returned to him.

He decided to start with one or two calls of his own. Fortunately, he'd kept all the phone numbers from that frantic Sunday morning while he tried to find Fabienne's agent.

Having no doubt that if Rita had discovered the truth about his guest; her intense scrutiny of Fabienne could mean little else: as a result, things would happen quickly. He wasn't about to be beaten, at least without a fight; he would move more quickly still. Clinging to the hope that she'd choose not to present in person, and perhaps would wait until the dust had settled; though he recognised intuitively that an early appearance in order to gloat, would be more consonant with the forces, which drove her.

Matt was correct in some of his assumptions, and the ravenous press were quick to act on Rita's information. Cars and vans with satellite dishes on long booms began to appear within two hours. He peeped through his window thinking it was a bit like mission control at NASA. Telephoning Fabienne, he asked her to take her time in returning.

"Okay, Matt, don't worry, I'm in this queue in Tesco, surrounded by all your patients. I think we're going to have to start a fan club for you, you know. Will you be able to do some photographs?"

"Listen, if you come back now, you'll be signing photographs, my girl," he replied seriously.

"Okay, Matt, received and understood: have fun."

Not for the first time had he taken over her worries; facing them as if they were his own, she contemplated, whilst wandering through the supermarket.

He telephoned Janice.

"Oh, hi Janice, sorry to trouble you on a Saturday. I need a favour. I wonder if you could pop round for some files and take them to the surgery for me, I'm a bit snowed under."

Janice lived a couple of miles away. It was an unusual request and not one that had ever been made before, but she was a simple, trusting soul; one who believed implicitly in her boss, and if he needed her to do something, then, that was reason enough. She grabbed her Dad's car keys, after asking his permission to borrow his car.

Matt replaced the receiver. Time to act. He opened the front door. Cameras clicked and flashes fired. His success now depended upon keeping a clear head and not wavering. He calmly walked down the drive. More cameras clicked.

"Doctor Sinclair."

"Doctor Sinclair, have you got Fabienne with you?"

"Who?" Doing his utmost to look very confused by unfamiliar words.

"Fabienne, the pop star," they offered as if clarifying who she was, would suddenly trigger his memory.

"Who's she? I've never heard of her, this 'Fabby Hen' you speak of. Why are you on my drive? There's no one here but me, and I don't know any pop stars. This is a sleepy village - not Broadway."

Keeping his words as simple and uninviting as possible, however, he spoke with a formality as one might expect from the commander of men, not used to being challenged. He didn't want to raise any sort of profile in the story, and by keeping things as low-key as possible, as boring and unemotional as he could, he hoped he'd get away with it. He'd deliberately chosen Broadway; knowing that Fabienne had performed in concerts all over the world - but never Broadway.

A car rounded the bend. This was the opportunity they were waiting for. Here she was! The GP had lied, and now the truth was about to be revealed. It was their duty to uncover that truth, expose him for a liar; thereby revealing Fabienne's whereabouts to the world. People had a right to know: of this they were all certain; this was their job, this was expected of them by the public who demanded knowledge, regardless of the price of its acquisition. They waited with intense interest as the sound of an engine was translated into the appearance of a little car. The car came closer, yes; it was turning, turning into the drive. There was a blonde girl at the wheel, with long hair.

Suddenly, the car stopped, with a bit of a jolt. Cameras clicked incontinently as thousands of shots were powered through hundreds of shutters; capturing as many images of the unfolding scene, as possible. Some photographers had brought steps to claim a better vantage point than their colleagues; others had faster cameras or more high-powered lenses; some had lights; some intense flashes: all concentrated their interest on this focal point, as the car door swung open with a rusty shriek.

Janice got out of the six-year-old, black Punto, and blinked against the intense lights as flashes and floodlights fired at her. Holding up her hand, her pigtails jingling as her head rocked a little under the impact of all those cameras and flashes, which seemed to be waiting for her. Janice had no idea why they were here, and what interest they had in her. She gave a little bow as most of them, realising their mistake, groaned and pointed their cameras back to the ground. The false alarm had somehow deflated them just at the moment when their expectation was at its height, which was precisely the outcome that Matt hoped for: their belief that the search was now over, comprehensively dashed.

Matt came to the door with the files.
"What's going on, Doctor Sinclair?"
"I wish I knew, Janice; they say there's a celebrity in the village."
"Who's that?" she asked, with confusion and shock vying for prominence across her features.
"I can't say, someone I've never heard of, I'm afraid. I'm no use with these pop stars' names," he offered, as if taxed

beyond his mind's capacity to take in the events that were unfolding.

"And they think she's here?" Janice queried incredulously.

"Yes I think they do, whoever she is," Matt said more calmly.

"How ridiculous!" she reasoned.

"It's so good of you to do this for me. Could you pop to the surgery, here are the keys, and place these files on my desk." He smiled gratefully, and also with thinly-disguised relief as he handed them over, with the care that he would afford any material that was precious and important.

Without telling Janice that the files were ones containing his gas and credit card bills, he reasoned, at least, they looked important, and she took them without question.

"My pleasure, Doctor Sinclair. I'll see you on Monday," she confirmed with simple honesty. Walking back to her car over the gravel drive, she bowed again; one or two photographers cheered good-naturedly, though their disappointment was palpable as it hung in the air.

Jim Duggan arrived late. It was unusual for his colleagues to get to a scoop before him. He'd had trouble with his car: a dog had run out in front of him whilst he was lighting a cigarette. Being in a foul mood, he swore viciously as he deserted his car more or less in the middle of the quiet road, just before Matt's house. Arriving just in time to hear the groans from all the photographers as they realised that the girl in the car was not Fabienne, Jim pushed his way past all the others.

"Too late Jim, false alarm," said one of them

"I'll be the judge of that, you old fart," said Jim without even stooping to look at his colleague.

"OK, Jim, no offence, just bein' friendly, like."

"Leave me alone, you old bastard, not fit to lick mi boots you bleeder," Jim affirmed with menace.

The other photographer shut up. Jim in this mood could be worse even than his usual vicious self. Stories held that he had once smashed a competitor's camera, in pursuit of a scoop, by hitting him with it in his face; breaking his nose.

"There's been a sighting in Hastings," said one, as he came out of the back of a van, the headset still on his head and connected to his communications hardware.

"I've got a sighting in Woolwich," said another, taking his mobile phone from his ear.

"No, I've got a report in Bradford."

"My contact says Edinburgh."

Jim swore again, spitting out his cigarette. No one, not even Jim, stopped to wonder why after all these weeks, so many sightings had been reported on this one day.

"Bleedin' dogs' breakfast," cursed Jim as he spat out heavily.

Matt could only smile as he waited on the porch for Janice to start the old Punto; doing her best to turn the car in the drive whilst they were gathered there. She smiled and waved as she left.

"Bloody amateurs, couldn't organise a shag in a bleedin 'arem these bleeders," continued Jim, to himself, as all others were ignoring him. Several of the photographers started packing up, sensing that they were in the wrong place and that the call was just one of many received that afternoon. They couldn't know that Matt had made each of those calls, save one; the one passed through by Rita. He was determined that she wasn't going to have the satisfaction of proving her otherwise accurate suspicions.

Jim Duggan saw Matt turn to go back in the house. "Seen 'im somewhere before, ain't we mi old son. Jim never forgets a bleedin' face. I'll find you 'andsome. I've seen you somewhere and I'll get yer. You wait till I get back to mi office: must have yer somewhere there. You know summat, ye bleeder, and Jim'll know soon enough. You ain't gonna beat me: somethin's appenin' 'ere and I'll find out. I'll have that soddin' scoop and that bonus, and you ain't gonna stop mi." Spitting out another copious quantity of spittle, he reached for another cigarette. Someone was having difficulty getting past his car, and Jim was ready to give him a piece of his mind and vent some of his frustration upon the hapless motorist, who had merely expected a right of way from an ordinary public road.

Darkness was gathering momentum as Fabienne returned after first telephoning Matt to ask him if all was clear. Matt looked out of the windows to confirm that everyone had by now drifted away, having sensed that there was nothing there, apart from a false alarm and a GP who'd never heard of Fabienne. He wondered if Rita was about to arrive, but he decided that she wouldn't know that her plan had been frustrated, and was no doubt waiting for the evening news to confirm her victorious piece of detection.

As the news came on that evening, she was to be found in front of her television, smiling to herself whilst waiting for the newscaster to deliver the news that she personally had uncovered, from under the noses of all those pathetic sheep in that village. Matt, no doubt, thought himself very clever. His cocksure manner would be in tatters at his feet, very soon, and that puerile bimbo would be packing her bags too, if she knew what was good for her! Rita drank deeply from her glass; a magnificent red; well worth celebrating with. The young man with her had gone to shower, which was a shame; still, he could always shower again later.

"No Sylvie, all clear here, there's no one in sight, it's all quiet and they've all cleared off. See you soon." Matt replaced the phone hurriedly and dived into the kitchen to start tea;

remembering that she'd gone to Tesco. His fear was that she was planning another evening meal, and he wasn't sure that, in its heightened state or otherwise, his stomach could take such an insult. Half an hour later Matt heard the Beetle coming to rest on the gravel. He switched the porch light off just in case there were any who'd decided to continue the surveillance. None had, a spectral calm had descended outside.

"Well, you missed the fun and games. We had everyone here," he said with a sense of glee crossing his face. "I gather though, that there were also sightings of you in some far-flung places and the guys here decided that it must have been a vicious and cruel hoax - they weren't that far off the mark. I'll get the bags; you sit down. I started tea, I hope you don't mind."

"Oh, Matt, I'd bought some food," she looked disappointed.

"I thought you'd be shattered, spending all afternoon away."

"I caught a movie, actually - had to take my cap off, but it was pretty dark in there," her pleasant tones confirmed.

Matt passed a hot plate towards her from out of the bottom oven.

"Here, I'll carry it into the conservatory for you. Do you fancy a glass of wine or something soft?"

"You know us rock stars, the strongest you have. Don't bother with the glasses."

"OK, start on the wine, and you can smash the place up later."

"Actually, we usually do that when we leave."

She seemed to pause for a moment, as if something important had just come to her: important but sombre. "Matt, I was planning to leave on Monday."

He made no reply: the silence that intervened, conveyed much more than any words.

"You know, I have to train, rehearse, prepare. I can't let the concert be anything other than the best they've ever seen."

"I know, Sylvie. It'll be more than that."

She grinned, "You're not going to fish out another magazine on me are you?"

"No Sylvie, just your tea. Here it is."

"So, do you think that Rita started all this?" she asked.

"Without a doubt," he confirmed, and continued. "When you don't appear, exposed to the world like some renegade, on the evening news, she'll know that we foiled her, at least temporarily; but she'll regroup and come up with something else in a day or two, so perhaps it's all for the best. We've bought time, I suppose, but not much." Optimistically; he believed, he'd bought her all the time that she'd need to begin her preparations.

Something else flashed into her mind at this point. "Just what is it about this place? Everyone who's worn a skirt at some time is an ex of yours."

"Sylvie, it was a long time ago," he said disarmingly, but couldn't quite meet her gaze.

"Rita seemed a bit more up to the minute to me." She poised with her fork in mid air as the concentration took over. "She certainly seemed a lot more intrusive than the others, very keen to know who I was, what I did, how long we'd been together and which toothpaste I used. Is there unfinished business between you two?" she asked perspicaciously.

Pausing for a moment, he wondered whether to attempt an abridged version of the truth. He'd seen first-hand the interest, in everyone and all things, that she displayed. When coupled with an ability to elicit the truth, not just from him but others too, it gave her a formidable sensibility: a skill which was at all times used with an almost child-like fascination that was more engaging than coy.

"I think she believes that, but not as far as I'm concerned; there's no further business between us." Detecting that she remained as unclear and curious in equal measure as to what exactly had passed between them, he continued, "Rita was very keen to have me join her practice. One of their senior partners was due to retire. As you know she works at Parkvale, it's a pretty big place, with eight partners. A large health centre like that; it wasn't really my cup of tea. I think Rita saw this as a weakness on my part, not wanting to join the cut-and-thrust of a modern practice. She told me in no uncertain terms that I'm a country yokel by their standards and suggested that this extends to my medicine too."

"Cheeky bugger, what does she know?" Fabienne said indignantly.

"I don't think Rita worries about what she knows. I think she isn't concerned by that; once her mouth is open; out it comes, and if you don't like what she has to say, then it's your problem not hers."

"Yes, I must say she came over just like that. I wouldn't fancy going to see her if my dog had just died."

"Let's just say that I suspect that 'snapping out of it' features strongly, in her medicine. As I said, we had a fling, a brief fling, some years ago. In other words, some years ago, a *brief fling*," he said emphatically.

She nodded, while acknowledging the point he was making.

"I think she thought that we could take up where we left off, and that joining her practice, no doubt moving house, changing my car and so on, were also high on her list of ways in which she was going to revolutionise my medicine, and bring me into the modern age from my antediluvian existence here in Perri."

"She strikes me as someone who doesn't want to hear bad news," she suggested.

"No, I suspect phoning Hitler to tell him you were turning back from Moscow would be easier!"

"She seemed to be quietly fuming when I led her to believe that I was your girlfriend; really started the twenty questions then," said Fabienne, smiling as she re-lived the encounter.

"Oh yes, she'd want to know all about the competition, I guess, and make sure she had the full measure of them," he advised.

Fabienne wasn't surprised to hear this information. It all added to the enigma surrounding him. Once again, here was a relationship firmly written in the past tense and yet, she was convinced that few men would be able to resist the sparkling green eyes, the glossy black hair and the perfect figure, coupled to the almost handsome good looks. Though she wouldn't be in a hurry to meet up with Doctor Letworth again, she could see that any man could be forgiven for thinking otherwise. There was no doubt that all sources had suggested that Matt had really been the lad about town: wherever she'd gone, she had bumped into an ex-girlfriend. The response was, by now, familiar. The glint in their eyes when she spoke of him, tinged with envy at the thought of her being his current lover. She could only guess, but her best estimate was that he hadn't had a serious relationship in over two years. The crumpled shorts half-mast up his long legs, and the mountain of clean but un-ironed laundry she'd discovered in the utility room, gave testament to this view. It seemed unlikely that his sexual ardour had cooled, given the number of occasions that she'd caught him surveying her, her legs or the line of her shirt, with a passion that appeared to be held in check behind those glances. Possibly he'd been hurt. Sometimes he'd look away, or apply his favourite tactic to divert the line of thought or conversation to other areas, so as not to give himself away. Her sensitive antennae had been aware of each of these attempts with some bemusement. Rita had obviously tried very hard to light the fuse within him, yet had failed - at least up to this point. The more she learned of this man, the more questions that remained.

They sipped another glass of wine as they finished their main course. Suddenly she leapt from her chair. "Stay right there. I have a pudding."
Groaning inwardly, as she disappeared into the hall, he could only worry as to what she was about to serve. Surely there wouldn't be enough time for her to cook anything. He smiled with barely disguised relief as she brought back a ready-made cream trifle a couple of dishes and two spoons. Sharing much of it between them, she sat facing him again. His stomach made a satisfying gurgle, as if grateful for its deliverance.
"You know what Mary told me?" she said tantalisingly.
"Go on, tell me more," he suggested.
"She's such a super cook, would you agree?"
"Not bad, I guess," Matt said as impassively as he could.
"Well, she says, if I return this way again, she'll show me how to cook like that." An air of satisfaction appeared in her voice.
Matt remembered, once more, all those things he had loved about Mary.
"Oh yes, but you can cook," he said, carefully applying his words: he didn't want to enthuse about her cooking too much, and reveal his lies for what they were.
"Well, maybe Matt, but not like that," she declared sincerely.
"Very well then, Sylvie; if you do return, you'll always be welcome to stay with me - if the Travelodge is full of course."
"I'll have to come back to make sure you're behaving yourself and not breaking more hearts."

Looking at her carefully, he synchronised the movements of his spoon to allow regular glances across the table. He could sense the many emotions that played across her face now, like clouds shooting by the face of the sun on an otherwise clear day. The sadness, the pain, the regrets as to what had happened, the sheer determination and, of course, the unmistakable hint of leaving. Lessons had undoubtedly been borne out of her pain, not all of them positive. She was perhaps a little more cynical, a little less trusting and also, vitally, a lot less confident. Suspecting that what had previously been second nature would now require supreme concentration, in order to recreate; he could only wonder whether the scars that lay beneath the surface would ever heal. Would she turn in the middle of the night, for years to come, and review and relive the horrors that she had seen, after Barry Miles hanged himself in pursuit of the ultimate ecstasy of sexual desire? These thoughts and more would no doubt be passing through her mind. Her crisis of confidence would seem very acute, especially when faced with a concert that simply *must* attract good reviews. A poor showing would do more damage than even the tabloids had unleashed in her life.

"Matt....." she paused, as if uncertain.
"Go on Sylvie, just tell me," he suggested.
"Are you okay with me leaving on Monday?"
He knew exactly what he wanted to say at this point, but by a supreme effort, objective analysis came to the fore. "Well, I think that you're as ready as you're going to be, to get this career of yours back on track. You know that I want for you, what is best for you."

The time element wasn't lost upon him. Disappearing was fine and had been a vital part of her immediate strategy, but the trick was knowing when to reappear: if she left it too long, she'd risk the possibility that people neither knew nor cared if and when she would return. Though he didn't doubt that there were many genuine fans, an even greater number would be more fickle, and no doubt would eye other artists as possibly worthy of their interest.

He was having more difficulty, however, with her reason for asking this question. Possibly she was indicating that she welcomed his views and valued his opinion, or was she suggesting something else, either an impending crisis of confidence within herself, or even in him as she departed? Her next words revealed a little more of her thoughts.

"You know that the next few weeks will be pretty busy. A lot rides on the sales of the new CD: if that goes badly our strategy will depend more on the MEN concert."

In that moment he understood either that she was preparing herself or, more likely, him for her absence from his life. She had no need to apologise for her single-minded aim to move forward. Though her plan was ultimately simple, she knew that any distraction would not only weaken her, but also her likelihood of success. He fully concurred, recognising, as did she, that there'd only be one chance, and the concert was, by any calculation, of crucial significance if she were to make a successful return.

"In any event, I'll hope to see you in Manchester."

"I'll be there. Front row, did you say?" he queried.

"I suppose you might just be the only one there," she said nervously.

"No, Sylvie; I can't see that somehow. If that is the case, however, I'll clap very hard."

Her smile was eclipsed by sadness – itself almost held in check by the determination upon her face.

From the day she first arrived, he'd made as few assumptions as possible; preparing himself for this point. They finished their meal and coffee in near silence, each with their own thoughts: she with preparations for survival, and he with acceptance of her need to go, despite wishing for it to be otherwise.

"Come on, let's catch the news," she suggested wickedly. The national news contained a very tiny snippet of news that Fabienne had been sighted in a variety of locations that day, but that all had proved to be a false alarm. Both he and Fabienne wondered privately whether Rita was watching the news and what her next step would be.

Rita had indeed watched each news item on every channel; her anger growing with each click of the remote. She wasn't used to being wrong-footed and would drive by Matt's house tomorrow to see for herself what was going on. In any event she wasn't in the habit of losing to anyone, and certainly not to Matt Sinclair and his blonde bimbo, whether inamorata, pop star or otherwise. Smirking, she wondered if he'd be foolish enough to be laughing at her now. In any event he wouldn't be laughing for long. She'd make him wish that he'd taken up her offer of partnership rather than embark on this misguided dalliance; though, for the life of her, she couldn't guess how he'd brought it about. Swearing at her young consort for spending too long in the shower, her mood had changed from calm expectation to vicious disappointment. It looked as if the young man with her would be the hapless victim upon whom she would dissipate some of that black mood.

After the news, the telephone rang. It was Steve. Nervousness modulated Matt's voice, being unsure as to how he would view things.

"Matt Sinclair, just what am I going to do with you? I might have known you were just too cheerful," he began, but quickly continued before Matt could speak, "Look, Matt, Mary's told me what happened, and I just want you to know that I'm not going to chew your ear over it. Mary says that

Fabienne told her that she won't be staying much longer; so if you want to talk then, that's fine. I do want you to know, though I shouldn't be feeding your obsession in this way, that we both think she's lovely and at the very least, you have good taste. Why you couldn't have found one just like that, who isn't a pop star being sought the country over, I'll never know, but I guess that's just you. So, my boy, call me when you're ready to talk, and Mary sends her love. Please pass on our best wishes to Fabienne, won't you?"

"I'll be sure to do that Steve, I'm pleased you're not angry, and I won't forget what we agreed."

Steve wondered if Matt's promise to him bore any relevance at all now, and whether Matt would always be submerged in worship of her, long after she'd departed. The only difference might be that he'd be afraid to tell him that that was the case. Contemplating an image of a sad and lonely old man, clutching memories of a few days he'd once spent in the company of someone he'd once worshipped; his life wasted with the ruin of regret at his feet. Steve would certainly do his best to steer Matt from that direction, but he'd seen it happen before and with disastrous consequences.

Fabienne left the room discreetly, so that he and Steve could continue their conversation in private. Though curiosity overwhelmed her, she sensed that to stay and make him feel awkward at this point was unforgivable, so she went to tidy the kitchen and made sure that a moderate amount of noise was made whilst she did so; thereby allowing him unfettered access to his friend.

"You can see what I can see now, can't you?" Matt asked of his friend, almost whispering. Steve remained silent; in truth he could see what Matt was driving at, he was impressed by the young woman and not just by her mien, her charm, her poise, but above all, by the way that the two of them seemed to be at complete peace with each other. Moreover, he could see what Matt had seen for so long. To communicate this to Matt, he reasoned, would have made his recovery even harder; when she departed with little chance of a return. Steve knew nothing of the life of pop stars, but he knew enough to know that this would be a temporary stop, and that once she'd moved on, there'd be little opportunity, or indeed desire, to retrace her route over such painful ground. He was filled with doubt whether she would ever contact Matt again. This wasn't in any way subterfuge on her part, but was rather like trying to cage a swan that was about to spread her wings.

He could never say this to Matt, but his silence might be a more cruel response than telling him what he considered he ought to know. In any event Steve didn't answer Matt's question: not having the heart to tell him what he really thought.

"Well, my boy, I just wanted to see how you were, and to say that I'm here if you should need me," Steve said slowly. Steve also had to confront some of his own feelings, having assured Matt that he'd never see her again after their meeting - and yet here she was in his house; how she came to be there, now in many ways irrelevant. Though accepting that the two complemented each other very well, Steve's plan would now be to help his friend to get over the prospect of never having her in his life again. This being more positive than admonishing him for daring to go ahead with the lunch meeting in the first place, as this obviously lay firmly in the past.

Ideally Matt would have wanted to talk more of Fabienne, to sample his friend's views, but Steve, sensing this was how it might go, couldn't risk having to remain silent over key lines of enquiry from his friend.

"Thanks for that Steve," Matt said simply.

"Speak to you soon," replied Steve, as he replaced the handset.

Fabienne returned a few moments later after detecting that the conversion had ended,

"Was that Steve?" she asked Matt as if to emphasise that his conversation had been private.

"Yes, he just wanted to say 'hello' and pass on Mary's regards."

Not being able to help but wonder if the conversation held much more detail than he alluded to, she remained intensely curious but couldn't bring herself to eavesdrop or to question him further.

CHAPTER XI

LOSS AND PROFIT

Sunday dawned bright but cool. Typically, they were up early; taking a leisurely breakfast while the sun did its best to exert its influence over the day.

"Come on, Sylvie do you fancy a walk? It might be your last walk here in Perrilymm," he said, as cheerfully as he could.

She hesitated for a second; there were many things she would have wanted to say, but knew that her constraining priorities would make them all redundant. She managed a weak smile, which perhaps made things easier than words might have done. Leaving the house, they went through the back gate and over the little bridge, but on this occasion turned left away from the village. Had they turned back they might have caught a glimpse of a charging red sports car screaming down the narrow and tortuous main road only to make a reckless turn into Matt's drive, barely missing his stone gatepost; the car mercifully engineered to save such a driver from disaster.

Rita was primed and ready to accost him; to assure the two of them that she and, as it seemed, she alone, had seen through their tawdry manoeuvres: she'd be back on to the press as soon as she'd tackled them both. She laughed to herself with unregenerate spite. Had she been a minute earlier she would have achieved this objective. As it was, seeing the two cars on the drive would only enrage her further: assuming that they wouldn't open the door, despite her persistent banging. Eventually, only by opening the front door and calling through the house, did she sublimate some of the anger within her, by discovering that nobody was home.

"If we follow this path for about five miles we'll eventually come to Miden: it's a slightly larger village than Perri and has a market once a week," Matt informed Fabienne. She asked him if it would be possible to find a nearby village that wasn't full of his ex-girlfriends, her playful grin now ever-present in their conversations. Rather than going on the defensive, he decided that the time had come to turn the tables a little, and ask the question that had been on his lips since the day she arrived.

"So then, Miss Megastar, is there no-one special in your life?"

He did his best to appear nonchalant and relaxed as if unperturbed, regardless of the reply. Had he looked at her at this point, instead of suddenly squinting towards the sun, he would have seen a hint of a blush, the delicate pink appearing more within the cheeks, but not quite matching the deep, vermillion of those lips. She tested him with a glance of her own, but found him still squinting away from her. Instead, she looked down as if making sure that her foot was on a secure hold, before transferring her weight.

"Oh, you know us rock stars. Another gig, another hotel room, loads of drugs, lots of sex, another bottle or three; smash it up, and we're on the road for our next stop," she offered breezily, but far from convincingly.

"That's not quite the image I have of you," he queried honestly.

"No, to tell the honest truth, there isn't time for relationships. I'm never in one place for long enough, and if I'm not performing, I'm rehearsing; if I'm not rehearsing then I'm travelling, and if I'm not travelling; then I'm asleep."

"Yes, yes I get the picture." He nodded to acknowledge the veracity of all that he'd just heard; his face remaining a study in impassivity, whilst excitement flourished, between each beat of his heart.

"As I told you, it's not something I can see myself doing forever, but for the moment it's fun - or it seemed so until just recently," she acknowledged pensively and wondered, as did he, whether it would ever be fun again or whether its allure had been indelibly asphyxiated, just like poor Barry Miles.

"Of course, if the concert goes badly, I may just be trying my hand as checkout girl or shop worker."

"I can always find room for you as a receptionist. Mrs Simpson, my practice manager, keeps looking at your picture, the one..." he hesitated, as he wondered if it would remind her of happier times, "... of us both in Luciano's. Pay isn't bad and I think you'll be able to keep up with all the gossip, somehow," he observed mischievously.

"Yes, I might just take you up on that, Matt: keep it open for me, I'll let you know," she replied engagingly and continued, "have I got to perfect my dragon receptionist line. 'No you can't have an appointment' and things like that?"

"Hopefully, not in my surgery," he advised, "but you can always practise those lines just in case."

Truth it might be, but Matt found himself deliberating in an agony of indecision as to whether the information she had given him reassured or worried him. Maybe he would have missed her just a little less, if he knew that she was in a happy, fulfilled relationship with some perfect hunk of a guy.

She didn't impart the information that first-hand experience of a failing marriage between her parents had always made her cautious about embarking on any relationship. Having seen what damage two people, who presumably had once been in love, could do to each other and to the product of their relationship, as it failed. She remembered all too clearly the time at the age of twelve, being moved from the independent school where she'd been happy to a local state school. It was just after her mother had announced that she'd embarked on a new relationship. Her father had declared that he could no longer afford the school fees, and she'd been plunged, mid-term, into a new school, where she was very much the outsider and constantly teased for having a name that seemed unusual. She'd been the weapon that each parent had used to bring about the mutually assured destruction of their relationship and their love, and by so doing to create the hatred that now existed between them.

As the sun became stronger they continued to walk, the time apparently passing seamlessly but remorselessly as they made progress towards Miden village. Only when they arrived at the outskirts of Miden did they turn back, after crossing the river, in order to begin their return journey. By this time Rita had long given up wondering where they might be, but assured herself that it was far from over; the confrontation with Matt Sinclair being postponed, rather than avoided. Driving from his house in a rage, she tore through the quiet village at a speed that reflected her anger.

Monday arrived all too quickly. After breakfast Fabienne raced upstairs to brush her teeth, and to finish her packing. He remained in the kitchen, handling the plates that she'd used that morning as he stacked the dishwasher. They seemed to bear special relevance that day, as he wondered if he'd ever see her again; would she succeed in re-floating her career, or would she simply decide that the struggle wasn't worth the effort, as many would have done? He considered leaving her plates, being the last things that she had touched whilst still involved with his life, a little like his classmate, all those years ago, who refused to wash the hand that had touched the footballer.

Slotting the plates in the dishwasher, he recognised that, for each of them, from different perspectives, tomorrow would be the first day of the rest of their lives. Though he'd had an interlude that even his wildest dreams couldn't have foreseen, he had to accept that it was now over; reality was about to sweep away the dream from which, given the choice, he wouldn't choose to awake. Reminding himself of the fact that she'd told him that his presence at Manchester was important. However, with such a big concert hall, he knew that she probably wouldn't be able to tell if he were there or otherwise, especially when she'd be fighting for her very survival, with thousands of spectators judging her performance. His thoughts were diverted by the sound of her struggling with bags on the stairs, and he rushed up to help her. He found places for the bags in the Beetle, and she arrived on the step, squinting a little as the morning sun hit her full on. Wondering if he'd ever see her standing at that spot again, and whether her feet would contribute to the smoothing of that sandstone at any point in the future: he concluded that it was unlikely.

She paused as she came down the step. Indecision racked him again and seemed more intense even than before. Should he shake her hand in a business-like fashion, hug her, or sweep her up in his arms and tell her something of his thoughts? She too seemed a little awkward, but the steel glinted in those lovely eyes of crystal that he would miss like oxygen itself.

"Matt, I think you're a lucky guy with this life in this village. I just want to thank you for giving me such insight into your life here, and all the people you know and for putting up with me, as you have, and hope that I haven't been a trouble to you." She smiled the mischievous smile that he'd seen so often and had slowly come to recognise as a central facet of her character.

"Now just before I go..." she paused on the cusp of indecision, as her query was forming.

"Go on, Sylvie; just tell me."

"Just what did you do with all those CDs you say you bought? There never were any, were there? Tell me Matt, I just need to know," she said, almost pleadingly.

"OK I'll do you a swap: you tell me what Jane Tomkins said, and I'll tell you what happened to all those CDs," Matt offered incautiously.

"Right then: fair swap," she agreed.

"You first," he suggested.

"OK, then, she's still love-struck, poor thing; just what do you do to them all? None of them have a bad word to say about you. All of them seemed very jealous of me as being seen as your latest! She said you were lively company, would do it all again tomorrow if she could, and had a really nice time with you. Oh yes, that's it, the sex, yes, the sex, she said, was marvellous!"

He blushed at her words, suddenly regretting having asked.

"What sex? All we did was hold hands," he suggested quickly, doing his best to hide his embarrassment.

"Now that, Doctor, I don't believe, and certainly she was getting excited just remembering it!" The playful grin was now held briefly but in abundance on that radiant face. The sheer joy of life and the compelling smile seemed restored to full intensity as she stood before him. "Okay. Now your turn," she reminded him as she looked intently upon him.

"Do I have to tell you?" he began.

"Yes, you have to tell me, your life depends on it, believe me."

"OK, then, well; I promise I have bought every single one you ever made. Must be twenty-four not counting the one that's about to be released."

She nodded encouragingly, with just a hint of surprise.

Suddenly his confidence failed, he couldn't tell her that they all went in the bin and even more crucially - why; which would be her very next question. She nodded as if encouraging him to continue; then more vigorously as she detected his hesitation. "Yes go, on, Matt, confession is good for the soul."

Suddenly an idea formed within his brain. "Oh, and then I gave them all to the church jumble sale."

"The church jumble sale! Are you sure?"

"They were desperate, what could I do?" he confirmed, doing his best to keep an impassive look.

His words had every appearance of verisimilitude. Looking intently at him, her eyes narrowing just a little as she brought more scrutiny to bear, whilst holding him tightly within their gaze. She sensed subterfuge: that somehow, though he'd started well, all hadn't been said. Effort on his part was applied and reapplied in keeping his face as neutral as possible. In those closing milliseconds he couldn't remember what people's faces were supposed to do when they lied, so he just had to hang on as best he could.

"A jumble sale?"

"A jumble sale," he confirmed, whilst attempting to restrain every muscle in his face.

"Well, I hope you got a few bob for them, the first ones are quite rare, these days, you know."

He knew, but looked surprised, as if he had been conned out of them by the vicar needing money for a higher purpose.

"I'm not sure whether to be flattered or insulted," she deliberated.

He sighed inwardly; she seemed to accept his version, which approximated the truth as closely as he was able.

"Later, Matt, we'll revisit this," she assured him, with a knowing nod.

He swallowed hard as he concluded, and not for the first time, that she was certainly no pushover, and if they were to meet again, her examination of him would be more intense.

There was no valedictory speech, no words true or apocryphal, that would change the reality that had forced itself back into their lives. The oasis in time was over, for each of them, and no words from either party could recreate it. He knew only, in those closing seconds that he couldn't ask her to stay. She knew only, that she couldn't say if she would return or when. She broke contact and was about to turn.

"Time for me to go," she said simply.

"Are you going to be OK?" He asked the same question she had asked him in Luciano's just as she left. It was almost as though she had handed him at that point, with her words, the baton of strength; a talisman that would protect him from harm most likely due to the raging thoughts within him that she had somehow detected. It was time for him to return that talisman to its rightful owner, as she now needed it more than he.

"I will be; now," she replied.

He bent down, grabbed her hand quickly but lightly as she turned, and kissed her. Strong arms held her to him for what his brain told him was an age, but his heart said was a fleeting moment. In any event as he let her go, the last image he had of her, was that of her walking to the rented blue Beetle, throwing the baseball cap on the back seat and starting the engine.

She drove through the gate and down the road, as she had come days before, without looking back. Smiling to himself, he heard the gearbox crunch just a little, as she attempted transfer of first to second gear. He had known loss on more occasions than would many in a relatively short life. His first year at medical school - leaving home at eighteen with his father just buried, and the death of his mother not that long ago. Those lonely and miserable times were as nothing compared to the loss he suffered now. He knew that in his parents' case he couldn't have altered their destiny or his. On this occasion all he could do was to torture himself with things he might have done or said, to persuade her to stay. This was almost an optional loss, something that he could have changed. The passing of his parents had been out of his hands, and purely in the lap of forces beyond his comprehension.

Returning to the large, now empty house, he saw her struggling in the kitchen, heard those heels on the stairs - wondered if they were still scratching the teak boards, queried if that rustle was the Beetle on his drive, and even if there were gentle sobs coming from her room. It was as if his whole life had shattered into a million tiny fragments that made no sense, and couldn't possibly interact in a useful way ever again. The only thing binding those loose and separating fragments together now, was abject misery. All his preparations, all his promises to be strong, were ineffectual in countering the torment and loneliness that accompanied him like an abyss into which he dared not look, in case it engulfed him completely.

He thought of phoning Steve, but he knew that this was something he would have to deal with on his own. Steve's criticism of him and of his life, had hurt like a body blow, but wasn't widely at variance with the truth. He'd hoped to prove that he was a better person than his self-centred stance had demonstrated hitherto, but these aspirations had departed in a blue Beetle. He went upstairs dejectedly to get his mobile phone and jacket, each step now a battle. As before, activity, one heartbeat at a time, one breath succeeding the one before, and one foot in front of another, was the only thing that would stop him from sinking into a catatonic state from which he knew he couldn't recover. Surely it would be easier to sink, to fail and to just let go, rather than struggle. Suddenly a reflection in the periphery of his vision demanded attention that swept away disquieting thoughts. By the side of his bed was a cube wrapped in bright paper, with a large metallic blue bow stuck on top. He picked it up and took the envelope that lay underneath it. The handwriting was unmistakable. Opening the envelope, he withdrew the card inside. His hands were shaking just a little more than he would have wished to admit, if he were describing the events to another person.

Dear Matt,
Well here we are, on a knife's edge. I'm really terrified and honestly don't know what the next few weeks will bring. I suppose I don't really know if I want to go back to the life that's bringing me so much pain at the moment. What I do know is that I'll never forget your kindness, the time and attention you gave me, and above all, your efforts to show me that there are real people on this planet, and that there are happy lives to be found in the most simple of places. You've been a true friend, when true friends seemed a little thin on the ground.

I'm sorry if I embarrassed you at all about some of your friends and some of your ex-girlfriends. Truth be told, everywhere I went people were pleased to know me, simply because I knew you, and I really wanted to find courage to say that to you before I left, so forgive me for bottling out on you and putting it in this card instead.

Please find in this little box a present I thought you might like. The one you have is not the sort of thing that a local GP should be seen wearing, so I've tried to put this right. I can't think of anyone, even Peter, on whom it would look better, and I do hope you like it. I hope each morning as you take it from its box and put it on, that you'll think of me as, I know, I'll be thinking of you.

Thanks, most of all for sharing a tiny slice of your life with me, and for rescuing me when it seemed I couldn't fall any further.

Love you loads.
Sylvie
PS. Give my Love to Mary and Steve

It was just as well that he was on his own at this point, as he knew that words wouldn't have come, the eyes were stinging again, and the fact that there was no-one from whom to hide that stinging, made it, in some way, even worse. Ripping open the paper, he withdrew a hinged leather case from its card sleeve. Inside the case was a Breitling Chronomat. A more magnificent timepiece he'd never held. Having seen them advertised in glossy magazines, he had never caressed one in his hands. He'd always assumed that their cost was above the ceiling that he could justify for a watch. Perhaps, as with the best presents, it was something he'd always inwardly desired, but had never been quite able to justify buying for himself. He took off his old watch, still keeping perfect time but looking on the distant side of cheap and nasty in comparison with the timepiece he now slipped around his wrist.

Self-reproach, charged with regrets flooded over him. How could he have let her go? Why had he not either screamed or begged her to stay? How could he have let her leave with so many words unspoken? There were several occasions on which he could have declared his feelings for her, swept her up in his arms and dissipated his sexual yearning. Moments had been wasted; moments when he could have capitalised on her low mood, vulnerable state or loneliness, to consummate those feelings that he had for her. His heart interceded to slow such racing thoughts. To pursue her and to win her in her weakened or distracted state might well have been possible. There had, indeed, been a great many opportunities: the long walks, the brushing of the hands, the occasions when she'd quickly kissed him, the drive back from Steve's house, or the dinners for two; he'd failed at each of these. In that cusp of indecision, clarity of thought prevailed. What his instinct told him he wanted held no place – this was about what *she* wanted, and what she needed, to repair damage that selfish people had inflicted. At that moment he shivered as he was reminded of the look of sexual intent that glowed from Rita's eyes, like some force that could neither be resisted nor controlled.

If he had made such advances and Fabienne hadn't responded, she might have felt compelled to vacate his house, a place where she'd sought protection and refuge, thereby compounding her problems, just at that most vulnerable time. Even if she had been willing to engage in a physical relationship, it would almost certainly have placed extra strain on her, and endangered the mutual regard that he told himself had been uppermost in his mind at all times.

Just before deconstructive analysis turned to self-loathing he realised that his duty as a doctor and his wish to help others had subjugated more base desires as a man. He brightened visibly, recognising his deliverance from thoughts that could only disappoint from their inception. A fleeting moment of optimism held that she would be in touch at some point in the future, though no assurances had been sought or given in this respect; such optimism was perhaps foolish and unwise. His heart could only tell him that he'd behaved correctly at all times, and that destiny possibly held more chapters for the two of them: accepting, ultimately, that it was impossible for either of them to say. No doubt all she could see of her own future at present was a concert in Manchester, looming large on the horizon.

He had tried very hard to hide his true feelings for her, from the precise enquiry of those eyes of glistening crystal, perhaps a window to her own soul, if one could summon the courage to engage with them for long enough. His brain was telling him that it would have to do; his heart undoubtedly had sought more, much more. She'd departed in a far stronger frame of mind than when she'd arrived. Much of this was due to his input and his unswerving adherence to a business-like agenda, which he'd hoped would be the approach most likely to restore her. He'd been correct in that assumption. The rest would just have to be dreamed about, or held fleetingly in his imagination before he recalled himself to reality. The ultimate truth had comfort for him; that he was grateful for, and would never regret, having known her: that he would do the same again, even if it meant that they were never to meet in the future.

A rusty old car appeared and pulled up on the verge outside his house. Jim Duggan vacated the car and kept station in the wooded area facing Matt's gateway; his pockets, as ever, crammed with powerful imaging and transmission equipment. Jim spat out, before placing yet another cigarette between the chapped lips and stained teeth. "Know who you are, old 'an'some, don't we mi boy. Yer won't escape this time yer strawberry puff. Jim'll have yer. No one does Jim out of 'is scoop, and certainly not some queer, quack doctor. I'm stayin' till she appears this time; think y're so clever, you two, but Jim'll 'ave yer *and* that bleedin' bonus."

Matt glanced at his new watch: he hadn't been aware of the time, but he was now brought back to focus with the reality that he was late. He gulped the remains of a cold mug of coffee and departed for work. His heart insisted that his best course of action was to wallow in regrets about what might have been, served with lashings of self-pity. His head, however, held most firmly the view that his only hope now lay within the work that he loved. As he neared work, his head finally won the argument - but only by the narrowest of margins and at the last minute, in deciding the balance of that argument by recalling the promise he had made to Steve.

Janice, as always, was gossiping to Mrs Simpson. She was imparting to her, for once, something that she hadn't known, and something so unusual that even at the last minute she couldn't step in and say that she'd known about it from the outset. In an unusual state of affairs, she was listening intently as Janice gave her version of events.

"I hear this new girlfriend is a real stunner. They say she's staying with him for a few days. Whole village is talking about her. All the old boys in the shops are lusting after her."

"Why the press? The old lech, what's he been up to?" queried Mrs Simpson, now so curious that she could not feign prior knowledge.

"He told me there was supposed to be someone famous in the village, and they had the wrong house or something."

"You don't think he's a Russian secret agent sent here as a sleeper at the time of the cold war?" put in Mrs Simpson.

Janice thought so long on this that Mrs Simpson wondered if she had the strength to explain it to her.

"He don't look that old does he, Mrs S?" Janice asked while doing her best to maintain the thread of the conversation.

"No, Janice," she said, summoning reserves of patience that were not at their deepest, "I was only joking." Suddenly, abjectly, regretting her light-hearted departure from the simple. "But you can be sure, there's something going on here, and my name isn't Monica Simpson if I don't find out pretty soon. Why did he ask you to collect those files? Why didn't he do it himself?"

"I don't know; he was ever so grateful," said Janice, as usual picking out the kindest aspect of her interaction with another.

"I've had a look at those files, and they're just utility bills and statements, things like that. No, no, Janice something's going on here, right under our noses." On this occasion the practice manager's instinct was much more accurate than her usual misconceived pronouncements.

Matt came in, determined not to look as miserable as he felt, and decided to keep things moving by avoiding getting caught in conversation: his timing made this easier.

"Sorry for being late: better start straight away. I'll call the first patient in now, if that's OK, but I'll get back to you after the surgery, Monica. Oh Janice, thanks for collecting those files for me at weekend. Just had my hands full and wanted to go through them today."

Mrs Simpson waited for him to go into his consulting room: "a likely story; something very, very, fishy here," she suggested, with more excitement than she would wish to reveal to her junior.

He was soon immersed in his work, and the patients, as usual, brought a mixture of the unusual, serious, humdrum and routine, as he sat in his consulting room. It was a fairly busy surgery, and the nice thing was that there was no time to think about anything else other than the patient coming through the door. After the visits he popped home for a quick lunch. The house seemed very quiet and he didn't remain longer there, than the time it took to make and consume a couple of sandwiches and a cup of coffee: black with a splash of cream. The joy and companionship that she'd brought in so short a space of time was now so sadly lacking. He'd never felt alone within his own home, having always preferred a solitary existence - until now. At no point had he foreseen a time when he would want to live anywhere else, but her absence brought into stark relief the fact that his home now seemed sterile and lonely. He could only hope that the feeling would pass in time.

Jim Duggan noticed the blue Jaguar returning. The house had been very quiet all morning. Jim had been telling himself that it was because 'the stupid bitch', as he had referred to her, couldn't get out of bed. On Matt's return, he reached quickly for his camera, sensing that this was the moment that he would claim his scoop. He had more words to say to himself when, thirty minutes later he saw Matt dart back to his car again, and head back to work.

"Lazy bleeder, does she never get up? No good, missee, I'm goin' nowhere. This time you ain't gonna 'oodwink me. I'll 'ave yer yet, and that puff of a boyfriend of yours."

It was to be two hours later that Jim's mobile phone would ring with the news that Fabienne was giving a press conference in London. Throwing down his expensive digital camera in a burst of unrestrained temper, he swore prolifically as he got into his car to begin the long drive back to London, for a story that would be old news by the time he got there. How he hated this job!

Matt met with Mrs Simpson after lunch. A busy few weeks lay in prospect at the surgery, and she and Matt finalised the plans. Matt was delighted that so much was to happen so quickly. The simple expedient of not letting his mind wander would stop him from thinking too much, and just at that point, it was the thinking that was painful. He wasn't looking forward to the nights, sensing that it would be harder, much harder, to cope with those, especially if sleep refused to remove him from those restless thoughts. The saving grace was that the only aspect of his life that she hadn't directly touched, was his work. Work would be the lodestar that he'd follow, as might a traveller of old in searching for Polaris shining from the heavens. By applying himself to that work, he could at least continue, without thinking of her every few minutes. His home life, he knew, wouldn't be so easy. A steady caseload waited for him in the afternoon's surgery, and he continued to concentrate with as much strength of will as he could muster, on each problem trivial or otherwise.

It was unusual for him to hang around after work. He bade all the staff a good night and stayed inputting data on to the computer system. Mrs Simpson's mind was speculating wildly as to the true reasons behind his sudden change of work pattern. Looking at him intently as he sat at the computer in the office: try as she might she just couldn't come up with any possible answers to the puzzle before her. Something was going on, and the only thing she did know, was that sooner or later she'd find out. She left quietly, still deep in thought. Matt stayed for a couple of hours; he'd never been so reluctant to return to his empty house. Eventually he could think of nothing else that needed doing, and he didn't feel hungry enough to stop off anywhere for his tea. He knew that he'd have to return home sooner or later, so he decided to do just that.

As he approached his house he saw that Steve's car was on the drive. Pulling up beside it, he saw that Steve and Mary were waiting in the car.
"Hi Matt, we were just about to go. You must be tired; we'll go and I'll phone you tomorrow," Steve offered.
"Sorry Steve, Hi Mary, I've been pretty busy at work, but please come inside and I'll make you a drink."
They looked at each other, as if to gauge the wisdom of disturbing him in this way.
"Come on, I'll get the kettle on," Matt cajoled.
Sensing his need for company, they followed him across the sandstone porch and into the house.
"So Matt, how's things?" Steve asked.
"Sylvie went back this morning."
"Yes," said Mary, "we saw her press conference on the telly. They've launched her new CD and the Manchester concert is on. Apparently, after that she's off to North America to do a further four concerts there."
"So how are you holding up?" said Steve solicitously, marking him more a friend than psychologist, which Matt appreciated.

"We think you did a really good job, Matt in providing a shelter for her. It seems she's really been through a bad time," suggested Mary.

Matt could tell that each of them wasn't quite sure what to say, as it was unusual for them to keep talking in this manner.

"Look, it's really good of you to come round." He knew that they just wanted to make sure he was coping and also to make sure that he wasn't lonely.

"I bet you were really shocked to see her on your doorstep," said Mary, a smile flickering on her round face. Matt told them of the events of that evening, and how she'd appeared, seeking a refuge where none would think to look. He described his pleasure at being in her company, but said nothing of the worry about her future, nor the strain of adopting a caring role when his hormones had demanded something very different. He also told them of her bluff theory, which Steve, in particular, found very interesting.

"One or two perceptive people, however, like you Mary, smelt a rat straight away," he voiced with the calm even respectful tones that one might use with an older sister, and habitually so when conversing with Mary.

"Matt, you looked so good together," her voice trailed off. Mary could see the turmoil and the sense of loss that he could barely hide from others who knew him less well, and certainly never from her.

"We think she's lovely. We had a really long chat, the day she popped round with those flowers. She's someone you think you've known all your life," Mary continued, "Are there any plans to see her again?"

Matt explained that it was impossible to say; that Fabienne could only see as far as her next concert and not much else apart from that, at the present time. Mary nodded by way of acknowledgment of the difficulties she faced. Only later when the couple were alone did they voice their view that any return would be on the less probable side of unlikely.

Matt spoke of his plans for the surgery and the imminent changes that would be taking place. He also informed them that he had put together an audacious bid for the contract of medical adviser to a large private nursing home that had just opened, barely a mile from Parkvale surgery. Both he and Greg realised that the partners at Parkvale, and especially Rita, would see the contract as being unequivocally within their grasp, and would under no circumstances expect it to be placed anywhere other than with them. Steve, in particular, remained quiet as Matt discussed his plans for the lucrative and high-profile role, whilst Mary found his enthusiasm nothing other than infectious. Mary could only conclude that Parkvale would be extremely unwise to discount him, as this was precisely when Matt was at his most potent.

They chatted for a little while longer before Steve suggested that they'd better be getting home. Both seemed a little sad to be leaving him, suspecting that he was about to have a bad night. Mary went to wait in the car after kissing him goodnight.

"Look, Matt it's going to be a tricky few days, I want you to know how proud I am of you, and I think you've done an excellent job here. You've done her a really good turn," Steve confessed and went on to say, "I couldn't believe it when Mary told me what had happened. I suppose it shows that these mega celebrities might have loads of money, but no real friends. If there's anything I can do, just give me a ring. I'll phone you in a few days," he said with finality, just as another thought came to him. "Oh, and by the way, we've got such good news: Mary's pregnant. We've not told anyone yet, because it's a bit early, but we thought that the Godparent ought to know."

Matt shook his hand and insisted on going out to the car to congratulate Mary. Steve got in while Matt leaned on the open window of Mary's side. "Thanks for coming, you two. I really do appreciate your support. Hope to speak to you in a few days and in the meanwhile you take care of yourself, Mary." Matt kissed her again; Steve eventually managed to start the car and Matt watched them depart.

Matt was delighted for them both. He thought about the time that he and Mary had been together. It was a long while ago. He'd always thought of her as a wonderful person, and time had enhanced, not diminished, those sentiments. She'd been an ECG technician when they met and he remembered the day that he'd suggested that Steve come out for a drink with them. Something had clicked as soon as they'd set eyes on each other, and he'd spent the rest of the evening playing gooseberry to the relationship that sizzled between them. Over the years they'd grown together; now he wasn't surprised that they'd set the seal on their marriage and relationship, by embarking on having children.

Looking up at the stairs as he went back into his house, he thought of the bedroom that now seemed uninviting, as if a battle was about to be joined there that would last all night. Matt toyed with the idea of taking a sleeping tablet. He knew that this would prevent the turmoil that he was expecting through the night, and he also knew that with modern sleeping tablets he would awake refreshed, rather than hung-over, which had been a problem with earlier tablets. Ultimately, he realised that relying on the dubious artifice of a tablet would create a false state within him, and he knew only that for better or worse, this was something he would have to work through.

He decided to sit in his lounge and go through his CD collection. Predictably, his mood was reflected in his choice of music. Puccini's *Madam Butterfly* seemed strangely appropriate, and *One Fine Day* was pumped up to such a volume, through the magnificent KEF monitor speakers, that neighbours down the street, had he had any, would have been able to hear it. He played the CD several times, and the tragic nature of the music and the story seemed to soothe some of his thoughts. After hearing it a few times, he settled for Michael Jackson's rendition of *Smile,* which also stopped unhelpful thoughts from racing round his frantic mind. He took a hot bath, went to bed even later than usual, tried to read; doing all the things that he told his patients to do, but ultimately failed to get to sleep, until his racing brain was granted absolution with the reward of sleep, thirty minutes before his alarm sounded.

Getting up the following morning could only be accomplished by a supreme effort. He sank to his knees by the side of the bed more in penance than in prayer. His sin? To have believed that he could ever have been truly happy. He wasn't sure that he had the strength to get up, let alone go on, as desolate feelings found fertile ground in his exhausted brain. Dragging himself towards the shower, he hoped that its jets would do for him, what they had done many times before; create some life in a body that seemed devoid of it. After negotiating the shower, he got dressed. However, it was only when he came to put on his new watch that his body and mind flickered, as if someone had just activated the 'on' switch. Smiling to himself, he re-read her words from the card.

'I hope you'll think of me, as I'll be thinking of you.'

She'd almost meant the gift to be something more; a constant reminder that would bridge the distance between them, both physically and emotionally. He gently rubbed the watch between his fingers and palm as if somehow it would summon her presence, like a genie from a rusty lamp. One thing was unmistakable; she seemed to have wisdom, and an insight into the character of other human beings, that was belied by her own tender years. How ironic that those around her had managed far less on the scale of humanity. He fastened the watch round his wrist. She had been correct in this too: it was a magnificent watch, and he was very lucky to have such a timepiece. Just looking at the Breitling for those few moments had given him more energy and strength of purpose. If he were to fail now, he'd be letting down not only himself and others who depended upon him, like his patients and his staff, but also, he could see now, Fabienne herself. A twinkle appeared on his face that would shine through those dark days – an emotion that Fabienne would very much approve.

He drove to work feeling much brighter. Dr Stevens was starting today, and Matt was keen to be early. A small surgery had been booked for the new doctor. Janice, having carefully checked each set of notes the evening before, arrived early: ensuring that she was on hand to meet the new doctor and help him with any queries. Matt smiled again to himself. He knew that Greg wasn't married, as of course did Janice, by this time. Even Mrs Simpson had pinned up her usually untidy brown hair and put on her best suit, the one she wore when Matt was meeting with members from the PCT, or when interviewing new staff.

Matt was in the office when Dr Stevens arrived. Janice rushed to the door to hold it open for him as he struggled a little with his briefcase; dashing off very quickly to make him a cup of tea. Matt considered that she must have re-boiled the kettle several times that morning already, as she returned in no time with a mug of tea and some biscuits. Matt noted that the tea seemed piping hot, and the biscuits were perfectly intact, unlike the offerings that were usually placed in front of him.

Greg was shorter than Matt, but what he lacked in height, was more than made up for by his stocky, muscular build. The shirt, though perfectly ironed, seemed just a little small for the substantial neck, and the tie seemed to be under considerable strain from the developed muscles. His white teeth shone like porcelain, in his rather rotund face, creating even more of a contrast with the smooth black skin.

"We've put you in my consulting room, but only booked half a surgery; we thought you'd want a bit of time to get to know some of the patients," Matt suggested helpfully.

"Many thanks, Matt. That's really good of you," Greg answered in his smooth, deep voice.

Matt took him down to the consulting room for a final run-through of things and a brief demonstration of his blood pressure machine, which was of an unusual design. He returned to the office just as a large truck pulled up outside. The builder had given a start date, and the temporary cabins were being delivered today, so that they could be up and running with services connected when the roof came off.

Patients started drifting in, but seemed bewildered by all the changes. Mrs Simpson despatched Janice to reassure them, and make sure that they were given details of the arrival of the new doctor and the start of the building work. The PCT had already written to each and every one of them to that effect, but Mrs Simpson warned Janice that nothing could be taken for granted. As soon as Dr Stevens started the surgery, Matt took the opportunity to nip out. He popped to Tesco in Merton to buy Fabienne's latest CD. Slotting it immediately into his CD changer in the boot, so that he could listen to it, out on his visits. He also noted a review in the morning paper, which he placed on the passenger seat with a view to reading over lunch. He thought that the CD was superb, but admitted to more than a little bias. He considered that he'd never heard a bad record of hers, unlike those of some artists who couldn't seem to attain that consistency that she'd maintained over the years.

Unfortunately, as he read later, the press took a different view. Reviews of the CD held that it lacked variety and sufficient interest, and whilst competent, didn't seem to contain any ground-breaking material. Almost as if damning it with faint praise, they considered that it was perfectly adequate for background music, but hardly up to her best work. The assistant on the audio counter had told him that sales had been slow, and Matt hoped that this wasn't representative of the national picture. Fabienne would be distraught if the sales and reviews were negative, as she'd been hoping that this would signal the start of her turnaround. If the sales were as poor as the assistant led him to believe, and this was reflected nationally, then Matt knew that she'd now be under intense pressure, with even more riding on the Manchester concert. She'd told him that she rarely read reviews, but with her career at a finely poised juncture he wondered whether this was a luxury she could still afford.

Matt finished off the visits and met up with Greg as his surgery finished. He seemed to have enjoyed his first morning, and Matt wasn't surprised to see that Janice had kept him supplied with regular cups of tea and biscuits. The cabins had been set down in the car park, and contractors were already on site, connecting the services. Computers, files and office equipment were to be transferred throughout the afternoon, as soon as the electricity was connected. Matt ran the afternoon surgery, which allowed Greg the opportunity to take a look round the practice area, and also to acquaint himself with some of the office procedures, as well as the computer system. Mrs Simpson had planned to do this introduction personally, but acquiesced after much pleading from Janice, who had offered to remain at work without pay, so that she could assume this role!

Matt remained behind after surgery. The temporary accommodation had been set up, and he told himself and others that he wanted to make sure that everything was ready for surgeries to take place in there the following day. The builder was due to start at the end of the week, and all were praying for a dry autumn so that the roof could come off without too much damage to the existing fabric of the building.

Matt arrived home late to find yet another car on his drive: this time the unmistakable red Boxster. As soon as she saw the Jaguar come to a halt, Rita got out of her car and walked over to him.

"Hi Rita, what brings you to this quiet backwater?"

He opened the door and Rita went in ahead of him.

"Nice place Matt," she said smoothly.

"Thanks Rita, not bad for a country yokel like myself."

"Look Matt, I didn't come here for a row." She hesitated almost as if traversing new, unfamiliar ground. "I miss you. I suppose, I've always wanted you in my life. I see you wasting your time with pipedreams - a person, let's face it, you'll never see again. First a concert in Manchester, then she flies out to the States to try to shore things up there. Word is that she's staked everything on this one concert. She's so up to her neck in lawsuits, with the venue owners who are suing for breach of contract; all the ticket refunds; and sponsors deserting the sinking ship. She's putting off the inevitable. She doesn't know if she's going to make it, and she certainly can't tell if she'll be back this way. Now come on. She must have a sailor in every port, and you in this village!"

Her logic, as always, was inescapable and wasn't far removed from what he'd told himself, albeit in more emollient terms. It wasn't necessarily that her words lacked truth, but the choice of those words, and the dispassionate, uncaring analysis with which they unceremoniously flowed from her tongue - that was hard to bear. Rita, as always, missed the nuances of human emotion, a person's need to be carefully won over with new ideas, and tempted by words as well as actions. She knew about temptation by visual stimulation, and obviously this method had worked well for her. The low-cut, diaphanous blouse, the delicate see-through lines of the bra supporting her full breasts, the crisp skirt, the tanned legs, and trim figure; all of these were used proficiently to excite the male sexual drive, so dependent on visual stimulation; and to make women feel jealous of her. Visual enticement, powerful though it was, was no longer sufficient to create the more lasting appeal that he realised his heart longed for. Having suspected as much before having Fabienne in his house: he now knew it to be a fact. He wondered, if Rita had found herself having to hide away in the house of a near stranger, what sort of note, if any, she would have written, and what sort of present, if any, she would have left.

Matt sat down next to her; for once it required no effort on his part to maintain those revealing legs at the periphery of his vision. As he looked at her the deep blue met those emeralds of sexual conflagration.

"Rita, don't think I'm not flattered by the offer and by the attention. I know you don't think it's much - but the life I lead here in this village, with these people, is as vital to me as I'm sure yours is to you. What we had was a long time ago. If I hurt you in some way, then that wasn't intentional." He remembered that she'd grown impatient for a more frequent sexual engagement than his studies permitted: eventually drifting into the bed of a contemporary - who promptly failed his finals.

"The person I was then, and am now, are very different; and I suspect the same is so for you too. I'm sorry, but I can't see us turning back the clock: as much as we might want to try, we're doomed to fail."

Carefully considered words were chosen so as to avoid insult, yet leave no doubt about what he was saying. "*You* know, and I know, that you'd be bored in no time: that the life you lead and the one I lead are very different things. We've both moved on from our student days and become two very different people, and the memories that we both share, happened a long time ago. I'm sorry if that isn't enough for you."

She glared at him, surveying him critically. There was a slight pause before her words gushed forth. "You're wasted here in this place, in this tiny village," she said forcibly.

"I'm happy here, Rita; happy and contented, " he replied calmly.

She continued, "You poor sod, you've gone soft on me. I can see you're soft on her. The person you'll never see. You'll sit here, waiting and waiting, while she travels the world, refloating this, or shoring up that, if she can, of course. There won't be any time for you, old Matt; you'll grow sad and lonely here, as well as boring, which you already are. Whatever did I see in you? Remember too, Matt, that *contentment* is a word used by those who can't admit to themselves that apathy and lack of ambition run their lives. That's you all over, at the moment."

Facing disappointment or hearing an opposing view was never her strong suit and such emotion was quickly subsumed by anger. Having finished her diatribe, she rose quickly as if she could bear no more contact with him, in case his ideas would somehow addle her mind.

"I'm sorry you feel that way Rita," he offered, sensing that her departure had an air of finality about it.

She turned as she said, "Goodbye, Matt, I hope you have a nice life: I know I will," and continued spitefully, "hope you manage to catch a glimpse of her on the telly every once in a while, maybe treat yourself to a new CD of hers - that's if she does make a comeback, which is in doubt after the rubbish she's just released."

Only then, as she turned to go, did she catch a glimpse of the magnificent timepiece on his wrist. "Nice watch, Matt," she said: "Enjoy it won't you: it'll measure your ageing very nicely."

He decided to say no more. The poison that was released when she heard something she didn't like was particularly hard to take: there was often just a hint of truth, perhaps a tiny seed of doubt that she could instil in a person. She was certainly adept at picking up others' doubts in a given situation, and such insight was used rather as a captain might use the lash on the back of an unruly crewman. He paused as he reflected to what effect Fabienne would use those same skills. Rita rushed from the house without looking back: though the door was left open, any lines of communication between them had been irrevocably closed. He shrugged as the Boxster screamed away. Upsetting her had been a function of simply telling her the truth, rather than any desire on his part to hurt her. At the final analysis, he would rather be on his own, with his memories - and his watch - than risk a relationship at any level with Rita.

Matt's strategy in those first, difficult days was very simple; to spend as much time as possible at work and in the company of others, and to arrive home as late as he could. Slowly, with the passage of time, things became easier. His home no longer triggered unhappy and unhelpful memories, but gradually, as time passed, he was able to spend longer and longer periods there. He'd taken to reading his paper in the conservatory again, and had started cooking at home, rather than eating out. Other thoughts persisted stubbornly, however. Laughing to himself, he suddenly realised that he would even be perfectly happy to sample more of her cooking -if it meant she was with him.

It was to be a few days before he could enter the spare room to remove the bedding and the towels neatly folded on the side of the bath. He could still smell that delicate perfume on the duvet, as he stripped the bed. Holding the pillow, he pictured her recumbent pretty face and gorgeous tresses. She'd affected every aspect of his life within the house, so that it was very hard not to picture her there, while he went about his old routines. He continued to take long walks after work. Just as he'd assured her that the walks and the calm that was to be found at night would restore her; he now took comfort from his own advice. Each morning, reaching for the case that contained the watch, became almost a ritual, as though she were there to speak to in person. Telling himself that she'd be thinking of him at this time of day, such thoughts, and the simple act of strapping on the watch, above all, helped him as the days slowly passed.

Fabienne had released another single which was available just before the concert was due to take place. Matt bought a copy as soon as it was released and found himself playing it repeatedly in his car and at home. The reviews, once again, were mixed and Matt knew too well that this would be more unwelcome news for her: raising the pressure on her to confound her critics by bringing about an outstanding performance in Manchester. He'd been hoping that he'd be able to spend a few minutes with her at the concert, though he knew that this was unlikely as there'd be so many people surrounding her, which might preclude such a meeting, even if she should want to see him.

The eve of the concert came at last. He'd been ticking the days off at first, on his year planner; but then as the days went by, he became busier and busier and more distracted, so that he neglected the planner. Eventually he was surprised to realise that the concert was the very next day. On that Friday an urgent call came through as he held his surgery in the temporary accommodation. He wasn't expecting to hear from Professor Harrison, the psychiatrist who had been treating Barry Miles.

"Hello, Dr Sinclair, it's Prof Harrison here. I'm sure you'll remember me. You telephoned me some weeks ago about Barry Miles.

"I'm sorry to trouble you, but something potentially serious has come up. You're our last hope," he said gravely.

Matt's thoughts were racing furiously, as he wondered just what these events were. He didn't have to wait long.

"Sheila Coombs was Barry Miles' girlfriend. She's psychotic and has a history of violence. She and Barry met while both had been sectioned, some months ago, in one of our secure units. Soon after his death Sheila, who'd been discharged into the community with regular reviews in clinic by this time, refused to have any further depot injections."

Matt knew that depot injections of anti-psychotics were often used to control the more serious cases, especially if there was a problem with tablet compliance. Some psychotic patients led chaotic lives and couldn't always guarantee to take medication regularly, even if they wanted to. Long-acting or depot injections were often used in such patients, with their consent, to ensure that the condition was controlled and as near normal a life as possible resumed.

Professor Harrison continued, "Sheila has refused to go back on the depot and has also refused to take any tablets. We believe that she's dangerous. Moreover, she blames Fabienne for trying to take Barry Miles away from her, and blames his death on her. We're of the view that the psychotic condition is responsible for these thoughts."

Matt's mind was racing, as the full impact of the professor's words hit him.

"She's defaulted on a number of clinic appointments. The duty assessment nurse has been out to her flat on several occasions, but she hasn't been in." He paused for a moment, so that Matt could take in what he was saying: "we were planning to section her, admit her, and administer treatment under compulsion."

Matt knew that this, 'certifying' of patients, as it was known, by doctors who were about to invoke the Mental

Health Act, usually as a last resort; was to protect a patient or members of the public, or indeed both. It was a very traumatic way to force patients into having treatment, and was used only for the most pressing of reasons and also in the most serious cases. Professor Harrison had more to tell. "Truth is, she's disappeared. We've put an alert out to the Police, as we believe that she may be dangerous. My reason for phoning you is that you told me that you were a friend of Fabienne's, and she may well try to make contact with her. Please advise Fabienne that she must make no attempt to get too close to her, and must phone the police immediately if any approach is made." The professor paused for a few seconds. Matt understood the implication even before his next words. "Fabienne should consider herself to be in danger. We have tried to contact her press secretary, but have been unable to get through. You were very much our last resort: forgive me for burdening you with this; we really have no other avenues open to us. It may be a false alarm, Sheila Coombs may well turn up in a week or two, but we thought that we'd better alert people to the possible dangers."

"I don't suppose you have a photograph of Sheila Coombs have you?" Matt enquired

"No, I'm sorry Dr Sinclair, we don't."

Matt knew that even serious drug addicts and people who were considered a risk to society never had their photographs on their files - it was considered a breach of their confidentiality, even though it would have helped enormously if they were being sought by medical or law-enforcement staff, as now.

"Well, many thanks for this professor," Matt offered somewhat ambivalently: it seemed strange to be thanking someone for such terrible news. "I'll try to warn Fabienne and her team."

Professor Harrison suggested: "The only information I can give you, is that she has long, lank, greasy, brown hair which is really untidy. Hygiene was never one of her strong points even when she was relatively well, and of course now she is poorly, she'll be more unkempt than usual. She usually wears T-shirt and jeans. Every time I've seen her she's been wearing an old FCUK T-shirt and jeans with torn-out knees. I know it's not going to be much help to you." His voice died away as he recognised Matt's difficulties.

"I have your number if I do hear anything," Matt confirmed. "Thanks again for letting me know."

Just before closing, professor Harrison offered sorrowfully, "please accept my apologies at burdening you with this; I hope it's all a false alarm. The poor girl, Fabienne, appears to have been through enough of late, from what I gather."

As he replaced the handset, deep in thought, Matt realised that the professor's emotions went deeper than simple regret. The court had entrusted Barry Miles' care to him so that he could make a proper assessment, recommendations and treatment. He'd then failed him by delaying treatment too long. Knowing that Fabienne was a target, he failed to inform her or the police, and delayed again when her very destruction seemed imminent, with some story about preserving patient confidentiality. Matt remembered from his own experience, that the medical defence unions would give an opinion about whether information could be divulged, on the same day, not a week later. Matt could now see that the Professor's overriding emotion was neither regret nor concern, but rather guilt; that could only arise in a clinician who'd been negligent. Having failed Fabienne once, he'd now failed her again, by neglecting the care of another patient entrusted to him. The difference this time, was that Fabienne stood to lose more than her career. If the professor was admitting so much so late, Matt had no doubt that she was in grave danger.

He thought furiously about the facts he could put in place. Remembering that Barry, was an unemployed stage constructor, and had most probably been in contact with Fabienne during the course of his work. Perhaps he'd seen her during concerts or rehearsals. His mind raced feverishly ahead, as it failed to accept the logical progression of those thoughts. How could he possibly find Sheila Coombs? She could be anywhere; Fabienne could be in danger at this minute. Matt reasoned, however, that, as Professor Harrison had trouble reaching anyone in her team, it was likely that she was keeping a low profile until the concert, and would hopefully be out of harm's way, at least for the time being.

Matt's surging and chaotic thoughts suddenly seemed to come into focus, and the more he thought, the more he realised that each of those deliberations led to the concert. This would be an ideal opportunity for someone to attack Fabienne. A concert in front of thousands of people could offer little protection. The whole attraction of a concert, as Fabienne had indicated at their meeting, was the proximity of the star to her fans: proximity that would be inevitably entwined with the danger that she faced. A scared and detached performer would be unlikely to engage with her audience and generate the favourable impressions she desperately needed. An armchair-theorist would instantly recognise the compelling dilemma, which was about to open up; the very place they didn't want Sheila, would be the place she would most likely appear. Matt reasoned that this, in fact, was their only practical hope of finding her. The concert might force her out in the open, although the corollary would be that Fabienne was in danger. He telephoned Lucy immediately.

"Hi Lucy, it's Matt."

"Hi Matt, nice to hear from you, are you well?" she asked.

"I'm fine. Look Lucy, I've come across some information that may mean that Fabienne is in danger." Matt related to Lucy the information as given to him by Professor Harrison. "Do you think she'd better cancel?" Matt suggested.

"To tell you frankly, Matt, if this concert doesn't go ahead, it'll be certain professional suicide for her," she said gravely and continued, "by all means, I'll pass on your message, but I don't think she'll cancel now. We'll probably hire extra security guards and protect her as much as we can, without reducing her visibility."

Matt recognised how vital such visibility was to pop stars like Fabienne, since she'd drawn his attention to the fact that it was one of her main reasons for agreeing to their lunch meeting. He couldn't bear the thought of her being endangered, but had to accept that there was probably no other way.

"We hope to see you there, Matt, and many thanks for letting me know."

"Pass on my ... best wishes won't you, and good luck."

"I'll be sure to do that, thanks for phoning, Matt."

Matt wasn't surprised at Lucy's assessment of the situation. Fabienne, he surmised, would make the decision, but was gambling just about everything on this one throw of the dice. Being aware that Fabienne must have worked tirelessly on preparations, rehearsals, new material and promotion. Her efforts had, no doubt, been redoubled since the disappointing sales of the latest CD and single. She told him once, that a star who was removed from his or her fans was in danger. He knew, however, that she hadn't intended that to include danger of this nature. Replacing the handset: though desperate to hear more of her, he knew that Lucy would have her work cut out, and that Fabienne would now be under intense pressure.

He felt redundant. Just what could he do to find this particular needle in a haystack? He didn't even know what she looked like. He could only reason that as the former girlfriend of someone who had, most likely, encountered Fabienne on stage and at concerts, she'd see this as familiar territory and therefore the most logical place to attack. Knowing that there'd be thousands of people at the concert, the difficulties in spotting an unknown assailant amongst them seemed insurmountable. He could only hope, as no doubt Fabienne would, that extra security would foil Sheila Coombs' plans in some way, and by so doing ensure the safety of pop star and patient alike. Matt realised, however, that psychotic minds were extremely unpredictable, and thus harder to reason with; such people often possessed great physical powers too, and though mentally in a turbulent state, they could never be underestimated. Tossing and turning all through the night, his thoughts raced along the lines of most significant probability.

Immediately before his alarm went off, which was just as sleep eventually came to him, he reasoned that Fabienne's destiny was now inextricably linked with the concert, and this would be the most likely point for her to face an attack. The only thing he could do, ultimately, was to take his place at the concert, and do his utmost to second-guess the disordered thought processes of Sheila Coombs, and attempt to detect and to stop her. Reasoning that this, though difficult, was the only way that he could make any sort of progress. Matt found himself praying that the warning was unnecessary, that Sheila Coombs was at this moment many miles away, with very different things on her mind. The shiver down his spine held a clue as to what was about to develop.

CHAPTER XII

LETHAL CONE

The day of the concert was a Saturday. His alarm sounded its usual shrill tone though he'd risen over an hour before. A vast panoply of emotions had passed through his mind for most of the night, and getting up and taking breakfast hadn't stemmed their flow. Excitement about the concert and also the prospect of seeing Fabienne again, even as a member of the audience, was counterbalanced by his dread that if she failed today, it would mean almost certain professional disaster for her. The one emotion that outweighed all others, however, was fear for her safety, and it was this that rendered all other considerations insignificant. He dressed, still deep in thought; he could only hope to help her in some way, but was unable to see how he could bring this about.

Steve telephoned to say that Mary hadn't been well, having experienced some bleeding. Although early scan hadn't shown any obvious problems, he wanted to stay close to home so that he could keep an eye on her. Matt understood perfectly while accepting that he'd have an empty seat next to him. Musing that, he could, in days gone by, have sold that ticket for a small fortune, but wondered if it would be in such demand today. Following a light breakfast, he joined the Motorway north, taking his time driving to Manchester, arriving there some hours before the concert was scheduled to begin. He wondered where in the great city, Fabienne could be. Possibly at the Midland or one of the other prestigious hotels. Without doubt security around her would be tight, but on the opposing side of this view was her need to be visible to her fans. Today this balance was even more critical than usual.

Matt walked around the north end of the city. So many changes had taken place since the IRA bomb some years before. Much had been rebuilt, nearly all areas had been revitalised, and the successful Commonwealth games had assisted in this, with many new businesses being attracted. Pavement terraces, cafes, up-market restaurants, high-profile retailers and residential developments had taken place; not unlike the changes in Salford Quays, a mile or two away, but on a much larger scale. Matt wandered through the Printworks, eating lunch in the Triangle. Walking helped to calm his racing thoughts. Knowing, too, that Sheila Coombs might well be in the city; even as he walked, she might be hoping to gain entry to the MEN Arena from where she could attack the star. One who was already betting everything on a successful outcome for today's concert.

Matt had parked his car in the Arena car park; its concrete spiral of ramps and low walls always very confusing, and the tight turns in the spiral never ceased to make him dizzy. Fortunately, his early arrival meant that he wasn't on too high a level and even managed to find a generous-sized spot for his car, though he didn't doubt that when he returned for it later, a rusty wreck would be parked next to it, as previous experience had shown. As the afternoon drew on, he decided to make a return to the MEN Arena. That area of town showed a carnival atmosphere when there was a large concert on, with lots of street vendors using the opportunity to sell everything from food to electronic devices with flashing lights and displays. Parking attendants suddenly appeared at the behest of car park owners who hoped to offer more parking spaces, which were now greatly in demand in the immediate vicinity of the Arena.

Matt wasn't fond of the MEN Arena. The car park set the scene for an explosion of concrete. There were concrete steps up to concrete terraces with rows of plastic seats, and a large concrete rim that skirted the arena allowing entry and exit for the fans, now starting to drift in. He remembered his first trip there some years earlier when the only seats he'd been able to get were right in the gods. The terrace was steeply sloped and very narrow at that point. A late arrival meant that he had to find his seat in semi-darkness, and all those who'd arrived on time were already in their seats and extremely unhappy at being disturbed. Only after some time, and by unsettling a great many of them, did he find his allocated seat, and he sank into it gratefully. Space was always at a premium in the loftier rows, and out of necessity he could only sit by allowing his long legs and large knees to protrude forward, which attracted further opprobrium from his near neighbours. He spent the entire performance clinging to his seat, frightened to move.

Today, he need have no such fears, as his seat was right near the stage. The one thing that allowed him to forgive the Arena's obvious deficiencies was the size and quality of that stage. This was a magnificent area: large, easily visible to just about the whole auditorium, and a perfect platform for artists to give of their best performance. The lighting and acoustics, all computer-controlled with leading-edge systems were first rate, and acts had all the space they needed to shine. Fabienne had promised him seats close to the stage. True to her word, he found that he was on the very front row; almost within touching distance. It was impossible to get any closer and still be a member of the audience.

He looked up to the massive lighting rigs with their arrays of spotlights, electronics, microphones and computer-controlled sound. He could see some of the engineers' panels, which no doubt coordinated some of the thousands and thousands of sophisticated lights and visual displays, that made up a modern concert of one of the big stars: and stars didn't come much bigger than Fabienne. Matt sat there, taking in the atmosphere. Psychiatric patients seemed miles away and he wanted to believe it impossible that Sheila Coombs would even be here, let alone that she'd be able to penetrate the tight security he'd witnessed in getting to his seat. In addition there were so many people back stage that surely she'd be challenged immediately. Matt continued to survey all around.

Recalling the words chosen by Professor Harrison in making the last-minute phone call to him: almost a panic measure after he'd clearly exhausted all other options for recovering his lost patient safely. Seething with anger, Matt wondered just how the Professor could have neglected firstly his patients and now Fabienne so signally. His tone meant that each word he'd uttered was laden with regret at finally admitting that he'd lost control of a vulnerable, yet potentially dangerous patient, in this way, who might be driven by a mental illness to attack Fabienne. Nor would his apologies help Fabienne now, on perhaps the most important night of her life.

If Sheila was present, Matt could only attempt to predict how she'd mount her attack. Recognising immediately the difficulty with such a strategy, he had so little experience of how such a patient would respond, and whether there could be a correlation between her mind and those who were not mentally ill. He acknowledged that the mind of such a patient couldn't even be compared with the evil forces that drove criminals who planned deliberate harm to others, but was based on abnormal perceptions of the world with which they interacted. Matt shivered as he remembered that most serial killers who had evaded capture to kill again, were in this group. They were often fast, agile of mind and body, and should never be underestimated. In any event, as he now concluded, he'd be unwise to allow the party atmosphere to lull him into lowering his guard. He just wished that he had a place to start.

After a few minutes, Matt turned around: hundreds and hundreds of people had filed in after him, and the rows and columns of seats were filling up rapidly. The speed of ingress and the density seemed encouraging; a sell-out crowd would be a good start. He glanced round at regular intervals and as he turned for about the fifth time, he witnessed a capacity crowd, sitting behind him, quietly leafing through programmes, drinking, munching or swirling hand-held devices sporting arrays of coloured lights. On looking to either side, however, he could see that there were many unoccupied seats in the front row. One of those belonged to Steve, but Matt wondered how many of the other seats should have been occupied by former 'friends' of Fabienne, who'd deserted her in every sense.

The lights dimmed, music started, the warm-up act were on. He'd never seen the four young artists before, but they were excellent. Performing for about half an hour, they left to uproarious applause. The lights dimmed briefly as Matt became aware of musicians and backing singers filing onto the stage. From his position he could feel the heat from the lighting, the amplifiers, the sound systems and, of course, the hordes packed in the arena. Though he'd struggled to convince Fabienne of his attendance, at just one, let alone every concert she had ever given, he recognised a familiar format. Using the darkened stage to position herself and her team, when the lights came back up she'd be standing there, before her audience: spectators on this occasion who'd be judge and jury for her future.

The familiar announcement came, "Ladies and Gentlemen, please be upstanding for Fabienne."

Suddenly, there she was; Matt was, once again, stupefied as he saw her. Having retained the short hair that Stella had reluctantly, but brilliantly, cut; she wore a tight, gypsy dress with lacework at the front, and high, thigh-length spiky boots. Matt's advantageous seating meant that he could view every inch of stage without fear of anyone obscuring his view - even for a moment. There was an eruption of applause as the whole auditorium rose to their feet, including Matt who, like most there, had acted involuntarily on the tide of movement, which stood to greet her.

The place was full to capacity; the applause was deafening. It seemed that apart from the first row, where he sat, there was no evidence of a fall-off in support for the girl; now staking all on one throw of the dice. Fabienne looked every inch the star as she took up the microphone. Wondering for a moment if she had looked down in his general direction, but with so many lights focussed on her, and the audience being in comparative darkness; he doubted that she'd be able to see him, let alone have the time to attempt to do so.

"Ladies and gentlemen, I'd just like to thank you all for joining us here at the magnificent MEN Arena." Applause once again reverberated around the auditorium as people acknowledged her words. Matt saw Peter standing by the side of the stage, his massive hands folded before him, an earpiece protruding with a little coiled wire from his right ear. There were more, similarly-suited, figures dotted around the perimeter; more than Matt could remember on previous occasions. No doubt, they'd got the message and were providing as much security as possible. By placing them around the stage, but at audience level, they formed an effective but less visible deterrent for any who might be present for reasons other than just enjoying the concert.

Fabienne replaced the microphone in its stand. She looked nervous. Matt had never witnessed this emotion on her face at any of her previous concerts, and yet, it was unmistakable now. After the events of the previous weeks, the scalding attacks on her by press that she'd previously regarded as supportive, and the crucial importance of this one concert, it was perhaps not surprising. He knew from his own experience that confidence was a fragile attribute. Nobody who'd been through what she'd experienced in those past few weeks could fail to have their confidence damaged, if not utterly destroyed. Here was the moment of discovery. He suspected that much of it would be self-discovery, and the crowd were hushed, as if waiting for a sermon from a prophet, which would lead the way out of the wilderness of uncertainty about her ability to continue to enthral them, as she had done for the past six years.

The momentary pause began to open before them into a chasm of time, which seemed more and more untenable. Looking about the throng before her, the crisis unfolding within, preventing both movement and speech. The dancers stood motionless in the semi-darkness behind her: still nothing. The crowd remained silent, as if even the slightest noise would shatter the delicate balance on which success or failure now rested. Matt's throat burned as if scorched by the blood pounding in his neck; speech had long ago become impossible for him as he gripped his seat, whilst locked, wide-eyed, into the scene unfolding. Suddenly, a young voice shouted, "C'mon Fabienne!" There were many cheers as if, in that instant, the spell had been broken. Her hand was raised, she touched the boom microphone suspended from her ear, and the musicians cut in immediately. The concert had begun.

Matt cheered furiously until hoarse, with the rest of the multitude. The dance moves began with faultless precision; her voice was loud and pure: the golden cord held taut by the Fates, from which success was hung precariously, for thousands to witness first-hand. Matt felt sure, or at least dared to hope, that her training and endless rehearsals would protect her, like some automatic system that would just cut in so that she wouldn't have to think. Timing of each component of the dance moves was crucial. As each revolution was completed, it had to be co-ordinated with her dance team and, exhausting though such moves must be, even to one who'd exposed herself to relentless training- they also had to allow for her to sing. In any event, it was far too late now for any sort of reflection or self-appraisal, the show had begun: the avalanche that would either take the crowd with it, or would bury her, now unstoppable. The first number was from her latest CD and, as always, the live version was better than that recorded. This was the essence that sold CDs; this was the beguiling power of the live performance.

Matt scanned the stage furiously; this would be the place to strike, but how? If he were the assailant, what would he do? This was the spot, sure enough, but the stage was well away from the seats, even those, like his, near the front. Fabienne was ringed by extra security he'd noted as he took his seat. Realising that they couldn't possibly keep an eye on everybody; their job was to make sure that no one got too close. The cordon around her would be un-breachable from the front. Matt thought quickly. *What if you could get in another way? What if you could get in close? What if you were already in?*

Perhaps Barry Miles had given Sheila information as to how she could get in close, breach that secure cordon; maybe he himself had done this at concert after concert, even when he wasn't authorised to be there, or even after he'd been dismissed. Suppose that he'd had a back-stage pass that he'd retained, one that was now in the possession of Sheila Coombs.

This simple possibility must surely open up countless other options, especially if one's target had assumed herself safe, at least during the performance, behind a protective barrier of security. Matt continued to think. Once within the barrier, you could be anyone: a stagehand, a member of the arena staff. No one person would know everybody who had a right to be there, and this meant that you could intermingle, and perhaps put yourself in a position to strike: but where and how? He'd been wrong to assume that a stranger would be immediately spotted behind stage: they were probably all strangers; some worked for Fabienne, some for the Arena, some for hired security. What would Sheila Coombs do next? Would she try sabotage of some sort, to bring the concert to a premature, but disastrous, close? No, she'd reject this: she was after one person, and she'd want that person to suffer in front of the fans who were there to support her.

The two big possibilities were, unshielded electricity and unrestrained fire. Either would be a very effective weapon, if access to them could be secured. Briefly, he considered an attack in close proximity; even a knife would suffice. He doubted that this would be possible. The stage was very large and was basically a flat, open platform, in full view. The security guards wouldn't allow a person, whose vague description they'd no doubt been given, to come close to Fabienne. Having seen the energies that she put into physical exercise, he knew that at the very least, she could run as fast as was needed to escape.

An enemy would need something else. The electricity cables snaking over the stage must, no doubt, carry high voltages and high currents, but how to get such unshielded forces in contact with a the performer who was moving very quickly on stage? A patch of water, a flammable liquid or accelerant perhaps; but that wouldn't work either, as there'd be no way of knowing which way she'd move next, especially as much of the material had been worked just for this concert. A bomb? He doubted that even the mind of a smart, psychotic killer could prepare, position and wire a bomb in the time available, especially as, no doubt, every inch of stage would have been checked beforehand, even with sniffer dogs for all Matt knew; assuming that the threat had been taken seriously.

Try as he might, he couldn't envisage a plan that would allow, such a person, to bring about the attack they were aiming for. His brain ran on an endless loop that couldn't provide answers; eventually he decided to sit back and enjoy the concert. The hypnotic power of her voice held him enthralled, just as it did every other member of the audience, who remained in a hushed reverie while she cast her spell. Could he dare to believe that Sheila Coombs was miles away, or had been picked up by Social Workers or the Police, and Professor Harrison's fears had been unfounded? Any number of events could have distracted her. She might well be back under treatment, though Matt conceded with a shiver that, this would most probably be applied compulsorily.

Track after track was reeled off. It was hard to know just how she kept so cool when performing such physically demanding moves as she sang. Recalling the questions that he'd wanted to ask her, whilst going through his own countless rehearsals prior to their first meeting. He remembered the fitness she was careful to restrain in the gym, so as not to embarrass him. The suffering that he'd endured for those few minutes as he'd tried to match her, paled beside the movement she demonstrated now. The physical performance that the dance steps alone would require, before even considering the singing, made his twice-weekly workout seem like a bask on a sun lounger by comparison.

He sat back and marvelled, just as thousands of others did; allowing himself to be immersed in a voice that seemed to take on a magical quality, created by the application of skills and a spell known to very few, and evidently practised by this incomparable performer, on a stage almost within reach. He hoped that there were lots of critics present, as they couldn't fail to be wowed as everyone else had been. Ultimately an audience made or broke a star. If his views of what was passing around him were anything to go by, they were witnessing a performance verging on the Messianic to justify their faith in the skill and talent of a star who deserved the accolades that had been heaped on her in happier times; and hopefully were being earned unequivocally once again.

Having seen most of Fabienne's concerts, this one raised her performance to the next level. He'd never seen her perform as well as this; he'd never witnessed *anyone* perform like this. Knowing that her contemporaries wouldn't wish to see her fail, in the way that the press involvement had precipitated, however, they'd be forgiven for seeing an opportunity to perhaps take up the vacuum, formed by her catastrophic fall from the pinnacle of her career. She'd done so much tonight to re-establish herself with a flawless performance, that kept the audience numbed with disbelief at the dance steps and the tracks: having brought them to life as only a live performance could. Matt had no doubt that although this was exhausting for her in every way; she was correct in her belief that a live concert gave the star a public face that couldn't be ignored.

All too soon the performance was drawing to a close. The dancers filed out to shattering applause, leaving two or three backers. This was often the part of the show for which she chose slower numbers, and she'd use a hand-held microphone as she sang alone, before them, assisted only by the backers. On previous occasions, at this point, Fabienne would address her audience, to thank them, the owners and employees of the venue, and, of course, the city hosting her concert. She would then acknowledge her own staff, before singing a final number.

Fabienne stood alone, just catching her breath a little before she spoke. Removing the small boom microphone suspended from her left ear, she picked up the one on the stand in front of her. This part of the concert she was obviously retaining, as it was very familiar to Matt. The only thing he didn't know: what would be her choice of final song. She waited for the crowd. As always, what elevated a good performer into a great one, was flawless timing, and she possessed this innate skill in abundance, thereby ensuring that such co-ordination was maintained with seamless precision.

"OK everyone, I'd just like to thank you all for coming tonight," she began. No trace of her nervousness remained, only the image of a giant star occupying an environment that very, very few could seek to inhabit. Pausing for the applause to die down: the crowd were on their feet. Matt rose, too, without realising that he'd done so, as everyone else had done while emotion swept throughout.

"I'd like to thank my production team for their unswerving loyalty and unstinting hard work. I couldn't have done this without them. Not forgetting the staff of the MEN Arena and, of course, the lovely city of Manchester."

More rapturous applause echoed thunderously around the arena.

"For my loyal fans, who stuck with me, I'd like to thank you all from the bottom of my heart."

If her voice faltered at this point, it was drowned in the tumult cascading through the concrete bowl that made up the Arena. The fans were at the height of elation. This was the passion that fuelled a star's rise, and kept it in an orbit not inhabited by ordinary people.

"My last song is dedicated to a very special friend, without whom, I wouldn't be here tonight. Matt, this one's for you."

Wondering, once again, if she looked in his direction, but so much was going on that he couldn't be sure. Only when the introduction from this track started, did people resume their seats, and a hush once again descended on the massive venue, no one wanting to miss any of the notes that were about to flow. He could feel his ears burn with the excitement and start ringing, as the noise abated around him. The emotion in being recognised in this way before so many fans overwhelmed him: a gesture that he would remember for the rest of his life. His eyes were stinging, once again, as the feelings welled within: he could only stare, wide-eyed with wonder as the song, just for him, or so it appeared, was crafted like a spell. He considered just how many people would know who Matt was; what his patients would say if they could see him at this moment. A carefree laugh came over him. It didn't matter who knew: this moment was his to treasure, and it required no witnesses to acknowledge it.

The first few bars of '*I'm not in love*' began to swell across the auditorium. The crowd went wild. Matt's eyes stung unequivocally as he nearly wept, grateful for the darkness to hide the emotion that he couldn't control. In those few seconds his total experience of her flashed before him. The talk show, the concerts, the magazines and her appearance on his sandstone porch; the millions of other memories he held of her. All these moments imploded into a single thought of unquantifiable significance, where the very focus of that amazing voice was projected forth for him alone. The crowd were hoarse with shouting. All Matt could do was to sit back.

Looking back on events, he'd never be able to say exactly what made him look up at that moment. Was he perhaps looking for angels in the girders above the stage, who could no more miss the performance, than vacate the very firmament? Certainly, something in the periphery of his vision attracted his attention as he attempted to bring it into focus. Perhaps a watch, or something made of glass, had caught a tiny sliver of reflected light in the darkness above. Looking up directly, he tried to pierce the radiation flooding down from the lighting arrays. The information arriving from the eyes was decoded by his feverishly-working brain.

Someone was moving about, up there in the gantries that supported the lighting rigs and electronic paraphernalia, as they were seamlessly manipulated in the darkness above the stage. If just one of those items could be dislodged, it would crush the person beneath. This was the part of the show where Fabienne would remain in one place; she'd be vulnerable to an attack coming from the vast space above her. Even a near-miss might suffice. Matt knew that the song was a long one, and he estimated that she'd be singing, at that spot, for as long as six minutes. He desperately looked about him to see if anyone else had noted what he'd seen; possibly a security guard. The crowd were spellbound, the backers crooned in time with the music, and everyone's heart was thumping, synchronised to the beat she set, as those angelic sounds emanated from her mouth. Fabienne's pure voice sailed serenely to all parts of the auditorium, almost as if it were carried by a medium other than air. Even the security guards seemed mesmerised.

No one saw Matt leap to his feet. Peter saw him but hesitated for so long that Matt was able to get through: perhaps he was shocked to see him as he flashed by, or simply he'd been transfixed by that song, as everyone else was. Matt was up on the stage in seconds. Gasps and startled noises came from the crowd, as they saw him there; Fabienne kept singing. Someone tried to follow Matt, but Peter intervened decisively, to dissuade him from the folly of making the attempt. Matt shot to the back of the stage, where he encountered a sound-recordist in the wings.

"How do I get up there?" he bellowed, as he pointed to the lighting rigs suspended high above the stage.

"You're not supposed..." the reply began.

"Life or death; she's in danger!" Matt screamed.

"That ladder," he indicated the ladder to his right.

Matt climbed as quickly as he could, and kept going with all the force he could muster: time was ticking away. Eventually, stepping out on to the gantry, he panicked as he realised that he could see no sign of her. Wires, cables, conduits and ducting surrounded him. Everything without exception was painted black, and it was very hot and very dark up there. The gantry on which he was standing supported other gantries, from where the paraphernalia of modern concerts was kept largely out of sight of the audience, who were far away. Complex and unfamiliar noises seemed to emanate from all directions; fans blew over sensitive electronic circuitry; relays clicked, motors whirred as they moved hundreds of lighting arrays; the sounds were in complete contrast to the pure notes which permeated from below. He felt unsteady as the suspended gantries moved to an uneasy rhythm. Crouching defensively, he tried to make urgent sense of his surroundings.

Fabienne, the true professional, continued as if nothing had happened. The song now finishing: she would replace the microphone in its stand, bow, and then address the audience. He continued to look feverishly around him, doing his best to pierce the darkness by looking away from the projected beams of light, so that his eyes would accommodate more quickly to the dark.

Suddenly, he saw her. The long, lank, greasy, brown hair; the driven, restless look in lustreless eyes: as if she were hunted or possessed by demons, deep within. What was that she was holding? The smell was unmistakeable - a petrol bomb! He swallowed hard; a near-miss would suffice, from such a lethal weapon within these confines. Even the most favourable outcome would still see Fabienne horribly burned.

With Sheila's other hand, she clicked furiously at a little gold lighter that, miraculously, was refusing to ignite. She stopped briefly, when she saw him.

"Too late, whoever you are: she took Barry away from me, and she'll burn in hell." Her face was blank, without malice, or any emotion that he could discern. Her movements were furious but automatic, as if pre-programmed by forces he could neither feel nor understand; her voice, a gruff monotone, no doubt due to a chain-smoking habit. The scene chilled him to the core as his mind desperately tried to bypass the shock that was engulfing him, and arrive with a coherent strategy in what would otherwise be the last seconds of Fabienne's life. He swallowed hard, as the dry throat cut him from within: his heart pounding, for once, not with desire or anticipation, but with the cold sweat of unrestrained fear. Knowing that words, any words, would come too late to cause even a moment's delay, he realised that direct force upon her, was now the only way in which he could secure the life of the person in unmitigated danger; on the stage thirty feet below.

He wondered about a desperate lunge on her, but he knew this would almost certainly be too late, destined to fail before he'd even set off. She clicked the lighter again, it lit with a lethal cone of flame, with a destructive potential far greater than its size would suggest. The light it gave off illuminated her face at an odd angle, creating an illusory smile on the otherwise expressionless countenance. Her galvanic hand-movement continued, as she approximated lighter to wick. He needed seconds, but events were certainly set fair to deny him even begging for mercy on Fabienne's behalf. Doubting that any words he could say would register within the unfeeling illness that now controlled the patient unequivocally.

She was directly over Fabienne, who was about to bow to the audience's earthquake of applause. All that was required now, was for her to light the wick and drop the bottle: the petrol would do the rest; no defence was possible. In a couple of seconds, even if he attempted to restrain her, the deadly payload would be on its way. The accelerant would consume

Fabienne horribly, with a passion that was totally belied by the unfeeling expression written to the face of her attacker. The idea of her immolation in this way, before thousands of her fans, nearly caused Matt to freeze as the ghastly image presented within his racing mind. In order to gain those seconds, he formed a desperate plan.

"I've spoken to Barry ... he's downstairs, says there's been a misunderstanding and wants to speak to you. He told me to find you, and bring you to him," Matt said, doing his best to remain calm, as if it were the most obvious thing in the world that he'd been despatched in this way. Vital seconds passed while she considered this: she lowered the lighter away from the bottle. Matt fumbled with the belt around his waist, feverishly unbuckling it in the semi-darkness, as she looked distractedly away. A flicker of emotion crossed her sterile visage. He desperately needed to keep her attention, but it was not to be. She might have gone with him at that point, but somehow the commotion in the front rows, who could, barely, see them illuminated in the blackness above the stage, distracted her long enough to realign her dreadful intent.

"Liar!" she said flatly," when I've burned her, I'll burn you to hell, too."

She moved the lighter towards the wick, its flame more than enough to complete the desired effect.

Matt committed himself to one desperate chance. He employed the belt as one would a lash. The heavy metal buckle was whipped forward along an arc as it gained terminal speed with considerable force, unfortunately missing the intended target - the lighter. By happy accident, however, it caught her full on the wrist. She screamed in pain as the buckle whipped the flesh like searing heat, as it gave up its momentum. No grip could withstand such agony.

She dropped the lighter, which fell harmlessly to the stage below. Somehow, she still hung on, with her left hand, to the petrol-filled bottle. Matt had created all the time he needed, however, using her pain and dismay at losing the lighter, as a distraction; he lunged forward, nearly stumbling over a cable, while aiming for the bottle.

Fabienne was thanking the crowd once again. Those on the first few rows could see the desperate struggle, taking place high above them. Though it was very dark up there, measure and countermeasure could still be seen as they were applied. Matt's dive forward brought gasps from the crowd. The gantry was narrow, and to those who were unaccustomed to working in such places threatened a variety of dangers, any of which could cause injury or death. He didn't have time to assess such factors: being totally preoccupied by the shadowy figure of Sheila Coombs - who retained a bottle full of petrol. As he leapt forward, she sneered, "Too late!" but Matt was faster than she'd assumed, and concentrated solely on that bottle, with all other factors, including his own safety, held in abeyance. He grabbed at the bottle; she was knocked backwards as he fell on top of her. With one final pull he wrenched it from her grasp. She hissed and spat at him, with coiled menace, but he knew that his actions had assured Fabienne's safety.

Peter and another security guard had followed Matt onto the gantry. The gentle undulations of the suspended metalwork became more vigorous with the unaccustomed weight on the precarious supports. Peter took the bottle from him, while his colleague restrained Sheila. Matt looked down. Fabienne was making her final bow. The audience were on their feet, the applause thunderous in its intensity; the whole auditorium seemed to be vibrating under the forces so released.

He remained, just staring at her from the shadowy depths of the scaffold. That she was in her natural element was certain, and the performance he'd witnessed was so impressive that anyone who'd expressed doubt as to the likelihood of her return had seen those thoughts expelled decisively. Down on the stage Fabienne raised her arm as she straightened from her bow. Initially she chose a typical self-deprecating wave of the hand, but then extended her arm above her, as high as she could, and pointed skyward, her form looking even more slender as she did so. Nobody could have resented her marking her moment of triumph in this way. A further cataclysmic roar swept through the arena, as people shouted and screamed from delight. She opened her hand: so close was the bond between her and her fans, that silence descended quickly; there was more that she had to say and she began, "Manchester, Manchester, I love you! To each end every one of you, I thank you for being here tonight." Eventually the roar began to subside and she continued whimsically, "Could you all bear just one more song?"

They erupted: an affirmation that could have levelled city walls with its intensity. In all of her concerts that Matt had attended, he'd never seen this before. Her smile bordered on giddiness as she sensed that her trial was over. Sheer relief exerted an intoxicating influence. A quick word with the orchestra, and the song began at once.

"*We never talked about it, but I hear the blame was mine…*
and I called you up to say I'm sorry, but I wouldn't want to waste your time.
'Cause I love you, but I can't take any more
There's a look I can't describe in your eyes.
If we could try like we tried before …"

Nobody in the whole auditorium, not even Matt in his elevated position, noticed the tiny tears that formed in the corners of her eyes. Had they done so, they might have assumed that her emotional moment was due to the relief from recent events, or even to a personal relationship that had failed, as was of course the case with Phil Collins, who wrote and performed the original. As the tears developed into a silent, unstoppable cascade, that now no one could miss; she knew that it was none of those things. She continued to sing, her voice faltering ever so slightly, and the more discerning noted a slight French accent forming on some of the words that she sang.

As the tears streamed down that pretty face, suddenly she was a little girl again in the midst of terrible rows between her parents, and she was the weapon that each used against the other. By hurting her, they hoped to inflict pain and spite on each other. Neither adult ever grasped just why, later, she had refused to speak French although, in the early days of their marriage, they'd worked hard on encouraging her to be bilingual. The ineluctable truth was that French was the language of the arguments between the two of them, and was used more and more in this way, as their feelings of love turned to loathing. Child logic desperately hoped that by confining conversations to English, they would all escape conflict and pain: how wrong she'd been. The inescapable fact that now emerged was, that her tears hadn't so much crystallised around memories that had recently resurfaced, but had simply grown from the realisation that there wasn't a single living soul to whom she could reveal such reminiscence.

She continued to sing..
"There are things we won't recall
feelings we'll never find
It's taken so long to see it

*'Cause we never seemed to have the time
There was always something more important to do
more important to say
But 'I love you' wasn't one of those things and now its too late.
Do you remember?"*

The question that Matt had wanted to ask her in Salford Quays, how could she sing and dance at the same time with such precision and speed, held a simple answer - concentration. Concentration that failed signally at this moment, as memories that had crept in, grew with malignant intent. Tears that fell now in rivulets bore witness to the forces within her. She remembered phoning her Dad as an excited teenager whose first record release was about to enter the charts. He'd ignored her words and her excitement, by launching into a tirade of abuse at her mother, who was planning to depart on holiday with her new consort, the onslaught being delivered in perfect clipped French as if he were talking to his ex-wife and not to a young girl. The bitter memory destroyed any concentration utterly.

She was now in a nexus of pain and torment from memories long repressed. Realising that she couldn't go on, she looked round at her orchestra like a person who'd suddenly strayed into quicksand. The backers, sensing catastrophe, raised their voices to cover what must be imminent total failure. Any likelihood of movement, other than sinking to her knees, as the tears dissolved her, was extremely remote: an abrupt termination of the song mid-verse, much more likely. A camera on a long boom floated right in front of her at that moment, bright beams from the lighting rigs followed the camera, illuminating her brutally; the camera that had measured her success in the concert, was now about to record her in a condition of mental distress, in high-definition close-up, not only in front of the fans present, but all those watching on television.

Just before failure was unleashed, she noticed a little girl near the front, being held aloft by her parents. Fabienne recognised Elisabeth, the young girl from Luciano's, who was waving the signed photo that Fabienne had given her. In scenes much beloved by science fiction writers, where power is rerouted to circuits that had long since gone critical, Elisabeth's smile had such an effect. Forces that could be neither comprehended nor described were summoned and applied, averting disaster between beats of her heart. In that iota of time, deliverance from suffering and failure beckoned, the voice returning with its usual clarity and volume. She wiped the tears with her hand, as her face brightened. The earthquake resumed as she finished the song; she bowed for a final time, thanking them once again as she turned to leave the stage. The lights faded on an unforgettable performance.

As Matt gazed down upon her from his vantage point, there was much that Tantalus himself would have recognised: images that could create desire and temptation in equal measure, but all firmly beyond reach and out of his grasp. Such thoughts would revisit him later, and unavoidably so. Matt slowly made his way back through the narrow passageway and found the ladder he'd ascended. It was with some relief that he stepped back on to the more secure stage, and became aware of Peter looking at him with a mixture of surprise and admiration; as if seeing him for the first time. He did his utmost to give off an air of imperturbability, belied by his shaking legs and pounding heart, which he was grateful that Peter, and others, could neither see nor feel. The police had been called to restrain, and the emergency mental health team to assess, Sheila. Matt waited backstage hoping to catch a glimpse of

Fabienne. A few moments later she joined him and gave him a hug.

"Are you Ok Sylvie?" he asked solicitously.

"I am now," she affirmed, as if realising something for the first time. "I see you made it on stage then, Doctor Sinclair," she mused, brightly.

"Yes, I wasn't sure who was more surprised, you, or Peter."

"For once, I'm glad that he was a bit slow off the mark. Not many can get past him, so count yourself fortunate, just as I do, of course. She could have done serious harm to me or a member of the crew with that," nodding to the petrol bomb, held by Peter. "You're forever saving me and I... I just can't thank you enough."

The flicker of emotion was held firmly in check. There was so much she wanted to say; yet she was only too well aware that time was severely limited. The reaction from the audience, whilst welcome, was only part of the success upon which any concert turned; the most vital consideration that she'd alluded to before, was publicity. Publicity whose flames could only be fanned by the interviews she gave to the media, who addressed a much larger audience. The performance had gone well, the crowds were ecstatic, yet there was a woman there who'd intended either to kill or to maim her. Wanting to stay and chat with the man who'd saved her, she knew, ultimately, that those interviews would not wait.

Sensing her turmoil, he spoke quickly, "I couldn't have her spoiling that performance now, could I? At least she's now in safe hands, and will begin treatment almost immediately. No doubt the police will investigate and take a lead from Professor Harrison as to whether she'll stand trial or not. I had a great view of the performance from up there: it's a shame I was kept so busy!"

"I was going to say that to you - were those seats I got you not good enough?" she asked. She linked her arm in his. He looked appreciatively at the very short, low-cut gypsy dress, which was also skin-tight, the long legs enhanced with spiky boots.

"Nice outfit." he said. "Didn't see you wear that around Perri?"

"Good job, they might have arrested me."

"It certainly would have caused a stir, I've no doubt."

"Come on, let's get a cup of tea or a G&T or something, to calm our nerves," she said as she led him towards her dressing room.

Despite the events, she seemed both delighted and relieved in equal measure with the way things had gone, and couldn't have had better reception from the audience. Matt could see that any trace of nervousness had been banished. Any self-doubt had been turned around, and from that slight pause at the beginning she hadn't looked back. Flowers were delivered to her dressing room as people appeared and disappeared with each knock on her door. Matt saw Lucy, Rupert and others whom he had not met, who all popped in to hug and congratulate her on the performance. Fabienne introduced him to them one by one, but there were so many that they flashed through his mind like a blur. There was, in truth, only one person that he could see.

At last they were alone, but Matt was acutely aware that she was wanted by a thousand people – each of whom had legitimate business to be there. Though desperately wanting to talk of old times in the village, he realised that such conversation was now out of place, and his final analysis revealed that this must apply to him also. It had been easy, whilst she had been with him at home, to think of her as just an ordinary girl; but here amongst her colleagues, her correlated team, he visualised the breadth and depth of her professional life, and it was far more than his mind could compass. A tiny but inescapable thought flashed within his brain and once there, couldn't be dismissed. 'Unattainable' was the thought. Press reviewers wanted interviews; several TV companies were waiting. Rupert came in respectfully to remind her of all these things, and also that their flight would be leaving that evening. Matt knew that Sylvie would be aware of that already. Moreover, he couldn't blame Rupert for emphasising those points, so that Matt himself would know that effective use of this time was, quite simply, crucial.

"Look, Sylvie, I'd better go. I hear you're off to North America tonight."

"Yes, we start a four-centre tour there in a couple of days, so we need to make sure the venue's all set, and of course there'll be last-minute rehearsals, as always." She continued, "the fans in North America weren't so affected by the stories in the press, and sales have held up fairly well, but it's such an important market for us. We have to be seen to be still out there, and not hiding away in London."

Matt understood perfectly; she need not have looked so apologetic. Her eyes met his, the vital crystal now shimmering with things to come, and a bright future that had been restored; his at their deepest, midnight blue, reflecting the sorrows and the lonely times that awaited him. His introspection continued, as clarity displaced ambiguity. Realising that the role that he'd played, though small in the wider panorama of her life that he could now visualise, had nevertheless been pivotal in securing her future. In return, he'd had the most wonderful time of his life, and though it was unlikely, he now understood, that he would see her again, there was no aspect of it that he regretted.

Holding his hands, she looked intently at him, as if reading his surging thoughts like a page of a book. "You know I couldn't have done this without you, and I'll be forever in your debt," served as part apology, and part consolation. He was sad, and desperately so, but neither jealousy nor bitterness resided within him. Sensing that she had a higher purpose, it was time for her to renew or fulfil that part of her life - a life without him.

"Sylvie, as I said to you, you're not finished yet, there's much more for you to go and do. If you ever find yourself driving a rented Beetle, with a gear lever, through the village, please feel free to call on me, and we'll talk about old times," he suggested, more in hope than in expectation, doing his best to generate a smile. He was determined not to let his sadness spoil her night, or intrude on her opportunity to capitalise on the first positive attention she'd received from the media in weeks: attention that would hopefully surface in the press and on TV the next day.

"You look magnificent Sylvie; welcome back to where you were always meant to be," he concluded magnanimously, knowing finally that it was a place he could not inhabit. He stood, grabbed her hand and kissed her quickly. Within seconds he'd departed, much to the relief of Rupert, who was busy trying to schedule as many people from as many agencies as possible for those interviews.

Matt continued to walk without looking back. He smiled to himself as a thought came to him. Rita had been correct. How she would laugh at him if she were here now. Knowing that his brief contact with the star had drawn to a close; he was unlikely to re-establish that contact ever again. Rita's analysis had been as accurate as it had been prescient. Analysis was probably the correct word, as this was how she perceived everything, including human emotion, like a balance-sheet on a computer, a profit and loss. He'd lost; there'd been no profit, therefore, no gain. Her delight at seeing him walk away lonely and wretched, would know no bounds.

The party atmosphere unleashed on the streets around the Arena was at complete variance with how he felt, and simply served to highlight his mood in cruel contrast. He could only cling to the belief that his, his memories, and the help he'd provided, would be with him forever, and would sooner or later enrich his life rather than burden it, as now, with regrets. The warmth that she'd shown, the sheer delirium of each breath that she took, would be a constant inspiration to him, now and in the future, and he could never regret that. That she'd gone was a very high price to pay, but that was inevitably a return to the life that she knew, and he did not. How could he ever begrudge her that freedom? Certainly he would never allow his own selfishness to make such an attempt.

He decided to stay in Manchester for a little while, so that the crowds could dissipate into the gathering night. He ate in one of the many new restaurants that had sprung up across the city in recent years, but didn't feel remotely hungry. Things were very different from the time when he was a medical student and in student accommodation in the 'toblerones', as they were known, down Oxford Road. It was very late when he walked back to his car. He toyed with the idea of staying over, rather than have the long drive home. Something about that late drive, however, seemed to draw him. Perhaps it reminded him of that time when he and Fabienne were on their way back from Steve and Mary's house - all he lacked was her chatter and warm company, that being just about everything, he reminded himself, with a shiver. Ultimately, he realised that night would be the cloak with which he could hide his thoughts and himself. He would run, before his desperate mood, into the night, which enveloped him like a tunnel as he sped southward, reaching home in the small hours of the morning.

Flopping on top of his bed, after using the last of his energy reserves to brush his teeth; he was pleased that he felt so exhausted. His last thought, before sleep claimed him, was whether she would be boarding a plane bound for the States just at that moment. He wondered if she'd have time or inclination to spare for a few thoughts of him.

Though most mornings, now, were greeted by a definite autumn chill to the air: the weather had remained dry and bright. Such days encouraged him to get up early, the sunshine flooding into his room at still quite an early hour. He walked down to the newsagent's. Though he was a regular customer and frequented the newsagent's most days, the owner would never omit to ask him about Sylvia, his girlfriend. In fact everywhere Matt went, people would still ask about her, even though it had been some weeks since her cheery presence had been amongst them. He didn't have the heart to tell them anything of the truth, but the constant stream of enquiry about how she was getting along, and when she'd be coming back to visit, was wearing him down. Wondering if he should perhaps tell them that the relationship was over, but he knew that most would be distraught to hear that, such was the effect that she'd had on them, in so short a span of time. He realised too, that his own judgement and integrity would be called into question if he should admit that they'd broken up. People would at the very least think him mad for letting such an angel on earth out of his sight; and perhaps at worst, question the very fundamentals of his judgement. If only it had been that simple.

Selecting all the Sunday broadsheets, he took them home. The conservatory remained warm and the bright sunshine streamed in, as it had done for most mornings over the past two weeks. He flicked quickly through the papers to look for the headlines and news of her concert. The reviews were fabulous. Picking out one or two for more detailed reading later, he wanted to get an idea of their overall impressions as expressed in the headings and bold print.

"*They Came, They saw, She Conquered,*" wrote one
"*Fabienne Wows the MEN, as only she can,*" another.
"*Welcome back - Queen of Pop,*" one more.
"*Fabienne re-launches her career with a Bravura performance.*"
"*A Matchless performance - Fabienne.*"

The only papers who were not carrying any comment at all of her concert were the *Sunday Scoop* and the *Daily Scorcher*, both of whom were embroiled in ferocious legal battles with Fabienne's lawyers, and had had injunctions served on them, forbidding them from printing anything at all about her, until the Press Complaints Committee had reached their judgement on the nature and extent of damages to be made. Rumour held that they were set to be the highest ever, and both papers were already squealing, in a late attempt to show contrition. Matt knew that Mervyn Boomer, their owner, would be far from pleased. Time to reap the whirlwind, he thought to himself with untempered satisfaction.

He continued to read the reviews.

'*The MEN arena has always attracted the finest stars and I have been fortunate to witness so many unforgettable performances. None however, in all my years as a reviewer, have come close to the performance I witnessed there yesterday. If Fabienne came out on stage looking a little awkward and uncertain, this did not last long. Within seconds the awesome tracks, many of them from her recent CD, were raising the rafters of the auditorium, and were backed up with flawless dance moves that were executed perfectly. If she has been accused in the past of perhaps sticking too much with her successful formula, she rewrote the rule-book yesterday, delivering an enthusiastic roof-raising concert, laced with more Chutzpah than has been seen in Manchester since the time of the Beatles.'*

Another paper wrote, '*The hushed audience before the performance began, seemed to know what a spectacle they were in for. Only seconds after she started, they were treated to one of the best performances that she has ever given. If people had written her off after her recent problems, as exposed painfully through some of the tabloids, they were wrong. Welcome back Fabienne, you certainly routed any that had doubted you, decisively.*'

One or two mentioned a scuffle at the end of the performance; reporting that a patient of the Nottingham Psychiatry unit, had been detained by a doctor and security guards. Matt smiled to himself, not regretting his anonymity for a second. He continued to read and to digest the words that were all in praise of the performance, her skill as a dancer, the power and purity of her voice, and the consummate professional that she was. He knew that Fabienne couldn't have hoped for a better return. Over the next few days he continued to follow the news, and learned that the CD sales had been propelled by the concert into the top spot as the fastest-selling CD of all time. There was even talk that its total sales could outstrip albums such as *Thriller*.

CHAPTER XIII

DOCTOR BROWN

Another Monday; another surgery box of patients' notes. Matt sighed wearily to himself as he gazed meditatively into the murky alembic of what must have been, initially at least, a hot mug of coffee. Since Dr Stevens' arrival, Matt's drinks were always cold and usually lacking in even a drop of milk. Janice seemed to have forgotten that he loved piping-hot coffee with lots of milk, if not a good splash of cream, unlike Greg who preferred his black, but lukewarm. Despite his momentary disquietude he had no cause for complaint. Looking more closely at the surgery list that Janice had finally mastered on the computer, he could see that it was only half full. Greg Stevens had made a superb start, winning over the patients very quickly. Many of the younger ones, especially women, would gravitate to his ever-lengthening surgeries, Janice eyeing them all suspiciously as they came to the desk to be entered as 'arrivals' into the computer. Matt had no worries about Greg's acceptability to all the patients; many of his regulars had told him what a kind, caring, person he was, and how they believed he'd complement the medicine and the care that Matt had always tried to give.

Whilst scrutinising the cold coffee and soggy biscuits on the tea tray, Matt reflected on recent events. Dispassionate analysis could only conclude that he must be a very happy man. Fortunate indeed. He'd rebuilt the practice; things were going very well, much more smoothly than he'd hoped. He had, once and for all, seen off Rita's unsparing assertion that his contentment was just a polite word for inaction, used by a sterile and ideologically bankrupt person. Her criticism of him, though borne more out of a desire to excoriate rather than convey objectivity, had conspicuously spurred him on to greater efforts, and as luck would have it, Doctor Stevens was cast in the same mould. Theirs was now the fastest growing practice in the region; the PCT were delighted with the quality indicators and the patient surveys, which had come back as being among the best that had ever been seen. He and Greg had won the contract with the new nursing home. With help from Mrs Simpson, they'd gone in with a computerised slide-show presentation, a full cost-benefit analysis and a business plan. He'd learned that Parkvale had simply turned up expecting that a little glad-handing would automatically grant them the contract.

He'd heard through one of the district nurses, visiting his surgery, that Doctor Letworth was pregnant. Matt wondered mischievously who the lucky man was, and whether the experience might just bring Rita in contact with the human race. Perhaps this incongruous development was what she'd needed all along, something to think about other than her own selfish desires. More sober analysis might question whether she could summon sufficient self-awareness to nurture the life that was to be entrusted to her care.

He'd also witnessed Fabienne's recovery both in person, at the concert, and also more recently by the items on television news, MTV and, of course, in the newspapers. Being both delighted and amazed by the wonderful publicity that now followed her, he would often gaze at the magnificent watch, or gently rub the pulp of his thumb over its hard crystalline surface that was said to be unscratchable. He'd pored over magazine and press articles, on the verge of a purchase, but recognised that Steve would see this as a retrograde step, and worry about whether he was going to slip into his celebrity worship pattern again. Matt, however, knew that such an assessment from the Psychologist was now out-dated and inaccurate, as he quietly congratulated himself on the progress he'd made. His house was no longer an empty place to be, while he waited to hear her voice, smell her cooking, or imagine another careful step from those very fine legs as they descended his staircase; but had reverted to being his home, refuge, and the place where he could find comfort and succour after hard and challenging days. The walks that he'd taken in increasing frequency, now held more interest and recreation for him: rather than being the re-enactment of times that he'd spent in her company. His dreams, too, had settled for at least a few nights a week, in tandem with an improving sleep pattern. Moreover, he no longer felt tempted to take the sleeping tablets that had been in his drawer for many months; and though he'd turned the alarm clock so that it faced away from him, he'd forgotten the last occasion that he'd woken in the small hours and been tempted to look at the time.

Inevitably, thoughts of Fabienne continued to stream through his mind in a fantastic panorama. Ultimately, he realised what Steve had known all along, as he now understood exactly what his feelings had been for her - pure infatuation. His on-going recovery forced him to confront, with a shiver, once again, some of the beliefs that he'd held with regards to Fabienne. He accepted that his views were not so far removed from those of Barry Miles. True, he had no desire to break into her house or to harm her in any way, but he would gladly have followed her from concert to concert. The nightmare that he'd repressed for a long time had surfaced some days before, forcing him ashamedly to face that truth. The memory, all those years ago, of waiting for hours on a rain-soaked pavement in Manchester; he tall and upright, standing stark and alone, amidst hundreds of screaming teenagers who'd waited, just as he had, for her to emerge from the stage door of the Palace Theatre, at one of her earliest concerts. What would Steve have said had he revealed to him this event? Having no idea of how and why she'd turned up at his door that night, he wondered if the whole thing had been imagined in a Miles-like delusion? He shivered vigorously, as this disquieting possibility occurred to him.

Whilst looking for something in his drawer a few days earlier, he'd chanced across Fiona Darling's card. She'd seemed very keen to take him to dinner; remembering with a smile, the flash of her stocking tops as she discussed her anti-inflammatory drug. Steve had continued to expound at some length the virtues of a meaningful relationship with an 'ordinary' girl, and Matt didn't doubt the wisdom or motives behind such advice. He'd had more than his fair share of unfulfilling liaisons in his past; surely he'd be better on his own than embarking on a relationship that he knew to be false. As he turned the embossed card on his desk with a spinning motion, his thoughts were elsewhere. Something told him that it was time, once again, at least to seek a relationship with a significant other, if only because it would stop Steve from nagging. He'd probably contact her this week, and see if she were still keen to dine with him. In the event that all else failed, he knew that the work he loved would continue to sustain him; if nothing, other than that was written in the stars for him; then, it would more than suffice - especially with what he now knew.

James Farquar had telephoned the previous Friday. James was an execution-only broker, and would never have occasion to phone a client in this way. Matt took the call with curiosity as to what had precipitated such an event. His broker had wanted to thank him for purchasing shares in *'Brite Lite Entertainment'*, having explained that he'd been so intrigued by Matt's massive purchase that he'd followed his example, albeit more conservatively. Though the price had drifted for some time, the success of Fabienne's concert and her re-launch on the world stage had caused the shares to recover sharply. James had made a twenty-fold profit and was now in a position to break free from his ex-wife, using the money he'd gained. He confessed to Matt, however, that they'd been getting on so well of late, that they were hoping to rekindle their relationship and even get back together! Matt had been amazed by such news, but conveyed his heartfelt congratulations, nevertheless. James informed Matt that his own holding was now worth just less than four million pounds, and wondered if there were any instructions.

Matt had laughed, explaining to James that he'd bought the shares as a mark of solidarity to a friend, and that the money wasn't important. The broker had gasped when Matt asked about tax-efficient ways of passing half of it to charity, and certainly couldn't understand why Matt had said that it was a bit too much like winning the lottery. Both men had ended the conversation with enough surprises to generate light-hearted puzzlement for the ensuing few days.

Anticipating many more Mondays, just like this one, where much of his time would be spent in thinking of Fabienne – he'd continue to be the person who'd worshipped her. However, more recently, he could at last see a time beyond that, where he'd begin to emerge from such narrow views that she'd unwittingly engendered, and the real person within, would emerge; a little older but very much the wiser. One who'd have broken free from such unproductive loops of thought.

She'd intimated that she'd be in touch with him, but he knew that such words were given at a time when she couldn't be sure of anything in her life, apart from the need to survive. Ultimately, he realised that he'd be the last person she'd be able to contact should she even wish to. He didn't feel in any way bitter, as he'd foreseen much of this on the day she leapt back into her rented blue Beetle; crunching the gears whilst driving down the road and out of his life. Objective analysis also told him that she might well see her time with him as a painful period in her life, rather than something wonderful - the perspective from where he saw things. He would never wish her to return under those circumstances: laughing aloud as his mind drifted over such an unlikely event.

Fabienne's *Vimto* advertisements had been released on the television by Nichols plc. They depicted a frightened young boy, running down the road away from a gang of bullies who were intent on catching him. On rounding the corner, he saw that another group were heading from the opposite direction. Racing in to a corner shop, he tried to evade them. The camera angle suggested that the shopkeeper was a little old lady, with her back to him as he entered. The bullies congregated around the shop, leering through the windows at the scared young boy, now frightened to leave. The shopkeeper turned. Fabienne's familiar face came into view as she straightened and left the counter to assist him. The mob could see her give him a can of *Vimto*, which he downed quickly. Suddenly, the crowd panicked and started to disperse as, emboldened by his drink, and swiftly followed by Fabienne, he came out, to face down his tormentors. As they fled before him, he handed the empty can to Fabienne who promptly tossed it over her shoulder into a recycling bin, but without looking. The caption coming up as the group dispersed and the boy walked safely home, was '*Stronger than It Looks*'. The simple advert had taken up something of a cult status, with its anti-bullying message, and had been enormously popular. Sales of the soft drink had rocketed, and there was talk of her participating in further advertisements. Billboards sprang up depicting Fabienne holding a can of *Vimto* with the message '*Stronger than It Looks*'. The images carried some resonance with the wider public, who'd been acutely aware of her being placed quite innocently at the centre of the storm that some newspapers had generated for their own gain. National advertisements had been also placed in all newspapers, with notable exceptions being the *Daily Scorcher* and the *Sunday Scoop*.

That there were a thousand mercies shown in each day, was becoming apparent once again. Matt was noticing the tiny things present in everyone's life in abundance, but that the preoccupied, the greedy and the self-absorbed would simply not see. The tender flower that opened as the sun rose; the rain that held off just long enough for a walker to find shelter; the rainstorm that created a beautiful rainbow over the meadows; or the brilliant disc of the de-crescent moon holding the promise of a warm, sunny day to come.

His earlier preoccupation with why he wasn't happy, when as a paper-based exercise he felt that he ought to be, had been confusing. Steve had assumed that he'd been driven by a search for more 'prizes' to put into a life that was already full and rich, but decadent. Rita had assumed that nothing was as important as what a person wanted, and how one went about securing it. They'd both underestimated him, albeit for entirely different reasons; and from Steve's viewpoint, less self-centred ones. Matt had been confused as well as worried by Steve's outburst when he learned of the meeting in Salford Quays, and it was only latterly that his mind had furnished the answers. In doing so he realised that his friend had misjudged him and his motives. Smiling, he pictured how each would have approached his day at the leisure-centre pool with Fabienne. Steve would have refused any contest; Rita would have done and said anything to ensure victory. That conquest, once secured, would be swift and crushing. Only Fabienne had held the true answer: that it was the joy of taking part, and the greater joy in allowing success to pass without fuss or fanfare into the hands of another person; this being the reward that she sought, above pursuit of personal triumph, especially when at another's expense. He could now see clearly that this was why she was so special.

Here lay the secret of his own happiness, which was right before him all along. It had taken Fabienne's presence and her example, to finally show him that it wasn't about finding time to accumulate material things, or generate a tick-list of accomplishments within a life. Rather, to take the time and trouble to consider what delights it already contained. Steve could no more see this, than Rita could. Fabienne had shown him the way to take on these subtle thoughts for himself; realising that, having learned this from her, he would not, of necessity, need her presence to continue them. She'd taught him all this, by her words, her actions and probably her every thought. It was almost as if she'd spotted a crack in the code, the human genome for happiness, that was now irrevocably flawed for so many. Having discovered the error in transcription, she'd set about restoring, single-handedly, that code, using every ounce of energy and resource that she possessed. Fleeting, wild thoughts held that this is really why she had appeared on his doorstep. However, reality soon cut in and he dismissed such a notion as he shrugged his shoulders and laughed aloud. If only she were here, so that he could show her that he now knew what she had known and practised, all along - in each breath that she took. No matter: he'd continue this process, using his recently acquired knowledge and skills.

The phone urgently disturbed his meandering thoughts. He reached for the handset.

"Doctor, it's Mrs Simpson here. I'm afraid we have a disturbance out in the waiting room," she paused for a sharp intake of breath, as if the encounter had already taxed her to the limit. "A young woman is standing in reception, refusing to sit down or to depart. She says that her boss has given her a letter that you must, the cheek of it, *must* read before you start your surgery. There's a young man here too, who says he wants to see you."

He felt a little irritated, either because of being interrupted in his eulogising over Fabienne, or because it sounded like something Mrs Simpson should be able to handle without the embarrassment of his direct intervention - before a waiting room full of patients. Mrs Simpson very rarely lost control of even unexpected events in Reception.

"Monica, can't you deal with it? Perhaps give her an appointment for a little later this morning? There are plenty of appointment slots left," he suggested, reasonably.

"I have offered her a same-day appointment in an hour's time, but she refuses, and she won't sit down. She says she's been given strict instructions by her boss and won't move until you've read this letter that, *she says*, is so important."

Matt thought this very unusual. Patients might well turn up at his door at midnight bringing a poorly child with a sore ear - that was part of village medicine, but disruptions in reception were extremely rare. It sounded as if he was going to have to deal with it after all. The male visitor was probably a drug representative who could always be given an appointment after surgery and would be perfectly happy provided Matt agreed to see him. He wondered why Mrs Simpson hadn't simply taken his card and asked him to return later, as was usual practice.

Getting up: all thoughts of Fabienne had now disappeared just as they always did when he was brought back to the reality of life as a GP. In many ways this was a good thing: reasoning that his recovery depended on it. He saw Janice, who must have been standing next to Mrs Simpson in reception before she had gone to telephone. Even now, the manager was scurrying back from the office; without doubt, so as not to miss any of the fun and games that were about to be unleashed in the normally quiet reception area. Facing Janice was a tall, nervous-looking, slim man in a pin-stripe suit that seemed ill-fitting, as if it had been bought off the peg, but in a hurry, or had even been bought by someone else. The pin-stripe made him look even taller and thinner. Matt thought that the only thing he lacked was a bowler hat. He clutched a briefcase, thereby supporting Matt's theory that he must be a drug representative. No doubt the case was full of samples and free pens and glossy sheets, so called 'detail aids' to allow him to emphasise the points about a particular drug. Matt couldn't see much of the woman standing to his right. She was clutching a crisp, white envelope, which presumably held the letter he was to read before starting his surgery: looking down, so that much of her face was hidden, partly by the red baseball cap she was wearing. He thought to himself, that after some gentle admonishment, so that his practice manager didn't lose face, it would probably be easier to just read the letter and get on with his surgery. Suddenly he recognised the cap - *'Wokingham Working Men's Club'.*

His face erupted in a smile that he could barely contain, as he bounded forward. Mrs Simpson was looking very annoyed, and Janice puzzled; the tall man seemed very nervous, and the woman in the cap, struggling to control a fit of the giggles! In an effort to put her case first and maximise her position of authority, Mrs Simpson stopped him before he could say a word: as if daring him to do anything other than give the two of them good carpeting.

"This woman *insists* that you read this letter before you start your surgery." She took it with a movement that was not far off a snatch from the young woman's hand. Incredulously Matt noticed that the tall man was also holding a letter. Matt managed, barely, to stay looking as solemn as his surging thoughts would allow, when faced with a scene that his overactive mind couldn't have glimpsed in his wildest imaginings. A strand of more logical thought interceded, with the view that he should perhaps read the letter.

He did manage a, "Now then, Miss," as he took the envelope from Monica Simpson, trying his utmost not to beam back at the face held in shadow by the peak of the cap.

"Very well, Miss, you see I've given him the letter as you insist," Mrs Simpson said perfunctorily, as she fixed a gaze, laden with admonishment, upon her. Matt wondered if she would fold her arms across her chest and nod disapprovingly to further enhance her displeasure at the crime that had been committed. Matt opened the envelope, and had to give a loud cough to diffuse the laugh that otherwise would have escaped him at this point.

Dear Matt,

I have a Gulfwing 2000 parked at Manchester Airport, fuelled and ready. We'll be leaving for Barbados at noon. There's a fast car (they tell me, even faster than yours) waiting outside. You have thirty minutes to pack; please don't forget your toothbrush and swim shorts - all else is optional. The gentleman has a letter for you.

Love you loads,
Sylvie.

Mrs Simpson was drawn quite involuntarily towards the letter. She could no more have stopped gazing curiously at it, than stop the world from turning. Matt folded it, doing his best to indicate that he'd just read something of crucial importance. Reflecting later, that this was precisely what he had read.

Patients had been drifting in steadily and were very curious as to exactly what was happening in the normally sedate pace of the surgery, where the arrival of the new doctor and the roof coming off, were the most significant events of the past thirty years. Their curiosity was as nought compared to the irresistible intensity of that emotion bubbling up within the practice manger, who stood there glowering at the rude young woman, who'd obviously tried to usurp her authority. She would learn. Doctor Sinclair was a very gentle man, but she had no doubt that this slip of a girl would feel the lash of his tongue any second.

Matt gave another forced cough and motioned to the young man to give up his envelope, which he did with some relief crossing his face. Opening the envelope, he discovered another letter.

"*Dear Dr Sinclair,*
My name is Dr Fergus Worthing. MBChB, DRCOG, DCH. I have been retained for a three-week, full-time, locum beginning today at 9am.
All relevant fees have been paid in full.
My GMC registration, certificates and MDU documentation are attached."

Matt, far from stifling a laugh at this point was plunged into uncharacteristic uncertainty, as so many factors washed over him simultaneously. "I'm not sure, I mean, let me see, well I suppose," was uttered in a garbled fashion as he struggled to bring coherent thought to a deluge of new information.

Mrs Simpson was horrified. She'd expected him to start shouting at this interloper, yet that response didn't seem to be in the offing. Looking her employer, her face reddening to even more than its usual livid hue; now aghast at the concentration that was being applied to what she'd assumed could only be a frivolous request of some sort. Perhaps she was wrong, perhaps this was indeed a life-or-death situation, and she'd treated the young woman harshly.

Fabienne looked up just enough, so as not to miss the turmoil on his face. She was desperately choking back a laugh, but couldn't filter out that awesome smile. He looked up from reading the letters, clearing his throat with as good an air of finality as his surging emotions would allow.
"Mrs Simpson. I've been called away on urgent business. This gentleman is Doctor Worthing and he's to start as a locum immediately. I expect that the business will take about three weeks to settle." Matt did his best to retain a grave note in his voice, whilst his lungs panted in time with the summersaults from his heart.

He shook the hand of the locum, who was looking very relieved now that he was on familiar territory and everyone knew what he was doing there.
"This is Mrs Simpson, practice manager, and Janice, one of our receptionists. They'll show you everything, and Dr Stevens will be consulting in the adjacent room to you. They'll be able to answer any questions you may have." An ecstatic urgency had found its way into his voice. "I'm afraid I must dash immediately with this young woman to attend to these urgent affairs. Please give my apologies to any of the patients who may be inconvenienced," he said as he slipped the letters in his inside pocket much to the chagrin of Mrs Simpson, who sensed that she'd never learn their contents.

Only unexpected shock allowed Matt to stifle the grin from crossing his face as he followed Fabienne, who had turned abruptly and headed for the door as soon as he stopped speaking. Mrs Simpson was speechless and unable to say just what she'd witnessed, other than that her employer had obviously been given information that required his immediate presence, and would last three weeks. Of course she couldn't say precisely what was involved, but she could clearly see that something of major importance was about to pass, if it required his absence from surgery for so long. Perhaps, it could have something to do, even with the Government. In any event she would find out, when he got back.

Janice spoke. "Do you think he's done a Dr Brown?"

"What?" said Mrs Simpson, who was now very irritated.

"You know, a 'Doctor Brown' over at Mitchelham - you told me, remember, where he's about to crawl through the window, and never be seen again."

"Don't be ridiculous, Janice, can't you see that this is serious business?"

Janice couldn't see that. She thought this far from serious. "She looks a bit like that woman in the photo." Janice realised suddenly in an epiphanic moment and continued, "that's where I've seen her before; I knew I'd seen her somewhere!" Janice stared, as if mesmerised.

"Close your mouth, Janice you look as though you're catching flies," suggested Mrs Simpson brusquely. Mrs Simpson's head was now hurting; her left temple felt as if it was about to burst from her skull. She decided to take the path of least resistance, showed the young doctor into the consulting room and retired to the office quickly, so that she wouldn't have to attempt any more deliberation on what had passed before her eyes. The patients sat, by and large, in silence through this time, none the wiser either.

The black Mercedes, with tinted windows, stood pulsating smoothly on the drive just outside the entrance to the surgery.

A driver held the door open, as the young woman removed her cap to reveal the shimmering hair, lit gloriously as it caught the morning rays of the autumn sunshine. Matt entered the car after her.

"To Doctor Sinclair's house, Tony, back the way we came through the village. I'll tell you when we get there."

"Yes Miss," he indicated, as he released the handbrake; and the car was underway without further ado.

There, next to him, at last, was that delirious smile: the smile that held undiluted joy of living, fully restored and as he'd always remembered. All his life he'd spent his nights, or so it seemed, with dreams of this person, and at this moment here she was; not because she had to be, nor because she needed to hide, but for the single, compelling reason that, of all the places in the world that she could be at that point in time; she'd chosen to be with him. He looked towards her. The usually placid blue, now ablaze as it met the blue crystal, full on. "That was exciting, what's next?" His face illuminated by joy and excitement in unrestrained quantity.

"Oh, more; much, much, more," she confirmed, ecstatically but slowly, as if savouring each of the words.

"Oh no, not Barbados again, another hotel room; more sex, drugs and Rock 'n' roll?"

"Well, not quite: I have a little place there, on the beach, and I'm hoping, perhaps, for two of the things on your list." Her eyes, widened with sensual intent.

He smiled again with rapturous exhilaration as he said, "Now, hand-holding only, you remember."

"Huh, that's what you say."

"Sylvie, I have missed you," he said, with as little sentimentality as he could manage.

"Me too," she replied, following a pause that said even more than those simple words. She leant over and kissed him; a longer and more lingering kiss than his heart could have dreamed he would ever experience. He hugged her to him, as would two survivors coming out of the water, after believing for so long that their rescue was never to be. The car made unruffled progress towards Matt's house.

"Matt, you've shown me your world, and it's lovely. That experience saved me, when I don't think anything, or anyone else, could have. Come with me, and I'll show you something of mine." She paused, "just one thing, I have to ask."

He looked at her - the eyes had him transfixed with their uninterrupted glow, like pure copper sulphate that had crystallised about a core of scintillating diamond.

"Well, go on Sylvie, just tell me."

"Just what did you do with all my CDs?"

He laughed with the sublimation of the fear as to what she'd been about to ask him.

"Sylvie, that's a long story, and it begins many, many months ago," he beamed.

"Don't worry, Matt; I'm very patient, a good listener, and I have a feeling we'll have all the time in the world. Nice watch," she said, as she touched the Breitling, her lips cooing like a child's on Christmas morning.

"Oh, from some old girlfriend of mine. Can't quite remember her name, but it must have been a long time ago."

The beatific smile held dominance on her face; even his dreams couldn't have quite captured its radiance. Words that he'd never dared dream, let alone utter, came forth, almost as if pre-programmed in his subconscious. He could no more control them, than he could stop his heart. Moreover, in the scintilla before the words appeared, he knew that it had always been so.

"I love you, Sylvie."

"Is that a serious diagnosis, then, Doctor?"

"Yes, I think I may have it for the rest of my life."

She kissed him again and again.
"You'd better."

THE END